KAREN ROBARDS

Tiger's Eye

This is a work of fiction. Names, characters, places, and incidents are products of the author's imagination or are used fictitiously and are not to be construed as real. Any resemblance to actual events, locales, organizations, or persons, living or dead, is entirely coincidental.

AVON BOOKS
An Imprint of HarperCollins*Publishers*
10 East 53rd Street
New York, New York 10022-5299

ISBN: 0-380-75555-6
www.avonromance.com

First Avon Books paperback printing: May 1989

Printed in the U.S.A.

20 19 18 17 16 15 14

Patsy

New York Times Bestselling Author

is

"IN THE TOP RANK OF ROMANCE WRITERS."
Louisville Courier-Journal

"KAREN ROBARDS . . . PENETRATES
THE STEAMIEST OF WOMEN'S FANTASIES. . . .
HER PARTICULAR BRAND
OF ROMANCE IS FASCINATING."
Chicago Sun-Times

"ROBARDS HAS A KNACK
FOR TELLING A STORY."
Knoxville News-Sentinel

"[ROBARDS] TURNS ROMANCE INSIDE OUT. . . .
SHE HAS THE ELEMENTS OF
GOOD WRITING DOWN."
Cincinnati Post

"ROMANCE—WITH A DIFFERENCE. . . .
[ROBARDS] CREATES A FUN SUMMER READ."
Orlando Sentinel

"KAREN ROBARDS IS ONE
TERRIFIC STORYTELLER."
Chicago Tribune

Other Avon Books by
Karen Robards

DARK OF THE MOON
DESIRE IN THE SUN
GREEN EYES
MORNING SONG

To Rusty and Iris—beloved friends.
And, as always, with much love
to Doug and Peter.

I

Thunder crashed. A great jagged bolt of lightning split the sky, its brilliant white light illuminating the muddy road ahead for no more than a few seconds. Still, it was time enough to reveal five ominous horsed figures leaping from the copse of oaks at the road's bend to gallop furiously toward the oncoming coach.

"Stand and deliver!"

The terrifying cry, hurtled from the storm-tossed night, put the final, dismal cap on what had been, for all four occupants of the coach, a most harrowing day. Even as four pairs of eyes widened, and four spines straightened, the command was punctuated by a musket blast. The crested brougham swayed violently as Will Coachman, caught by surprise as he all but dozed on the high seat, snapped upright, his hands tightening reflexively on the reins. Beside him Jonas, the young groom pressed into service as outrider for this odd start of the earl's, almost went off the bench seat as the coach's wheels slipped in the mud. Saving himself with a hasty grab, he fumbled for the ancient fowling piece that Will had tucked beneath the seat at the last minute before departure. Before his hand did more than touch the cold metal, another musket barked, the ball whistling too close to the groom's head for comfort. Jonas ducked, swearing, and abandoned all thoughts of heroics.

For his part, Will thought for a moment of whipping up

the horses and making a run for it, but the beasts had travelled clear from Thetford that day and were as tired as he was. The earl's instructions had stated clearly that they were to take no more than this single day upon the road. His lordship was of no mind to pay for a night's stay at a hostelry when there was no need. He wished to see my lady in London on this very date, February the twenty-sixth. Will and the rest of the staff, as well as the lady herself, had all done their collective bests to comply with the earl's instructions, though my lady had had only two days to prepare for her journey. And yet just look where such praiseworthy obedience had brought them: to a perilous clash on a dark, deserted road with near a half-dozen highwaymen brandishing muskets! Had ever there been such an ill-fated day?

First one of the horses had gone lame, which meant that the beast had had to be replaced with a post horse, an expense with which the clutch-fisted earl would not be pleased. Then the rain had started, an icy downpour that turned the post-road into a quagmire and sent the coach slipping off into a ditch. It had taken the stout backs of a willing farmer and his son, plus Jonas and himself, to get the coach back on the road again. Which mishaps, of course, had made them far later than they should have been in getting to London. At that very moment it was nigh onto ten o'clock, and here was yet another delay!

Perhaps that was not quite the right way to think of an attack by five armed bandits, but that was how Will saw it, at least in the first few, surprised minutes. After all, in this the year of our Lord 1814, with Napoleon Bonaparte running wild all over the Continent and England bereft of near all but lawless men, being held up was not so uncommon. If they did but cooperate, the old man thought hopefully, they would suffer no hurt but the loss of the lady's valuables. And, bless her, she was not one to take on about that, nor blame him for that which he could not help.

Black-cloaked figures swirling out of the darkness to encircle the moving coach resolved his dilemma. Clearly, the only thing that an attempt to flee would accomplish would be his own and Jonas's ruination. With a silent, heartfelt apology to the lady within, Will bowed to the inevitable and pulled the coach up. Two of the thieving rogues immediately grabbed at his reins; his horses, unused to such cavalier treatment, reared up in the shafts, whickering shrilly with fright.

Inside, Lady Isabella Georgiana Albans St. Just sat a little straighter on the plush velvet seat as the coach jolted to a stop. The widening of her soft blue eyes was one of the very few hints of perturbation she revealed. Like Will on the box, she had been near dozing. Allowing her head to rest against the curved seat back had caused the masses of baby-fine brown hair that had plagued her since earliest childhood to work free of its pins, as it frequently did. Tickling tendrils straggled distractingly around her face as she blinked awake. It was a moment before she was certain that the muffled noises which had awakened her came from outside the coach and were real, not part of some disturbing dream.

If her pale skin went a shade whiter at the knowledge, the light from the single carriage lamp that was still lit was too uncertain to reveal it. Her fine-boned body in the unfashionably plain blue woolen frock remained stiffly erect but unmoving as she listened to the commotion outside. Long, slender white fingers tightened fractionally over the reticule she held in her lap, but the convulsive movement was covered by the lap robe that was tucked around her waist. The tip of her tongue appeared to wet lips that were far too wide for beauty. The nostrils of her narrow-bridged nose flared as she drew in a deep breath, for a moment calling attention to the dusting of freckles that had plagued her as long and persistently as her disobedient hair.

Then her breathing steadied. One hand emerged from the lap robe and rose in a gesture so automatic that it required no thought to brush the wayward strands of hair from her delicately boned face. She lifted her pointed chin a scant fraction of an inch, squared her narrow shoulders, and waited with outward composure for what would come.

"My lady, what . . . ?"

Across from Isabella, riding backwards, Jessup, her thin, sallow-skinned maid, was far less resolute. The first musket shot brought her starting from deep sleep. As the coach lurched to a stop she stared wildly around, clasping her bony hands so tightly together that the knuckles showed white. There was an odd rasp to her breathing as she grasped what was happening in the darkness beyond the confines of the cozily lit carriage.

"Calm yourself, Jessup, if you please! I cannot think you'll be of any use to me or yourself if you give way to panic."

"My lady, my lady, we're being held up; we'll likely be ravished by the rogues and murdered! Oh! Oh! To think that we should come to this!" Jessup was beyond being calmed as she sought to convince her mistress of their danger.

A faint crease of displeasure appeared between Isabella's brows. Such fear was contagious, and she had no wish to lose her own composure. A stout heart would get one through most trials, she had found.

"Don't be silly; they've no reason to harm us! They are simply thieves. If we give them what they want, they'll be gone in a trice. I've a little money in my reticule, and you must give them my jewel case if they ask. If we do that, I'm sure we have nothing to fear."

Isabella was not quite as unruffled as she sounded, but she had borne the many vicissitudes visited on her in twenty-three years of life with fortitude, and she saw no reason to lose her head over what, after all, would likely be a very brief, if admittedly unpleasant, encounter. 'Twould all be over very quickly, she was sure, and then another hour or so would see them safe in London.

" 'Tis unnatural, my lady, so calm as you always are!" Jessup sounded almost accusing. Her own agitation was obvious as she all but bounced up and down on the seat.

Isabella, with the majority of her attention focused on

trying to hear what was happening outside rather than her maid's upset, supposed vaguely that Jessup had a point. Most ladies of quality were reputed to be possessed of exquisite sensibilities, and certainly any lady of sensibility would be giving way to the vapors about now, as shots and shouts sounded outside her carriage. But she had never had much sensibility, only sound common sense. Sensible Isabella, she had once heard her father describe her, to the man who was then, though she did not know it at the time, her prospective husband. Thinking back on it, Isabella supposed that her father's description of her was far more accurate than she had known at the time. At any rate, she had never seen any good come from an unrestrained display of emotion. Certainly all her tears and pleas had not managed to save her from being married off to Bernard—or save her from Bernard himself, once they were wed. After the humiliating disaster of her wedding night, she had vowed to have done with tears. She had not wept since.

"My lady . . . !"

The door was jerked open. A man stood in the aperture, one hand holding the door wide, the other grasping a pistol. Even Isabella gasped. Jessup squealed, and shrank back against the rolled squab. The dense blackness of the night outside shrouded all beyond the intruder in mystery. He stood, large and menacing, in the wavering pool of light that spilled from the coach. Masked and hooded as he was, Isabella could not distinguish a single feature, not even so much as an ear. All she could tell was that he was a man of some girth, not fat but solid and square-built, and his eyes, glinting through the slits in his mask, were a hard, flat brown.

"Lady Isabella?" He was looking at her as he spoke, his voice as hard and flat as his eyes. Isabella felt the sudden, sharp bite of real fear. He knew her name. But how could that be . . . ?

"Here, this is all I have." She forced the words out around the sudden dryness in her mouth, thrusting her reticule at him at the same time. "Take it and be gone!"

"Nah! You'll not be rid of me so easy-like, my lady."

His accent was sharp and unfamiliar to her ears, not the well-modulated syllables of the well-bred nor the soft Norfolk burr she'd grown accustomed to since her marriage. But she had no time to ponder his origins. Despite his words, he snatched the reticule from her hand and stuffed it into a pocket well hidden by his enveloping cloak. Then he looked at her again. Though she could see nothing save his eyes, she gained the impression that he was grinning. An evil grin . . .

For a long moment they stared at one another. Isabella's heartbeat quickened, and she felt her stomach clench.

"Jessup, give him the jewel case."

If her words were sharp, it was because it was all she could do to keep her voice from shaking. Jessup blanched as the man's eyes slid around to her, but she reached into the little hidey-hole in the upholstery for the leather-bound case.

"Here 'tis." Jessup's voice was scarcely more than a squeak as she thrust the case at the man. He took it in his left hand, hefted it.

" 'Tis a rich prize," Isabella said steadily.

The man nodded. "Aye," he said, apparently impressed by the weight of it. Then he shouted over his shoulder to a henchman, tossed the jewel case to him, and turned his eyes back to Isabella. She had to fight not to shrink away from his gaze.

"You have it all now, so you may take yourself off." Her voice was surprisingly steady.

"Nah."

To Isabella's horror, he reached in to close a large, meaty hand around her upper arm. He dug his fingers into the soft flesh beneath her sleeve, hurting her and not caring if he did. Isabella knew in that moment that there was to be no speedy end to this nightmarish encounter, after all.

"Unhand me!" she cried, truly frightened now, beating at his arm with her free hand. She might as well have beaten her fist against an oak tree for all the effect it had.

Jessup screamed and cowered back in a corner as her mistress was dragged from the coach.

Only the hand on her arm kept Isabella from falling headlong into the muddy road. Her shoes sank deep and her skirt trailed in slimy ooze. The cold needles of an icy rain beat down on her uncovered head, wetting her to the skin in a matter of moments. An equally cold fear chilled her heart.

As she found her feet, Isabella was just able to make out three or four shadowy forms on horseback milling around the coach. Searching further, she discovered Will Coachman and Jonas, bound as neat as Christmas geese, lying in the tall grass at the side of the road. They were uncovered and, if left to lie thus in the rain for very long, would be in grave danger of contracting an inflammation of the lungs, or worse.

But at the moment Isabella harbored fears of a far more immediate danger, to herself as well as her servants. No highwaymen who chanced to rob a coach at random would know their victim's name—nor would they go to the trouble of tying up her servants. Stomach churning, Isabella reached the inescapable conclusion that her coach had not been chosen at random. These men had a purpose. . . .

"What do you want from me?" she demanded, her voice suddenly grown hoarse. Freezing cold from fear as much as from the rain, she turned and swept the dripping tails of hair from her face, looking up at her captor with what dignity she could muster as she struggled to quell a burgeoning panic. Her fright was rapidly assuming monstrous proportions. Instinctively she fought to remain calm. It was the only defense she had left to her.

He laughed, the sound coarse, and shoved her brutally on the shoulder, spinning her around, making her stagger and nearly fall. Then he caught one wrist, dragging it behind her back to yank her upright. Isabella cried out as he caught the other one, too, and bound them both with a leather strap. In the next instant a sour-smelling rag was tied roughly over her eyes, blinding her. Terror brought a bitter taste surging into her mouth. Whatever these men intended, it was not simple robbery. . . .

With her eyes rendered useless, her hearing was suddenly more acute. Over the sounds of the rain and the wind she heard a rhythmic splashing that warned of the approach of horses. At least two . . .

"What do you want?" she asked again, her nerve nearly broken. A grunt was her only answer. There were presences around her, horses and men; she could feel them, hear them. . . .

Without warning she was spun around. Isabella cried out, staggered. Her cry was cut off by a wad of dry cloth thrust between her teeth. Her head swam sickeningly as in the next instant she was lifted off her feet to dangle head down over a man's shoulder. Instinct warned her to lie perfectly still as he strode away with her, one arm holding her about the thighs. In the background, Jessup's screams as she was dragged from the coach were abruptly silenced by what sounded like a blow. Such or worse would be her own fate if she gave her captor any trouble at all, Isabella sensed. Struggling mindlessly would avail her nothing. Better to remain calm so that, if an opportunity presented itself, she could use her wits to escape. To give way to the panic that threatened to overwhelm her would be useless.

With no care at all for her delicate bones or tender skin, Isabella found herself tossed facedown over a saddle. The leather creaked as a man mounted behind her. Isabella turned her head from the smell of wet horse and wet leather, her cheek resting against the beast's soaked, heaving side. Then, with a surge of muscles, the horse was off, bounding over the ground in great jolting leaps.

Held in place as she was by the man's hand on her back while her head spun sickeningly and her stomach churned, the truth of the matter occurred to Isabella in a blinding flash: for whatever purpose, she had just been kidnapped!

II

After a bruising ride over rough terrain, the horses—for her hearing told her that there were other horses and riders with them—at last stopped. The man behind her swung down, as did the others, she thought. The rain had stopped, but the smell of it was everywhere. The cold grew worse as the clock approached what must have been midnight or beyond.

With about as much care as if she had been a sack of grain, Isabella was lifted down from the horse and hefted over a man's shoulder again. Wordlessly he carried her inside what she assumed to be a house from the countless smells that assailed her nostrils as she passed out of the cold: cooking spices and peat-fueled fire, dust and tallow and a faint mustiness overlying all.

"Ye 'ave 'er, then?" It was a woman's voice, coarse and low.

"As ye see."

"Good, good. My, she be a wee little thing, ain't she? Not dressed as fine as I thought, for a countess. Ye sure ye got the right one?"

"She be the countess, right enough."

"Take 'er up, then. I got the room ready."

Isabella was borne up a steep, narrow flight of stairs. Its dimensions became painfully obvious to her because her head banged against the wall several times during the ascent. When he reached the top he took only a few steps.

There was the sound of a door opening, and he walked through it. Without warning, Isabella felt herself falling, to land on her back on a prickly, straw-stuffed mattress. She cried out at the unexpectedness of it, the sound muffled by the gag.

The woman *tch-tch*ed. "No more need for that, is there? There's none to 'ear 'er no matter if she screams. No need to suffocate the poor thing."

The man apparently shrugged, because the gag was fished from Isabella's mouth. Her lips and tongue felt dry and swollen. Her jaws ached. She closed her mouth, swallowing painfully, even as she was flipped over onto her back and her hands were untied.

"She's wet through. I s'pose she'd be glad to get them clothes off 'er."

"I don't see as it makes no difference whether she's wet or not."

"Ain't you that 'as to nurse 'er if she sickens, is it?" the woman retorted.

"Do what you want," the man replied, clearly indifferent.

"Besides, them clothes might look right nice on me." The woman reached out to finger Isabella's skirt. " 'Tis good cloth, it is."

The man snorted. "Aye, and you might just get the dress on, too, if you was to split yerself in 'alf!"

The woman gave an indignant cry. There was the sound of a slap, and half-playful wrestling. Isabella, her hands free, turned over cautiously, hoping they were too intent on themselves to notice her. Instinctively one hand rose to her blindfold. . . .

"Nah!" The man's hand knocked hers away, the blow so hard that her fingers went numb from it. Then his hands were on her shoulders, shaking her. "You try that again, lady, and I'll beat you clear to London and back. You understand me?"

"I—I understand!"

He stopped shaking her, pushing her back down against the mattress instead.

"What are you doing?" Isabella could feel him leaning over her, and her heart stood still. He said nothing in reply, but caught one wrist and lifted it high above her head. Isabella felt a rope pass around her wrist, and realized with a sinking feeling that she was being tied to the bed frame.

"But 'ow am I to get 'er dress off, then?" The woman sounded disappointed as Isabella was secured wrists and ankles.

"That's your affair. But you're not to untie 'er without me 'ere, understand? If she was to get loose, it would go 'ard with you."

"Don't you threaten me, you—"

"Understand?" His voice was suddenly cold. The woman quieted.

"Aye, aye then. I understand." She sighed. "I s'pose I could cut the dress off 'er—but what good's a cut dress?"

"You'll 'ave to cut it to get into it anyway," the man said without sympathy. The pair of them sounded as if they were moving away from the bed. Isabella heard the creak of floorboards, followed by the sound of the door being shut and the click of a key in the lock. She was left alone in the dark, bound hand and foot to a bedframe that her fingers told her was made of solid iron. She was wet through, shivering with cold, and more afraid than she had ever been in her life.

What was to come to her now?

III

As hours of captivity turned into days, physical misery was as constant a companion to Isabella as stark fear. She was untied twice a day, and permitted to remove her blindfold to use a chamber pot in relative privacy. She was left alone in the room for this business, while one of her captors—she thought it was always the same man, the one who had carried her inside that first night—remained in the hall just outside the open door until she was finished. When her blindfold was retied (which Isabella did herself on the man's orders) he would come back in, and thrust a piece of bread and sometimes a bit of fish or game into her hand. Isabella would eat standing up, wolfing the food down so as to have time to finish. Then she would be permitted to drain the water from a mug, and retied in the same position as before. Her muscles screamed a protest each time, but she did not. The man's brutal indifference gave her the feeling that he would have no compunction about clouting her over the head, did she give him any cause.

The room where she was being held was tiny, furnished only with the single iron bedstead, a rickety candlestand and a washstand with a pitcher and bowl, which she was never given the opportunity to use. Everything from the cobwebbed ceiling to the dusty plank floor was filthy. Under other circumstances, Isabella would have cringed at the idea of lying on the grimy mattress. It was bare of any bedding save the tattered quilt, gray with age and dirt, which they threw over her for warmth. Despite its condition, the coverlet's protection was welcome against the icy nights passed without a fire lit in the blackened stone hearth. Shivering, glad of the bedding that would have revolted her under any other conditions, Isabella knew that she had more things to worry about than the possibility of nits. Like her life . . .

The woman—Isabella had overheard one of the men call her Molly—ordered Isabella out of her dress the first time she was untied, thus for Molly neatly solving the problem of whether or not to cut the much-admired cloth. Isabella protested timorously that she had nothing to put on instead, and after a moment was tossed what, from its width and lack of length, was one of Molly's own gowns. It was of coarse kerseymere, in a truly dreadful shade of brown, and was so large it could wrap around Isabella twice. She looked at it in revulsion, but from her position in the hallway Molly warned that Isabella would be forcibly stripped if she did not obey. Horrified at the prospect, Isabella quickly took off her clothes—Molly wanted "every blessed stitch"—and donned Molly's scratchy, dirty gown. It barely covered her calves, but in every other respect was so huge and shapeless on her that Isabella could have been any size beneath it. Molly was clearly a female of ample proportions. Isabella was allowed to keep her half-boots—Molly apparently had no hope of squeezing her feet into Isabella's narrow shoes—but that was all. Even her stockings were taken from her! Scantily clad as she was after that exchange, Isabella suffered even more from the cold than she had before.

Once Molly got her hands on Isabella's clothes, she seemed to lose all interest in her. Sometimes Isabella was aware of her presence as she performed some task in the room, but the woman never approached Isabella nor spoke to her directly. Isabella came to believe her primary purpose was to cook for the men, and care for their needs in other ways. Ways which Isabella tried not to think about. Although her fear of being intimately attacked by one of her captors receded as days passed without it happening, the possibility remained always in the back of her mind. If the other woman was there to take care of the men's carnal needs, Isabella could only be thankful for her presence.

From the voices she sometimes heard below, Isabella speculated that there were at least five men, and possibly six, holding her captive. Scraps of conversation she overheard led her to the conclusion that she was being held for ransom. On the surface, Isabella supposed she seemed an ideal candidate: the much younger wife of an earl, the oldest daughter of a duke. Her captors would have no way of knowing how tenuous her hold was on either man. Her husband openly admitted that he had married her for her large dowry, which had towed him, a hardened gamester, out of the River Tick. Her father had married her off to please Sarah, his new young duchess, who had, in six years of wedlock, already presented him with a brood of three, including the newest infant, his long-awaited heir, making Isabella herself both unneeded and unwanted. Neither man would be overly enthusiastic about parting with a large sum to regain that which they did not particularly value in the first place.

Although they would, Isabella was almost certain, pay the ransom. Not to do so would be embarrassing. If word of Isabella's fate should ever leak out, a refusal would not look good to the *ton*. Sarah, the young duchess, might take to her bed over the expense, but the money would be handed over, however reluctantly. It was possible that the earl would be induced to pay it all out of what remained of Isabella's dowry. Certainly that would be the solution Sarah would prefer.

At any rate, despite the possible slight impediment of a family quarrel, the ransom would certainly be forthcoming sooner or later. So all Isabella had to do was remain calm, cooperate with her captors, and cause no trouble, and she would eventually be released. She could continue her journey to London—though why her husband, Bernard, wanted her there still mystified her—as if nothing had happened.

Or perhaps she would even be permitted to return home to Blakely Park. In any case, all she really had to fear was her husband's wrath if he was forced to use her dowry. Nothing aroused Bernard's anger more than having to part with funds on his wife's behalf.

The first small indication Isabella had that change was in the wind came that evening, her sixth in captivity, when the man came as usual to release her to eat and use the chamber pot. When she was finished and he had re-entered the room, he did not check the tightness of the blindfold as he always did. Thankful to be spared a tightening of the knot—she had kept it loose in deference to the headache that throbbed at her temples—Isabella did not wonder at his lapse until he was retying her to the bed. Her head turned sideways against the mattress in silent protest against the screaming pain of muscles forced to assume the same unnatural position in which they had been stretched for three endless days. The blindfold slipped. Isabella found herself looking right into her captor's black-bearded face.

Isabella stared up at him in growing horror; he was looking back at her with a gathering scowl. Their eyes met. Isabella felt panic tighten her chest. Would he kill her, now that she had seen his face?

"Oh, the light is blinding me!" she babbled, her mind pricked into renewed sharpness by pure terror. Quickly she shut her eyes, hoping and praying that he would believe that the feeble glow cast by the candle he'd set on the bedside table was in truth enough to blind someone who'd been deprived of light as long as she.

To her surprise, instead of striking her, or retying the blindfold, he pulled it from her head and dropped it on the floor by the bed.

"Don't matter, not no more. 'Tis at an end, anyroad." He seemed to be talking more to himself than her. Then, candle in hand, he turned to leave the room.

"Do you mean—did you get the money, then? Am I to be released?" Isabella's eyes flew open. With sudden, wild hope, she watched as the man looked back over his massive shoulder at her, his blunt-featured face twisting into a grimacing smile.

"Oh, aye, we'll be settin' you free, sure," he said, and turned away.

"When?" Her voice rose shrilly. To be free again . . . ! Only now, when the prospect of being safely released was at hand, did she realize how truly frightened she had been.

A careless wave of his hand was her only answer. He lumbered from the room, closing the door behind him as he left her alone again in the dark. Isabella lay there for long moments, flooded with relief. Soon she would be free of fear—free!

Then, slowly, she frowned. Her giddy anticipation faded as she realized that something did not seem quite right.

She had seen him clearly, could identify each and every feature. He knew it, and didn't care. What did that tell her?

As Isabella worked it out in her mind, she began to shiver. There was only one possible interpretation: they had indeed gotten what they wanted—the ransom—but instead of releasing her as agreed, she was to be killed. That was the only solution that made any sense. The man had been so careful not to let her see him, or any of them, up until now, when it was all over. If they meant to let her go, common sense dictated that they should be doubly worried about concealing their identities. Once free, she could go to the authorities and identify them. If caught, they would certainly spend a long time in gaol. They might even hang.

The more she thought about it, the more certain Isabella was that she was right: the man didn't care if she saw his face because they had already made up their minds to kill her.

Her heart seemed to stop. She could barely draw breath. Bound hand and foot, she was helpless to resist in any way. At any moment they might come in and shoot her, or strangle her, or smother her with a pillow, or . . .

Panic clouded her mind, sent her thrashing wildly on the bed. Frantically she jerked against her bonds, not caring how the rope cut into the flesh of her wrists and ankles, kicking and writhing with all her might as she fought to get free. The bedstead banged against the wall. . . .

"What's goin' on in 'ere?" Her captor was back, glaring at her from the open door, the candle held high as he surveyed her frenzied movements. Until now, she had been an ideal prisoner, causing no trouble, hoping that her meekness would make it easy for them to let her go when the time came. Now she knew that the time would never come. Again he had not bothered to conceal his face. Isabella stilled for a moment, fighting panic. She had to think!

Her eyes were wild as she stared at him, her chest heaving with terror that she fought to control. Would he divine that she had guessed what they intended to do? If he did, would he kill her now? She could not allow panic to consume her. If she did, she would stand no chance at all. There must be something she could do, some way . . .

"I said, what you kickin' up such a dust about?" He took a step into the room. The candle's golden glow bathed the bed. Above it, his face looked fiendlike, menacing. It was all Isabella could do to bite back a scream.

She could not give way to panic. Her wits were the only weapon she had.

"There—there's a mouse in the bed," she gasped in a squeaky voice that was caused by true fright. The inspiration had come upon her from nowhere. She let it take her, hoping, praying. . . . "Oh, please, it's burrowing in the bedclothes! You must help me! Oh!"

Desperately she began to writhe again, jerking and thrashing and crying out, "Oh! Oh! Oh!" in shrill fear. The bedstead banged against the wall, scooted over the dusty floorboards. Scowling, the man approached.

"Help me! Help me! Oh! It's—it's right under me! Oh!"

"Oh, for Gawd's sake," the man muttered, and set the candlestick down on the bedside table. Isabella continued to whimper and thrash as he bent to untie her ankles. When they were free, she kicked wildly at the bedclothes, doing a praiseworthy imitation of a featherheaded female crazed with fear of a small rodent.

"Be still, or I'll—" The threat was accompanied by a grunt as he freed her hands. Isabella catapulted off the bed, visibly shaking, while he scowled at her, then turned his attention to the rumpled quilt.

This was the moment, the only chance she might get. She had to incapacitate this big, burly man who was easily twice her size—but how?

"I don't see no mouse." He was pawing rather gingerly at the quilt. Isabella's eyes settled on the filthy pitcher in its equally filthy bowl on the washstand not more than a pace to her left. From their grimy state, neither had held water for at least a year.

"It's there, it's there!" she cried, pointing as he cast a suspicious look at her over his shoulder. "Get it, oh, please, get it!"

Thus adjured, he turned back to the bedclothes. Isabella took a lightning step toward the washstand and grabbed the pitcher. He was still bent over the bed, but he was turning his head to look at her again.

"You—" What he was going to say, she never knew. Strengthened by terror, she brought the pitcher crashing down on the side of his head. It shattered. The man blinked once as she watched with horror, dreadfully afraid that she had done no more than annoy him and he would straighten up to his awful height and murder her on the spot.

Then he collapsed like a punctured balloon, sprawling facedown across the bed.

IV

For a moment Isabella stood frozen. But only for a moment. She had no idea how long he would remain unconscious, but she didn't think it would be for very long. Should she tie him up? Foolish to waste precious time, especially when she doubted that any knot she tied would hold him. Her best use of these precious minutes would be to flee into the night.

Isabella raced to the door, stopped, and listened. She could hear the sound of voices from below. Of course, the other men would be down there, and Molly as well. If her caretaker didn't appear shortly, one of them would undoubtedly come looking for him.

On that thought, Isabella closed the door and turned the key in the lock. On the bed, the man groaned and stirred. Heart pounding, Isabella ran back to hover over him. He was waking up!

Snatching up the brass candlestick he had carried upstairs with him, she snuffed the flame. Then, when he groaned again and lifted his head, she bit her lip so hard it bled and brought the candlestick crashing down on the back of his skull with all her might.

He sank like a stone.

Going out the door and through the house was out of the question. That left the window.

After bludgeoning him a third time with the candlestick

for good measure, Isabella went to the window. It was high, and narrow, and thick with dust.

Praying it would open, she tugged at the sash. At last it moved one inch, two, with great reluctance. Finally she managed to force a wide enough opening to permit her to wriggle through.

The man groaned again. Cold sweat broke out on Isabella's forehead. She ran back to the bed, lifted the candlestick high in the air, and brought it crashing down on his skull for the fourth time. This time the blow was so hard that his head bounced against the mattress.

He made no further sound as she went back to the window and slipped out. Only when her feet dangled far above the ground below did Isabella realize just how high up she was. The house was a two-story, rickety farmhouse; the ground sloped away from the foundation, making the drop seem much farther than it actually was.

There was no alternative. She had to let go and pray she didn't break a leg, or her neck. Holding her breath, she squirmed backwards until only her head and shoulders remained inside the room. With another silent prayer and a last, fearful look at the still figure on the bed, she wriggled one last time, until her entire body was dangling from the window and she was hanging from the sill by her hands.

The edge of the sill bit into her palms. There was a tremendous strain on her shoulders. She could not hang on for long. Yet she was suddenly, wildly, afraid to let go.

Her feet in the soft half-boots scrabbled wildly for a toehold. There was none. The wind hit her, making her body sway. . . .

Isabella risked a look down. It was a mistake. Even through the wisps of mist that floated like ghosts through the darkness, she could see that the ground was far, far away, studded with what looked like rocks, and without so much as a bush to break her fall.

From inside the window came a groan. She let go.

Isabella landed with tremendous force on the balls of her feet, then pitched forward onto her knees. Her legs screamed a protest—but they worked. She didn't waste so much as a second scrambling away from the house.

Behind her there were no sounds of pursuit. She cast one haunted look at the lighted window in the front of the house, then fled toward the line of trees that marked the end of the yard. She was just one long stride short of the woods, her skirt hiked around her bare knees as she ran like a hare with the hounds after it, when a tall shape stepped from the shadows to loom in front of her.

Isabella screamed.

V

"Hush, now! Avast, lassie, don't shriek!"

But the whispered words might as well have been in Arabic for all the attention she paid them. Thoroughly unnerved, Isabella let loose with another night-shattering scream even as the man grabbed her and clamped his hand over her mouth.

"Damn it, shut her up, Paddy! Why don't we just send in a bloody bugle corps to announce our coming and be done with it?" The order and disgusted mutter that followed it came from another man, not quite so tall or massive as the first, but tall and massive enough to cow Isabella. Like the first man, he just seemed to materialize from the shadowy woods.

Caught in the grip of enormous arms that held her against a chest wide enough to belong to two men, Isabella knew when she was beaten. She went very still, her eyes huge with fright over the ham-sized hand that covered most of her lower face as well as her mouth. With her back to the first man, she was able to gain no impression of him except for his enormous size. But even by the wavering, mist-filtered light of the slivered moon, Isabella could see that the second man was riveting. He was tall, broad-shouldered and hard-looking, with an arrogant tilt to a head that was as perfect of feature as an ancient Greek coin. His hair was tawny gold, waving a little in the mist and secured at his nape, and if she wasn't mistaken, if the fragmented moonlight was not playing tricks on her eyes, his eyes were the same tawny gold as his hair.

Another man joined them, then another, and another. Five men in all. They stared at her with varying degrees of suspicion and hostility. The man with the golden eyes was running them over her in a nasty, speculative way that frightened Isabella. As if he was considering how best to dispose of her . . .

With a horrible sinking feeling Isabella faced the fact that she had been captured once more. How had they known of her escape? Or had they? She could have sworn that at least three of the brigands were downstairs when she went out the window. And the fourth man, her caretaker, had certainly not managed to outflank her and wait, hidden, in the woods. So were there more of them than she knew? Were these men guards who kept watch in the woods? But they had been afraid that her scream would alert the men in the house. . . .

Who they were didn't matter. Surviving did. Isabella opened her mouth to ask them their intentions toward her, but all that emerged from behind that suffocating hand was a wordless whimper.

''Paddy!'' It was a sharp alert to keep her quiet, given by the golden-eyed man in a hoarse whisper.

''Be still, lassie.'' The words muttered in her ear carried a hint of a plea, as well as clear warning. His hold was unbreakable; she was helpless as a child against him. But he seemed to be exerting very little of what she felt sure was his enormous strength. It was as if he was trying not to hurt her, being deliberately gentle with her. Would he be sorry when the other man ordered him to break her neck? Even if he was, Isabella knew instinctively that he would obey without question. The golden-eyed man's authority had been apparent the instant he appeared. The giant and the rest of the men would do as he said.

''Christ, what the hell is a bloody female doing in these woods at night? The nearest village is five miles away! Hell and the devil, what are we to do with her?'' The golden-eyed man addressed these half-savage mutters to himself as much as Paddy, but Paddy answered.

"We could let 'er go. . . ."

"Aye, and have her screaming her head off again, or mayhap sneaking around to warn Parren and his men of our presence? Look at how she's dressed! 'Tis certain she's no honest maid. Likely she's a doxy belonging to one of them."

He turned those eyes on Isabella. She met them, her own huge over Paddy's silencing hand. The golden-eyed man scowled at her.

"Scream, and Paddy there will break your neck like a twig. He's going to take his hand away from your mouth, and you are going to answer some questions. If your answers are truthful, why, we may just let you go."

He had no more intention of letting her go than he did of jumping over the moon, Isabella could tell from his tone. But she could not let him know that she knew that. She nodded her acceptance of his terms.

At a signal from the golden-eyed man, Paddy slowly lifted his hand from her mouth. Isabella drew in a long, shuddering breath. Paddy's hold on her was as secure as ever, but at least she could breathe again.

"How many are in the house?" The question was fired at her like a bullet. Isabella swallowed to moisten her dry throat, and also to give herself time to think. She would answer the questions as well as she could, as long as they didn't deal with herself. Clearly they had no idea who she was. If they even knew that Lady Isabella St. Just had been kidnapped, they obviously did not associate her with the lady. Molly's awful dress had thrown them off. Until she knew more of what was going on, she was better off keeping her identity to herself. To this group of brigands as well as the other, she could very well be nothing more than a rich prize.

"Well?" His frown was fiercer. Isabella looked up at him with what she hoped was a guileless expression.

"Five. I think."

"Who are they?"

"I—I don't know their names. Three or four men, and a woman. I think she's called Molly."

"What were you doing running from the house in the middle of the night?"

"I—I was frightened. I—I wanted to go home." That was no less than the truth. Taking advantage of a sudden flicker in his eyes, she rushed on. "If you let me go, I will go home, and never bother you again, nor tell anyone I saw you. You have my word."

"Why were you frightened?" His eyes ran over her again, and his frown deepened. He completely ignored the last, breathlessly hopeful part of her speech. "Were you raped?"

"No!" It was an indignant denial, uttered without thought even as her face turned scarlet with embarrassment. A gentleman never, ever, broached such a topic to a lady. But of course, it was quite obvious that he was no gentleman—and he didn't know that she was a lady. Not, she thought, that he would have bridled his speech if he did.

"You're naked under that dress. Why?"

"I am not . . . ! How dare you . . . ? Oh!" This last was a squeak, uttered as he, ignoring her flustered denial, reached out and laid a hand on her breast. The contact was fleeting, but her nipple, already hardened by the cold that had long since penetrated the thin cloth, responded to the sudden cupping warmth like a soldier snapping to attention. Isabella jerked away, her movements severely limited by Paddy's silent hold. But the instinctive recoil was unnecessary. He was already removing his hand with leisurely indifference to both her humiliation and response.

"There's not a stitch under your dress. You were running away from the house, half-naked, and you say you were frightened. Are you Parren's doxy? I hear he's rough with women."

"No!"

He made an impatient sound. "Suppose you tell me who you are, then, and what you were doing running from the house without further roundaboutation. And I warn you, I have very little tolerance for lies, or liars."

Isabella hesitated, looking up at him with enormous eyes. For the life of her, she could not lay claim to being a maidservant or some such. She had the feeling he would know she was lying the minute she opened her mouth.

At her silence the gleam in his eyes hardened, and he looked over her head at Paddy.

"This is a waste of time, and we've little enough of that if we want to be back in London by daybreak, but she can't be let go. Take her back in the woods and keep her quiet."

"Aye."

The golden-eyed man turned away without another glance at Isabella. The other men, except for Paddy, who still held her immobile, followed him.

"Be a good wench, now, and I won't have to hurt you." Paddy released his bear-hug grip to catch her arm and tug her toward the woods. Isabella went meekly until she was just inside a sheltering overhang. Then it occurred to her that, if she was ever going to break away, now, with Paddy's grip almost gentle and his eyes on the path ahead, was the time.

She had to escape a second time. It would take only a little cunning. . . .

Pretending to stumble over a root that thrust up from the path, she fell to her knees. Paddy's hand dropped from her arm. Even as he released his grip she was away, scrambling out of his reach, snatching up her skirts and flying down the path with a fleetness that had been hers since she was a little girl.

"Come back here, wench! Blast and damn!" Paddy was crashing through the trees behind her. With his great size, he would be slow, she hoped.

Her hair streamed behind her like a banner. Her heart pounded. The wan moonlight did not penetrate the trees, making the woods as dark as a cave. A branch clawed her face; she ducked and cried out. Her stride broke, but she faltered for no more than an instant. Yet in that instant she became aware of footsteps pounding close behind her. They were too light and too swift to belong to Paddy.

Isabella was just turning her head to cast a scared look over her shoulder when a hand tangled in the flying mane of her hair, tightened, and jerked her off balance. She screamed reflexively, the sound piercing as a whistle in the still night, even as she was pulled back hard against a man's broad chest. Immediately an iron arm encircled her throat, ruthlessly choking off the sound, cutting off her breath. The scent of leather, bay rum and tobacco filled her nostrils as she gasped for air. He held her so tightly that the buttons of his coat dug into her back. Isabella struggled, clawing at the arm that would squeeze the life from her, to no avail. Even before she looked up to see the golden eyes gleaming furiously down at her through the darkness, she knew who it was. Knew it and went suddenly limp.

VI

"Troublesome bitch. Scream again and I'll bloody well break your neck, understand?"

His voice lost some of its polish in his fury. Isabella realized again that, whoever he was, he was certainly no gentleman. There was an undertone of Cockney to his speech, an accent of the streets. She straightened, again clawing at the hard arm that threatened to strangle her, and his grip on her throat eased.

Isabella drew a deep, shuddering breath as Paddy thundered down the path. When he saw the pair of them, he slowed, his chest heaving as he drew in great gulps of air.

"Sorry, Alec," the big man muttered as he came up to them, sounding both shamefaced and winded. " 'Tis a good thing you're quicker afoot than me."

Alec snorted, but whatever he might have said by way of a reply was cut off by a hiss from one of the other men, who was galloping down the path in Paddy's wake.

"There's sommit going on up at the 'ouse," he hissed. Alec stiffened and thrust Isabella at Paddy.

"Hold on to the damned noisy wench this time, would you? I've no more time to chase her down for you." With that he swung back down the path with the third man trotting along at his heels like a pet dog.

Paddy wrapped his huge hand around Isabella's wrist. She was shackled to him as securely as if by an iron bracelet. Clearly he did not mean to let her get away again.

Isabella didn't much blame him. She had only just become acquainted with Alec's wrath, but it was enough to frighten her.

"What you did wasn't nice," Paddy muttered reproachfully, dragging her after him back up the path. He stopped in the lee of the trees, near where Alec stood with the other men, his eyes fixed on what was happening at the house. Isabella, stumbling to a halt at his side, had perforce to watch the sudden flurry of activity as well.

Whether alerted by her screams or through some other means, it was clear that the people in the house had just learned of her escape. One man was standing in front of the house holding his head, looking wildly around. A lantern rested on the frozen ground at his feet. Two other men quartered the open field armed with lanterns, while a fourth stood near the first man, who was shouting in his rage.

"She got away! The bitch got away! Bloody 'ell, what do we do now?"

"Find 'er, that's what! You great lummox, how could you have let that scrawny gentry-mort get away from you? 'Twill be your neck if 'e finds out we've let 'er escape!"

"Tricked me, she did!"

"Bah! 'Tis the brains of a bloody bullfrog you've got, 'Arris, and no mistake! All of you spread out and look for 'er! She can't have got far!"

It was suddenly clear to Isabella that she had indeed managed to escape from the cutthroats in the house. They clearly had no idea that there was another group of men in the woods, watching their every move. The men who held her were not part of her original captors' band. Who, then, were they? Perhaps a rescue force, hired by her father or Bernard? Bow Street Runners, even? She dismissed that idea instantly. Whoever or whatever they were, she did not think that they were on the side of the authorities. If they had indeed come to rescue her, there would be time enough to alert them to her identity. At the thought of Alec's consternation when he realized how he had hurt and insulted his employer's wife or daughter, she smiled. The arrogant creature deserved a comeuppance. . . . But then her smile died. With the best will in the world, she did not think he had come to rescue her.

Alec stepped out of the trees, into the open field. The pale moonlight silvered his hair. With the now well-lit house for a backdrop, he was in silhouette, his back to her. Isabella saw that his hair was confined with a black ribbon, and that he was broad-shouldered and lean of hip. He appeared to be reasonably well-dressed, in a frock coat and breeches that were fashionably snug, hugging long, muscular legs. Dusty boots rose almost to his knees, and he carried a pistol in his right hand.

Isabella's eyes fastened on the pistol. Her heart speeded up again as she saw that the three men following him were armed too, and ready.

Another man emerged from the house, followed by Molly for a total of six. Each now carried a lantern—and a pistol.

"Spread out and find 'er. But don't shoot unless you must. 'E don't want it messy. No blood."

Isabella recognized the voice. It belonged to the man who had dragged her from her coach, and it sent shivers down her spine. Apparently he was the leader. But who was the "he" the man kept referring to? The ultimate boss? Perhaps—horrors!—Alec? Had there been a falling out among thieves? That seemed more likely than the possibility that he was the leader of a benevolent rescue force.

"Good evening to you, Parren."

Except for the hard undertone that laced the words, Isabella would almost have described Alec's voice as affable. The effect on the man who had just emerged from the house was immediate. He froze, swivelling toward the speaker as if he'd heard a voice from heaven—or hell. The other men whirled in their tracks as well.

"God's bones, it be the Tiger!"

"Damn it to bloody 'ell!"

"I done tol' you 'e 'ad the second sight!"

"Shut up!" This last was muttered by the man who had dragged her from the coach—Parren, Alec had called him. They responded by sidling toward their leader, who stood still as a rabbit in peril from a snake as Alec strolled toward him. The darkness made it impossible for Isabella to see the burly Parren's expression, but the tension of his stance made his apprehension obvious. The lantern he was holding suddenly seemed to vibrate. Isabella wondered if his hand trembled.

"I, uh, didn't expect, uh . . ." Parren seemed utterly discomposed as he stared at Alec.

"Are you trying to say that you didn't expect to see me this far from London on such a fine night? Why, Parren, how shortsighted of you!" Alec's voice was pure silk, so polished that if she had not heard him earlier, she might have mistaken him for a gentleman after all. But something sinister buried just below the surface made even Isabella shiver. The lantern Parren was holding quivered again.

"We . . . we never meant to do you out of your cut, Tiger. I . . . I swear it. We would 'ave give it to you, just as soon as we got back to Lunnon. But the gent whut wanted the job done was in a powerful 'urry, and . . ." Parren's voice trailed off as Alec—Tiger?—shook his head almost regretfully.

"But you know how much I like to be informed of these things in advance. I'm afraid that you've made a slight error in judgement, Parren. And it's going to cost you. Dearly."

" 'Ow much? 'Ell, Tiger, you can 'ave 'alf our take. . . ."

"I want it all."

"All?" It was an outraged croak.

"And the lady, too. Alive."

"But—but we already made a deal with 'er da, and got our cash. 'Ard bloody work it was, too. Believe me, Tiger, there'll be no more paid for that one."

"There is no deal made out of London unless it's approved by me. You know that."

Parren was silent.

"You shouldn't have tried to cheat me, Parren. I don't like that. Ask anyone. Ask Harry Givens."

"But 'e's crabbed."

"He is dead, isn't he? And that's what you're going to

be if I ever set eyes on you again. I'm very much afraid that from now on you'll have to carry out your dirty little jobs in another town, Parren. London's just been closed to you."

"You can't do that! 'Ell, even you don't own the whole bloody town!"

"Don't I?" The voice was almost a purr. Alec lifted his pistol almost idly, and the men behind him immediately did the same. The tension in the air was palpable. In the sudden silence Isabella thought she heard a metallic click. . . .

"Watch it!"

All of a sudden Parren dropped his lantern. Isabella was following its downward trajectory with her eyes when there was another hoarse shout and the staccato bark of a pistol.

Paddy cursed, and thrust her toward the woods. "Run, wench!" he growled at her. Yanking a pair of pistols from his waistband, he sprinted for the field. There were more shouts, more pistol shots. As Paddy emerged from the woods, pistols blasting, Isabella realized that Alec lay on his belly on the frost-bitten ground. The other men had either taken cover in the woods or were, like Alec, lying sprawled in the open.

Run, Paddy had said. Isabella needed no second urging. She lifted her skirt clear of her legs and fled as exploding pistols and men's screams rent the night.

She was just leaping over a rotten log fallen across her path when something struck her with the force of a mule kick square between the shoulder blades.

Isabella cried out, was spun around by the force of the blow. Instinctively her hand twisted, clawing up her back for the site of the spreading, burning pain. She could not reach it, but there was a wetness soaking the back of her gown. Her fingers touched something warm, something wet and sticky. She withdrew them to look down with shock at the thick, dark liquid that stained them.

"Why, I've been shot," she thought, horrified, just before she crumpled senseless to the ground.

VII

Alec Tyron got to his feet, dusted off his breeches, and stood looking down at the body of Cook Parren with cold disinterest. The fool should never have tried to play him false. Others had attempted it before, and most had paid with their lives, as had Parren.

Alec had not risen to be the overlord of London's seamy underworld on the strength of his jolly good humor or remarkable looks. It took a strong man, a ruthless and clever one, to claw his way up to the position of ruler of the Spitalfields-Whitechapel-Kensington district. A smile tugged at the corner of his mouth as he thought that over. Royalty, that's what he was. At least, of the slum rat variety. King of Whitechapel. Maybe he should get himself a crown.

"What're you grinning at?" Paddy came up beside him, frowning. Paddy was a chapel-going sort, not at all suited for the life of riding herd over the pickpockets, murderers, brigands and bawds among whom he found himself. He had a conscience, and a most inconvenient set of morals which Alec, with his quicker brain, had found himself talking around most of his life. Paddy and he had been together since the time when both had been grimy urchins barely breeched, roaming the streets of London doing whatever they must for crusts of bread to keep body and soul in one piece. They'd complemented each other, Paddy with his enormous size and huge muscles, and Alec, for all that he was some few years the younger, with his agile brain. It was that combination of brain and muscle which had got them to where they were. And it was that combination of brain and muscle that would keep them there. Paddy was the only human being in the world besides himself that Alec completely trusted.

"Where's the gentry-mort—the lady?" Alec had worked hard and long to rid himself of the cant speech of the streets, but sometimes he slipped. It usually occurred in times of stress, and he was always severely disappointed in himself when it happened. Speech habits marked a man, labeled him as clearly as slovenliness or a cringing mien. To rise above the lowest of the low, the class to which he'd been born, it had been necessary to change the way he spoke as well as nearly everything else about himself. He'd done it, by dint of much effort. But still, when he least expected it, hints of his origins would emerge, to his secret shame.

"The little wench? When the shooting started, I told her to run. I saw you go down, and I thought Parren might have done for you at last."

"Not bloody likely. And the little wench is no wench, at least not by birth. It's become clear to me that she is the very lady we came seeking."

"What?" Paddy was skeptical.

"Parren and his men lost her, and we found her. Just how many females do you think go running about these woods at night, anyway?"

"She didn't look like no lady I've ever seen. Not—not fancy enough." Paddy frowned doubtfully at Alec.

Alec shook his head, pocketed his pistol and knelt by Parren's sprawled body. "You great looby, it's the bawds that wear the fancy dresses and perfume. Ladies—real ladies, born-to-it ladies—don't dress like that. They dress real plain."

"She was dressed plain, all right." Paddy began to grin. "You put your hand on her—"

"Aye, well, I thought she was a doxy." The memory of how that small breast with its taut, eager nipple had felt against his palm made him uncomfortable suddenly. He looked away from Paddy, down at the body whose pockets he was systematically turning out. "She was near naked. Threw me off, or I'd have tumbled to who she was sooner."

"You going to apologize?" Paddy's smile was wide as he thrust his own pistols into the waistband of his breeches. Alec had never apologized to anyone for anything in his life, and Paddy knew it. Alec flicked him a dampening look.

"Saving her from Parren is apology enough. He meant to kill her."

"Aye." Paddy sobered momentarily. "I don't hold with killing females, Alec."

"I know."

For all his size, Paddy was a peaceable man. He didn't find it easy to be rough with men, much less women, as Alec well knew. Alec straightened away from his cursory search of Parren's body, and gave Paddy a clip on the shoulder.

"We saved her life, if it makes you feel any better. Now all we—*you*—have to do is find her."

"What do you mean, *I* have to find her?" Paddy looked aggrieved.

Alec shrugged, and started walking toward the house. "You let her go, you find her. Or not, as you please. 'Tis not exactly sporting to save her from Parren and then leave her to freeze, to my way of thinking. But 'tis up to you."

"She could be anywhere in those woods!"

"I doubt it. Besides, 'tis not a very big woods. Take some of the men with you, and I don't doubt you'll have her back in a trice."

"We've already frightened her half to death. She'll go to ground like a fox, does she know we're after her."

"So tell her you mean to restore her to the bosom of her family."

Paddy snorted. " 'Tis likely she'll let me get close enough for conversation, isn't it? Besides, we don't know who her family is. Or even her name. All we know is that

Parren was hired to kidnap a high-born lady and kill her. Hell, if he'd gone through the proper channels, we wouldn't even have cared."

" 'Tis the way things work."

"Pray tell me just what you mean to do while I'm freezing my backside off searching for the lady."

Alec ostentatiously fastened his frock coat, shivering, to tease Paddy about the cold. "I'll be searching for something else, of course. Something that interests me infinitely more than a skinny little female."

"The ransom." Sometimes Paddy was surprisingly perceptive, given his usual obtuseness. But then, he knew Alec very well.

"Aye," Alec said with a quick grin.

"And of a surety we'll be keeping the ransom for ourselves?" There was more than a hint of sarcasm beneath the question.

"What would you have me do with it? Parren, who I suppose would technically be considered its rightful owner, is dead. The lady's family will be getting her back unharmed, which is more than they would have without our intervention. 'Tis money well earned, in my opinion."

"You're a sad case, Alec," Paddy said, shaking his head.

"Aye, I know it, and the knowledge sends me weeping to bed every night. Go on, go find the lady. I'll see to the cleaning up here. Can't leave bodies lying about, you know. 'Tis not hygienic."

They were nearing the house. Even as he said the last few words, Alec felt a sudden tingle crawl up his spine. Usually that tingle meant danger. It was another gift that had helped him survive to climb as high as he had. He continued to walk, but with his eyes and ears on the alert for anything out of the ordinary. Looking around, carefully casual, he saw from the fallen bodies lying about the field that all but one of the men who had been in on this attempt at subverting his authority were down. Only a heavyset woman and a single man remained on their feet, and they were being herded toward the house by his men.

All his enemies were accounted for. Why, then, could he not shake the sense of danger?

"You and your big words," Paddy complained, shaking his head in equal parts admiration and annoyance. Intent on pinpointing the source of the eerie feeling that refused to leave him, Alec barely heard him. "Half the time a body don't know what you're nattering on about."

When Alec responded with no more than a grunt, Paddy surrendered to the inevitable and took himself off, calling to Deems and Ogilvy to follow him. The rest of the men stayed behind, to dispose of the dead and ransack the house for the ransom and any other items of interest or value under Alec's direction.

Rat-face Hardy, a runt of a man whose name described him perfectly, came up to Alec for orders about what to do with the bodies. Alec spent a few moments considering the available alternatives. Perhaps they should be transported back to London, and left to rot on the streets as a grim warning to those who would emulate Parren's foolhardiness? But no, that would cause Bow Street to go into a flap, which might be a nuisance in some of his operations. Besides, transporting corpses was sure to rub Paddy's scruples the wrong way, and would be an awkward task at best. Still bothered by that niggling tingle, Alec chose the easiest solution, directing that a shallow grave be dug in the woods and the corpses buried together therein. No stink would be raised about the disappearance of such vermin, but they would be missed, and the talk on the streets would be enough to serve his purpose of deterrence.

Problem solved, he was just walking up the steps when at last the reason for the tingle became clear. Behind him came a stealthy movement, and the click of metal on metal. He would recognize the sound of a pistol being cocked in his dreams. . . .

Alec whirled, grabbing for his own pistol.

The movement was too late. Even as his hand closed over the polished wood muzzle, Rat-face Hardy fired.

The ball hit Alec like a fist in the chest, first cold and

then burning hot as it churned deep within his flesh. Alec staggered backward to be brought up short against the doorjamb, his pistol still in his hand. Even as Hardy dropped the first smoking pistol and lifted a second for another go at him, all hell erupted around them. Men loyal to the Tiger shouted, running toward the scene, drawing their own pistols as they tried to figure out who was doing what to whom. Alec heard his name, shouted in Paddy's voice. Hardy was apparently unnerved by the commotion. Forgetting to fire a second time, he looked about him, turned to run. . . .

Alec lifted his own pistol, pulled the trigger. The ball hit the little bastard right between the shoulder blades, exploding the back of his coat as it tore a great bloody hole through his flesh. Alec smiled as Hardy staggered and fell. It wasn't the first time he'd ever shot a man in the back, but it was the first time it had ever felt so good.

What happened after that, Alec didn't know. The world began to swim around him, go black. The pistol fell from his suddenly nerveless fingers. Clutching his chest, he felt himself losing his balance, and with his balance went his consciousness.

His last rational thought before he rolled down the steps into a void of nothingness was that it was of all things most ironic that the Tiger should be brought down at last by one of his own trusted men.

VIII

When Isabella opened her eyes again, her first thought was that she must have died and gone to heaven. Plump cherubs strumming on golden harps flitted about before her eyes, their white wings soft as clouds on a field of celestial blue. For a moment she simply stared. Then fright made her screw her eyes tightly shut. She didn't want to be dead!

Her back throbbed like a sore tooth. That fact was borne in on her as she took a deep, shuddering breath, only to cringe from the pain. Dead people didn't feel pain, she was almost certain. And they certainly didn't hear thunderous snores.

The acknowledgement of that sound brought her eyes open again. Now that she was prepared for the sight of naked angels, she was able to discern after only an instant's blinking that they were delicately painted onto blue silk bed hangings, and that she was, in fact, lying on her stomach on a sumptuous bed. Her eyes travelled around the room, still seeking the source of the snoring that had not abated. Perhaps Bernard . . . ? But he never snored, so far as she knew. Impossible to imagine a man as fastidious as he, victim to such a lowering fault. Besides, when had he ever slept in the same room with her? The few times he had taken her to wife, it had been quickly over with and then he'd left her to sleep alone.

Besides being crude, the sound was too rawly masculine

to be coming from Bernard. Wincing, Isabella lifted her head from the pillow and looked carefully around. The room was large and lavishly appointed, the walls all hung with blue silk. The furniture, including the enormous canopied four-poster in which she lay, appeared to be made of gilded wood. A white chaise covered in what looked like satin stretched before the dying fire that was the room's single source of illumination. Isabella realized from the deep shadows that crept about the corners of the chamber that it must be night.

But there was nothing on that side of the room to account for the snores, so Isabella carefully turned her head to the right, wincing at the stiffness of her neck and back. On that side of the room stood a gilded washstand which held a dainty porcelain bowl and pitcher. Beside the washstand was a partially open door. It was on this door that Isabella's eyes fastened, widening.

Just visible beyond the door was an enormous pair of men's boots. From the angle at which they stretched across the opening, it was obvious that they were attached to a man. An enormous man, if the size of the boots was anything to judge by.

Fascinated, Isabella stared at the boots. Wherever she was, it was no place she had ever been before. Except for her wedding night and a few isolated nights thereafter when Bernard, either too bored or too far into dun territory to abide London for a while, had visited the country and subjected her to his husbandly demands, she had never had a man in her room. Now here she was, in a strange and overly ornate bedchamber, lying in an enormous bed that seemed to be scented with lavender and was dressed with silk and lace-trimmed sheets, with a man snoring in the antechamber next door.

What on earth had happened to her? And what did she do now?

Resting her cheek back on the silk-and-lace pillow, careful to keep her eyes on the motionless boots, Isabella frowned as she tried to make sense of her surroundings. She remembered being kidnapped, remembered the horror of learning that they meant to kill her, remembered escaping, being recaptured, running and being shot. Of course, that accounted for the pain in her back.

She also remembered two men, a relatively gentle giant named Paddy and a golden-eyed, wickedly handsome villain named Alec.

The question now was, where was she? Was she in danger? And to whom did those enormous boots belong?

She was not bound in any way, Isabella discovered as she experimentally moved her feet beneath the bedclothes. Surely, if she was being held for some sinister purpose, she would be bound.

Or maybe not. Not if they thought she was unconscious and thus unable to attempt escape.

Escape. That's what she must do. Wherever she was, it was no place she had been before and thus no place she wished to be. Safety lay in making her way back to Blakely Park, back to the faithful servants who would protect her with their lives, and sending word to her father and Bernard of all that she had endured. Despite their mutual lack of abiding affection for her, they would protect her from whatever ruffians had her in hand now.

The man beyond the door was asleep, no one was watching her and she was not bound. Now was the time to attempt escape, before they discovered her return to consciousness and restrained her. Whoever they were, which really didn't matter at the moment, it was a certain bet that they meant her no good.

She wanted to go home. Her throat tightened at the thought of Pressy, her former governess and present companion who had been like a mother to her since her own mother died. Pressy would be wild with anxiety about her, as to a lesser degree would be all of the servants who took care of her at Blakely Park. With no real family of her own, she had come to think of them as family, and they had the same regard for her. Will Coachman, if he still lived, would be hounded by guilt at having let her be taken. Jonas, the young footman, would wonder if there wasn't more he could have done to save her. Jessup would be having endless days of hysterics because she had failed her mistress when she was most needed. All, all, would be glad to see her home again.

Even Russell, the enormous black hound she had taken in as a starving puppy and raised to galloping adulthood, would be missing her. And oh, how she missed all of them!

She had to get home. She just had to!

Moving carefully, the care motivated as much by pain as by fear of discovery, Isabella very gingerly managed to maneuver herself into a sitting position. Her head swam, but by means of sheer determination she forced her mind to function. This might be her only chance to escape. She could not allow bodily weakness to cheat her of it. Not if she ever wanted to get home again.

By clinging to the bedpost nearest her head, she managed to get to her feet. She stood still for a moment, leaning against the wall, waiting for her head to clear. The room was cool enough to make her shiver, despite the fire that burned steadily in the hearth. Her bare feet curled in protest against the cold boards of the floor. But the room's chill had one benefit: it helped to clear her head a little more.

She took a step, and then another. Her knees threatened to buckle at any minute, but will power leavened with a healthy dollop of fright kept her going.

Isabella managed to make it to the door, only to discover, as she tried the knob, that it was securely locked.

She tried it a second and a third time before she was convinced: there would be no escaping through this particular portal. There were two windows in the room, one on either side of the bed, shrouded with heavy silk draperies in the same celestial blue as the walls and bed hangings. If she could not leave by the door, perhaps she could get out through a window.

Casting a quick look at the booted feet still clearly visible through the half-open door to the antechamber, Isabella was relieved to find them unmoving. The snores continued unabated. Leaning against the wall, battling the weakness that tried to claim her, Isabella made her way to the nearest window. Thrusting aside the heavy draperies, she made a chilling discovery: on the outside of the frosted glass the window was fitted with iron bars. There would be no escape this way.

Fighting down panic, Isabella stumbled to the other window. It, too, was barred.

What did she do now?

The snoring remained loud and rhythmic. Whoever the man was beyond the door, he was certainly deeply asleep. It was very likely that the key to the door was somewhere on his person, or perhaps lying nearby. She had knocked a man unconscious once before. And that man had not been asleep.

Looking wildly around, fighting the twin demons of panic and weakness that threatened to overwhelm her, Isabella spied an intricately wrought triple candelabra on the floor by the bed. It was only a matter of moments before she had it in her hand. The thing was satisfyingly heavy.

Now all she had to do was step inside that doorway and bash the sleeping man over the head.

Panic cramped her stomach. Clutching the candelabra like a talisman, she told herself to be calm and sensible. She had only to be quiet, and careful, and from somewhere summon the strength of an ox. . . .

Gritting her teeth, fighting against the weakness that clouded her mind and threatened to send her to her knees, she got to the half-open door. She could see only a little bit of the room beyond, enough to notice that it was a dressing room, perhaps, and every bit as elaborately decorated as the bedroom it served.

In order to view any more of the sleeping man besides his boots, much less knock him unconscious, she was going to have to push the door farther open and slip inside the room.

Isabella pushed at the door. It opened soundlessly, leaving her staring at a squashed-face giant of a man sprawled out in an uncomfortable-looking chair. His head was thrown back against the striped silk of the chair's top, and from his yawning mouth issued the ear-splitting snores.

He was the biggest man she had ever seen, and there was no mistaking his identity: Paddy.

He had let her go, and she was going to repay him by hitting him over the head with a candlestick. But he had only let her go because a gun battle had erupted; if it hadn't, sooner or later he probably would have wrung her neck, whether he'd wanted to or not.

That hardened her heart quite effectively. Isabella only prayed that she had the strength to do the job properly. She shuddered to think of his wrath at being clubbed over the head should she not succeed in rendering him unconscious.

Isabella crept almost to the big man's shoulder. She took a deep breath, raised the candlestick high . . .

"Don't make another move!" commanded a harsh voice from the end of the narrow room. Isabella was so shocked that she jumped, her eyes flying to discover a single bed shrouded in shadows against the far wall. In her concentration on the giant, who'd been illuminated by the small pool of light coming through the door from her own room, she had completely failed to see anything else.

A light flared in the charged darkness, was touched by long male fingers to a candle by the bed. Isabella blinked at the sudden spreading light, her eyes fastened to the bed and its occupant.

The man in it was bare-chested except for a white bandage wrapped around his middle, with tousled tawny hair, and several days growth of beard darkening his jaw. He had struggled up on one elbow, and looked as if he would have trouble staying in that position for long.

She recognized him at once despite the shadows that hung over the bed. There was no mistaking those cameo-perfect features—or the gleam of golden eyes.

He held a pistol in his hand, and despite his obvious weakness, it was pointed straight at her wildly beating heart.

IX

His eyes moved over her, widened. Looking down at herself, Isabella saw why. She was clad in the most indecent nightdress she had ever beheld in her life. It was pure virginal white, but its color was the only virginal thing about it. Made of diaphanous gauze, it constituted the sheerest of veils over her body. Its neckline was demure, its sleeves long. Its hem reached her ankles. And yet she might as well have been naked.

Her small breasts pressed wantonly against the fabric. Either the chill of the room or the sudden heat of his eyes caused her nipples to thrust against the sheer cloth like hard little buds. Their rosy color, and the darkness of the circles surrounding them, were perfectly visible to her eyes—and, she had no doubt at all, to his.

The lithe line of her rib cage, the narrowness of her waist, the gentle flare of her hips, all were revealed to him. She followed his eyes down over the very slight convexity of her stomach, down the length of her slender legs, to her bare white toes, and up again.

When she saw that he was staring at the sable triangle between her legs, she thought her body would catch fire from embarrassment.

Drawing a quick breath, she sidestepped so that Paddy and his chair were between them. Her hair was tumbling in a wild tangle down her back to her waist. Shaking it forward, she used the fawn-colored mass to shield her body still further from his view. Still clutching the candlestick, her face a flaming red, Isabella at last dared to meet those golden eyes over the top of Paddy's sleeping head.

What she saw in them made her remember, with heart-stopping immediacy, the scalding heat of his hand cupping her breast.

Then, as suddenly as they had blazed, his eyes cooled, hardened. It was as if he were mentally drawing rein on whatever thoughts had caused that sudden hot flare.

"Put the candlestick down!" he ordered, his voice grim. Then, in a sharper voice, he called, "Paddy!"

Isabella meekly set the candlestick on a table beside the chair, her eyes never leaving the man in the bed. He seemed very weak, almost as weak as she suddenly felt. She clung to the chairback, watching him wide-eyed as he cursed his sleeping friend. His language was enough to singe her ears, but she scarcely heard any of it.

It occurred to Isabella suddenly that she had never before seen a man's bare chest. Bernard had always come to her bed in the dark, and even then he had not fully undressed. This man—Alec—had wide shoulders, wide enough to block more than half of the simple iron rungs of the headboard from her view. They were heavy with muscle, powerful-looking. His arms were as muscled as his shoulders, corded with them as he leaned on one elbow. His chest tapered down from his shoulders in a wide, deep vee, narrowing until the pale blue satin duvet which covered the bed abruptly cut off her view at his waist. A wedge of curling hair several shades darker than his tawny head covered his chest. It was bisected by the pristine white of a bandage. The bandage had been wrapped around his body several times, and was positioned just below his nipples. His nipples. Isabella stared at the brown circles peeking through the nest of hair, and felt herself go even hotter than before.

Her eyes flew back to his, ashamed of where they had been, to find that he was watching her. His eyes were still cool, still guarded and faintly hostile, but there was an awareness of her in them that made her suddenly catch her breath.

The pistol he pointed at her wavered suddenly before being snapped to attention again. Alec frowned at her over its gleaming barrel. Luxuriously thick, tawny eyebrows nearly met over the bridge of his nose.

"Paddy!" The call was louder this time, then was repeated at almost a shout. The giant stopped snoring, snorted and blinked.

"Damn it, Paddy, wake up, will you? Fine bloody bodyguard you turn out to be!" This last was said under his breath, in a disgusted murmur.

"What?" Paddy sat up, shaking his head to clear it. "Did you say something, Alec?"

"I said wake up, lummox, and look about you. The lady there was on the verge of making mincemeat out of your brains!"

Paddy turned to see Isabella standing behind him, staring down at him with an expression of utter terror on her face. He swore, and jumped to his feet, facing her.

Isabella shrank back against the wall, dragging the chair with her both as a shield from his eyes and as protection from any forthcoming violence. He was huge, at least six and a half feet tall, hulking with muscle for all the semi-civilization of a crumpled frock coat and breeches. His hair was a brown so dark it was almost black, grizzled in places with gray, and cropped close against his skull. His features were nothing short of homely: a broad low forehead set like a shelf over small, deepset eyes; a short nose that might once have been pug but now merely looked squashed, as if it had been on the receiving end of too many blows; a wide mouth and an even wider jaw that jutted out into a square, prominent chin with, absurdly, an off-center dimple. A frown on such a face was unnecessary, but he was wearing one. Her back flattened against the smooth, cool plaster of the wall.

Paddy's frown turned to a full-blown scowl, and he took a step forward. Isabella felt fear clench her stomach. She drew a great, ragged breath, pressing even harder against the wall.

"What are you doing out of bed, miss?" he asked gently, as if she were an errant child caught out in a misdemeanor. Isabella opened her mouth, but no sound came out. Her eyes, huge and very blue with fright, slid guiltily to the tell-tale candelabra, then jerked back up to his battered face.

"She was on the verge of braining you with that candlestick there, friend. Fortunately for us both, I don't sleep like the dead."

Paddy turned reproachful eyes on her. Isabella saw that they were brown, and soulful. Strangely kind eyes for such a monster of a man.

"Aw, Alec, she's frightened." He might have been speaking of a puppy.

Alec snorted. "She wasn't frightened until you woke up. She was bent on murder—yours, and probably mine after that."

"You weren't really going to hit me with that, were you, miss?"

"I—I . . ."

Lying had never come easily to her, but she was learning fast. Before she could frame a denial, though, she was interrupted by the sound of a key turning in the lock of the bedroom where she'd been.

All three of them listened as the door was locked again. Then soft footsteps crossed the other room, paused.

"Oh my heavens, where'd she get to?" The voice was female, slightly husky, and annoyed.

"In here, Pearl," Paddy called. Isabella was vastly relieved to have attention diverted from herself. She was feeling muzzy-headed, and it took all her strength just to remain on her feet, much less defend herself against the giant and his handsome friend.

The woman came to the door of the dressing room and looked at the trio inside with obvious surprise. Isabella's eyes widened at the sight of her. It wasn't just that she was beautiful, which she was. Her hair was so blonde it was almost white. Her face was soft and round like a child's, with the requisite cupid's bow mouth, artfully reddened, pouting prettily below a nose that might have been a hair too retroussé but was lovely for all that. Her eyes were midnight blue, framed by incredible lashes that were astonishingly dark for such a fair-haired woman. It wasn't any of that, or the amazing quality of her white skin, or the soft pink flush in her cheeks, that made Isabella's eyes grow round. It wasn't the trio of towering purple plumes in the elaborately upswept hair, or even the necklace of what appeared to be enormous, genuine sapphires around her neck.

It was her gown. Or rather, what wasn't covered by her gown.

The woman had a figure that would stop a full-grown bull moose in its tracks. And a large portion of it was on display.

Full white breasts flowed lushly over the scanty bodice, which was of purple brocade edged with black lace. Above it her neck and shoulders and all of her breasts down to the very nipple were bare. Isabella could actually see the crescents of dark pink areolas.

After a shocked stare, Isabella finally managed to drag her eyes lower. Beneath the magnificent bosom the woman had a tiny waist that curved into generous hips clearly outlined by the clinging, ruched brocade. The dress hugged her lushly curved thighs until it reached her knees, where the purple brocade parted to reveal a petticoat of tiered black lace. The lace was semitransparent, allowing the viewer a peek at plump, silk-stockinged legs with a garter tied daringly just below one dimpled knee.

Never in her life had Isabella seen such a costume. The word indecent barely did it justice. Clearly designed to engender lust in a man, it was provocative, tantalizing, simmering with promise. Isabella thought of the two men in the room with her, undoubtedly ogling this flaunting exhibition, and her face flamed a brilliant red.

X

"My lord, angel, what're you blushin' for? We all got the same equipment, ain't we?" Pearl addressed that question to Isabella with lively surprise.

"But some of you are . . . more abundantly equipped than others," Alec intervened with a wry grin. Pearl's eyes flew to him.

"Oh, Alec, you're better! It's so good to see you sittin' up, darlin'!"

She rustled across the room, dropping to her knees beside the bed. Throwing her arms around him, the purple plumes scraping the wall as she lowered her head, she kissed him lingeringly on the mouth. Watching, Isabella felt a strange discomfort somewhere in the vicinity of her belly, and hastily averted her eyes. Then, when at last the kiss was done and Isabella thought it was safe to look again, Pearl pressed Alec's head to her bare white bosom in a gesture so intimate that Isabella felt her face burn anew. Her eyes dropped to the floor for the second time in as many minutes.

"Ahem." Apparently also embarrassed, Paddy cleared his throat and shifted his eyes from the embracing couple to Isabella. His cheeks, like hers, were a shade pinker than they had been before.

He shook his head at her. "You shouldn't've got outa bed, you know. You've been lying there, out of your head delirious, for nigh on a fortnight. Wearing yourself to the bone ain't gonna help you recover."

Isabella fixed her eyes on him with a certain desperation. Rustling sounds and a soft giggle from the direction of the bed warned her that the embrace had resumed. For some reason her eyes wanted to turn in that direction, and she had to battle to keep them fastened on Paddy. If she hoped to make head or tails out of the situation in which she found herself, she had best keep her wits about her, and watching that woman's lascivious display with Alec certainly did not help clear her mind. She understood nothing of what was going on, but clung to one fact: so far these people had shown no disposition to harm her. They might, though. Remembering the original kidnappers' plan to murder her, she felt a cold frisson of fear quiver along the back of her neck.

Until she was safe at home again, no one could be trusted.

Her eyes slid past Paddy to the bedchamber beyond.

"I—I think I will go back to bed. If you'll turn your back, that is. I'm not dressed," she explained hesitantly, gesturing down at herself as he looked at her with a growing frown. The chair and her hair still shielded her body from view, but if she stepped out from behind the chair, her hair would cover only so much. Alec and Pearl were clearly too preoccupied to notice anything but themselves, but Paddy was not. She gazed at him pleadingly. To her surprise, he turned his back.

Risking a quick glance at Alec and Pearl—she was lying sprawled on the bed with him, and Isabella didn't even want to think about what his hands were doing—she stepped out from behind the chair. As she walked toward the bedroom, her head began to swim. Her knees shook, and she suddenly felt icy cold. Another step and she had to catch hold of the doorknob to keep from falling to the floor. She must have made a slight sound, because Paddy was by her side in an instant, seemingly oblivious to her state of undress as he looked anxiously into her face. Isabella was not oblivious, though, and despite her weakness, tried to cover herself with her hair, cringing away when he would have touched her.

"Pearl, leave off fawning over Alec and come help this chit back to bed," Paddy said.

"You do it, Paddy. You don't need me—but I think Alec does." A throaty, suggestive giggle punctuated the words.

"Go help the lady to bed, Pearl. I'm not up to much right now, anyway."

"Oh, Alec!" Pearl protested, pouting.

"Do as I say, now. I need to talk to Paddy. Business."

"Oh, you and your damned business! That's all you ever think about!" Pearl snapped, flouncing off the bed. Out of the corner of her eye Isabella could not help but see Alec's next appeasing gesture.

"All, Pearl?" He squeezed her bottom, his grin beguiling.

Pearl giggled, turned, and planted a kiss full on his chiselled mouth. "Well, maybe not all," she agreed, relenting. Her good nature thus restored, she adjusted a drooping plume while apparently wasting little thought on the bosom that was even more daringly exposed than before. Then she moved over to where Isabella watched her with half-frightened fascination.

"Come on, angel, let's mind Alec and tuck you back into bed."

Isabella instinctively shrank as Pearl slid an arm around her waist. She was not used to being touched, especially by strangers. Especially not by a stranger like Pearl, who was absolutely scandalous in dress and behavior. But after a moment she permitted herself to be helped away from the door and led into the bedroom. Her weakness was not feigned, but her meekness was. Such meekness had helped her to escape before, by lulling the suspicions of her captors. It might help her again.

Although she was a little lightheaded, she was not so far gone that she did not notice the key that Pearl had left in the lock on the inside of the door. If she could just get away from Pearl, she could be out that door in a trice. And through that door lay the way home. . . .

If she took the key with her, and locked the door from

the outside, Pearl and Paddy and Alec would be unable to follow her.

She would be free.

Behind them, Paddy shut the door to the dressing room, leaving the two women alone. Pearl helped Isabella toward the bed. Isabella's thoughts were becoming sluggish even as her body was growing increasingly weak, but she fought to stay alert. Should she try, or bide her time?

She might never get another chance.

Isabella took a deep breath, inhaled Pearl's pungent floral perfume, and succumbed to a totally unexpected fit of sneezing that nearly sent her to her knees. Pearl jumped back, shaking her head, and when the sneezes subsided, withdrew a lace-trimmed handkerchief from her bosom and passed it to Isabella.

"Here, angel, use this."

Like Pearl herself, the handkerchief was drenched with scent. Isabella tried not to inhale as she accepted it.

"Come on, then, let's get you into bed."

Pearl put her arm around Isabella's waist again. Isabella, realizing that it was now or never, prayed that her last remaining reserves of strength would be equal to the task. Then, gritting her teeth, she shoved the unsuspecting Pearl as hard as she could. Taken by surprise, Pearl staggered backwards and, tripping over the long train of her gown, crashed to the floor.

"Why, you little slut!" she cried, but Isabella was already at the door, fumbling with the key.

"Alec, Paddy, help! Quick!"

Pearl came after her, scrambling on all fours. The door to the dressing room flew open just as Isabella managed to turn the key in the lock. She jerked at the knob, got the door open. Paddy barreled through the dressing room door. Behind him, Alec had managed to get out of bed and was leaning, panting, against the jamb of the dressing room door, clearly able to go no farther. He was as white-faced and weak-looking as Isabella felt.

Stumbling through the opening, Isabella was felled by a violent jerk on the hem of her nightdress. She staggered forward, falling. Her knees hit the polished wood floor of the hall, and she cried out. A young female in a nightdress as diaphanous as her own was in the hall with a well-dressed gentleman in tow.

"What. . . ?" the gentleman said, starting forward. Isabella noticed that Paddy had faded back into the bedroom, while Pearl hurried forward to yank Isabella to her feet.

" 'Tis only one of my girls, out of her head with child-bed fever. And she lost the child, too, poor creature." Pearl jerked Isabella back toward the room.

"Can I help you, Miss Pearl?" the girl asked in a soft, dreamy voice.

"No, Suzy, you just take care of your gentleman," Pearl snapped, then smiled at the gentleman as if to soften her words. Isabella, knowing herself defeated and too dizzy and exhausted to struggle against her fate anymore, allowed herself to be pulled back inside the bedroom.

"Ungrateful little besom," Pearl muttered, shoving her to the center of the room. Isabella fell to her knees again, not caring any longer that Alec and Paddy were seeing her near nakedness or that they were all angry with her. She didn't even care that she had failed to escape. . . .

"Be careful, Pearl, you'll hurt her," Paddy said in a scolding tone as he bent to pick Isabella up.

"If she gives Alec's hiding place away, I'll do more than hurt her." Pearl carefully locked the door, then turned to glare at Isabella. "I'll kill her!"

"Such fierceness, sweeting. I'm flattered," Alec murmured from where he still leaned against the doorway.

"Darlin', you shouldn't've got out of bed!" Pearl remonstrated, flying to his side, casting Isabella a fulminating look as she did.

Isabella, held awkwardly in Paddy's arms, glanced at the pair, then away. Paddy laid her on the bed, looming over her.

"Please don't hurt me," Isabella whispered, and amazingly, Paddy straightened away.

For the moment, it seemed, she was to be spared. Giving in to the weakness that now washed over her, she closed her eyes, and let exhaustion claim her.

XI

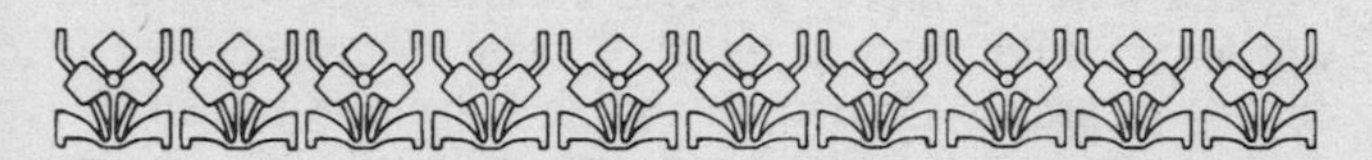

When Isabella awoke the next time, the room was once again shrouded in darkness. Had she slept the clock round? Only a soft orange glow from the dying embers in the hearth provided any light at all. Disoriented, dry-mouthed and in some pain, she stared at the dark shadows around the bed, wondering what had awakened her. Then, for no reason at all that she could think of, she had the disquieting sensation that she was not alone.

Holding her breath so as to listen for the faintest sound, Isabella was conscious of her heart knocking against her chest. Lying on her stomach, her head sliding sideways off a deep, downy pillow, she was frighteningly aware of her own vulnerability. Someone was in the room with her, she knew it. And if they were creeping about under cover of darkness, what could their intent be but evil? Was she to be strangled—smothered—bludgeoned—while she slept?

A shadow moved near the foot of the bed, separating itself from the voluminous bed-curtains.

Isabella gasped, and wound or no wound, turned over onto her back, swarming up over the mound of pillows piled against the headboard.

"For God's sake, don't start screaming."

She would know that voice with its dry intonation anywhere. It belonged to Alec, and immediately, though for no solid reason that she knew, a great deal of her panic left her. Although his intentions toward her were most likely less than benign, she did not fear that he personally would murder her in cold blood. At least, not tonight. She hoped.

"What . . . what are you doing in here?" she whispered, staring at him. He was no more than a denser darkness against the gray-black of the room.

"You were whimpering like a kicked pup. I listened to you for a while, then decided I'd better check and see if ought was amiss. Obviously not, so I'll return to bed."

He made a movement as though to leave. The idea of being left alone in the dark suddenly frightened Isabella far more than he did.

"Wait!"

"What is it?" His voice was harsher, and she remembered that he, like she, had been confined to a sickbed the last time she had set eyes on him. Perhaps it was an ordeal for him to stand.

"Could . . . could you tell me where I am? And what's happened? And what you intend to do with me? Please?" This last was said in a tiny voice as he made no response to her questions. There was a few moments' silence, and then he moved again. Isabella thought he would leave without responding, but to her surprise he sank down on the end of her bed.

She squeaked, unable to help herself as Alec made himself at home on her bed, and hitched herself up higher against the headboard. Having him in her bedroom was bad enough, going against every tenet of decency Isabella had ever learned, but for him to actually sit on her bed. . . ! Only a husband was accorded such privileges, and then only rarely.

"If you want to talk, I'm willing, because God knows you must be frightened to death and I hadn't considered that, but if you let loose with one more squeal I'm likely to throttle you. My head aches like bloody hell." The warning came grumpily out of the darkness.

His language in her presence was almost as unsettling as his presence on her bed. Certainly no gentleman would swear so in front of a lady. But since she had been kidnapped the proprieties had been flouted so many times in so many ways that bad language was a mere bagatelle.

"I'm sorry. I didn't mean to scream. But—you're sitting on my bed."

"It's either sit on your bed or go back to my own. I'm not exactly in ruddy good health at the moment, you know. But I can bloody well leave if you wish."

"No!"

From the satisfied quality of his silence, Isabella guessed that that was the response he had expected.

"All right then. If the idea of being ravished out of hand is what's making you so nervous, pray dismiss it from your mind. Even if I wished to—which I don't—and were capable—which I don't think I am just at present—I don't go in for forcing myself on unwilling females. There are too many willing ones."

Isabella was both embarrassed at his plain speaking, and shocked at what she perceived as his uncanny ability to read her mind. Ever since she had become aware of his presence, a tiny part of her mind had been afraid that he had come into her room in the middle of the night for just such a purpose. After watching him disport himself so shockingly with Pearl, and remembering how his eyes had heated as they'd moved over her own body, she felt she had good reason to be wary. Alec obviously liked women, and she could rely on neither his morals (she was convinced he had none) nor his breeding (he had none of that either) to keep him in check. But he had said he did not force himself on women, and to her surprise, she discovered that she took him at his word. He might order her murder, but she believed him when he assured her that he didn't indulge in rape.

"Now that we have that settled, what do you want to know?" His disembodied voice was curiously comforting. It was nice to know that there was someone with her, that she was no longer alone in the dark. She would be quite comfortable with him, if only she could be assured that he felt toward murder as he felt toward rape.

"What happened? How did I get here, and why are you . . . hiding . . . in the dressing room?"

Isabella could feel him looking at her. "I don't much like the word 'hiding,' " he said finally. "Though I suppose it's true enough. I was shot by a man who's worked for me for years, someone I thought was totally loyal. From what he said before he died, he was paid by someone else within my organization to kill me. Hardy—that was his name, Rat-face Hardy—died before he could identify the man who hired him. With me half-dead, Paddy got his protective instincts up. Not knowing who the traitor was, he elected to trust nobody with my precious person but himself.

"You were felled by what I can only assume was a stray bullet, so Paddy had on his hands two badly bleeding bodies that he didn't know quite what to do with. He bundled the pair of us up and brought us to Pearl, who is as shrewd as she can hold together. Paddy trusts Pearl, and so do I. She's one of the few people that I absolve of a wish to harm me. Pearl came up with the idea of putting you and me into a single bedchamber, you quite openly as one of her girls taken ill, and me in secret. Whoever wants me dead had a taste of success, and he's likely to try it again if he can. Until I'm up to full strength again we decided that it was best if I lay low. Paddy is playing bodyguard while my men try to ferret out the weasel who wants to take over the organization. With me out of the way, we figure he's bound to get nervous and make his move. Then we'll have him."

"What kind of organization do you run?" He did not seem overly concerned that someone was trying to kill him. From her own experience, Isabella knew that facing one's own prospective murder was terrifying. But perhaps killing was an everyday matter to him.

He hesitated. She could sense him mentally drawing rein on himself again, as he debated what to answer. Isabella realized suddenly just how little she knew of this man, and how misleading her earlier sense of familiarity might be.

"Are . . . are you going to kill me?" Her deepest fear came blurting out before she could stop herself. Isabella sat with her hand pressed to her mouth, eyes wide with horror at what she had said. She should have pretended to have no such notion, and waited for another chance to escape. . . .

Unexpectedly he chuckled. The sound was oddly engaging. "So, far from fearing rape, you thought I came in here to put a pillow over your face, eh? That's not a bad idea, considering the noise you were making."

Isabella sat mute. After a moment she could feel him peering at her through the darkness.

"That was a joke, you know. You don't have to fear being murdered. At least, not by me."

"What do you mean?" The last part of that statement was definitely sinister. Isabella stared at him through the darkness, feeling less than reassured.

"You and I are in the same boat, my dear. Someone wants you dead quite badly too."

Isabella must have made a protesting sound, because he continued with a touch of impatience. "I'm assuming you know that the bastards who kidnapped you meant murder."

It was a statement more than a question, but Isabella nodded, forgetting that he couldn't see her through the darkness. But apparently he sensed her movements as she sensed his.

"Aye, then. Well, somebody hired them—Cook Parren never took a step in his life unless there was somebody to pay him for it. He meant to kill you right enough, but it wasn't his idea. Before we restore you to the bosom of your family, you should know that somebody in your life wants you dead."

Isabella stared at him. "That's impossible! Who?"

From a slight movement of the mattress she thought that he might have shrugged. "Now, that I don't know. Not knowing you, or your family."

"My family wouldn't want me dead."

Again she had the sense that he shrugged.

''They wouldn't! You must be mistaken.''

''You know your family better than I do. But Parren was hired to kidnap you for ransom, which he did, and then paid more to kill you, which he would have. Somebody hired him, somebody with something to gain. Who stands to benefit from your death?''

''Benefit? You mean financially? No one. My husband got my dowry when we married. I have very little in my own name. And my father . . . my father wouldn't do that. Besides, he certainly has nothing to gain. Sarah—my stepmother—doesn't like me, but she wouldn't hire someone to murder me. There's no one. I'm sure of it. No one.''

''Believe me, there is someone, someone who wants you dead badly enough to pay a goodly sum to have it done. I can try to find out who for you, if you wish. One of the advantages of my position is that I can ferret out any amount of unsavory facts. If someone knows who hired Parren, and why, my men will find him sooner or later. And then you'll know the worst. Of course, if you'd rather not know, that's up to you. I can have you sent home to your family as soon as we no longer need you for cover, if that's what you want. You'll have to provide me with your name and direction, of course.''

''You don't know who I am?'' Isabella's eyes widened as she realized that he didn't even know her name. And here she'd been feeling more at ease with him than she had ever felt with a man. Certainly more comfortable than she ever felt with Bernard.

''We got word that Parren had contracted to kidnap a lady without going through the proper channels, so to speak. I'm the proper channel, so I moved to put an end to his insubordination. Your identity was incidental.'' His voice was almost apologetic.

''Well, that's very nice to know!'' She was unaccountably nettled, and it showed in her voice.

''Are you going to tell me your name, or not?''

''Oh, yes. I'm Isabella St. Just, Lady Blakely.''

''Oh, my, a lady! Just what kind of lady are you?''

''My husband is the Earl of Blakely.''

"You're married to Bernard St. Just?" His voice was fractionally sharper.

Forgetting again that he couldn't see, Isabella nodded.

"Well?" He was impatient.

"Yes."

There was a silence. Then, "How in hell did you end up married to him? You're not much more than a just-hatched chick!"

"I am three-and-twenty!" Isabella retorted. "Bernard is forty-five. My father says 'tis the prime of life."

"And just who is your father?"

"The Duke of Portland."

"Ahhh. So you're a very juicy plum for the picking, indeed."

"I beg your pardon?" His cant went over her head.

"Never mind. Is your marriage happy?"

"Whether it is or not is certainly none of your concern!" Isabella replied, taken aback.

"I'm simply attempting to determine who would want you dead. If your marriage is unhappy, then that needs to be considered along with everything else."

"I told you, none of my family would want me dead."

"St. Just dropped a packet at the tables a few months back." It sounded like an idle observation, but in the context of the conversation it was sinister. Isabella blinked.

"How do you know that?"

"Let's just say that it's my business to know what goes on in London."

"Who are you, anyway? You don't sound like a—a . . ." Her voice trailed away as she recollected that what she had been going to call him might just possibly be considered an insult.

"A . . . ?" he prompted. She thought he might be amused again.

"A ruffian," she came up with, and this time he laughed aloud.

"Oh, I'm very definitely a 'ruffian,' my lady, believe me. Although I've never thought of myself in exactly that way."

"I beg your pardon if I offended you."

"Not in the least. I've never been one to quibble at calling a spade a spade—or a ruffian a ruffian."

He was grinning; she could tell he was. Her eyes narrowed. She was providing him with a great deal of amusement, it seemed!

"Besides 'ruffian,' do you have another name?"

"Indeed I do, my lady. Alec Tyron, at your service."

"How do you do, Mr. Tyron?"

"Very well, thank you, my lady. And now that the formalities have been observed, and your fears of imminent murder have been laid to rest, may I suggest that we light a candle? If we are to continue this fascinating conversation, that is."

"Oh, no!" His suggestion brought home all the hideous impropriety of the situation. Clad in another of the diaphanous nightdresses, she was the next thing to naked—and he was a (probably dangerous, and certainly wicked) stranger, for all he was sitting so companionably on the end of her bed, and for all the unaccountable feeling of security he gave her in doing so.

"Why not?" The question was reasonable.

"I am not . . . dressed."

"Are you trying to tell me you're sitting there talking to me stark naked? Dear me, I'm shocked!" From the mock-horrified tone of his voice, Isabella knew that he was teasing her. But the image his words conjured up was vivid, and caused a queer little tightening in her belly. Mortified at both the conversation and her response, she struggled for words.

"No, I am not na—completely unclothed! Of course I am not! I have on a nightrail, but it is—it is not . . ." He knew perfectly well what she was trying to say, she thought. After all, he had seen her nightrail—and what lay beneath it—for himself. The memory made her flush.

"You relieve my mind. For a minute there I thought that I was to be subjected to the sight of a naked—no, I beg your pardon, the word was 'unclothed,' wasn't it?—an unclothed lady."

"You are not to be subjected to the sight of a lady at all, for I refuse to allow the candle lit!"

"And if I insist?"

That silenced her. For all his good-humored bantering, he had the upper hand here, not she. If he chose to light the candle, she had not the means to prevent him.

He must have sensed the uneasy quality of her silence, because after a moment he sighed.

"Nay, I was but teasing you. I forgot you're just a chick, not yet up to snuff. You've naught to fear from me, I give you my word. If you do not wish the candle lit, why, then it will stay unlit. Never let it be said that I failed to honor a lady's wishes."

"I wish you will let me go home." The plea, born of her confusion, the growing flame of liking she felt for him and the dying embers of fear, sounded heartfelt.

"Certainly you may go home, in no more than a day or two. I give you my word on that, too. Although, were I you, I would want to know who was trying to put a period to my existence before I put myself within their reach again."

"I cannot believe—"

There was a sound at the door, then the grating of a key turning in the lock. Isabella's eyes riveted on that dark portal as light slowly began to show around the edge of it. At her feet, she felt Alec tense.

XII

The man who stepped through the door was carrying an oil lamp in one hand. The wick was turned down low, so that the lamp shed just enough light to permit him to find his way. His features were in shadow, but there was no mistaking that huge form.

"Over here, Paddy," said Alec, confirming Isabella's guess.

Paddy turned up the lamp. Isabella blinked, then gasped as she realized what the lamp must reveal. Hurriedly she grabbed at the bedclothes and jerked them up around her neck, where she held them securely in place. Her unconfined hair tumbled in a riotous mass over the blue silk coverlet which she held to her chin. Above it her eyes were wide, and a softer, deeper shade of blue when she dared look first at Alec and then at Paddy. As she had feared, both men's eyes were upon her, and she wondered just how much of her person they had seen. Although, she thought with dubious comfort, they could not have seen more of her than they had already, the night before.

"I fear you've compromised the lady's modesty with your lamp, Paddy." There was a wealth of amusement in Alec's voice. Those golden eyes shifted from her to twinkle at his friend.

"What are you doing from bed? The sawbones told you to stay put for at least another week." Paddy frowned at Alec as he took another step into the room. Then, apparently remembering, he reached around to turn the key so that the door was securely locked again. He was dressed in what appeared to be the same crumpled frock coat and breeches he had worn the day before, but he was clean-shaven and his linen was fresh. A bottle of what appeared to be brandy was tucked under one arm, and both pockets of his coat bulged suspiciously. From the clinking sound the contents made when he moved, Isabella suspected that one pocket held glasses. What was in the other pocket, she couldn't be sure, but from the shape of the object, she would guess it was a pistol.

Alec shrugged. Lamplight played on the bare width of his shoulders, delineating solid muscles and painting them gold. The hairs on his chest were tipped with gold by the light as well, and for a moment, forgetting herself, Isabella stared. He was so very masculine, so completely different from herself. His skin looked as if it would be sleek to the touch. . . . Her fingers curled into involuntary fists as if she fought the sudden impulse to discover the texture of that skin for herself. Such thoughts must be a product of some lingering weakness of the brain from her delirium, she decided, because she had never had any remotely resembling them before.

Except for the sheet he had twisted around his middle, and the bandage around his chest, Alec was as bare as a babe. Apparently he had not taken time to pull on his breeches before coming to check on her. At the thought that she'd been sitting here in the darkness, visiting cozily with him when they were both next to naked, Isabella felt her throat grow dry.

She decided she still must be weaker than she knew. There was no other way she could think of to account for such disturbing physical symptoms.

"To hell with the bloody sawbones." Alec's voice was still perfectly amiable, but there was a steely note to it that told Isabella that he was accustomed to having his preferences deferred to. She eyed his profile with reluctant interest as he frowned at Paddy over one shoulder. His features were as perfectly carved from the side as they were from the front, his forehead high, his nose long and straight, his chin firm. What appeared to be a good week's growth of beard roughened his jaw, making him look in truth like the ruffian she had called him. His tawny hair, like hers unconfined, waved almost to his shoulders. "I've had a bellyful of skulking in here."

"You know what we decided. Until we discover who put Hardy up to shooting you, you're to remain in hiding. 'Tis best, Alec, and you know it."

"To hell with what we decided. I'll find the bloody blighter in my own way."

"They'll be on you like jackals on a corpse if they see a chance to get to you while you're weakened. 'Twill be easier to smoke them out if they don't know where you are, or whether or not you still live."

There was a moment's silence as Alec scowled at Paddy. Paddy met the golden eyes steadily, and after a moment Alec sighed.

"Aye, I know it. But it chafes me to hide away, while you're out scouring the woodwork for the vermin who got to Hardy."

"Can't be helped, Alec. Unless you've a hankering for a pine box instead of the gibbet I've always said would be your earthly reward."

Isabella made a sound of shock at such plain speaking between friends, and Alec's attention shifted back to her. Embarrassed to be caught ogling him, she quickly switched her attention to Paddy. But despite her best efforts to be as seemingly nonchalant about their unconventional situation as Alec was—although, of course, sitting half-naked on a bed with an equally unclothed female was probably nothing out of the ordinary for him—she felt warm color stain her cheeks.

"Now, why is she blushing?" Alec remarked on a surprised note, apparently to the world at large.

Of course, this made Isabella color up still more.

"I—I . . ." Isabella could come up with no response to that. How did one tell a gentleman—no, he was certainly no gentleman!—but a man, that his lack of clothing bothered her in the most inexplicable way? Isabella was lost for words. Her eyes met Alec's almost shyly. He returned her look, his own eyes suddenly intent.

Paddy cleared his throat. "Well, we'd best be letting you get back to sleep, miss. Alec had no business waking you in the first place."

Alec's eyes shifted to Paddy, and when he spoke his words were light. But Isabella could not shake the notion that something—she didn't know quite what, but something—had just passed between Alec and herself that was quite beyond her experience. Something that was hot, and secret, and sent the heat that had blushed her cheeks surging clear down to her toes.

"The shoe's on the other foot, my friend. She woke me, squalling like a bloody kitten. And she's 'my lady,' not miss, Paddy."

"Beg pardon, my lady," Paddy said, bowing in her direction and turning an inquiring eye on Alec.

"Countess of Blakely. St. Just's relic."

"Oh." Paddy frowned, started to say something, and apparently thought better of it.

"Is something the matter, Paddy?"

"Tell you later," Paddy said under his breath, with a warning look at Alec. Isabella sat a little straighter. As she pressed against the headboard, her back throbbed beneath the neat square bandage that protected the healing wound, but she ignored the pain, fixing Paddy with wide eyes.

"If it is something to do with me, I would prefer that you tell me as well as Mr. Tyron," she said with quiet dignity.

Paddy looked unhappy.

"Go on, Paddy, it can't be too bad for her ladyship to hear, can it?"

"Alec . . ."

"Tell her." Despite the quiet timbre of Alec's voice, it was an order.

"St. Just was below tonight."

"What?" Isabella could not believe she had heard correctly. Paddy obligingly repeated what he had said, more loudly this time.

"But why? What is this place? Why would Bernard come here? Is he looking for me?" She felt strangely disappointed that that should be so. Bernard was her husband; if he had come looking for her, she would have to go to him. And she was astonished to discover that, all of a sudden, she had no wish to go home after all.

Alec and Paddy exchanged long looks.

"I don't think he was looking for you," Paddy said slowly, watching her face with troubled eyes.

"Then why was he here? What is this place?"

Alec frowned. Those golden eyes gleamed at her in the candlelight.

"Have you ever been to the theatre? In London?" he asked.

"I've never even been to London," she admitted slowly.

"Well, we're in London's theatre district."

"Sort of," Paddy amended, sounding uneasy. Alec flashed him a look. Isabella couldn't decipher its meaning.

"If there's something you're having trouble telling me, I wish you'd just say it." Isabella was looking at Alec, who unexpectedly gave a wry grin. "Why don't you start with where we are. Precisely. I'm already aware that this is not—not a respectable place."

"No, it's not respectable," Alec agreed. Paddy looked embarrassed. "It's called the Golden Carousel, and it's a combination gaming hell and bawdy house."

A hell was bad enough—indeed, she had never expected to be inside one—but a bawdy house! Her eyes widened as she remembered the young female in the hall—and Pearl. Why, they must be . . . Her face went scarlet.

"Oh," Isabella said faintly after a moment, feeling that some response was called for, and unable to think of anything more adequate. Then she frowned. "I suppose Bernard came to gamble, then."

Paddy looked uneasy, but nodded.

"There's more, isn't there?" she asked, her eyes on his face. "If he came to . . . to . . . if he came for . . . female companionship, you needn't try to hide it. I'm more up to snuff than either of you think. I know such things are common with gentlemen."

Alec made a sound under his breath. Isabella saw that his eyes were dark with pity for her. She lifted her chin at him.

" 'Tis the way of the world," she said steadily.

"Alec, could I see you for a minute?" Paddy still looked uneasy.

"If you have anything else to report on Lord Blakely, you can say it in front of me. After all, he is my husband."

"Say what you have to say, Paddy. Whatever it is, 'tis best that she knows." Alec's voice was abrupt.

Paddy looked at Isabella sorrowfully. "St. Just was dressed in full mourning, my lady. He told one of the bawds that he was newly widowed."

"What?" Isabella was stunned. "But . . . how could he say that? He is certainly not!"

"Apparently he thinks you dead." Alec got up from the bed, absently hitching the sheet higher around his waist. "If I were you, I'd think about that."

Isabella said nothing. There was nothing she could say. That Bernard was calling himself a widower had many possible ramifications. She had to examine them all before she knew what to think.

Alec watched her for a moment, then turned to Paddy.

"Let's go crack open that bottle, friend, and let the lady go back to sleep."

Isabella was scarcely aware as they padded silently toward the dressing room. She was too busy turning what she had learned over in her mind. Did the fact that Bernard thought her dead mean that it was he who had schemed to have her killed? But why? Surely, surely, there was some other explanation. . . .

"You don't have to be afraid, you know. We have you safe here, and you can stay as long as you like." It was Alec who spoke from just outside the dressing room door. As she looked in the direction of his voice, Isabella became aware that Paddy had carried the lamp away with him, and the room was once again dark. Alec was no more than a tall silhouette against the light that now shone from the dressing room behind him.

She could find nothing to say to that. She merely stared blindly at the tall, dark shape of him without answering. He waited a minute, then turned away, speaking over his shoulder as he left her alone.

"Good-night, then," he said softly. Then, softer still, he added, "Isabella."

XIII

Isabella slept for most of the next week. Pearl, Paddy, and Alec were in and out of her chamber, but she was only occasionally aware of them. Finally, she was awakened, rudely, by a hand shaking her shoulder. Isabella blinked, and opened her eyes to see Pearl bending over her.

"What is it?" Isabella asked, turning over gingerly. The soreness in her back was much lessened, she discovered, but it still ached if she put too much pressure on it. The bedclothes fell away from her shoulders as she moved, and Isabella was left looking down at a vast expanse of her own bare skin. Though she was grateful for the use of the nightrails (and wondered if perhaps they were standard issue for the girls at the Golden Carousel), she would much have preferred something a little more similar to her own neatly pin-tucked muslin ones. Or if such was not available, and upon reflection, she did not suppose it would be in a bawdy house, then at least something with a modicum of decency to it.

Pearl was thoughtful as her eyes ran over Isabella. "If you find yourself in need of employment, angel, I can always use you belowstairs. A great many gentlemen seem to enjoy the young, innocent-looking ones. Probably reminds them of their daughters."

Isabella gasped and grabbed the bedclothes to tuck around herself.

"No, I thank you," she managed. Pearl shrugged, and went to part the curtains so that pale, cold sunlight filled the room. Through the frosted panes of glass Isabella could see a coating of ice on the iron bars that caged both windows.

"Why are the windows barred?" From what Alec had said, there had been no time to fit the windows with bars just to keep her imprisoned, even if they had wanted to, which Alec had assured her they did not. Strangely enough, Isabella found that she trusted Alec to tell her the truth, however painful. Though the truth as he saw it might not always be the truth as it was. . . .

"Oh, sometimes 'tis necessary to lock a new girl in until she learns the rules of the establishment and gets used to her duties, so to speak. Not that I have to do it very often, but the room's here when 'tis needed. And a good thing, too, for Alec. He don't have to worry about anyone comin' in the windows after him. That just leaves the door to watch."

"Do you really think someone will be coming here to try to kill him?"

"They would if they knew where he was, that's for sure. But they don't, and they won't find out if I have anything to say about it. I'm allowin' none of my girls in this room until Alec's safe, and no one else knows where he is but me and Paddy and the sawbones—and you."

She gave Isabella a measuring look.

"I wouldn't do anything to betray him," Isabella said hastily. "How could I, even if I wanted to?"

Pearl pursed her lips. "You could've given him away the other night, running out like that. But what's past is past, and I won't hold it against you. Paddy explained it all to me, and I understand where you might have thought you were in a bad situation. As long as you don't do it again."

"No, I won't," Isabella promised. Pearl stood looking at her for a moment, as if weighing the truthfulness of her words. Then she shrugged, and turned her attention to a silver tray which she must have placed on the bedside table before awakening Isabella.

Isabella sat up a little higher, tugging the coverlet with her, and absently lifted a hand to smooth an errant strand of hair from her face. She watched Pearl with some fascination as the other woman's hands fluttered over the contents of the tray. Pearl's white-blonde hair was dressed in girlish ringlets which fell from a pink satin bow adorning the top of her head. Her face was the exquisite white of the night before, but by daylight Isabella could see that at least some degree of her skin's porcelain perfection was due to the careful application of a light layer of maquillage. Her cheeks bloomed rosily, her mouth was rouged a soft red, and the lashes surrounding her midnight eyes were long and sooty black. The heavy scent of roses enveloped her. Isabella had to strain to keep her nose from wrinkling. Painted and perfumed, Pearl was like no female, lady or maid or peasant, Isabella had ever laid eyes on before.

"I've brought your breakfast. I feel like a bloody chambermaid doing it, too, I don't mind telling you. Waiting on females is not what I'm used to."

"I'm sorry," Isabella offered, feeling that the response was inadequate but not knowing what else to say. She offered the other woman a tentative smile.

Pearl grimaced, then sighed. " 'Tis none of your fault, I suppose," she said as she lifted the cover from a silver dish to peer at the contents. Apparently satisfied, she replaced the cover and started to lift the tray.

"Wait, please!" Isabella held up a hand. She could not eat with her breasts more naked than not, barely veiled as they were by sheer gauze. And she could not eat and hold the bedclothes around her neck at the same time, either. And she was really hungry. She supposed she had taken nourishment during the time she'd been ill, but she had no recollection of it. "I hate to ask, as you've been so kind to lend your clothes already, but do you have a wrapper or shawl or something I could use to put over this nightdress?"

"You cold?" Pearl asked, sounding surprised. "Oh, I forgot, you're a lady, aren't you? Sure, I've got something, angel. Just hold on a minute."

Pearl crossed to rummage in the tall wardrobe opposite the bed. When she returned, she was holding a small, fluffy jacket made of lavender satin and trimmed with downy feathers that had been dyed to match.

" 'Tis a bed jacket," she said, holding it up for Isabella's inspection. "Is it not the most cunning thing? I had my dressmaker make some up for my girls—you know, for mornings when they want to take breakfast in bed with a gentleman."

Pearl was so matter-of-fact that Isabella realized that, to her, taking breakfast in bed with a gentleman was as commonplace as breathing. Probably it was something she often did with Alec. . . .

The thought and the image that accompanied it were unsettling. Isabella tried to banish both, murmuring something incoherent by way of thanks as she reached for the bed jacket. She needed Pearl's assistance to get it on properly, and the movements caused a stab of discomfort in her back. But it was discomfort only, not pain, and Isabella was encouraged to realize that her wound really was healing.

The satin felt luxuriously cool and smooth against her skin, and to her relief, bore only a faint scent of lilies. From the gentle smell she tended to think the garment did not belong to Pearl, whose preference seemed to be for the headier scent of roses.

"Is this yours?" Isabella asked, doing up the ribbons that secured the garment.

"Oh, no. That belonged to Lily. Each of my girls has her own distinctive color and scent, and Lily's was lavender and lilies. Of course, her real name was Doreen but when she chose the scent, she changed her name to match. She was real popular with the gents, once she got the hang of it."

"What happened to her?"

"She got a protector who set her up in a little house of

her own. A lot of my girls do that. I don't mind; it helps to keep the Carousel fresh. Gentlemen do like variety, you know."

Pearl placed the breakfast tray across Isabella's lap. Isabella sniffed the heady aroma of rolls and conserve, and felt her mouth water. Quickly she spread a roll and took a large bite. Her attention returned to Pearl.

This morning she was wearing a breathtaking dress of pink gauze trimmed with silver lace, which, except for the heart-stoppingly low neckline, was unexceptional. Isabella loved pretty clothes, although she did not own many herself. As Bernard had very reasonably pointed out—and Isabella agreed—finery was wasted in the country. But she had always had a sneaking longing to have a wardrobe that was slap up to the nines, and she could not help but wonder how Pearl's dress—with a filled-in neckline, of course—would look on herself.

"That's a lovely gown," she said, sounding a little wistful. "Is pink your color?" She remembered that Pearl had worn deep purple the other night, and wondered.

Pearl looked sharply at her, as if to gauge whether or not she was being made sport of. When she saw that Isabella was sincere, her expression softened.

"I get to wear whatever I want. I'm the mistress of the establishment, not one of the girls."

As Isabella spread conserve on a second roll, having demolished the first, Pearl moved to stand before the cheval glass in the corner of the room, preening as she examined her reflection.

"The dress is pretty, isn't it? I had it made up special, to give Alec something to think about other than the spot he's in. Pink's his favorite color."

"Is . . . is it?" Isabella managed faintly, swallowing the bite of roll that had suddenly lost much of its taste. Pearl's tone could not have made it plainer that she was Alec's mistress—unless, the horrible thought suddenly occurred to Isabella, she was his wife?

Isabella was surprised at how much she disliked the notion of that.

"You and he are not married, are you?" The question was out before she could stop it.

Pearl laughed, flounced over, and sat down plump on the edge of the bed in almost the very spot that Alec had occupied the night before. Isabella had to grab for her teacup to keep the brew from sloshing over.

"No, angel, though I'm not sayin' I'm not workin' on it. But Alec's a slippery fish to catch."

"He seems very fond of you," Isabella said.

"Oh, he's fond of me, all right. He'll come round to marriage one day, I guess. Eat up now."

"Have you known him long?"

"Twenty years, or thereabouts. Since we was kids."

"It's very nice of you to let him—and me—recover in your house. Or, ah, whatever."

Pearl laughed again. "The Carousel ain't mine. It belongs to Alec, just like half o' London. A regular Midas, he is."

"Is he?" Fascinated, Isabella quite forgot about the teacup suspended in one hand, and blinked at Pearl over it.

"Angel, you don't know nothin', do you? Where've you been, that you never heard of Alec Tyron, the Tiger?" Pearl's voice was mildly scandalized.

"I've never been out of Norfolk," Isabella admitted. "And I've certainly never heard of anyone called the Tiger. Why do they call him that, anyway?"

"Because of his eyes—don't they give you the shivers? And because he's the boss around here—the boss of London, really."

"I don't understand."

"Why, Alec does it all—runs the hells, like the Carousel, and the bawds, like me and my girls, and the sneaks and cracks and cheats, and the hoisters—"

"That's enough out of you, my girl," Alec interrupted suddenly. Isabella looked up to see him standing in the doorway between the rooms. This time, though he was barefoot, he was clad in black breeches and a half-open white shirt. His tawny hair had been neatly secured at the nape with a ribbon, and he had shaved. His golden eyes gleamed as he looked the women over. Isabella felt oddly embarrassed at having been caught talking about him, and lowered her eyes back to her tray.

At the sound of his voice, Pearl jumped off the bed and looked guilty. Then she gave a little gurgling laugh and tripped toward him.

"Oh, Alec, what's the harm in a little gossip? Darlin', should you be out of bed? You know what the sawbones said."

"Don't you start, too," he said, suffering her to plant a kiss on his mouth and then stand pressed against his side, her arms wrapped around his waist. "You're starting to sound like Paddy, and Paddy might as well put in to be my ma."

"I can't help it if I worry about you." Pearl pouted. It made her red lips look deliciously small and curved, Isabella noted, and guessed Pearl was well aware of the effect. Just as she was aware of the shimmery allure of her lovely pink dress, and the temptation of her exposed white bosom pressed against Alec's muscled arm. Though it was early in their acquaintance, Isabella was sure that Pearl did very little without being aware of its effect on her audience.

"I know, and I appreciate it. I guess I'm just cross because I'm hungry. Where's my breakfast, wench?" He slid an arm around her waist and gave her an affectionate squeeze. Isabella had to look away, assailed by a sudden pang of discomfort as she watched Alec smile down into Pearl's eyes.

"I'll get it. I'd've brought it with me, but I thought you'd still be sleeping."

"Now, when have you ever known me to sleep in?"

"Never—but then, I've never known you to be hurt or sick before, either."

"True enough, but I'm almost up to full strength again. If you feed me, who knows what I might be capable of?"

"Really?" Pearl said, brightening. She rubbed herself against his side with blatant provocation, and smiled widely up at him. "I'll get your breakfast."

"And tell Paddy I need to see him," Alec called after her as she let herself out. Pearl nodded, and closed the door behind her. Isabella noted that she was careful to lock it as she left, and wondered that they were still so bent on keeping her locked in. Of course, Pearl would not know about the events of the night. Until she knew the truth about Bernard, Isabella couldn't go home. . . . Then it occurred to her that they were not locking her in so much as they were locking Alec's enemies out. Such elaborate precautions were not on her behalf at all.

"Pearl's a wonderful woman, but she has a tendency to jabber when she should be silent. I hope you'll strive to forget what she told you about me."

"I couldn't understand half of it, anyway," Isabella admitted. "When she started talking about sneaks and cracks and cheats, I was lost."

Alec shook his head, and came to stand at the foot of the bed, his hands casually curled around the gilded footrail. Isabella realized that this was the first time she had ever seen him by daylight. Unlike Pearl, he was even handsomer by the frosty light of the sun than he had been by candlelight. The pale sunlight gleamed off the smooth, firm textures of his bronzed skin, and picked up golden highlights in his tawny hair. His eyes gleamed too, bright and predatory as they moved over her. Isabella could quite see how he came to be known as the Tiger.

"That's as well. What are you eating? It smells good."

"Rolls with orange conserve. And tea. There's plenty, if you'd like some."

Aware of his eyes on her, she felt strangely flustered, and was conscious of a strong, almost painful wish that she were the kind of woman to make him catch his breath. For the first time in her life she sincerely longed for the gift of beauty. But even as she wished it she knew that she was being ridiculous. Those heart-stopping golden eyes were seeing her just as she was: a too slender, big-eyed slip of a girl in an incongruously luxurious lavender satin bed jacket, her wayward hair, more untidy than ever from not having been properly dressed in more than a week, sending itchy tendrils to tickle her nose while the mass of it cascaded in a tangle down her back. She knew that she was nothing out of the ordinary, with her pale skin and freckles and delicate, pointy face. Certainly her looks paled to insignificance beside Alec's dazzling golden handsomeness, or Pearl's outlandish blonde beauty.

"Thank you, but I'll wait for Pearl to come back," Alec said abruptly. Startled at something in his tone, Isabella lifted her eyes to his face. He was frowning slightly, though not so much at her, she thought, as his own thoughts. Or perhaps he was in pain. There was such a vitality about him that it was easy to forget that he had been shot in the chest not so long ago.

As suddenly as it had appeared, his frown vanished. His eyes were keen on her face.

"Have you decided? Shall I try to find out who it is that would see you dead?"

The question caught Isabella by surprise. But it seemed that during the long, sleepless night she had indeed decided.

"Yes, please," she said.

He inclined his head, accepting her decision without comment. "If you'll excuse me, then, I'll finish dressing."

Isabella nodded. He turned on his heel and strode with easy grace to the dressing room door. There he paused for an instant, looking at her with a frown as if he would say something more. He apparently thought better of it, shook his head, and left her alone.

Isabella was left staring after him. The image of those broad shoulders and muscular legs as they had looked walking away from her remained with her long after he had vanished from her sight.

XIV

A quarter of an hour later, Paddy had joined Alec in the dressing room, and Pearl had returned with his breakfast. The three of them were closeted together. It gave Isabella an odd sense of lonesomeness to be on the wrong side of that closed door.

She looked down with distaste at the remainder of her breakfast. Her appetite had quite deserted her, and she wasn't sure why. It might be because she was facing the very real possibility that someone, most likely her husband, had paid to have her killed. Or it might be that she, a married woman, a lady, was growing all too disturbingly aware of Alec.

Just because he was the handsomest man she had ever seen in her life was no reason to lose her sound common sense, she scolded herself. Even were she not married, he was not for her. The gulf that separated them was far too wide. She was a lady of the *ton,* a countess of noble parentage. He was . . . what? Certainly he was not of her ilk.

Isabella was beginning to realize that she had been sheltered too long at Blakely Park. In the six years since her marriage to Bernard, she had seen few people besides the servants, and no attractive men whatsoever. She was a normal young woman, after all, and perhaps her attraction to Alec merely meant that she was starved for compatible company. It was possible that Pressy and the servants and her animals weren't enough for her. Perhaps what she needed was someone of her own age and kind, to talk with and laugh with and experience life with a little.

Maybe Bernard had known that, and that was why he had so inexplicably summoned her to London.

Although Bernard, in the years she had been wed to him, had never showed the slightest degree of perception where she was concerned.

A knock at the door interrupted her thoughts, and despite the sudden surge of alarm she felt—after all, with Alec and Paddy and Pearl all in the dressing room, who was left to knock at the door?—she was glad to have them interrupted.

The knock sounded again, more loudly this time. Isabella stared at the door. What should she do? She couldn't answer it—it might be someone who would do harm to Alec.

Quickly she got out of bed, padded to the dressing room door, and tapped on it. The door opened, and Paddy looked out at Isabella inquiringly.

"Someone's at the door," she mouthed, pointing.

Paddy looked over his shoulder, and frowned. "Pearl, if you'd let Alec be, he might recover faster. Anyway, there's someone at the door."

There was a rustle of cloth, and then Pearl was beside Paddy, going on tiptoe as she reached up to tweak his cheek. "You're getting to be a regular spoil-sport, aren't you, lackwit?"

Paddy apparently took no offense at the mocking nickname, because his frown faded as he looked down into her face. Isabella was struck by something that flashed briefly in his eyes. Was it possible that Paddy was attracted to Pearl, and deferred his interest to Alec's prior claim?

This intriguing notion was interrupted by a banging on the door that defied anyone not to answer it. Isabella, suddenly recalled to a sense of her dishabille, scurried for the bed and clambered in.

Paddy swung to face the door, his hand reaching for his

pocket where Isabella assumed he kept his pistol. Pearl shook her head at him.

" 'Tis Mr. Heath, the sawbones," she said, and Paddy relaxed as she went to open the door.

Mr. Heath was not quite as tall as Pearl, and he was so rotund that he gave the appearance of being nearly as wide as he was tall. Despite the chill of the day, he was red and perspiring, the floridness of his complexion extending clear past his face to his balding pate. Scant strands of ginger hair were combed back into a skimpy tail. His coat and waistcoat were unfastened, his shirt was crumpled and looked as though might pop its buttons at any moment, and his breeches were stretched to the limit. All in all he was not a figure to inspire confidence in any who might be his patients, but Pearl greeted him blithely and hustled him inside, carefully locking the door behind him.

"And how is the Tiger?" Mr. Heath asked, referring to Alec in what Isabella could only think of as a reverential tone. He had spared not a glance for Isabella, who assumed that she was his patient as much as Alec, and felt a small degree of affront, as she was not used to being ignored. But clearly, to Mr. Heath, it was the Tiger who mattered.

"He says he is much recovered, and won't stay abed," Pearl reported, leading the way to the dressing room.

Mr. Heath frowned. "So I feared."

With that he was ushered into the dressing room. Paddy and Pearl disappeared with him, and the door was closed on Isabella's interested eyes.

Mr. Heath remained in the dressing room for some three quarters of an hour. The only clue Isabella had to what was transpiring within was Alec's shout of "I absolutely refuse to be blooded by this money-grubbing leech!" halfway through the proceedings. When Mr. Heath emerged at last, accompanied by Pearl, he looked flustered, and his florid face was even redder than before.

His subsequent examination of Isabella was cursory, and after he replaced the bandage covering her wound with a smaller one, he pronounced her well on the road to recovery.

" 'Tis fortunate that the bullet only grazed you, young woman. You've nothing more than three inches or so of skin gouged out of your back. Had fever not set in, I daresay you would have been on your feet again within a day or two. But then, fever often accompanies these cases. I'm glad to see that my powders have brought you to the right-about."

"I've been giving 'em to her just like you said," Pearl asserted virtuously, although so far as Isabella was aware, Pearl had done no such thing.

"Good, good. Keep her in bed for the remainder of the day, and then by tomorrow she should be able to begin sitting for an hour or so in a chair. It doesn't do to hurry these things, you know. The renewing of the body can't be rushed. Though try telling that to him in there." This was accompanied by a rolling of Mr. Heath's eyes in the direction of the dressing room. Pearl responded with a sympathetic murmur, and ushered Mr. Heath to the door.

"Remember, tell no one," Pearl said to Mr. Heath at the door. She pressed a large wad of pound notes into his hand.

"As if I would betray the Tiger," Mr. Heath responded, very much on his dignity as he pocketed the money. Pearl smiled at him, and opened the door so that he could leave. Once the door was locked again, Paddy emerged from the dressing room.

"How is he?" Pearl would have pushed by Paddy to see for herself, but Paddy stopped her with a hand on her arm.

"Grumpy as a badger. You know how he gets. We'd best let him alone for a bit."

"Like that, is he?" Pearl made a face. "Well, I have some things I need to see to downstairs. Let me get the breakfast trays, and I'll get out of here."

She went into the dressing room, and emerged in a few minutes grimacing, tray piled with empty dishes.

"Told you," Paddy said with equal parts humor and sympathy.

"Well, at least he gets over it quick," she sighed, and came to get Isabella's tray from where it had been removed to the bedside table. "Can I get you anything before I go downstairs?"

"If you have a brush and some pins, I would tidy my hair."

"I can manage that, I guess."

Pearl set down both trays and crossed to the wardrobe. Rummaging within, she came up with a silver brush and comb set, some pins and a mirror, which she dropped on Isabella's lap.

"That do?"

"Yes. Thank you, Pearl. You've been more than kind, really."

Pearl, pausing in the act of picking up the trays, looked surprised. Then she laughed. "That's certainly the first time I've been called *that,*" she said, and grinned at Isabella. Then, her spirits apparently restored, she took herself out of the room. Paddy followed, carrying the crockery-piled trays.

As Isabella brushed out her hair, struggling with tangles she feared might be permanent, she was all too conscious that she had been left alone with Alec. Only the closed dressing room door separated them, and she half expected him to emerge at any minute. She didn't know how she would deal with him in a temper, and the thought made her jumpy.

But he didn't emerge, and she at last managed to get her hair tamed into a semblance of obedience. After twisting it up and securing it with pins in a soft roll at the back of her head, she studied her reflection critically.

She was even paler than usual, which made the scattering of freckles across her nose seem more noticeable. She was thinner too, which made her mouth look wider than ever and put shadows beneath her cheekbones and collarbone. But the lavender eiderdown encircling her neck did wonderful things for her eyes. Always before they had been just a plain, gentle blue. Somehow, though, they seemed to have picked up the bed jacket's color, and the soft blue sparkled with lavender lights. Her hair looked better too, probably because it had not yet had time to straggle. But it seemed softer and fuller around her face, framing it with light brown waves. . . .

The dressing room door opened without warning. Isabella looked up to find Alec standing there frowning at her. Hastily she put down the mirror, embarrassed to be caught staring so raptly at her reflection. Bright color flooded her cheeks at the idea that he might think her vain.

"Where's Pearl?" he demanded without preamble, his brows coming together over his nose as his eyes moved over her.

"She went downstairs."

He was shirtless, his broad shoulders filling the opening, the white bandage around his chest the only thing that kept him from being completely naked above the waist. As always, he seemed totally unconcerned about his lack of proper clothing. Isabella only wished that she could be as blasé as he was about his immodest display. Her color deepened as she averted her eyes from his chest.

"She did, eh?" His eyes raked over her again, then he turned to go back into the dressing room. It was then that Isabella noticed a new bandage wrapped around his elbow.

"What happened to your arm?" she asked before she thought.

He glared at her over his shoulder. "Pearl and Paddy between them managed to talk me into letting that damned sawbones bleed me. Now I feel as weak as a puling infant."

"Maybe you should stay in bed," Isabella offered, trying not to smile as the reason for his grumpiness became clear.

"To hell with that," he growled, and went back inside the dressing room, shutting the door behind him with an audible bang.

Left to herself again, Isabella put the toilet articles aside and reached for the book on the bedside table. She had done no more than look at the title when the dressing room door banged open again. Alec stalked into the room, still clad only in his breeches, and stopped at the foot of her bed to glare at her. Isabella looked up at him with a question in her eyes, at a loss to think of how she might have offended him.

"Is ought the matter?"

"The knot in this damned bandage is coming untied. Does it come off, if I know Paddy and Pearl, they will have the bloody sawbones to me again. 'Tis just like Pearl not to be around when I need her, while the rest of the time she sticks to me like day-old porridge."

"Would you like me to retie it for you?" It was all she could do not to smile at the note of aggrieved complaint in his voice, but she feared that an inauspicious smile might provoke him to an explosion of wrath.

"You?" He looked down at her in disbelief.

"I assure you I can tie a knot," Isabella answered, her chin lifting haughtily.

"Getting on your high horse, are you, Countess? I warn you I'm in no mood to put up with fancy airs from a wet-behind-the-ears miss."

"I'll try not to subject you to any," Isabella said sweetly, when what she really wanted to do was chuck her book at him. "Do you want me to retie it, or not?"

Thus adjured, he came around and seated himself on the edge of the bed, his back to her. Isabella looked at that strong back with its satiny bronze skin, and felt her skin heat. He was within touch of her hand. . . . She would have to touch him, were she to retie his bandage. And, as he had said, the knot was on the verge of working itself loose.

"Are you going to tie it or not?" he demanded impatiently, frowning over his shoulder at her.

Isabella drew on all the calm, good sense she'd ever had in her life to reply in a cool voice, "Certainly I am, if you will but hold still."

He held still. She reached out and unraveled the failing

knot, careful not to allow her fingers to touch him. But she was so close that she could see the smooth texture of his skin where it stretched over the indentation of his spine. Further up, his shoulders at close quarters were so wide and heavy with muscle that they took her breath.

As she fumbled with the knot, her fingers grown suddenly clumsy, she felt in truth the wet-behind-the-ears miss he had called her. No matter that she was a countess and he a commoner, or that he was surely no more than ten years her senior, if that. He was so much her superior in worldly experience that, compared to him, she was a mere babe. He sat calmly waiting for her to tie the knot of his bandage, no more affected by her nearness than he would have been by that of Mr. Heath. While she—she could scarcely draw breath, because when she did she inhaled the musky scent of him. She felt as though her bones would melt as the heat of his body enveloped her in waves.

Tugging at the ends of the knot to make sure it was tight, her knuckles brushed his skin. Immediately she jerked her hands away.

"All finished?" He slewed around to look at her, apparently not the least aware of her discomposure. Those golden eyes met hers. Helplessly, horribly, she felt herself turning a fiery shade of red.

His eyebrows snapped together, and he got off the bed. "Why do you blush every time I set eyes on you? You're not shy, I'd swear."

Terrified that he was about to ferret out the shameful effect he had on her, she snapped up her chin and looked him full in the eyes. "Perhaps 'tis just that I am unused to gentlemen who take such pleasure in flaunting their . . . persons . . . before a lady. Indeed, I have rarely seen you fully clothed, and I admit that I find such immodesty discomposing."

His eyes widened on her face as the sense of that sank in, and his lips compressed. "Since you are a married woman, Countess, I wouldn't have thought that you would find the sight of a man without his shirt so 'discomposing.' As you do, I'll do my best not to offend you until you can find some other, more gentlemanly fellow to shelter you from your murderous relatives."

As he finished biting off the last words, he turned on his heel, stalked into the dressing room, and slammed the door in earnest. Isabella was left to her book, which she determinedly picked up and opened. A considerable time passed before she realized that, of what she read, she had not comprehended a single word.

XV

By the afternoon of the next day, Isabella was as heartily sick of her forced confinement with "the handsomest man she had ever seen in her life" as Alec obviously was of being cooped up with her. Unable to leave the confines of the bedchamber or dressing room while Paddy and his cohorts scoured London for news of who it was who was out to kill him, and feeling more fit with every passing hour, Alec was as grouchy as a large bear in a small cage. He growled at everyone, and scowled at Isabella, for whom he obviously felt particular ire, every time he emerged from the dressing room.

Isabella, for her part, regretted their quarrel, and would have apologized had he given her the least opportunity. But he did not. His fit of the sullens did not go unremarked by Paddy or Pearl, but as they knew nothing of what had passed between Alec and herself, they attributed his ill temper entirely to the sawbones's visit, and vowed they would not summon Mr. Heath again unless Alec lay dying.

As a result of Alec's surliness, and her own guilt over adding to it, Isabella was as jumpy as a cat on hot bricks. Whenever Alec emerged from the dressing room—which he did frequently, pacing about the bedchamber and cursing his confinement—Isabella would either watch him with wide, wary eyes or, if he scowled at her, studiously avoid looking at him. Either way, it seemed her actions maddened him.

He seemed to be waiting for her to remark on the fact that, since their quarrel, he wore a decently buttoned-up shirt and breeches whenever he entered her chamber. From the looks he shot her, Isabella thought he was daring her to comment. Prudently she refrained.

When he stalked into her chamber for the fourth time in an hour, she, who had been trying to read a book for that same hour, flashed him a displeased look and sighed loudly.

He caught her eyes for the first time that day. Isabella, thoroughly annoyed herself by that time, refused to back down. For a long moment neither gave an inch. Then an unwilling smile tugged at the corner of Alec's mouth. Isabella, determined not to be coaxed from the ill temper he had at last reduced her to, lifted her eyebrows at him with all the haughty disdain she could summon.

His smile widened. She gritted her teeth, and sniffed audibly. He laughed out loud. His amusement, Isabella knew, was at her expense. Her temper, usually so serene, heated still further.

"And how, pray, have I displeased you now, Countess? Behold me fully dressed, even to my boots."

"I am glad you find me amusing, Mr. Tyron. 'Tis worth it if it will serve to sweeten your temper. For my part, I am trying to read, and will continue to do so if you will make yourself less of a nuisance."

"You can call me Alec, you know. In fact, I wish you would, for I have every intention of calling you Isabella—at least when you're behaving yourself. When you're not, I shall have to call you Countess."

Alec grinned broadly as her eyes flashed at his baiting, and came to stand at the foot of the bed. His eyes gleamed at her as she lay propped on a mound of pillows. Isabella's hand clutched at the neck of the lavender bed jacket as those eyes moved over her. Still determined not to be lured from the ill humor he had succeeded in driving her to, she found she could ignore him no longer. Lifting her eyes, she regarded him with obvious displeasure.

"And I wish you would take yourself back to your room. I am not accustomed to gentlemen making free of my bedchamber." The look she gave him was disdainful.

His eyebrows rose, and he whistled through his teeth.

"Come now, Countess, climb off your high horse and cry friends. We're stuck with each other for the nonce, so we might as well make the best of it."

"That," said Isabella through gritted teeth, "is quite impossible."

Instead of being angered by her obdurateness, Alec seated himself on the end of the bed, grinning engagingly.

"I'm bored," he complained. "Put that bloody book aside and talk to me. Tell me how you came to be married to that bounder St. Just, to start."

"Pearl will be up to see you before long, I am sure. If you wish to talk, talk to her. I am trying to read. And I wish you will refrain from using bad language in my presence, and cease referring to my husband as a bounder."

"Talking is not what Pearl and I do best together."

"Indeed?" she replied frigidly, and reached for her book.

"What Pearl and I do best together I cannot do properly with your big ears listening in the next room," he said wickedly, and to her fury, Isabella felt herself blush. He had meant to shock her, she knew, and she was almost as angry with herself for letting him get under her skin as she was with him for his deliberate baiting.

"Your bad taste in making such a remark is appalling," she sniffed, her voice dripping icicles, and turned her eyes to her book again. Without warning he snatched it from her, holding it away from her when she would have grabbed it back.

"Mr. Tyron!" Out of all patience with him, she held out her hand for the book.

"Alec," he corrected. His eyes were devils of merriment as they laughed at her. "If you want the book back, Isabella, you must say, 'Please, Alec.' "

"You can . . . read that book yourself for all I care," Isabella hissed, her eyes shooting sparks of real fury because she could not think of any words bad enough to annihilate the maddening creature.

"I see I shall have to teach you to swear, Countess," he said softly, and then when she thought her temper must explode, he meekly handed her the book. She accepted it and buried her nose in it. He stretched out comfortably along the end of the bed, propping his head on his hand, watching her read.

Of course, with him lying across the end of her bed, she could not make sense of a single word.

"Would you please go away?" she gritted at last, shooting him a look of pure loathing.

He smiled at her then, a charming lopsided smile that, against her will, threatened to melt her bones.

"Talk to me," he wheedled. Then, when she still scowled at him, though it was an effort in the face of that engaging grin, he added softly, "Please?"

"About what?" she sighed, acknowledging defeat, and leaned her head back against the pillows as she eyed him. If truth were told, she would much rather talk to him than read. Alec was infinitely more interesting than her novel.

"Tell me how you come to be wed to St. Just," he said again, disposing himself more comfortably. By the time he was settled he was lying flat on his back along the foot of the bed, his hands linked comfortably behind his head and his booted feet extending off the other side of the mattress. His eyes were turned in her direction, and he seemed to be studying her face. Isabella knew that she should object to his posture. But she didn't.

An odd thrill went through her at his nearness. Such proximity to a man who was not her husband was scandalous, of course, but then the whole situation in which she had found herself since being rescued by Alec was scandalous. He'd slept in the dressing room of her chamber for a fortnight now, wandering through her room in various stages of undress, beheld her more nearly naked than anyone except her maid had seen her since she was a tiny child, and now he sprawled on the end of her bed for a cozy chat. If word of this ever got out, her reputation would be irretrievably ruined. But the mere fact that she had passed a fortnight in a bawdy house would ruin her as surely as anything else, so Isabella relaxed, and allowed herself to enjoy—though not without some guilt—the sheer pleasure of his company.

XVI

"Well?" Alec prompted when she didn't immediately respond. Isabella, recalled to her surroundings, made a face.

" 'Tis not very interesting," she warned.

"Tell me anyway."

"All right." Absently she smoothed a wayward strand of hair away from her face. Without her maid to dress it for her, it was less likely than ever to stay tidy for any length of time. "Bernard's property marches along my father's holdings in Norfolk. My family has known his family for years. I came of an age to be married, Bernard offered for me, Papa accepted, and we wed. And that's all there is to that."

Alec looked skeptical. "Why would your da be willing to let you wed a bounder—oh, forgive me, I'm not to call a spade a spade in this case, am I?—a man like St. Just? He's been wed before, and he's a generation older than you are—"

Isabella gave him a warning look for his mockingly retracted description of Bernard, but answered anyway. "As I said, my father has known his family for years. When Bernard's first wife died, he was devastated. Shortly after that, my papa wed for the second time, and Sarah—my stepmama—promptly got with child."

"That still doesn't explain why your da married you off to St. Just."

Isabella sighed. "To be truthful, I expect Papa accepted Bernard's suit to get me out of his household. Sarah made it rather clear that she found my presence upsetting."

"Why would she find your presence upsetting? You're one of the least offensive people I've ever known."

"Why, thank you, sir—I think." Isabella smiled at him. "But I look like my mama, you see. Almost exactly. Apparently Sarah found it a hardship to be faced with a replica of her predecessor day in and day out."

"So your da got rid of you for her?"

Isabella shook her head. "It wasn't like that, exactly. I didn't enjoy sharing a household with Sarah, either."

"You weren't in love with St. Just?"

Isabella shook her head, and smiled a little ruefully. "He was a neighbor, but I didn't really know him. He's a very attractive man, of course, I quite see that, but he was so much older and so experienced. I was frightened of him, to tell you the truth, and I begged my papa to call off the wedding. But Sarah was getting closer to her time, and he would not."

"Fine, loving da you have." It was a disgusted mutter, but Isabella heard.

"I never saw much of him, not even when my mother was alive. I don't think they were very happy together. And he dotes on Sarah. And the new babies."

"Babies? Good God, how many has she had?"

"Three. The youngest, Nathaniel, is a boy. The heir at last. Papa must be over the moon."

"Don't you know?"

Isabella shook her head. A slight sadness shadowed her eyes. "I've only seen Papa twice since my marriage. He's been . . . busy with other things, you see."

"Oh, aye, I see." Alec's voice was grim. His golden eyes narrowed as they met hers and saw the faint darkening in the soft blue depths. "So tell me about being married. Was it as bad as you expected? From what I've seen of St. Just, he'd make the devil of a husband for a chit like you."

Isabella shook her head. "Oh, no, I don't want you to

think that Bernard has been unkind to me. He's in London most of the year, but when he does come down to Blakely Park he is perfectly civil to me. That's why I cannot believe he would hire someone to kill me. He doesn't hate me or anything, you know. He treats me with the respect due his wife."

Alec gave her a derisive look, but forbore to comment. Instead he asked, "Have you any children?"

Isabella shook her head. Alec forbore to comment on that, too, to her relief.

"So tell me about Blakely Park. Is that your home?"

Isabella eagerly accepted that inoffensive conversational gambit. "Yes, and it is the most beautiful place! Acres and acres of moor with pine trees and babbling brooks and a beautiful blue lake to fish in. I love it there."

"Were you coming from there when you were kidnapped?"

Isabella nodded.

"Who knew you were on the road? Do you always travel to London at this time of year?" He frowned as she shook her head, then continued more slowly. "Oh, that's right, you said you'd never been to London before. So what prompted you to decide to come?"

"Bernard sent me a note asking me to join him." Isabella smiled faintly. "I was so excited! I'm still looking forward to seeing it. The Tower, and the wild beasts at the Exchange, and the theatre and the opera and—" She broke off, laughing at her own enthusiasm. "Hinkel, the head groom at Blakely Park, is a Londoner born and bred, and he's been filling my head with tales, as you can see."

"St. Just has never before brought you to London, and he just happened to want you to join him, and you just happened to get kidnapped on the road? And you don't find anything the least odd about that?" Alec's voice was sharp with disbelief.

Isabella looked at him with dignity. "There is such a thing as coincidence, you know."

Alec snorted, then after a moment said, "This Hinkel—did he know you were coming to London?"

"Yes. All the servants at Blakely Park did. Why?"

"Who else knew?" He ignored her question, his eyes intent.

"I don't know. It wasn't a secret. I suppose my servants may have told someone in the village; or Bernard's servants in London, who must have been expecting me, may have told someone."

"They might have, I suppose." Alec sounded unconvinced.

Isabella sighed. "You are determined to think that Bernard hired those men to kidnap and kill me, aren't you? Well, I think you're wrong. Ours was not a love match, true, but he has no reason to wish me dead."

"Your money?" Alec suggested.

Isabella shook her head. "Papa paid him a perfectly enormous dowry when he married me. I cannot think he'd have any more to gain if I died."

"So he married you for your money?" Alec probed.

Isabella shrugged. "Yes, I suppose. But that's hardly unusual. Nor does it make him a killer."

"Why do you defend him?" Alec looked at her curiously.

"He is my husband, after all. Though the marriage might not be what I would have wished, it is still a marriage, binding in the eyes of God and man."

"Noble sentiments," Alec sneered.

"True, nonetheless," Isabella insisted quietly. "And so far you've told me nothing that convinces me that Bernard is conniving at my murder. Just because he was dressed in mourning, and told one of Pearl's girls that he was a widower, is no proof that he himself planned to kill me. It only means that he thinks me dead. Why, I don't know. But there could very well be an excellent reason, just as there could be an excellent reason why he wished me to join him just at this time. Until we know that there is not, I cannot convict him in my own mind on so little evidence."

"What a loyal little wife you are!"

Isabella met his gaze steadily. "If you would quit sneering and think, you would see that it is far likelier that the ruffians who kidnapped me merely heard through a servant's perfectly innocent gossip that I would be travelling to London, knew that I was the daughter of a duke—my papa is very flush in the pocket, you know—and the wife of an earl. Then, when the ransom was paid, the kidnappers decided—on their own—to dispose of the evidence: me. Admit it; that scenario is far more plausible than your contention that my husband, for no earthly reason that comes to mind, paid those men to kill me."

Alec was silent for a moment. "Yes, it's more plausible, I suppose," he said, and the very tone of his voice told Isabella that he thought otherwise.

She sighed, unwilling to quarrel with him again. "Since we are obviously not going to agree on this, we must agree to disagree and change the subject. Tell me about yourself. How you got to be the Tiger, or whatever."

Unexpectedly Alec grinned, and rolled on his side to prop his head up on one hand. The movement brought him nearer, so close that his chest nearly touched her small feet where they burrowed beneath the covers. Isabella looked at him, so handsome and so familiar and so close, and felt her heart speed up just a little. But he was talking, and she forced herself to ignore her sudden tingly awareness of him to listen.

"I detect a lamentable lack of respect in your voice when you call me that, my girl. I'll have you know that strong men the length and breadth of England—aye, and some on the Continent, too—cringe at the mere mention of the Tiger."

"Ah, but I am not a strong man—and you don't look very dangerous to me." Her eyes twinkled as she bantered with him.

Alec's grin broadened. His golden eyes gleamed at her. "I don't, eh? I can see I'll have to work on my image where your ladyship is concerned."

"So tell me," she prompted when Alec fell silent again. "You've heard the story of my life. The least you can do is reciprocate."

"Such big words as you use, Countess," he mocked. "Clearly you've had the advantage of a proper education."

"A governess, is all," Isabella replied. "Did you not have a tutor? Or go to school? You're very well spoken, for a—" She broke off abruptly, afraid of hurting his feelings with her thoughtless words.

"For a ruffian?" he guessed, smiling again but without the humor that had sparked the last grin. "Aye, I suppose I am, but I owe it neither to school nor tutor, for I had none."

Isabella looked at him inquiringly. Obligingly, he went on.

"As a young lad, I . . . uh . . . made the acquaintance of an old bawd—uh, female—who had once been an actress. Not a beauty, was Cecily, nor ever had been, but she had a wonderful way with words. She took me under her wing a little, and bullied me until I learned to not drop my *h*'s nor add them where they weren't needed. As to other education, why, I learned as I could. I did a fair amount of reading—where I learned that, I couldn't tell you, just picked it up—and read what I could find. Most of which would singe your eyeballs, I'm sure."

"What of your parents?" Her voice was soft as she tried to picture the young man he had been. Thin, she thought, but still so handsome, and eager to learn. . . .

Alec shrugged. "I'm sure I had some, but I never knew them. I've been on my own since I was a wee lad. I ran the streets as a youngster, eating what scraps I found in the gutter, sleeping in doorways or barrels or whatever I could find. There were lots of us out there, and we kind of hung together. That's where I met Paddy. I must have been about five when he pulled a bigger boy off me when we were fighting to the death over a meat pasty that I had pinched and the other boy wanted. Paddy was bigger even than the other boy, and he knocked the daylights out of him. We've been friends ever since, fought our way out of the slum together."

"What of Pearl?"

Alec smiled reminiscently. "Ah, Pearl's a right one,

ain't she? She was a regular little spitfire when she was younger, out on the streets with the rest of us. Of course, she sold what she had to sell, but she didn't turn to the bottle or get caught with the pox like a lot of 'em do. She always had more to eat than the rest of us because she was earning money, and she'd share what she had with Paddy and me. When we went, we took her with us."

"She's very beautiful."

"Aye, she is. And rare popular with the gentlemen belowstairs. Of course, nowadays she can afford to be choosy about who she shares her favors with."

As the sense of this sank in, Isabella blinked at him. "Don't you care?" she blurted before she could catch back the words. As he looked at her, brows raised, she turned a bright pink.

"I've got no leading reins on Pearl, just as she has none on me. She can do as she pleases, just as she has been for years. Indeed, I'd like to see the man who could stop her."

Alec chuckled, apparently picturing such a scenario. Isabella concluded that, however Pearl felt about Alec, he had no intention of wedding her. Unless, of course, ruffians were less than nice in their notions of proper marital fidelity.

"How did you get to be what you are? The Tiger?"

" 'Tis naught but a silly nickname." His tone was repressive.

"You know what I mean." Isabella refused to be sidetracked.

"Aye, I know what you mean." Alec's eyes slowly narrowed as if in thought, and then he shook his head. "No, Countess, I'll not sully your ears by recounting the details of that. Suffice it to say that I found, as I grew, that I'd a knack for thinking of things quicker than most, for running operations that were successful, for directing things. I was a good leader, Paddy a good enforcer. We climbed through the ranks together, and here we are."

Isabella guessed that the "details" he refused to recount were both extremely interesting and extremely unsavory, but she was willing to let it pass for the moment. There was one thing, however, that was piquing her curiosity.

"Mr. Tyron . . ."

"Alec, Isabella. Come, 'tis an easy name. Al—ec." As his mouth teasingly formed the syllables, Isabella had to smile.

"Alec, then. Would you please tell me what is a—a sneak?"

Alec looked at her hard, then laughed. "So Pearl's jabbering didn't go totally over your head after all, hmm? Very well, Countess, let me educate you. A sneak is one who'll pull the gold watch from a gent's pocket, or the pound notes from your reticule one bright afternoon in Piccadilly. A pickpocket."

"Oh." Isabella was fascinated. "So you're the boss of the pickpockets?"

Alec sighed. "I'm the boss of all the games there are in London: the pickpockets and burglars and thugs-for-hire like the ones who kidnapped you. I watch over the bawds, and the abbesses, the Charley-boys, and the Lazarus lay—"

"Lazarus lay?" Isabella breathed, fascinated.

"There are those who sell dead bodies for anatomy lessons," he answered. "And those who don't care if the bodies are killed for precisely that purpose, though I'm no advocate of that. I oversee most of the back-street hells, and I know all the men who lose money in them, like your Bernard. I'm the one men come to when they need a job done, and if I accept the commission, I choose the men to do it. Nothing gets done out of London without my say-so."

"So then the men who kidnapped me usually worked for you—"

Alec nodded. "In your case, they were freelancing. Not to do so is a lesson well learned in my ken. But Parren and his fellows were never particularly bright."

"What else do you do?" Isabella stared at him wide-eyed. The fear of him that she'd completely gotten over days ago stirred again as she realized just how truly wicked his mode of living was.

Seeing the sudden shadow darken her eyes, Alec frowned, then gave her a lopsided smile.

"I play a mean hand of piquet."

"Piquet?"

Alec sighed. " 'Tis a card game, Countess. I can see you've never played it."

"No."

"Then I'll teach you."

"But . . ."

"But what? Have you anything better to do? A pressing appointment, perhaps?"

Isabella had to laugh. "No."

"Well, then."

Still Isabella shook her head. She'd never played at cards in her life, and to do so with Alec could not be a fit and proper way to pass an afternoon.

XVII

It was long after dark by the time Pearl and Paddy, both bearing loaded supper trays for the invalids, interrupted the game. Isabella, having lost every one of her hairpins to Alec, was laughing, her hair tumbling around her face, her cheeks flushed rosily, her eyes sparkling. Alec was laughing too, his eyes gleaming at Isabella as he soundly trounced her for the dozenth time that afternoon. With thirty-two cards higher than seven to keep track of, piquet was a complicated game, and Alec was a master at it. The stack of guineas he had wagered against her hairpins had not suffered a single loss. But even as she lost repeatedly, Isabella had fun. More fun, she thought, than she had ever had in her life.

Pearl preceded Paddy into the room, and stopped short on the threshold, her eyes widening as she took in the pair on the bed. Behind her, Paddy nearly bumped into her, just managing to stop in the nick of time with a clatter of dishes. He, too, stared at the scene before him in amazement.

Alec was sprawled lazily on his side, a hand of cards in front of him and more spread out on the blue silk coverlet, looking more relaxed than either of them had seen him in years. As they watched, he slapped a card down with an air of triumph, grinning broadly as he took a final trick. Given his grumpiness over the last twenty-four hours, his present good humor was even more amazing.

Isabella, who both Paddy and Pearl had privately considered a little mouse of a thing, was giggling like a child, her eyes alight with mischief as she plaintively accused Alec of cheating. As she laughed at him, wrinkling her delicately freckled nose, exposing small teeth as white and even as a row of matched pearls, it occurred to both Pearl and Paddy at the same time that she was a very taking little creature after all.

Alec apparently thought so, because as she held out empty hands and shook her head to indicate that she was out of something he claimed as forfeit, he grinned at her devilishly. Paddy, for one, had seen that grin before, and knew what it signified.

Pearl wouldn't like it that Alec was interested in the little countess. In fact, knowing Pearl, she was likely to be mad as hell.

Hurriedly Paddy cleared his throat, the sound making a loud "Harumph!" that could hardly fail to be heard. Both Alec and Isabella looked around, becoming aware of their audience at the same time, which was exactly the effect Paddy had hoped for. Pearl was staring at the pair of them with narrowed eyes. Moving quickly and gracefully despite his great size, Paddy sidestepped around her, blocking her view of the transgressors and their view of her, lifting his tray high.

"I've been pressed into maid service, as ya see," he said mock-plaintively, his back unconsciously tensed as he waited for Pearl's reaction to the unexpectedly cozy scene they had interrupted. Very possessive of Alec, was Pearl, and very quick of temper, too.

"And here I thought we'd been left to starve to death." Alec levered himself up off the bed with easy grace, and negligently began to gather up the cards. He grinned at Isabella as she scooped up her forfeited hairpins and began to twist up her hair. Her expression was self-conscious as she felt herself scrutinized by three pairs of eyes, one smiling, one dismayed, and one actively hostile.

"Alec—Mr. Tyron—has been teaching me piquet," Isabella offered, feeling compelled to explain the obvious as both Paddy and Pearl stared at her. Pearl set the tray she was carrying down with a clatter on the dressing table near the door.

"Oh, aye, our Alec's a wonderful teacher. He's taught me scores of things over the years." Pearl's lip curled, and she threw a hard look at Isabella, whose eyes widened in response. "Take care he don't do the same for you, angel. I doubt you're up to his weight."

"And just what does that mean, exactly?" Alec frowned at her. Pearl tossed her head at him, making her curls bob fetchingly even as she glared.

"You're so smart, you figure it out. I'm needed below. I do have other gentlemen who need taking care of besides you, you know. Just because you own the place doesn't mean you have me at your beck and call," she said coldly. Alec said nothing, just stared after her as she stomped from the room.

"What the devil ails her?" he asked Paddy after Pearl had left. Paddy, still holding the second tray, shook his head. He had no intention of getting involved in a clash between the two people he cared for most in the world. Either one of them was perfectly capable of annihilating him in the scramble for the other's throat.

Alec shrugged. "Well, whatever it is, she'll get over it, I suppose. She always does."

"Aye," Paddy said, sounding strangled. Isabella, feeling guilty as she, not being a dense male, had no trouble divining the cause of Pearl's annoyance, looked up at Paddy with large, troubled eyes.

"If you'll bring me my tray, please, I would eat and then read awhile. I'm quite tired." Her voice was very small.

"Of course, miss. Uh, my lady."

Alec looked from Isabella's uncomfortable face to Paddy's equally uncomfortable one as Paddy deposited the tray across Isabella's lap.

"Would someone please tell me what the hell is going on? I suddenly feel like I'm at a funeral." Alec's eyes swung to fasten on Isabella. "You weren't tired a minute ago."

Isabella's chin came up. "Well, I am now."

If he didn't recognize Pearl's very obvious jealousy, she was not going to point it out to him. It was too ticklish a topic, implying as it did that Pearl had thought Alec found her, Isabella, attractive. The thought was both unsettling and exciting, but Isabella had no intention of dwelling on it. She would eat her supper, read and go to sleep. Alec Tyron's opinion of her, for good or ill, interested her not at all. Or so, at least, she told herself.

"I take it that you would prefer to dine alone?" Alec's voice had a clipped undertone to it that told her that he was not pleased, to put it mildly.

"Yes." Her voice and eyes were both steady. The cheerful camaraderie that had enveloped them during the afternoon had dissipated like fog in the sun. Blue and gold eyes were equally cool as they took each other's measure.

"Very well, Countess, you may certainly have all the privacy you wish." Alec's fingers clenched around the neat deck of regrouped cards as he turned toward the dressing room. "Paddy, would you care to join me, or do you, too, have a pressing desire to dine alone?"

"I'll join you," Paddy said, casting an apologetic glance at Isabella as he picked up the other tray and followed Alec into the dressing room. Once inside, he shut the door.

Isabella was left alone to eat her dinner, read her book and fall asleep, just as she'd stated was her wish.

But the supper was tasteless, the book dull, and her sleep troubled by dreams in which she knew she was in mortal danger, knew she would be killed if she did not run, but was rooted to the spot as the killer, whose identity remained horrifyingly secret, approached.

She awoke with a cry in the shadowy stillness of her bedroom. A dark shape loomed over her. Reflexively she gasped.

"Al . . . Alec?" she squeaked. But she knew his identity before he even said a word. Of course, who else would be in her bedchamber in the middle of the night? But logic wasn't how she knew the shadow's identity. There was an aura about him that would have identified him to her in the bowels of the darkest cave anywhere on earth.

"You were having another nightmare." His voice was even, low. Isabella abruptly sat up, her mind still befuddled from the dream. The darkness with its shadows closed menacingly about her. Only Alec was real.

"I—someone—or something—was chasing me." Remembering the dream, she shivered, wrapping her arms around herself for warmth.

"Are you cold?" He was still speaking in that same low, emotionless voice.

"A little. Yes."

He moved away from her. She could see him, then, as he crouched before the dying red embers of the fire. He was shirtless, his breeches only partially buttoned. She supposed she could consider herself lucky that he had bothered to pull them on at all. He was barefoot, and his hair, unconfined, was tousled. The white bandage that was the only visible reminder of his wound bisected his chest. As he tossed more wood onto the fire, stirring it with a poker, Isabella watched him. The growing light touched his hair, outlining the tawny color of it in pure gold as it hung in deep waves almost to his shoulders. The firelight touched his shoulders and arms, too, burnishing them with the same gold as his hair. The strong planes of his back were deep in shadow, but she could still see the indentation of his spine, and the sharpness of his shoulder blades above the bandage. As he moved, his biceps bulged and rippled. Isabella watched the firelight play over his muscles with growing fascination.

She had touched that strong back. The memory made her tremble.

"Better?" He turned to look at her suddenly. Embarrassed to be caught staring at him, Isabella just managed to nod. He replaced the poker, and got lithely to his feet. Standing in front of the fireplace with only his breeches covering his nakedness from just above his hipbones to his calves, he was an impressive sight. Isabella felt her heartbeat quicken as she looked at him. Never in her wildest dreams would she have imagined that the mere sight of an unclothed male body could affect her so.

"Then I'll say good-night."

He headed toward the dressing room. Isabella felt a sudden clutch of loss. She didn't want him to go. . . .

"Alec." It was out before she could stop it. He had taken no more than a few steps, so that he was still between her bed and the fire, while the open dressing room door was clear on the other side of the room.

He stopped walking and turned to look at her.

Now that she had his attention, Isabella did not know what to say. She only knew that she did not want him to leave. And it was not only that she was afraid of the dark. . . .

"I enjoyed myself, this afternoon."

"Did you now?"

He was giving her no encouragement at all. Isabella could feel his eyes moving over her face, but she still could not read his expression through the shadows.

"Yes. It was kind of you to teach me piquet."

"I wasn't being kind. I'm not kind."

"Oh, but you are! You were kind to save me from those dreadful men, and kind to give me shelter until we know something about why it happened, and kind the other night when I was so frightened, and—"

"And none of that means that I am kind. I am not, I assure you." He sounded as though something was setting his teeth on edge.

"No?" It was a tiny question.

He made a sound midway between a snort and a grunt. "No. Now go back to sleep."

He started to move away again.

"Alec!" She reacted in almost a panic.

He stopped, turned. "What now?" He sounded exasperated, but still his voice was low.

"I'm frightened."

It was the truth, but not the whole truth. The rest of what she felt was something she had not quite worked out for herself yet. Even when she did, she doubted that she would share the information with him.

Alec muttered a word under his breath that Isabella didn't quite catch, but she didn't have to understand it to know that he swore. He moved toward her, coming to stand beside the bed looking down at her, his hands planted in loose fists on his hips. The shifting glow of the firelight behind him cast a red glow over the muscles of his shoulders and arms, and made him look enormously tall. Again his face was in shadow, but she got the impression that now he was positively scowling at her.

"Alec?" she ventured when he didn't say anything.

"I'm not your father, you know. Or your brother, or your cousin, or any kind of relation to you at all."

Those abrupt, puzzling words brought a frown to Isabella's face. "I know that. Of course I know that."

"You should be telling me to get the hell out of your bedroom, not encouraging me to stay. Unless you mean it, of course."

Isabella's eyes grew huge as she stared up at his shadowed face so far above her. "But . . . but you said—"

"I said I don't force myself on unwilling females. I never said I wouldn't take what's offered me. So unless you're purposely putting yourself on offer, quit making sheep's eyes at me and cover yourself up and let me the hell alone."

This last was said in such a savage tone that Isabella flinched. His eyes shifted deliberately from her face to her chest, and her eyes flew downward in the wake of his.

In her fascination with his body, she had completely overlooked the fact that the replenished fire might be revealing hers as well. Now, as she looked down at herself, her eyes widened. She was sitting up, the bedclothes a rumpled mass around her waist. Her hair, braided for sleep, trailed down her back. She wore another of the diaphanous nightrails, and in it she might as well have been bare to the waist.

As it had done with his, the firelight painted her skin gold. The nightdress was no more than a sheer, sensuous veil covering the creamy peaks of her breasts. Isabella was shocked to find her nipples distended, the small buds pushing wantonly against the inadequate cloth.

Crimsoning, she pulled the covers up to her neck.

"Isabella." This was said in a soft voice when she refused to look at him.

Still she kept her eyes on her knees where they tented the silken coverlet. The shock of feeling she'd experienced when she'd realized that he was seeing her near-naked flesh left her tongue-tied. Well-bred ladies are not subject to such tumultuous quickenings. . . .

"Isabella. Shall I stay?"

The question electrified her. Ashamed to look at him for fear he might read what she was feeling in her eyes, she stared steadfastly at her knees, replying with a single, negative shake of her head.

She could feel him staring down at her. Her heart pounded. Shall I stay? The question wormed itself into her heart and mind and soul. She closed her eyes.

"Oh, God, you are so young that you break my heart," he said in a strange, abrupt tone, and before she knew what he was about, he was sitting on the bed beside her, his hand sliding beneath her chin to lift it. "I didn't know there were chits like you anywhere in the world."

With his hand under her chin tilting her head up, she at last looked at him. What she saw made her knees tremble. He was close, so close she could see the darker streaks marbleizing the golden eyes. Isabella stared into those flickering depths, and was lost. Her fingers, suddenly nerveless, released their death grip on the coverlet. It slithered downward. Alec's eyes followed its path, then moved up to pin hers again. His lashes were thick, several shades darker than his hair, casting shadows on his high cheekbones. His lips were slightly parted. As he stared at her, Isabella saw that tiny flames had ignited in the golden depths. Mesmerized, she couldn't move as those blazing eyes fastened on her mouth.

"You take my breath away," he murmured. And then he leaned forward to touch his mouth to hers.

XVIII

If Isabella had died in that moment, she would have died happy. The feel of his lips against her mouth was the most exquisite sensation she had ever experienced. Fire shot through her, searing her senses, curling her toes. In a response that came as naturally to her as breathing, her eyelids fluttered down and her lips parted.

It was the briefest of kisses.

Even as Isabella's world rocked on its axis, Alec withdrew his mouth, sitting up again. His hand still cupped her chin. His thumb caressed the fragile line of her jaw.

After a long moment, her eyes slowly opened and she stared at him. He had barely kissed her, and yet the whole world looked different. She was different. For the first time in her life, she knew what it was to want a man's hands on her.

He stared back at her, his golden eyes slightly narrowed. He looked like a man who had received a shock, and not a particularly pleasant one.

His mouth opened as if to say something. Isabella, not wanting to be brought back to reality just yet, lifted a hand to touch his face. Her fingers just brushed his cheek, and yet the contact set off shock waves of feeling deep inside her. Although he'd shaved earlier, the beginnings of a beard roughened his skin. His face was very warm. Her fingers tingled where she touched him. Quickly she drew her hand away.

He caught that fugitive hand and brought it to his mouth, kissing the backs of her knuckles. Then, as she watched, her eyes darkening with feeling, he kissed each separate finger, drawing the tip of it into his mouth and sucking on it lightly. By the time he was finished, Isabella was holding her breath. Never in her life had she experienced the sensations she was experiencing now.

"Alec . . ." When he reached for her other hand to repeat the performance, she shook her head and put it childishly behind her back. A kind of panic assailed her as she realized that the pit of her stomach was quivering helplessly. With as much volition over her own actions as a straw caught up in a raging river, she realized that she was being drawn into treacherous currents way beyond her depth.

Then Alec smiled at her, a lazy, sleepy smile as seductive as his kisses had been.

"Shy, Countess?" he asked softly, the word both a taunt and a caress.

He was smiling at her, holding her hand in his, his thumb stroking over the backs of her knuckles. The firelight glinted off his golden eyes and illuminated features that had been chiselled by a master hand. Tawny hair waved down to shoulders so wide that they blocked her view of the hearth. The hard contours of his chest were in shadow, darkened more by whorls of crisp hair that curled over the edges of the bandage. The muscles of his arms rippled and gleamed, outlined in orange by the fire. He was so handsome that just looking at the man made her mouth go dry.

"You're gorgeous," she whispered, shaken, and her other hand emerged blindly to do what she had been wanting to do for days: touch him. Her fingers sought his arm, resting lightly where the muscle bulged just above his elbow. The skin there was warm and satiny smooth against her fingertips, the muscle beneath iron-hard. He stayed motionless as she ran her fingers along the length of his arm, but she thought he suddenly seemed to cease to breathe. The knowledge that she could stir him as he stirred her was enthralling. She smiled at him, tremulously, as her hand withdrew from his arm. He caught her hand, his eyes blazing into hers. Then he leaned forward, slowly, oh, so slowly, to catch her lips again.

She made no effort to evade him. Instead, her heart seemed to stop as she waited for the touch of those perfectly sculpted lips.

His mouth was very warm, and very soft, and very gentle. Isabella felt the heat of it clear down to her toes. She sighed her abject surrender, her eyes closing. The sensation evoked by his lips was the most exquisite she had ever experienced.

He let go of her hands, and they moved of their own accord to rest on his wide, bare shoulders, her nails curling ever so slightly into his flesh. His left hand came up to burrow beneath her hair, his long fingers curling around her skull, holding her head cradled for his mouth. His right hand tilted her face up to his.

This time, when he kissed her, the pressure of his lips was firmer. He angled her head for a better fit, his lips parting hers, the kiss still leisurely, unhurried. His tongue came out to touch her lower lip, run along the line of her teeth, which remained closed to him.

"Open your mouth for me."

The words were a mere breath against her lips, but Isabella heard. For a moment the tumultuous excitement building inside her quavered, and threatened to collapse. She had been kissed in just such a fashion before, by Bernard. His tongue, tasting of the wine served at their wedding supper, had thrust almost all the way down her throat, making her gag. . . .

But the warm sweetness of Alec's lips against hers blotted out the memory of Bernard's. This kiss was like no other. It made her long for more. Obediently she let him in.

Alec's tongue was slow and hot and gentle, sliding between her lips, touching her teeth, the roof of her mouth, the insides of her cheeks. He tasted faintly of tobacco and brandy, and as he tutored her in the sweet art of kissing, she drew a deep, shuddering breath. With her nose so close to his smooth, warm cheek, she drew in the heady aroma of bay rum.

His tongue touched hers as it cowered behind her lower teeth, stroked it, and then was withdrawn.

"You're supposed to kiss me back," he complained in a half-teasing, shaken-sounding whisper against her lips. Without giving her time to reply, he drew her lower lip into his mouth and sucked on it. Isabella trembled. A series of tiny, rhythmic contractions began to build from somewhere inside the very center of her being.

"I don't know what to do," she confessed, murmuring into his ear as he traced kisses along the line of her jaw. He pulled back to look at her, frowning. Terrified suddenly that her confession of inadequacy would drive him away, she slid her hands along his shoulders to lock behind his neck, pulling him toward her again. He came willingly, but still he frowned.

This time it was she who pressed her lips to his.

This time, when his head slanted over hers and his tongue entered her mouth, she relaxed, allowing her head to lie heavily in his cradling hand, arching her throat and letting him explore her mouth as he would.

This time, when his tongue stroked hers, her breath caught. Then her tongue moved to return the caress, meeting his, touching it.

And to her amazement, from the sudden erratic sound of his breathing, she realized that she did know how to kiss a man after all.

Just doing what came naturally.

It was the most erotic thing she had ever done in her life.

With Bernard, she had lain on her back, suffered his quick, hurtful invasion of her body, and thought of England to keep from screaming with revulsion as he had grunted over her.

She had consoled herself with the knowledge that, by suffering Bernard, she was fulfilling her wifely duty. If what he was doing to her was distasteful in the extreme, why, then, that was the lot of married ladies of her class.

Ladies did not enjoy the darker side of marriage. Only gentlemen did.

But Alec's soft, hot kisses were making her head swim. They were making her body burn. They were making her insides quake, and her toes curl into the mattress, and her breasts swell. It could not be her, Isabella Georgiana Albans St. Just, Countess of Blakely, who was experiencing such tremulous longings in the hands of a man who was certainly no gentleman.

But it was. And suddenly her perceptions of the world and her role in it shattered like the glass of a dropped mirror. Under Alec's tender ministrations, she felt herself changing, breaking out of the mold forced on her by convention, coming alive.

Her hands tightened on his neck, pulling him closer. She kissed him back with newborn passion while her bones turned to water and her flesh turned to fire.

His hand no longer cradled her head but slid down her back, touching her spine through the thin nightdress, easing her down on the bed. Then he was lying beside her. In gold-outlined silhouette he looked very large, his shoulders wide as they loomed above her, the muscles on his arms taut and formidable in their silent testament to his strength. Isabella felt the hard length of his body all along her side. Her shoulder butted under his armpit, her right breast grazed his rib cage, her right thigh pressed against the iron muscles of his, and the toes of her bare foot brushed the hair-roughened skin of his calf below his breeches.

Never had she lain so intimately with a man. Though Bernard had taken her to wife as was his right, he had never spent more than a quarter of an hour at a time in her bed. He had come to her room in the dead of night, climbed into her bed, lifted her nightgown and had his way with her. And then he'd returned to his own room with scarcely a word or touch exchanged between them.

Just the act. And always she'd been sorry to see him come, and glad to see him go.

His possession of her body had been a thankfully rare occurrence that she'd had no choice but to endure.

But this—this feeling of skin against skin, of hard male muscles against soft female curves—was something she had never experienced. Something she'd never dreamed she could or would experience. Something she'd never dreamed existed between men and women.

Something intoxicating.

Something enthralling.

Her eyes lifted from his body to his face to find that he was watching her intently. She stared up at him, incapable of speech, her neck cradled on the hard arm that stretched beneath her.

His right hand, his free hand, came up to lazily stroke curling tendrils of hair from her face. Then he touched her eyelashes, the tip of her nose, her mouth.

"You have the most beautiful mouth." He traced its lines with the pad of his thumb.

"It's too wide," Isabella whispered, shaken to the bone by both the compliment to the feature she'd always despaired of and the soft friction of his touch.

He shook his head. "God made it expressly for kissing," he whispered back, and to demonstrate his point, dipped his head and kissed her again.

Isabella made a sound like a moan deep in her throat, and parted her lips for him before he had done more than touch them with his. Her arms wrapped around his neck as his tongue entered her mouth. Her fingers twined in the rough silk of his hair.

As before, his kiss was slow and hot and dizzyingly sweet. Isabella shut her eyes and clung to him, giving herself over to the sheer magic of the way he could make her feel.

She kissed him back, doing to him what he had done to her. Her tongue darted shyly inside his mouth, touched the line of strong, smooth teeth, explored the insides of his cheeks and the roof of his mouth.

When he lifted his head at last, and she opened her eyes, it was to find him breathing as though he had run for miles, his eyes pools of pure golden flame.

They stared at each other. Then, moving slowly, so slowly, his right hand trailed over the slender arch of her neck, traced the line where the lace collar of her nightdress met her skin, fingered the delicate muslin below it. Then his fingers moved lower still, testing the fragility of her collarbone, sliding over the first faint rise of her chest.

At last his hand settled on her breast, fitting snugly over the small, swollen mound so that she filled his palm, her nipple stabbing into the very center of his hand.

Isabella's breath stopped.

He had touched her like this before, and made her aware of him. But that had been an impersonal touch, indifferent, detached, insulting. She had hated and feared him then. Now—now she wanted him more than she had ever wanted anything in her life. His hand on her breast was shockingly, shamefully intimate, and she loved the feel of it. It sent tremors coursing along her nerve endings from head to toe.

For a long moment his hand cupped her breast without moving. The heat in his eyes flamed over her face as he watched her. Chest heaving as she fought to draw breath, Isabella looked down at the long-fingered hand covering her breast, and then up at the cameo-perfect face.

"That feels wonderful," she breathed, even as her hand came up to cover his, pressing it more firmly against her.

Alec's breath caught sharply. His eyes blazed at her for a moment before his mouth came down on hers again, harder this time, demanding entry. She kissed him with a passion that she never would have suspected herself capable of. Her arms wrapped around his neck, holding him to her. Her heart pounded so fiercely that she could feel it knocking against her ribs.

"I think we can do without this, fetching though it is," he murmured, lifting his mouth from hers after a long, drugging moment. Isabella did not demur as he caught the hem of the nightdress and lifted it over her head.

Then, under the guidance of his hands, she lay back, naked, and quaked with longing as his eyes moved over her.

" 'Tis lovely you are," he murmured at last in a shaken tone, his accent roughened as she had already learned it tended to do when he was in the grip of strong emotion. His hand stroked over the flesh he praised. His fingers found her nipples, rubbed over them, gently pinched the tiny nubs.

Isabella cried out, her legs moving restlessly as an ache the like of which she had never felt before throbbed to life between them.

"Shh, now, love. Shh."

He gentled her with voice and hands, tracing light circles over her breasts until she was quivering beneath his touch. Then his hand slid down her body, stroking over her belly, delving into her navel for a moment while she squirmed and moaned, and at last finding the soft nest of hair at the apex of her thighs. Isabella shut her eyes as his fingers threaded through the tiny curls, then slid down between her thighs. The flat of his palm pressing against her inflamed the ache into a burning, almost painful pleasure that made her writhe.

"That's right, love. Part your legs for me."

With her eyes shut tight and her body on fire, Isabella could do nothing else but obey that soft, seductive voice. She parted her legs for him, her slender, pale thighs quivering as he stroked their soft insides. When he found the moist, secret place that he sought and stroked over that, too, then slid a finger a little way inside, she gasped in misery. The sensation was too exquisite to be borne. Her legs clamped together in reflexive reaction, but he would not remove his hand. Instead he pressed against her again with the flat of his palm. Shafts of fire shot upward through her body from that one central point, and she trembled all over.

Then, when she still would not relent, he wormed his finger even deeper. Isabella moaned, and her legs relaxed at last.

She was his to do with what he would.

He kept his finger moving inside her even as his head bent to nuzzle at her breasts. Taking a nipple in his mouth, he bit it gently, suckling her like a babe. The exquisite heat of his mouth brought her eyes fluttering open. The sight that greeted them made them widen with shock.

She was naked, her body gleaming white in the darkness. He loomed above her, his eyes mere golden slits as they focused on her body, his skin a rich tawny bronze where it rested against the paleness of hers. Her slender legs were parted wantonly, and the darkness of his hand moved between her pale thighs. As she watched, dazed with passion, he switched his attentions from one quivering breast to the other. Gently he kissed her nipple. Then his tongue came out to stroke it, twirling over the hardened bud before at last he drew it completely into his mouth.

His mouth at her breast was at the same time the most indecent and the most stirring sight she had ever seen in her life.

XIX

The tiny contractions grew stronger, making her body quake with their force. Isabella drew in a deep, shaken breath, and acting out of deepest instinct, slid her hands up over the back of his neck to his head, pressing it more closely still to her breast.

As he suckled her, she groaned.

The muscles of the arm that supported her head suddenly clenched, going iron-hard beneath her neck. Then, deliciously, it began to tremble.

Isabella felt that tremor with every fiber of her being. Trembling herself, she stroked her hands over his hair. He took a deep, shuddering breath, and lifted his head from her breast. The hand that had been doing unimaginable things to her person lifted too, and moved to the buttons on his breeches.

They stared at each other, wordlessly, while he freed himself from his breeches. Isabella's heart was pounding so loudly that it sounded like drumbeats in her ears. She knew what came next—he would put the male part of himself inside her and pump until he had spewed his seed.

She knew that. Bernard had done it more than once, and each subsequent time had been more distasteful than the last.

Now Alec was watching her, giving her time to object if she would, giving her time to change her mind.

She could refuse him, and he would stop. He had said he did not force unwilling women, and she believed him.

But she was not unwilling. And he was not Bernard.

He was trembling. She could see the unsteadiness in the hand that worked the buttons of his breeches.

Her body ached for him, burned for him, melted for him.

The male part that he bared was enormous with wanting her.

And yet he was merely watching her, those golden eyes aflame, giving her time to object.

She made a tiny mewling sound deep in her throat, and arched her back toward him in wordless offering. Her eyes closed. Her breath stopped.

"Isabella." He was on her in seconds, huge and hot and heavy as he pressed her into the mattress, his hand sliding between their bodies as he sought to position himself for entry.

She breathed finally, a great, ragged sigh, and parted her legs farther for him. Her knees bent instinctively, and he pushed his way inside. Isabella's teeth clenched on her lower lip. Her arms went around his body, her nails digging into the shoulder blades she had so admired. Her head tilted back as her body arched. He buried his face in the curve between her neck and shoulder. His mouth was open and wet and warm as he kissed her neck.

And then he began to move.

Isabella moaned as a fire storm built inside her. When at last it exploded into a million tiny flames, she cried out.

"Alec?"

The voice, just faintly heard, impinged on Isabella's consciousness as she floated back to earth.

At first she thought it was her imagination.

"Alec?"

Then she recognized the voice. It was sultry, heavy with sleep, and unmistakably Pearl's.

Lying atop her, heavier than ever now that his passion was spent, Alec heard it too. He left off from lazily suckling at her earlobe, and lifted his head.

"Darlin', where are you?"

Alec cursed viciously under his breath as he withdrew himself from Isabella and rolled off the bed, all in a single fluid movement.

"Go back to sleep, Pearl; everything's all right," he called back, yanking up his breeches and doing up the buttons as he spoke.

It was only then, as she saw the direction in which he addressed his words, that Isabella realized the true perfidiousness of the womanizing beast.

Pearl was in the dressing room. She was clearly sleeping in his bed. The dirty bounder had made love to her, Isabella, with his longtime mistress, whom he'd almost certainly bedded earlier in the evening, still asleep in the adjoining room in his bed!

"You *swine,*" she hissed at him, sitting bolt upright and snatching at the covers to shield herself from his eyes.

He turned glinting eyes on her. His mouth was compressed into a hard, straight line.

"You filthy rotten bounder!" She was spitting the words under her breath. The last thing she wanted was for Pearl to hear, and arrive on the scene to witness the degradation to which she, Isabella, had sunk. She thought she could not bear it should anyone save herself and Alec be privy to her shame.

"Isabella . . ." Alec was frowning at her, his breeches fastened now, his hands on his hips as he stood by the bed. Shirtless, barefoot, and tousled, he was impossibly handsome. Isabella gnashed her teeth at him.

"Cad!"

"Now wait—"

"Alec?"

"Rakehell!"

"Damn it, Isabella—"

"Alec! Are you coming back to bed? I'm cold!"

"Blackguard!"

"May God damn all women to bloody 'ell!" Alec lost his temper at last. She could hear it in the roughening of his accent, see it in his eyes. Still he did not raise his voice, but the tone of it was enough to raise the hairs on her neck.

Except that she was too blindly furious to be frightened of him.

"Scoundrel! Villain! Rogue!" Isabella's fists clenched over the coverlet she clutched to her breast. Her eyes shot bullets of pure rage at him. Never in her life had she been so angry—or so ashamed.

"Damn it, Isabella, I—"

"Ale-e-ec!" It was a wail.

"Cur!"

Alec's eyes blazed furiously at her. His hands clenched into fists. Then he was bending, snatching up her nightrail from where it had ended up on the floor and throwing it in her face. The soft muslin wrapped itself around her head like a cloud, temporarily both silencing and blinding her.

"Put that on, woman, and shut up, before I wrap the bloody garment around your bloody neck!"

Isabella yanked the nightrail from her face.

"Pervert!" she spat.

Alec was already striding toward the dressing room door. As her insult hit him, he turned back to glare at her. Even through the shadows darkening that corner of the room she could see the savage gleam in the golden eyes.

"Remind me one day soon to teach you to swear, Countess," he gritted. Although it seemed he had regained control of his accent, his fists were still clenched with rage as he turned his back to her again and stalked into the dressing room.

XX

Had there ever been such a bloody damned disaster? Alec slammed the dressing room door with enough force to shake the rafters and found, to his increased fury, that he was left in total darkness. The only illumination had come from the fire in the other room. The saber-tongued little shrew's room.

"Alec? What's the matter, darlin'? Where've you been?"

The sleepy voice from his bed made him grit his teeth. Before he could give vent to the fury he felt in the explosive manner it deserved, he had to get Pearl out of the way. Should she guess exactly what it was that had kept him so long from bed, she would explode in a shrieking tantrum that would be heard clear to Kensington Palace. Then he would have two bloody women furious at him, and at each other.

Christ, how had a canny chap like himself ever got caught up in such a tangle of petticoats? It was like to be the death of him—if he didn't strangle one or both of them first.

"The countess had a nightmare. Her caterwauling woke me up, and I went to see what ailed her." His voice was carefully even, carefully indifferent as he struck flint on steel and lit the candle near the bed.

Pearl, stretched out flat on her back, lifted her head and blinked at him.

"Ow! What'd you do that for?"

"Since the little—Countess—woke me, I might as well do some work. You know how I am about going back to sleep."

"Aye, I know." Alec's insomnia was something that Pearl and Paddy had long since learned to live with. He prowled the world when others slept, and thereby got twice as much accomplished as an ordinary man.

She sat up, stretching and yawning, arching her back provocatively. Alec saw that she was dressed in a silk nightrail in a shade of emerald green that did wonderful things for her dark blue eyes. Her white-blonde hair was a mass of curls about her face, and her body—that magnificent body that was her fortune—was temptingly on view. Dispassionately Alec decided that he'd never seen a better pair of tits on a woman. They were nearly bared now, falling enticingly out of the neckline of that provocative nightdress, lush, tantalizing white globes the size of melons with nearly the whole of her nipples popping out over that tiny excuse for a bodice.

Alec stared at them, at all of Pearl's voluptuous beauty, and was dismayed to find himself totally unmoved. Then, unbidden, came the thought of breasts small enough to fit into his cupped palm, of delicious strawberry nipples and a slim, lithe body, and eyes the size of saucers and the soft color of a pigeon's wing. Alec gritted his teeth, and banished the image with a curse.

"What're you swearin' about?"

To his chagrin, Alec realized that he had muttered the curse aloud. Now Pearl was staring at him, a frown gathering on her brow. To soothe her, he ruffled a hand through her curls, and forced a smile.

"Nothing. 'Tis just that I've been feeling a trifle out of sorts lately. My temper's not of the sweetest, as you may have noticed."

" 'Ave I ever!" Pearl giggled, and reached up to run a hand across his bristly cheek. "Darlin', I know just the cure."

Alec remembered another hand, smaller and much more

hesitant, that had touched his face in just such a way not an hour earlier, and before he could stop himself, he jerked his head back beyond her reach.

"My, you are grumpy!" Pearl pouted at him. As much because he was genuinely fond of her as because he wanted to distract her—whatever else she was, Pearl was nobody's fool—he leaned over and planted a quick kiss on her mouth. Then he grabbed her hand and hauled her from his bed.

"Alec!" she protested, swaying slightly as he pulled her to her feet.

"Now, you know I'd never get anything done with you in my bed distracting me. Go to your own room and go back to sleep, Pearl. I'll see you in the morning."

"But I don't want to sleep. Not now." She was smiling at him, a wicked little curve of her lips, and reached out to thread provocative fingers through the hair on his chest. She tugged, meaning to bring him closer. He frowned at her, and removed her hand from his chest.

"Alec!"

"I'm no fit company for man or beast tonight," he said, a little apologetically because it was rather beyond the line to turn her out of his bed in the middle of the night when she'd done nothing to give offense, and he knew it. But there was no way he was going to be able to sleep with Pearl when what he really wanted to do was go back in that bedroom and ring the little countess's bloody soft neck.

"Well!" Pearl stared at him, eyes narrowing. Most of the sleepy softness had fled her face. "If you don't want me, Alec Tyron, there's plenty who do! And maybe I'll just go find one of 'em!"

"Aw, Pearl . . ." Now Alec felt like the cad he'd so recently (and unjustly) been called. But even as he tried to think of a way to take the edge off his dismissal of her, Pearl stomped off in a huff. Her rounded hips swayed enticingly beneath the clinging silk, but Alec was in no mood to be enticed.

"Good-night," Pearl said with immense dignity, and

jerked open the door to the bedroom. It was only as she walked through it that Alec realized that in order to leave the room, she would have to pass through Isabella's bedroom. He rushed to the door after Pearl, holding his breath as she stalked across the bedroom to the door that led to the hallway and beyond. Isabella, a small mound completely hidden by covers, was motionless. Alec thanked heaven for small mercies.

Pearl reached the bedroom door and, without so much as a backward look in his direction, let herself out. Alec listened with relief combined with a healthy dose of guilt as her footsteps disappeared along the hall.

Then, when he was sure he was alone with the real object of his ire, he turned his attention to the lump in the bed.

It took only three strides to reach the foot of the bed.

She was totally hidden beneath the piled bedcoverings. Not so much as an eyelash or the tip of a toe showed. How she was breathing under there was a mystery, but one which Alec had no patience for solving at the moment.

"Wake up, Countess!" he growled, and brutally pulled the covers from her recumbent form.

She gasped, and jacknifed into a sitting position. There were tear-streaks on her cheeks, which would have made him feel like a bastard had there not been a regular forest fire of fury spitting from her eyes.

"How dare you!" she hissed. Her fists were clenched as they rested against the mattress on either side of her, and those soft blue eyes shot sparks of pure rage as she glared at him. Her hair was still confined in that childish plait that fell forward over her shoulder to end in her lap. Although a lavender ribbon confined the end of it, soft tendrils of hair escaped to wave around her face, making her look very young.

Some of Alec's anger died as he looked her over. In that transparent excuse for a nightdress that all the bawds except Pearl wore at the Carousel, she seemed very small and fragile. He'd seen the nightdress or its like before, of course, on many occasions, but never had it had the impact on him that this one did. And under the circumstances, his involuntary reaction did a great deal to revive his failing anger.

''Oh, I dare,'' he said grimly, tossing the covers to the floor in a deliberate gesture and coming around the side of the bed to stand, fists on hips, glaring down at her. By rights she should have been frightened to death of him, not just because his size and strength were many times greater than hers, but because he was the Tiger, and she'd put him into a flaming temper, and because she was, after all, completely in his power. But the snippy little miss scowled right back at him for all the world as if she was the lady of the manor and he was nothing more than a peasant born to grovel at her feet.

The comparison infuriated him, and the perfectly reasonable explanation he'd meant to offer her (in the heat of passion, he'd completely forgotten that Pearl was even in his bed) was lost as his temper flamed.

''I dare,'' he said again, and reached down to seize her by her upper arms and haul her out of that bed to stand in front of him. She fought, of course, kicking and squirming to be free, but her puny efforts in the face of his strength were laughable.

''Unhand me, you conscienceless libertine!'' she spat.

The utter inadequacy of the insult would have amused him at any other time, but he was beyond being amused at the moment. Furious or not, her nearness was having a definite effect on him, and he didn't like it one bit. Firelight made that damnable nightgown so transparent it might as well not even have been between them, and his body responded instinctively despite the best efforts of his mind.

''Make me,'' he said through his teeth, his hands tightening fractionally over her arms to draw her up on her toes and thus demonstrate the totality of his power over her.

He was looming over her, holding her so that they were practically nose to nose, his hands powerful enough to snap her fragile bones like twigs.

''You disgust me,'' she hissed at him.

''Do I now?'' he growled, yanking her even closer so

that her body was brushing against his. Feeling the softness of her breasts pressing into his chest, the bloody nightgown more provocation than barrier as they stood practically skin to skin, made his blood heat. And that made him madder than ever.

"Yes!"

"I didn't disgust you earlier. 'You're gorgeous,' you said, and 'That feels wonderful' when I put my hand on your—"

"Stop it!"

"Oh, no! I've not the slightest intention of stopping until I'm bloody good and ready!"

"Let me go!"

Alec smiled evilly into her eyes. Then, holding her gaze just to demonstrate how extremely helpless she was against him, he bent his head and put his mouth to hers.

Her mouth was soft, and warm, and tasted as honey-sweet as he knew her to be. As he kissed her he forgot everything but the rising passion that made him ache, God, he wanted her. . . .

And she wanted him too. She quivered in his arms, and her lips parted to let his tongue in.

Alec groaned, and released his grip on her to slide his arms around her, tilting her practically off her feet as he crushed her to him and drank his fill of her mouth.

His right hand slid around to her breast.

She made an inarticulate sound into his mouth and squirmed against him. The friction against that part of him that was already badly swollen for want of her made his passion blaze.

The hand that supported her back slid down to catch her buttocks and press her more fully against him. The hand that held her breast ever so gently squeezed. . . .

She shoved against his shoulders, violently, taking advantage of his loosened hold as she managed to jerk herself out of his arms. Then, incredibly, a fist exploded into his unsuspecting face just below his right eye.

"Damn it to bloody 'ell!" he yelped, staggering back a pace, a hand flying to his eye. The whole area surrounding it felt numb, but he'd been on the receiving end of enough punches to know that this one would leave its mark in the guise of a fourteen-carat shiner.

"You 'ell-born little bitch!" he gritted, the streets surfacing to color his voice as he took his hand from his eye to glare at her with equal amounts fury and awe. No female but Pearl had ever dared to hit him, and even she of the truly volcanic temper had never landed more than the occasional ringing (and usually well-deserved) slap. Now this little scrap of freckle-faced femininity had actually dared to plant him a facer! "I ought to paddle you until you can't sit!"

"Just you try it!" she panted at him, leaping with the agility of a cat from the floor straight to the center of the bed and standing there, fists clenched, daring him to come after her.

Alec eyed her, lips compressed into a tight, straight line. Never in his wildest dreams would he have suspected her capable of landing the kind of blow she'd dealt him. The little countess had a wealth of unsuspected depths, it seemed.

"Pray accept my congratulations, Countess." He had his voice with its hard-earned accent well under control again. "You punch almost as well as you rut."

It was a low blow, and he knew it, but he was too incensed to care. She gasped, and her cheeks flamed.

"Get out of here, you cretin!" There was true venom in the words.

Alec laughed, the sound grating.

"Such a vocabulary as you possess, love," he jeered.

"Don't you dare call me that! Get out! Get out, I said!"

"Oh, I'm going, you may be sure. Now that we've had a good tumble and I've found out for myself what lies beneath that strumpet's garment, I've no more reason at all to stay."

"Get out!" It was practically a screech.

With one more sizzling stare at her, Alec turned on his heel and stalked back into the dressing room. This time he closed the door very, very carefully behind him. Not for anything would he give her the satisfaction of seeing him succumb to the temptation to give it another vicious slam.

The candle was still burning in the dressing room. Alec threw himself in the chair Paddy had occupied that night that Isabella had tried to brain him—thus showing her true colors, if only he'd had the sense to see!—and felt for the bottle of brandy that was kept hidden under the skirt.

He meant to get good and drunk.

It was only later, much later, when the bottle was nearly three-quarters gone and the candle had melted down to a guttering nub, that Alec felt it.

He was so jug-bitten that at first he didn't recognize it for what it was.

When at last he did, he frowned, trying to clear his head of the awful sensation.

But it stubbornly refused to leave. He was experiencing that omniscient tingle of danger again.

XXI

If nothing else, that last dreadful exchange with Alec left her too angry to cry.

For a long time Isabella sat huddled in the center of the bed, calling him every vile name she could think of under her breath and waiting with a belligerent kind of trepidation for him to emerge from the dressing room again.

An hour passed, and more, and he didn't come out. Gradually she began to realize that he didn't mean to come out. That he meant to brood or sleep or fume or whatever he was doing in there all alone.

Until morning, she hoped.

That gave her the rest of the night to figure out what to do.

She could not stay here under his protection any longer. She would not. Whether or not he needed her presence as cover for his own, he could not force her to stay. Not after what they had done. If he tried, she would . . . she would . . . She didn't know what she would do, but she would think of something.

But then, the lowering thought occurred to her, he probably would not have the least objection to her removing herself from his vicinity. After all, as he had tauntingly pointed out, now that he had got what he wanted from her, what reason had he to want to keep her around?

None, that she could see. She would be just one more

in his line of discarded mistresses. An embarrassment perhaps. Or, more likely, an object of complete indifference.

She was glad she had punched him.

She would insist on going home at first light.

Home—where someone wanted her dead. Isabella's determination faltered, remembering that. How could she go home if someone there wanted her dead? If, indeed, someone truly did. Bernard had been wearing mourning—according to Paddy. But Paddy was Alec's right hand; could she believe him? After all, she only had Alec's word for it that anyone other than the original kidnappers had been involved in the plan to kill her. The question that occurred to her now that she had discovered the truth about his lecherous, untrustworthy nature was: Could she believe what Alec told her? Or had he said what he had for his own ends?

It was incredible to believe that Bernard or, for that matter, anyone else in her family was willing to pay to have her killed.

The only reasonable conclusion to be reached was that Alec was wrong. Either he was genuinely mistaken, or he had an ulterior motive in keeping her with him.

Perhaps he had meant to seduce her all along.

Isabella shuddered at the thought. Had she succumbed to the wiles of an experienced debaucher of women? She very much feared so.

True, she was not beautiful, but she was a lady, and as such, very much outside Alec Tyron's normal ken. He seemed to have a hankering for the outward signs of gentility. He had worked hard to raise himself out of the gutter, and on the way had acquired many of the trappings of a gentleman: a well-bred manner of speaking, usually; a modicum of good manners (which she guessed could vanish as quickly as the upper-class accent); and wealth.

Did it not make sense that he might wish to secure for himself that ultimate proof of gentility, a titled mistress?

The gutter boy had bedded the countess.

How could she have allowed such a thing to happen?

Although her marriage with Bernard was far from a love

match, it was a legal marriage, binding in the eyes of God and man. As her husband, Bernard was the only man who had the right to come into her bed, and join his flesh with hers.

No matter how she tried to wrap it up in clean linen, what she had done was no more or less than adultery. She had lain with a man not her husband of her own free will. She had not been forced, nor coerced in any way.

If she really cared to face the truth, what she had done made her no better than the girls who worked for Pearl. No better than Pearl herself.

She was a light-skirt, a strumpet, a woman of loose morals.

An adulteress.

And the worst part about it was that, if Pearl had not been sleeping in the dressing room to expose the full extent of Alec's depravity, she would have revelled in the things he had done. She would have rejoiced in the feel of his lips on hers, his hands on her body, and even in the marriage act, which had seemed so disgusting when Bernard did it and so marvelous when the man moving over her was Alec. . . .

Never in her life had she thought to experience the blinding pleasure that she had experienced with him. Never had she even dreamed that such physical ecstasy existed.

Isabella took a deep, calming breath. She would force that incendiary enchantment from her mind, banish the memory of it as surely as she would remove herself from this world of harlotry and dissipation.

She would go home, back to Blakely Park and the quietly happy life she had made for herself there. Soon last night—indeed, all that had happened over the past fortnight—would be no more than an unpleasant memory.

She would never so much as think of Alec Tyron again.

Clinging to that determination like a drowning man to a lifeline, Isabella put her head down on the pillow and surrendered to the welcoming lure of sleep.

Until something reached down into her troubled dreams at last and pulled her back to wakefulness.

She did not know how long she had slept, but she did know, almost immediately, what it was that woke her.

A man stood beside her bed, looking down at her.

The fire had died down, leaving the room alive with dense charcoal shadows. But the fact that she couldn't see anything more than his outline didn't matter. Even if she hadn't bothered to open her eyes, she would have known he was there.

Alec, come to her bed again for the Lord only knew what. To continue their argument—or her debauchery?

"Go away," she said fiercely, sitting up and glaring at the menacing figure. And then, to her amazement, without any warning at all, the tall shadow detached itself from the darkness and leaped on top of her, wrapping its hands around her throat.

Isabella screamed once before the hands tightened, cutting off her breath.

XXII

Alec nearly choked on his brandy. He spluttered, dribbling the fiery liquid down his chin, where it dripped onto his chest.

Damn the bitch anyway, for screaming like a banshee in the middle of the night and almost making him choke to death. He'd be damned if he'd go comfort her from any more bloody nightmares! The last time had cost him dear.

She could scream until hell froze over!

He wiped the drops of brandy from his chest with the flat of his hand, and ran the back of the same hand over his mouth and chin. God, he needed a shave, and a bath. He felt grimy, sticky, and out of sorts. All of which could be laid at her door.

She was making a god-awful racket in there. From the sound of it, she was having a hell of a bad dream.

Probably about him, Alec concluded with a jeering grin, and saluted the notion by raising the brandy bottle high before swilling down another huge mouthful.

It was damn fine brandy. Too bad it was giving him absolutely no pleasure at all. And that was her fault, too.

The only thing that would give him pleasure would be to rid himself of the self-righteous little vixen, preferably by putting a pillow over her face as she squalled her lungs out in the adjoining room.

Let her go back to her murderous husband. What bloody

difference did it make to him? Hell, he quite sympathized with the fellow!

There was a great deal of thumping and bumping going on in the next room. She must be flopping all over the bed, struggling to wake up from the dream.

Listening to the din, Alec's scowl deepened.

Damned noisy little bitch. Gave a man no peace.

His eye was swollen almost shut, and it hurt like hell. He should have played her tit for tat. Although hitting a woman—even such an infuriating one as she—went against his grain. But if he ever were to succumb to the urge to commit violent mayhem on female flesh, hers would be the flesh he would start with.

She screamed again, the sound abruptly cut off.

Alec cursed. He would be damned if he'd let her torment him all bloody night.

He had every right to get drunk in peace.

His lips compressed, he nodded to himself, and got to his feet. The walls of the room seemed to recede, and Alec had to catch the chairback to steady himself.

So far he'd done a pretty good job of drowning his sorrows. Once he got her quieted down again, he would finish the job properly.

With luck, he'd drink himself unconscious. Oblivion was a blessedly peaceful state.

Letting go of the chair, Alec made it to the door and fumbled for the knob, still clutching the bottle in one hand.

As he stepped through the door, squinting into the shadowy darkness of her bedroom toward the big bed, where she seemed to be flailing about in a positive frenzy, that nagging tingle came back in full force. It was strong enough to make him take a step backwards.

And that step backwards probably saved his life.

A knife hurtled through the darkness out of nowhere, thunking into the doorjamb near his chest, right where his heart would have been if he hadn't moved. For a split second Alec stared at the quivering blade wedged solidly in the wood. Then a muffled curse and the sound of feet rushing toward him told him that he was under attack.

His mind struggled to surface through the fog of brandy that dulled it. A man loomed up out of the darkness, rushing toward him, swinging a club at his head. Alec ducked, and the club slammed harmlessly into the doorjamb.

His mind was clouded, but his instincts were intact. Twice they had saved him.

The man with the club swung again. Alec struck out with the only weapon he had readily to hand, the brandy bottle, crashing it into the attacker's face. The glass broke with a tinkle, and Alec could feel the jagged edge of it slicing through soft flesh.

The man screamed, cursing as he dropped the club and clutched at his maimed face. His other hand fumbled at his waist for what Alec did not doubt was a pistol.

Alec dropped the bottle, which shattered with a crash on the floor. He grabbed the hilt of the knife that protruded from the doorway, wresting it from the wood just as the man jerked his hand up. . . .

Before he could get off a shot, Alec lunged forward, knife in hand. The blade sank satisfyingly deep into his opponent's belly. Even as Alec twisted it, the motion vicious and designed to gut the victim as efficiently as a fisherman might his catch, his mind was clearing enough to assimilate the true meaning of the sounds that had lured him from his cocoon of brandy.

Isabella had not been crying out in the throes of a nightmare. She had been fighting off an attack.

The knowledge scared him sober. Even before he had the knife properly withdrawn from the shrieking attacker's belly, he was running for the bed. . . .

He never made it. He was tackled en route, by a man big enough to knock him to the ground. Alec went skidding across the floor on his back, the knife flying from his hand to clatter across the floor. The enormous dark bulk of a man slid with him, grabbing at his legs, trying to heave himself on top of him. As Alec crashed into the wall, the man succeeded in straddling him, pinning him to the floor.

Near the hearth now, Alec could see the silver blade of

a wicked-looking knife as it was lifted high above him. He was about to have his throat slit like a slaughtered calf's. Getting his heels beneath him, he heaved, upsetting his would-be assassin's balance. As the blade started down, he managed to lunge to one side. The blade missed his throat by inches, slicing instead into his shoulder.

Alec grunted with pain. The knife was withdrawn, raised again for the killing blow. . . .

At that precise moment, Isabella screamed.

The attacker's attention was momentarily distracted, giving Alec a chance to punch ferociously upward. The blow caught the man on the chin, sending him reeling backwards while Alec grabbed the hand with the knife.

The man fought him, and he was strong. Even at full strength, Alec would have had a hard time besting him, and Alec was not at full strength. But he was fighting for his life, and Isabella's, and that gave him the extra impetus he needed. Bit by bit, inexorably, he brought the man's hand down to the level of his own face. Then, in a burst of strength, Alec slammed the hand holding the knife into the raised edge of the stone hearth. The man cried out, and released his grip on the knife.

Alec took advantage of the man's pain to punch him in the throat, once, twice, as hard as he could from such an awkward position. The man choked, his body snapping back away from the blows. Alec used the man's loss of center to get his heels beneath him once more and heave the attacker up and off his body.

In seconds Alec had him pinned on his stomach on the floor and was on top of him, his own arm closing about the other's neck.

There was a sound at the door leading to the hall. Even as Alec registered it, the door burst open, flying back on its hinges, crashing into the wall. Alec tensed, looking at the site of this new threat with savage eyes. His arm tightened reflexively around his prisoner's neck.

"What the bloody 'ell . . . ?"

"Alec, are you all right?"

It was Paddy, with Pearl right behind him. The fight

had completely gone out of the man beneath Alec. Keeping a wary eye on him, Alec sat up and put a hand to his injured shoulder, wincing.

"They had another go at murdering me," he said grimly, addressing Paddy, then looked in the direction of the bed, which seemed to be empty. Fear tightened his throat. "Isabella . . . "

Paddy lit a candle and held it high, illuminating the room. His other hand gripped a pistol. Pearl ran toward Alec where he sat cross-legged on the floor, breathing hard as he tried to catch his breath.

There was no doubt that the assassination attempt had been aimed at him. But had they killed Isabella instead?

XXIII

"Right behind you," Paddy said dryly. Alec turned his head to find Isabella, candlestick clutched in hand, standing motionless by the hearth.

"Thank God," Alec said, closing his eyes in a momentary wash of relief.

"I couldn't tell which one of you was which. I was afraid I would hit the wrong man," she said, her voice oddly hoarse. She dropped the candlestick with a clatter to the hearth. Then she sat down beside it, as though her knees had suddenly given out. Her head lolled forward to rest on her knees. Her hair, loosened from its braid, fell in a curtain of waves to the floor.

"Oh, Alec, you're bleedin'!"

Pearl dropped to her knees at his side and dabbed at the bloody puncture in his shoulder with the hem of her extravagant nightdress.

"I've had worse," Alec said impatiently, although the blood ran down his arm and chest, and his shoulder ached. Still, he'd been in fights enough to know that the injury wasn't mortal, not anywhere near the same degree of seriousness as the ball he'd recently taken through the chest. He had a feeling that the wooziness he was beginning to feel was more a result of the brandy he had consumed than the wound.

"Goddamn, Alec, 'e's dead! You broke 'is bloody neck!" Paddy, examining the man Alec had felled last, sounded disgusted. Straightening with a shake of his head, Paddy crossed to the bloody corpse blocking the entrance to the dressing room.

" 'Ell, you've done for this rotter too! 'Ow do you expect to find out who's behind this if you keep crabbing 'em before we can question 'em?"

Alec sat up, suffering Pearl to dab at his shoulder as he grimaced at Paddy.

"I beg your pardon, I'm sure. Next time I have a fight to the death, I'll try to be more careful." Irony lay heavy in his voice, but as was usual with such nuances, it was lost on Paddy, who was going through the dead man's pockets with a disgruntled look on his face.

"I'll send for Mr. 'Eath," Pearl said.

"The hell you will," Alec said fiercely. Then he added more slowly, "At least, not for me. Isabella . . ."

Pearl's eyes narrowed. Isabella lifted her head from her knees. Great blue eyes met his.

"I'm all right. Just shaken up a bit."

"You're not injured in any way?" Alec asked.

Isabella shook her head. "My throat aches a little, where he tried to strangle me, but I'm not hurt." Her lips quivered. "Dear God, who were they, and what did they want? They weren't after me. Were they?"

This last was said in a tiny voice that begged for reassurance. It made Alec wish the bastards were alive so that he could kill them again.

" 'Tis certain they were after Alec. After all, your people all think you dead. You're safe enough, as long as they continue to think so," Paddy answered.

"Do you recognize them, Paddy?" Alec asked.

"Nah. Though there's something about this one . . ." Paddy's voice trailed off as he stared at the corpse at his feet.

Alec's eyes narrowed on the dead man. He was almost sure he'd never seen either of them before—but as Paddy said, there was something . . . "Somehow they found out I was here. But how?"

Paddy shook his head. "No one knew where you were

but Pearl and me—and the countess 'ere. We didn't tell, and she couldn't 'ave. Someone must 'ave seen something and gotten suspicious."

"I know what it was!" Pearl exclaimed. "That night she ran out into the 'all! One of the girls saw 'er, and the gent saw 'er too, and they figured out that we were using 'er to 'ide you!"

Alec's eyes moved to rest thoughtfully on Isabella as he considered Pearl's theory. Paddy stared at her too. Isabella looked guilt-stricken at the mere idea. Alec quickly shook his head.

"That's not likely. There's no one to connect Isabella with me. 'Tis more likely that Paddy's been seen coming and going here more than is usual, and someone drew conclusions from that."

Paddy nodded. "That's possible."

Pearl looked disappointed. Isabella looked relieved.

"Well, we can puzzle it out later," Pearl said as she got briskly to her feet. She noticed the small crowd of half-clad girls and their gents who, attracted by the commotion, had gathered in the open doorway to stare.

"You girls go on about your business! Take your gentlemen with you! Go on now! Shoo!"

"But Miss Pearl, all this blood . . . !" One wide-eyed chit with improbable red hair swept the room with her eyes, and made a distasteful moue. "What 'appened? Who's the gents who've been offed?"

" 'Tis none of your business, is it now, Daisy? I don't pay you—any of you—to ask questions. Gentlemen, unless you care to pass the remainder of the evening in some other establishment, I suggest you return to your entertainment. Girls, take your gents and get back to work!"

Pearl's threat had the effect of making the girls scatter, pulling their men with them. As they left, Alec got to his feet. His legs were a little rubbery, and blood spurted from the gash in his shoulder as he moved. He looked at the wound, disgusted.

"Get something to tie this up with, would you, Pearl?"

"Darlin', let me send for the sawbones! You took quite

a beatin'! Besides your arm, your eye's all swollen! Please, Alec?''

Her earlier ire at him was forgotten in the face of his present condition, Alec realized. Pearl really was a very good sort. So he smiled at her even as he reiterated his firm no to the sawbones. That smile did the trick. She practically cooed at him before hurrying away to get bandages and medicines.

Paddy was busying himself with searching the bodies. With a cursory glance at him, Alec crossed to where Isabella sat huddled on the raised hearth.

As he crouched down in front of her, her eyes met his, and a faint color stained her cheeks.

''Let me see your throat.''

''I'm fine. Really.''

''Let me see.'' He was insistent. The look she gave him from big, dark-shadowed eyes was inscrutable. But she obediently lifted her chin and let him see her throat. Alec winced.

The delicate skin was scraped and red. There were three long scratches down the side of her neck where the slimy bastard's fingernails had raked her.

Alec felt that fierce urge to kill again as he raised a hand to touch the raw scratches. Isabella flinched.

''Don't touch me,'' she said quietly. Her eyes were very blue suddenly. The light smattering of freckles that dusted the bridge of her delicate nose stood out more than usual against the shocked paleness of her skin. Her mouth looked slightly swollen and very soft. From his kisses, of course. Staring at those lush red lips, Alec suddenly thought how very much he wanted to kiss her again.

Something of what he felt must have shown in his eyes, because she drew away from him.

''Don't ever touch me again.'' Her voice was steady.

He looked up from her mouth to meet her eyes. ''Isabella . . .'' he began, impatient to have her come off her high ropes and smile at him as she usually did. Hell, he could explain about Pearl, and if an explanation was not enough, he would even apologize. Anything to stop her from looking at him like he was something that had just crawled out from under a rock.

"Alec, come over here! I think I recognize this chap after all!"

Paddy's summons interrupted him before he could put his intentions into words. His eyes flickered in Paddy's direction with some annoyance, and his lips compressed.

"Alec!"

"Go on," Isabella said, and her eyes shifted away from his. Again that fugitive wash of color stained her cheeks and receded.

Alec cursed under his breath as he got to his feet. When he explained to Isabella all the ins and outs of the situation in which he'd found himself, he wanted to do so in privacy. And now was definitely not the time for the kind of discussion he had in mind.

"I'm coming," he said to Paddy, then quickly stepped to the bed and pulled the blue silk coverlet from it.

"Wrap up in this. You look cold," he said brusquely, dropping it around Isabella's shoulders. She looked at him without speaking, her eyes guarded, but she did pull the coverlet around her shoulders, cocooning herself in its soft folds.

XXIV

Isabella pulled the blue silk coverlet closer about her body, trying to stop herself from shaking. But with the best will in the world she could not.

It had been, in every sense of the word, a hideous evening.

Alec had killed two men tonight. She had known that he was capable of violence—of course, he had to be to come up as he had through London's slum hierarchy—but somehow it had never seemed real before. Even the shootings she had witnessed when he had confronted her kidnappers had not seemed real. But this—this bloodbath was real. He had fought for his life and hers, killed two men, painted the walls and floors of her chamber with blood, and sustained a dreadful-looking wound himself. Yet he did not seem particularly shaken.

Certainly he was not racked with remorse, or trembling with reaction as she was.

Pearl was his mistress, yet he had bedded her, Isabella, as casually as he might change his boots. Like the violence, her surrender to him appeared to have affected him not at all.

Which brought her to the inevitable question: Just what kind of man was Alec Tyron anyway?

Isabella made a sound that was almost a sob under her breath.

Giving herself to him had been a monumental act, one that would haunt her the rest of her life.

She doubted if he would remember it by the morrow.

That was the kind of man he was: a handsome thug, a charming brute. A user, especially of women. His easy charm was only camouflage masking the cold steel of the man beneath.

Witness how he had dispatched the two would-be assassins: with utter ruthlessness. And in bedding her without any emotion save lust, he had displayed the same ruthlessness.

Tears began to fill her eyes. Isabella closed them tightly, willing herself not to cry. She was not the first woman to make a fool of herself over a man. And she would not be the last.

Despite her best efforts, a tear forced its way past her closed lids, rolled down her cheek. Without making a sound she huddled on the hearth, blue silk coverlet wrapping her to her chin, face buried in her knees so that no one would see the tears streaking her cheeks.

"There, now, angel, you've got no cause to cry."

Isabella looked up in surprise as Pearl, her nightdress covered now by a feather-trimmed emerald wrapper, sat down beside her, draping an arm around her shoulders. The other woman's eyes were surprisingly compassionate. Isabella took a deep breath, fighting to control her voice.

"I . . . I'm just being silly, I know. But I . . . I can't seem to stop."

"Shock," Pearl said knowledgeably. "You need to lie down. Come on, into bed with you!"

Isabella looked at that bed where so many unspeakable things had happened to her in that one night, and shuddered. She could not lie there again.

"I . . . Could I have another room, do you think, just for the rest of the night? The blood . . ."

"Sure, angel. Sure. I don't blame you, neither. Come on, you can share with me." Pearl was warmly understanding.

"Thank you. That's very kind of you."

"You've kind of got 'kind' on the brain, don't you? But all right, if you like, I'm being kind. Can you stand up?"

Isabella managed to get to her feet. Her knees shook, but with the support of Pearl's arm around her waist, she was able to walk. Alec crouched on one knee near the door. His shoulder now sported a bandage similar to the one around his chest, which Isabella supposed Pearl had applied for him while she sat with her head dropped on her knees. As she and Pearl approached, he looked up from his examination of some items apparently culled from the pockets of one of the dead man's clothes.

"Where are you going?"

"She's going to sleep the rest of the night with me," Pearl answered.

Alec's eyes fastened on Isabella. She quickly averted her face, refusing to meet his gaze. His lips compressed, but then he nodded.

" 'Tis probably a good idea. Pearl will take care of you."

Isabella didn't say anything, and her face was expressionless as she and Pearl walked slowly out the door and down the hall.

One or two of the girls were leaning out into the hall, watching with interest as Pearl, in her elaborate wrapper, and Isabella, still wrapped in the coverlet, came their way. Pearl sent them popping back inside their rooms with no more than a searing look. No doubt the locked room and the mysteriously ill "new girl" had been the object of much speculation amongst the Carousel's denizens. And the night's noisy excitement would have added to their curiosity. Isabella was conscious of eyes boring into her back as she started down the stairs.

They descended two flights of stairs to end up in a wide hallway, the walls of which were covered with red flocked paper. Two large parlors opened off either side of the hall, and a dignified-looking butler was just closing the door after seeing a gentleman on his way into the inky blackness of the street beyond. A chandelier flickered overhead, and large gilt mirrors were everywhere.

Even so late at night—or early in the morning, depending upon how one looked at it, as it had to be nearly dawn—the downstairs rooms were filled with people. Well-dressed gentlemen strolled about the elegantly furnished parlors, looking over the shoulders of others of their sort as they played at cards or dice. Liveried footmen offered various liqueurs to the gaming gentlemen. Females in gaudy, low-cut gowns hung about the men, rubbing their shoulders and whispering in their ears as they made their wagers.

"Is anything the matter, Miss Pearl?" the butler asked, hurrying forward with a worried expression.

"There's been trouble abovestairs, Sharp. Some men found their way up to the third floor who should never even 'ave been admitted to the Carousel in the first place. The Tiger is up there now, and I imagine 'e'll want to be talkin' to you about it."

Sharp seemed to pale. "The . . . the Tiger is abovestairs? But, Miss Pearl, I've been at the door all night and I never even saw him come in. And you know I'd never admit anyone—not anyone!—who wasn't on the admission list!"

"Well, they got up there some'ow." Pearl shook her head. "And the Tiger's up there, too. Take a footman with you and go up to 'im. There's quite a mess to be tidied up, as well."

"I'm sorry, Miss Pearl." Sharp sounded as miserable as he looked.

"You tell that to the Tiger," Pearl said, and steered Isabella away, leaving the butler practically wringing his hands as he signaled to a passing footman.

Pearl's chamber—really a suite, consisting of a bedroom and sitting room—was located on the ground floor at the rear. A maid, pockmarked and ill favored, came toward them as Pearl opened the door, but Pearl dismissed her with a gesture. The maid curtsied and took herself off, closing the door behind her.

The rooms were decorated entirely in shades of white and gold. Isabella looked around, impressed with the sheer sumptuousness of everything. Pearl helped her to a gold-silk-upholstered settee that dominated the sitting room. Isabella sank down upon it thankfully.

"Brandy, angel?" Pearl asked, crossing to a table topped with a silver tray holding several bottles and glasses.

Isabella shook her head. Pearl poured the brandy anyway, into two large snifters.

"Take it. It'll do you good," she said, holding out the glass. Isabella took it. Pearl sat down in an elaborately carved chair at the settee's right and sipped the golden liquid in her glass. After a moment, Isabella followed suit. The liquid had a taste that was not unpleasant, and it was certainly warming going down. She took another sip, and Pearl nodded approval.

"Better?"

"Yes, thank you."

Pearl smiled wryly. "You're a real lady, aren't you? Always so polite, butter wouldn't melt in your mouth. I shoulda guessed from the first that Alec would come sniffin' after you. 'E's always 'ad a hankerin' to better 'imself any way 'e could."

Isabella looked across at Pearl, her eyes widening with guilt. She said nothing, because she could think of nothing to say. Pearl studied her surprised expression for a minute, then smiled wryly.

"Did you think I wouldn't figure out that somethin' was goin' on with you and Alec? With 'im always so protective of you, and callin' you Isabella in that way 'e 'as? I've known Alec since we were kids. I can tell when 'e's gettin' a boner in 'is breeches."

Such plain speaking embarrassed Isabella, but looking at Pearl's face, she felt her embarrassment die. For all Pearl's calm statement, there was a look in her eyes that spoke of pain carefully suppressed.

"If you're hurt, Pearl, I'm terribly sorry. I never meant—"

Pearl laughed, the sound tinged with bitterness. "Don't apologize, angel. I'm not one to begrudge you your fun.

Alec's been goin' 'is own way for a long time now, and I don't mind that 'e 'as other women. 'E's a real man, 'e is, and likes the ladies, but 'e always comes back to me in the end. I thought you should know that."

Isabella felt her stomach tighten. Pearl's voice was oddly gentle, and Isabella did not doubt she told the truth. Indeed, Isabella had known that she was no more than a passing fancy for Alec, a novelty. The idea made her wince.

Pearl's eyes sharpened. Then she dropped them back to her brandy, which she swirled thoughtfully around the glass. She looked at the pale gold liquid instead of Isabella as she spoke.

" 'E'll wed me one day, 'e will, and we'll 'ave kids just like us. We're the same breed, Alec and me. Survivors. You're just somethin' a little out of the common way for 'im, and as soon as 'e beds you a few times, you'll be out of 'is system for good. Just like all the rest."

The image of being bedded by Alec a second time, let alone the few times that Pearl envisioned, panicked Isabella. She would not, could not, sink any lower than she already had. To surrender to temptation once was contemptible; for a married, decent lady such as herself to become a man's mistress was utterly depraved.

"I have to get away from here," she said miserably, feeling sick as she too stared down at the brandy in her glass. "Will you help me?"

Pearl smiled, and took a sip of brandy before answering.

"Sure, angel. Sure I will."

XXV

Isabella huddled inside the hackney, pulling the hood of the blue velvet cloak Pearl had lent her around her face. Beneath the cloak, she was wearing a relatively proper morning gown of the same color and material. The clothes were much too large, but they were well made and clean and, best of all, warm. The first weeks of March usually saw a warming of the temperature, but this morning was bitterly cold.

Pearl had been all that was kind, ordering a footman to summon a hackney for her, lending her clothes, giving the address of the St. Just townhouse to the driver, even pressing money into her hand to pay the fare.

As the hackney rattled over the cobbled streets toward the fashionable townhouse that she had never so much as seen, Isabella stared out the grimy window and tried not to think.

She was sore afraid that she was making a mistake.

The sun was just peeping over the tallest of the narrow brick buildings, its rays turning the thick wisps of mist that floated over the streets to a dull yellow-gray. Chimney pots spewed plumes of gray smoke into the sky, and fat flakes of soot drifted down like small, gray autumn leaves to settle on everything below. A few hardy individuals were already out and about. Servants mostly, bundled up to their eyebrows against the cold. One plump old woman pushed a battered handcart down the street. Her cries of

"Butter and cheese! Butter and cheese! Buy, if you please, my butter and cheese!" echoed off the houses lining the fashionable residential square.

As the hackney pulled to a halt in front of an elegant townhouse, Isabella realized with a growing sense of trepidation that she had arrived at her destination.

The wizened cabby opened the door for her and stood waiting, blowing on his cold hands, his breath making little clouds of smoke in the cold air.

"This be it, miss," he said, impatience in his voice as he shifted from foot to foot, waiting for her to alight.

Isabella swallowed. What choice had she? It was either go in to her legal husband, or return to the Golden Carousel—and Alec.

She never wanted to see Alec again in her life. And she wouldn't, once she walked through the townhouse's lofty portal. Her life would resume as if he had never existed.

But what if Bernard had really tried to have her killed?

Absurd! said the logical part of her brain.

But what if . . . ? The question lingered almost audibly on the air.

Alec had firmly planted the seeds of doubt, ridiculous though they probably were, and all her common sense could not dislodge them.

Perhaps she should go to her father, and lay all before him, and beg him to determine what was true and what was not.

But he would say that a married woman's place was with her husband, and send her back to Bernard post-haste. She doubted that he would even wait to hear her story out.

Of course, Paddy said that her family thought her dead. Having her turn up very much alive on their doorstep might soften their hearts toward her.

Isabella smiled wryly. More likely her father would scold her for putting him to the unnecessary expense of purchasing mourning clothes. And Bernard would doubtless complain of the same thing.

And everybody would want to know what had happened, and where she had been.

"You gettin' out, miss, or not?" The cabby was scowling.

Isabella took a deep breath. She had to make a decision, now.

She got out, and stood looking up at the townhouse that towered three stories above her. It really was a most impressive residence.

"That'll be two bob, miss."

The cabby was holding out his hand for the fare. She gave him the coins, and scarcely noticed when he climbed back on the box and drove away.

Her attention was all on what she must do.

Walk past the marble whippets that guarded the steps, up the shallow stairs to the white-painted door, then knock.

A butler would doubtless answer. She would tell him who she was, and he would let her in.

The problem would be resolved. She would be back where she belonged, and Alec Tyron and his dire warnings would be behind her, soon to be forgotten.

Taking a deep breath, Isabella picked up the too long skirts of her borrowed cloak and dress, and walked steadily past the whippets and up the stairs.

She stopped on the landing, and reached up to knock—only to stare at the door with some confusion.

The knocker was off the door.

Isabella lacked town bronze, but she knew what that meant. For whatever reason, the house was closed. Bernard was not there.

Feeling almost lighthearted, she knocked anyway. She heard the sound echo through the rooms inside, but no one came to the door. The house was empty. Smiling faintly, she turned away.

Only to stop stock-still in the street, eyes widening, as she realized the position she was in.

She was alone in London with only a coin or two in her pocket and nowhere to go.

What did she do now?

XXVI

Hours later Isabella had still come up with no satisfactory solution to her dilemma. She had wandered down one labyrinthian street after another until she was hopelessly, totally lost. The streets had grown steadily shabbier, and as the day waned; Isabella realized that she was no longer in the fashionable part of town.

A sign swung in the wind that was just starting to pick up. "The Nag's Head Coffee House," it proclaimed. For all the building's cracked plaster and dingy windows, it was at least a place where she could get in out of the cold, sip a cup of tea and ponder her situation.

Carefully Isabella felt the few coins remaining in her pocket. Surely things were not so expensive in London that she could not have a cup of tea with a bit left over.

The Nag's Head was nothing more than a back-street pub, Isabella saw as she entered. The interior was dark and gloomy, and an assortment of scruffy looking characters sat at the crowded tables. First one and then another glanced at her as she passed to an empty table near the window. Isabella was made uncomfortable by the looks she received, and hastily sat, striving to make herself as inconspicuous as possible.

"What'll it be, me dear?" A stout woman in a gingham dress with an apron that was none too clean appeared at tableside, bearing a tray holding two foaming mugs of ale. As she waited for Isabella's order, she deftly slid the mugs onto the table behind her, where two sly-looking men talked in whispers.

"Well, ducks?"

"A cup of tea, please," Isabella said low. She saw nothing strange about her request, but the woman's eyes opened wider, and moved swiftly over her before coming to rest again on her face.

"A cup o' tea? If you say so, ducks."

The woman shrugged, and went to the rear of the establishment, presumably to fetch the tea. Isabella tried to ignore the covert looks of the other customers as she waited, keeping her eyes firmly trained on what she could see of the street through the window. As the glass was covered with a thick layer of grit, this wasn't too much.

" 'Ere you go, ducks." The woman put the tea down in front of her.

"How—how much is it?" Isabella asked, almost afraid to find out. What would happen if she couldn't afford to pay? To her surprise, the woman shook her head.

"No charge for a cuppa for you, ducks. You look like you're kinda down on your luck."

"Why, thank you."

Isabella stared after the woman as she took herself off toward the rear of the shop again. Kindness was everywhere, it seemed.

She settled down to drink her tea, and consider her options.

As she saw it, she could return to the Golden Carousel. Surely it would not be difficult to get someone to direct her there.

Or she could make her way to the nearest stagecoach house, and try to get back to Norfolk, where she could then decide whether to throw herself on her father's mercy or go straight to Blakely Park.

It was always possible that Bernard was in Norfolk, either at Blakely Park or at Portland House, her father's estate. Perhaps his absence was something to do with her supposed death?

She didn't know. She didn't even really care. All she

knew was that she was tired, hungry and confused, and wanted to be somewhere safe.

As she thought the word "safe," Alec's rakishly handsome face flashed before her mind's eye.

Now, why, she thought wrathfully, should she associate being safe with that blackguard?

Resolutely she banished him from her thoughts, as she had done about a dozen times that day.

Her best bet, she decided after more deliberation, was to go home to Blakely Park. Pressy would be there, and the servants, all of whom were her friends. If Bernard was truly trying to kill her, he would not do it there. And if it was someone else who wanted her dead, he would be confounded—for the time being, at least.

Drat Alec anyway, for putting such thoughts in her mind! Isabella knew that she would never pass another peaceful night in the vicinity of her husband or family for as long as she lived.

Glaring through the glass, Isabella abruptly sat up straighter. A tilbury was driving up the narrow street. The driver was a well set up man in a many-caped driving coat with a wealth of wavy tawny-gold hair left bare of any hat.

There could not be two heads of hair like that in England.

Alec!

Standing up so quickly that the remnants of her tea sloshed into the saucer, Isabella looked wildly around. The other customers were staring at her curiously, but Isabella paid them no mind.

Alec's presence in this particular street might be a coincidence. But she didn't mean to take the chance. She almost ran toward the back of the shop.

" 'Ere , where you goin' now, ducks?" The stout barmaid was hurrying toward her, her round face alarmed.

"Have you a back entrance?" Isabella gasped. But as she spoke, she saw it. A dark, narrow doorway that opened onto an alley behind the shop.

"Wait, now, you can't do that!" the woman cried, but Isabella was already out in the alley and running.

The alley was dark and filled with garbage. A foul smell thickened the air. An ancient drunk slept inside a doorway a little way along the street. Isabella flew past him, trying not to trip on the icy, uneven cobblestones.

''Isabella!''

She had known that his arrival in that particular street was not a coincidence. Now here he was, coming after her, his booted feet thudding loudly against the pavement as he ran.

He had caught her once before. She did not mean to let him do so again.

Picking up her skirts, she fled as if the hounds of hell were on her heels.

XXVII

"Damn it, Isabella!"

His hand closed on the folds of her cloak billowing out behind her, jerking her to a halt. Isabella whirled, snatching her cloak from his grip. Panting, she glared at him. Alec was scowling at her from less than an arm's length away. Even in the murkiness of the alley, he looked very big, very tough, and very handsome, and she had to squash a wayward flicker of pleasure and relief at his presence.

"Let me go!"

"Let you go? You're damned lucky I found you! I've had the word out on the streets all day. Do you have any idea what could have happened to you . . . ? No, of course you don't!" He was nearly as out of breath as she. "Just what the bloody hell did you think you were about, anyway? Where did you think you were going?"

"Home!"

They were practically shouting at each other. Alec took a deep breath, and when he spoke again his voice had moderated somewhat.

"You can't go home, and you know it."

"I'm not staying at the Carousel any longer! You can't make me! I will go home, I will!"

"Stop being such a spoiled little miss, and think what you're doing for a minute!"

"I will go home! I will!"

"Someone—very likely your husband—wants you dead, Isabella. Until we find out who it is, you cannot go home."

"I don't believe you!"

"You don't believe me?" His eyes narrowed.

"No, I don't!"

"Why would I lie?"

"To get me to . . . to keep me as . . . to . . . to . . . you know!"

Alec studied her for a moment, and Isabella felt her face pinken as she realized just what memories her words had stirred up in him.

"From that nearly indecipherable speech, I gather that you're asking yourself if my lust for you is such that I would keep you from kith and kin until it is slaked."

Uttered in such a satirical voice, the notion sounded absurd, Isabella had to admit. Still, she stubbornly lifted her chin.

"Yes!"

Alec laughed, but his eyes glittered at her almost as if he were angry. "No. The answer is no! You're a fine piece in bed, Countess, but I would not go to such lengths as that to keep you in mine."

Isabella felt her cheeks glow positively red. She glared at him. "You're vile!"

"And you're a bloody little fool, so I'd say we're well matched!"

"Stop swearing at me!"

"I'll bloody well swear if I feel like it!"

"You may certainly swear, but I don't have to listen to it!"

With that, Isabella turned on her heel, the cloak swirling about her, and marched off.

"Stop right there!" His voice was tight with suppressed anger. Isabella ignored him, and kept walking.

" 'Twould serve you bloody right if I left you 'ere," he called after her. She knew from his slipping accent that he was on the verge of losing his temper. Still she kept going, stalking down that cesspool of an alley with her back ramrod straight and her head high, not caring that the drunk in the doorway had awakened to blink at her with befuddled eyes, or that a small crowd had spilled out of the back of the Nag's Head to watch.

"Isabella! I'm giving you one last bloody chance to turn around and come back 'ere!"

She said not a word, but continued to walk. With a sound midway between a roar and a growl, he came after her. Isabella heard him behind her and, abandoning her dignity, started to run. He scooped her up in midstride, and slung her up and over his shoulder like a sack of grain before she could even regain enough presence of mind to struggle.

"Put me down! How dare you! What do you think you're doing?"

She kicked furiously as he carried her back toward where the crowd guffawed outside the Nag's Head.

"You mean you don't recognize the feeling?" He clamped her legs to his chest with one arm to still her kicking. "I'm kidnapping you, Countess!"

XXVIII

"Put me down!"

"Presently."

"Now!"

He ignored that as he carried her through the coffee shop and out into the street. The crowd of onlookers had fallen respectfully silent as he had raked them with his eyes, and now they trailed behind him, whispering amongst themselves with great care and even greater amusement.

Isabella was not amused. Alec had tossed a coin to the stout barmaid, thanking her for sending him word and telling her that if she ever needed a favor, she had only to ask for him. The woman had practically licked his boots in response, while Isabella, in her humiliating position, had seethed.

The Tiger was a force to be reckoned with in the slums of London, it seemed.

Alec gave another coin to the grubby urchin who was holding his horses—the Tiger didn't have to worry about harm coming to his equipage even in such a run-down section of the city; who would dare?—and deposited Isabella on the seat.

She immediately scrambled for the other side of the carriage, determined to take advantage of his momentary distraction with the horses to get away. For her pride's sake if nothing else, she could not let him treat her so high-handedly.

He caught her skirt with one hand, and yanked her unceremoniously back into a sitting position.

"Try that again, and I'll tie you hand and foot. See if I don't," he promised through his teeth.

Isabella did not doubt him. She had seen that look on his face before. She sank back in the seat, pulled the hood of her cloak over her head, and scowled at the pair of horses now carrying them briskly along the street.

"What would you say if I told you I had proof that St. Just paid Parren to murder you?"

Isabella cast a quick glance up at him. He was driving easily, competently, but he seemed to favor his right hand. She remembered that it was his left shoulder that had been wounded only that morning, and felt a slight pang of concern for him. But only a slight one.

"I would say, show me." Her voice was very cold.

"All right, I will." His mouth was set in a hard, straight line, and his eyes were suddenly very grim.

Neither of them said another word until he pulled the tilbury to a halt and threw the reins to another urchin who almost magically materialized from the ragged throng crowding the street.

"Watch 'em," Alec said briefly to the lad as he stepped down and turned to help Isabella down.

"Aye, Tiger, sir. Nobut will touch 'em with 'Ank Soames a-guardin' 'em for ye!"

Alec said nothing in reply to this fervent speech, but held out his hand for Isabella. When she sat there for a moment, just staring at his outstretched hand, he said impatiently, "Well, do you want to know or don't you?"

Isabella put her hand in his.

The street that was home to the Nag's Head looked like the epitome of fashionable London compared to this one. What seemed to be crowds of raggedly dressed, filthy people swarmed around a makeshift market of handcarts in its center, babbling in a nearly incomprehensible slaughtering of the King's English as they fought over prices. Isabella goggled at the sights and sounds, and tried to ignore the smell, which seemed to be coming from the overflowing gutters that ran along both sides of the street.

"This is where I grew up," Alec told her with what seemed to be grim pleasure as he took in her wide eyes and wrinkled nose. "But it's much nicer now, of course."

Isabella turned to gape at him, and thus missed noticing much about the entrance to the dark hole of an establishment where Alec led her. Impossible to imagine Alec as one of the filthy, rag-tag urchins darting about that unruly throng.

"This is what's called a flash-house," Alec said. Isabella blinked at her surroundings, not knowing whether to be frightened or appalled at what she saw. Men and women who looked like nothing so much as human refuse scrounged about in the cavelike gloom which was barely pierced by a few guttering, smelly candles. The odor of stale ale and, yes, vomit and possibly even excrement joined the awful aroma of the candles for a stink that was indescribable. As they entered, a man near the door stood up, took one look at Alec, and sank back down abruptly. Isabella instinctively clutched Alec's arm.

"Do you recognize that woman?" His voice was quiet. Isabella followed the direction of his eyes.

A short, stout woman in a patched-together, too tight blue wool dress huddled in a chair in the corner, cackling as she laughed at something a hulking man beside her said. Isabella stared at her, but shook her head.

"I'm sure I've never seen her before in my life."

Alec's mouth tightened.

"Look again."

Isabella did. There was something about the way the woman laughed. . . .

"Molly!" she gasped, and felt as if a fist had suddenly slammed into her stomach.

XXIX

Molly was clearly terrified to see Alec, and spilled her guts at his first quiet suggestion that she do so. Although she had never been told the identity of the man who had hired Parren, she did know that he was a "fancy lordship" who had wanted the lady killed after the ransom was paid. There was quite a wealth of detail, which Isabella couldn't think about without feeling sick, and all of it pointed to Bernard. Molly's whining insistence that she personally had never intended any harm to Isabella was treated with the contempt it deserved.

"Did I know she was your wench, Tiger, I'd a treated her like spun gold, I would!" Molly wailed, her voice shrill with fright as Alec listened to her story with eyes that grew steadily more arctic. Alec fixed her with a frightening look in his eyes, and Molly fell to her knees right there, babbling for mercy.

In the end, to Isabella's relief, he left the woman groveling on the floor. Even to such a one as Molly, Isabella would not like to see harm done.

"Damn it, Isabella, will you speak? Do you still want to go home?"

They were outside now, bowling through a maze of cobbled streets as Alec drove away from the worst of the slums. It was growing dark, and the wind was icy cold. Alec's perfectly sculpted face looked austere and a little bleak as the biting wind brought color to his cheeks and ruffled his tawny hair. Isabella's own hair had long since lost its battle with the pins that confined it, allowing wispy tendrils to straggle around her face. She brushed them aside, and glanced distractedly at Alec.

Alec met her eyes, his own hard and cold. "Isabella?"

"I can't go home, can I?"

"Stop looking so damned forlorn. You know I'll see you safe." His voice was rough.

"I can't stay with you."

"I don't see that you have a great deal of choice."

That was so true that she was left without a ready answer. Still, she tried.

"I must find employment. Surely there is something I can do to support myself."

"Don't be a fool, Isabella." He was glaring at her. She looked back at him calmly. All the emotions had been drained from her by Molly's bloodcurdling recital.

"I cannot let you support me. It's not proper."

"I think we've gone rather beyond the line of what is proper, don't you?"

Again Isabella was left without a ready answer.

"I won't let you keep me, Alec. Nor will I be your mistress."

His face tightened, and his eyes flashed as they moved over her face. "I'd wait till I was asked, were I you, Countess. I meant to offer you a job, nothing more."

"A job? What kind of job?"

Despite herself, Isabella was morbidly interested. No doubt he saw her as a bawd at the Carousel, or some such. Such an offer would be the final humiliation. Nothing would hurt as much.

"As a tutor."

His words were so unexpected that she blinked at him stupidly.

"A tutor?" Her voice was incredulous. "For whom?"

If it was possible, she would have sworn he looked slightly embarrassed.

"Me."

"You?"

"Yes, me. You're an educated woman, and I've decided I'm in need of . . . educating."

"You must be joking," she said at last, staring at him.

"Devil a bit."

Isabella frowned. "Are you really serious?"

"As serious as a grave. I bought a property in Horsham some time back, and I propose to rusticate there awhile as my presence at the Carousel is apparently an open secret. You can come down with me, and . . . uh . . . teach me whatever it is a gentleman should know, and I don't."

Isabella looked at him warily. "You have to understand that I have no intention of . . . that I won't . . ."

Alec smiled wryly. "That you won't repeat that delightful experience we so lately shared? Very well, Countess. Will you accept my offer if I give you my word that the arrangement between us is strictly business?"

Isabella looked at him a moment longer. Then she took a deep breath of the cold, crisp air.

"Yes," she said. "I will."

XXX

The day already being far advanced, the journey to Horsham was put off until the following morning. Upon their return to the Carousel, Pearl was conspicuous by her nonappearance, but since Alec's presence in the brothel was an open secret after the events of the previous night, there were servants aplenty to see to their needs. Isabella was given a room on a lower floor, and a maid to wait on her. Where Alec slept, she preferred not to speculate. Surely not with Pearl . . . But whether he did or not was none of her concern. Their relationship henceforth would be strictly business.

Isabella spent most of the evening trying to put together some reasonable facsimile of a wardrobe. With the maid's assistance, clothes were not hard to come by, but such clothes! Few were suitable for wearing by a female not intent on the seduction of the entire male gender.

When, not long after first light, Isabella descended the stairs into the Carousel's deserted front parlor, she was clad in a fur-trimmed bottle green pelisse that she wore buttoned to the throat to conceal the décolletage of the gown beneath. Of the same green wool as the pelisse, the garment was obviously intended for day wear—but not by a lady. It was long-sleeved, high-necked—and graced with a braid-trimmed cutout that bared her chest from her collarbone to halfway down her small breasts. With the pelisse, the outfit was unexceptional and could have been designed specifically for travel. Without the pelisse, the gown was indecent, as were most of the half dozen others she had selected as the best of a hopeless array. Certainly she could wear none of them with ease in a public place—or for viewing by Alec.

Isabella clutched the carpetbag containing the rest of her borrowed finery as she made her way down the stairs. On the last landing, she paused uncertainly. Pearl was crossing the hall on the floor below, and Isabella was not sure of what her reception might be. Pearl looked up then, saw Isabella and stopped. Then she walked purposefully to the foot of the stairs, where she stood with her hand resting on the well-polished newel post. For a moment she merely stared at Isabella, unspeaking, her beautiful eyes slightly narrowed. Then she smiled, and shook her head regretfully.

"So you didn't get away after all, angel."

Isabella, relieved at this mild greeting, smiled too, and continued down the stairs. There was nothing in Pearl's manner that was less than friendly, although for a minute there, anger seemed to have flashed in her eyes. Or maybe not. Although it was full daylight now, the hall had no windows, and the heavy curtains were pulled shut in the rooms on either side. In the resulting gloom, it was hard to be certain of anything, much less a fleeting look in someone's eyes.

"No. Bernard was from home. The knocker was off the door."

Pearl grimaced. "Alec was wild when 'e 'eard you'd gone. 'E gave me a tongue-lashing I won't soon forget, let me tell you."

"I . . . I'm sorry."

"No need for you to be. Alec and I've quarreled before, and we'll doubtless quarrel many more times afore we're through. Both 'ot-'eaded, we are."

Isabella could find nothing to say to that, so she smiled again, nervously fingering the soft brown fur framing her throat. The idea of Alec and Pearl quarreling repeatedly over many years to come bothered her in some odd way that she refused to even allow herself to consider. She could not be jealous of a street thug and his bawd. She would not even consider the possibility.

"I hope you don't mind that I've borrowed a few things to wear. Alec said it would be all right."

"Did 'e?" Again Isabella had the impression that something ugly flashed in Pearl's midnight blue eyes. Then the other woman shrugged. "You're welcome to anything you like, o' course. I only 'ope you know what you're gettin' into, is all."

"What do you mean?" Isabella's hand tightened over the fur.

Pearl pursed her lips. Compressed, they formed a perfect carmine red rosebud in the white oval of her face. The only flaw in her loveliness was the wrinkle on either side of her mouth, created momentarily by her expression and accentuated horribly by the cracking of the exquisite maquillage. "A gent dearly loves a bit of novelty, you know, in food or females. Still, I wouldn't 'ave thought a lady like you'd go along with 'aving Alec set you up as 'is mistress. But then, ladies ain't no different from the rest of us females when it comes to a 'andsome gent, I guess."

Isabella caught her breath. "Alec is not—I am not to be his mistress. You are quite mistaken, Pearl, believe me." She blushed horribly, and hated herself for doing so.

Pearl noted the blush, and a mocking expression came over her face.

"Oh, ain't you? Then why is 'e takin' you to Amberwood? It's grand—so grand Alec never even goes there 'imself. But I guess 'e thinks that since you're a countess and all, only the best will do for you."

"I—" Isabella began, and then stopped short. She suddenly discovered that she was at a loss for words to explain her new position in Alec's life. It occurred to her that he might not like to have it widely known that he felt himself in need of tutoring. So what could she say that would appease Pearl, salvage her own self-respect, and at the same time shield Alec?

"You're talkin' out of turn, Pearl." The chiding voice belonged to Paddy, who entered from the direction of the front parlor and stopped, arms folded over his chest, just behind Pearl. As Pearl threw a poisonous glare over her shoulder at him, he shifted his attention to Isabella with seeming indifference to Pearl's ill humor. "Alec is waiting for you out front. You'd best 'urry along."

Thankful for the interruption, Isabella murmured quick good-byes and moved toward the front door, which a chastened-looking Sharp, materializing out of seemingly nowhere, held open for her.

"My lady." Paddy's voice was gruff. Pausing with one foot on the threshold, Isabella looked at him questioningly. Unlike Pearl, Paddy seemed to bear her no trace of ill will. He came up behind her, moving lightly for such a huge man, his brown eyes sober as they met hers. "Whoever it is that wants Alec dead is still out there. 'Ave an eye to 'im, will you? 'E's a bit on the reckless side where 'is own safety is concerned." He paused, frowning. "You 'ave only to send word 'ere to the Carousel to reach me if there's need. I'll come at once."

Paddy's concern for Alec touched her. Smiling at him, Isabella nodded.

"I'll do that," she promised, then turned and walked out the door and down the steps to the street, where Alec waited impatiently with the tilbury.

XXXI

The distance to Horsham was not overlong, not more than a six-hour drive including time for a stop for a leisurely luncheon that the cook at the Carousel had prepared and packed in a basket for them to enjoy at their convenience. The day was warm and bright, the sky was blue, and the fields in the countryside were already starting to turn green. Small yellow crocuses butted their heads against the softened earth, here and there springing forth in solitary glory. Robins and bluebirds pecked busily on the ground between budding trees, searching for twigs and other necessities with which to build their nests. Despite the uncertainty of her position, Isabella felt strangely lighthearted. With a sidelong glance at the man beside her, comfortably silent as he handled the reins with practiced ease, she wondered suddenly if it was not he who was responsible for her unexpected happiness. If so, the implications were unsettling in the extreme. Isabella refused to be unsettled on such a beautiful day, and so she banished the thought.

As they left London farther and farther behind, the sun rose higher and brighter in the sky, and the roads roughened. Isabella's euphoria evaporated somewhat. When after a couple of hours Alec suggested stopping at the next likely spot they passed, Isabella was all too ready to agree. The road, battered by the incessant downpours that had marked February and March, was pocked with holes and crisscrossed by ruts, making even the well-sprung tilbury lurch and pitch continuously, like a ship in a storm. That alone would not have bothered Isabella so much—she was not usually prone to carriage sickness—were it not for the unseasonable warmth of the day. It was only the second week in April, but if one judged by temperature alone, it might have been high summer.

"You're looking a tad pale, Countess," Alec observed as the tilbury bounced energetically around a bend. "No doubt you'll be glad to get down for a bit and stretch your legs."

"Yes," Isabella agreed, trying not to sound too fervent. In truth, she was dreadfully hot and faintly nauseous, but she thought that if she could just sit for a minute under the shade of a tree on something that did not move, she would recover in no time at all.

"You're in luck. Look there." With the whip he pointed ahead to a grassy spot in a semicircle of trees.

"It looks wonderful."

"Whoa, there, Blaze. Whoa, Boyd."

Alec pulled up his horses, secured the reins, jumped down and helped Isabella to alight. She clung tightly to the hand he held up to her, knowing that her own was probably clammy.

But Alec appeared to notice nothing amiss with her. "If you should need to relieve yourself, you may go into those trees over there, but don't wander too far. I should hate to have to rescue you from a crazed wild boar, or some such creature."

This sally coaxed a faint smile from Isabella, but her voice was severe as she answered. "There are no boars in the vicinity, as you know very well. And a gentleman should never, ever, refer to a lady's . . . er . . . bodily needs. Gentlemen are supposed to believe that ladies have none. Or at least they pretend to believe that."

"Gentlemen are damned fools, then," Alec retorted good-humoredly, retrieving a pair of oat-filled feed bags from beneath the seat. "And you may leave off your tutoring until we arrive at Amberwood. Your employment does not officially begin until then. For the nonce we are merely a man and a maid enjoying one another's company."

Isabella shrugged. "As you wish."

She settled herself on a stump beneath the spreading branches of an oak tree while Alec saw to the horses. With the motion stopped, she felt a degree better, but the heat was stifling, and the fur closing around her throat was choking her. With one eye on Alec as he pulled a picnic basket from the carriage, she undid the first four hooks of the pelisse, parting the edges of the garment so that what small breeze there was might hit her sweat-dampened skin. The resulting opening bared a sliver-thin vee of flesh from her throat to the hollow between her breasts. Showing more would be indecent. But she was still sickeningly hot, trapped in close-fitting, fur-trimmed wool on a day that was, against all logical expectations, as uncomfortable as an August noon.

Alec came toward her, picnic basket in hand. He had shed his coat, and in shirt sleeves and breeches he looked both devastatingly handsome and maddeningly cool. Not a single bead of sweat dampened his brow as he set the basket at her feet.

"Would you care to join me for a light repast, Countess?" he asked with a sweeping bow and a wicked grin.

"I'm really not very hungry," Isabella said, averting her face from the delicious aromas arising from the basket. "You go ahead."

His eyes narrowed at her. "You look pale. Are you ill?" The joking note was gone, replaced by concern.

She smiled at him then, a little weakly but still a smile. Not many people in her life had shown much concern for her comfort or well-being, regardless of how closely connected they were to her. Coming from Alec, on whom she had no claim whatsoever aside from the odd friendship they had struck up, such attention was doubly sweet.

"I'm just a trifle queasy from the rough road. If I sit here for a minute, it will pass, I'm sure."

Still he frowned at her. "You're sweating. You should take off that fur thing."

"It's called a pelisse—and I prefer to keep it on."

"That's foolishness."

"Perhaps so. Nevertheless, I prefer to wear it."

"Well, I prefer that you don't. 'Tis bloody hot out."

Soft blue eyes met determined gold ones. "I shall take leave to tell you that it is not the thing for a gentleman to comment on a lady's attire."

He snorted. "Don't try to fob me off with that twaddle. Why won't you take off the fur thing? If there is a sensible reason, pray enlighten me."

Isabella sighed. "Would you please just sit down and eat? I would remove the pelisse if I could, but I cannot."

Fists resting on his hips, he cocked his golden head to the side and studied her as one might an odd type of bug. Even battling incipient nausea, she could not help but be aware of how dazzlingly handsome he was. In white shirt, buff breeches and tall, well-polished boots, he looked so fit and vigorous that just looking at him tired her. He also looked very young, younger than she had supposed he could possibly be, and carefree, like a high-spirited boy.

"How old are you? You've never said, and I've never thought to ask."

He looked surprised at the question. "Older than you, my girl, believe me, so don't try to change the subject. Why can you not take off that thrice-damned pelisse?"

"How much older? I am three-and-twenty, you know." She persisted with sweet indifference to both his swearing in her presence and his preoccupation with her pelisse.

His eyebrows came together. He looked her up and down, his expression weighing. She met that look with serenity—and determination.

"If I satisfy your curiosity, will you satisfy mine?"

"About what?" She was cautious.

"About why you cannot take off that pelisse."

Isabella hesitated, then nodded. "Yes."

"Well, then, I am as close to thirty as makes no difference."

Her eyes widened. "Are you telling me that you are no more than nine-and-twenty?"

"If I am, what of it?"

A smile tugged at the corners of her lips, broadened into a grin. "Why, you are just six years older than I!"

"I am centuries older in experience, believe me." His expression told her that her amused delight in his relative youth disgruntled him.

"You are scarcely more than a lad!"

"And you, my girl, are a wet-behind-the-ears miss in search of a good set-down."

As she giggled at his obvious discomfiture, Alec squatted beside the picnic basket, opened the lid, and began to rifle through the contents. A cloth had been included. He spread it out, and began to lay the picnic on it. Suddenly he looked across at her. "You have not honored your part of the bargain, Countess. You seem to find my age very amusing, but I still have no idea why you are idiotic enough to wrap yourself up in fur in this infernal heat."

A bargain was a bargain. She took a deep breath, and searched for the words to delicately describe her dilemma. "The dress I am wearing . . . it's not mine, you know, and . . . and it's not really the thing."

Disgusted, he said, "Are you telling me that the dress is so unfashionable that you would wear that stifling garment over it rather than reveal it to me?"

"No, of course not! It's not that the dress is unfashionable. Rather, it is . . . indecent." Try as she would to be matter-of-fact about it, she had to look away from him as she said the last word.

His eyebrows rose, and he scanned her outfit with renewed interest. "Really? Let me see."

"No!"

He stood up then, with the picnic half spread out at his feet. While she watched him warily, a single lithe step brought him beside her. Seated as she was, he towered above her, and she had to crane her neck back to see his face. He grinned at her, a wicked grin that caused those golden eyes to dance. Isabella observed that grin with more than a little misgiving.

"Come, Isabella, take it off. Your gown cannot be that

indecent, and 'tis nothing short of folly for you to wrap yourself from chin to wrists in wool on such a day. There is no one here to be shocked, you know. As for me—why, I can promise you that I'm too hungry to notice anything save my food."

That virtuous note made her smile, but still she shook her head at him.

"Eat, Alec, and leave me be. I am determined not to come out of this pelisse, and there's an end to it."

"And I am determined that you shall. You are making yourself ill, to no purpose. And you are keeping me from my meal."

"In my role as your tutor, I take leave to tell you that such persistence as you display is annoyingly ill-bred. A gentleman, knowing his importunities to be unwelcome, would desist at once."

"Fortunately for you, Madame Tutor, I am not a gentleman. And I refuse to let you suffer for so ridiculous a cause."

Isabella sighed. "I'm tired of bandying words with you. I am quite comfortable, I assure you, so let us find some other topic to discuss as we eat."

"I'm tired of bandying words about, too."

Before she knew what he was about, he bent, scooped her off the stump, and deposited her flat on her back on the just-greening ground quicker than she could squeal his name. Even as she squeaked with surprised protest he was kneeling over her, straddling her, catching her hands in one of his and pinioning them over her head.

"What the . . . the blazes do you think you're doing?" Struggling was useless, she knew, and she refused to give him the satisfaction of subduing her when no good could come of it. But her eyes bespoke her emotions as they shot blue daggers at him.

"You really are going to have to learn to swear, Countess. If you mean bloody hell, say it."

Alec's eyes teased her. His free hand moved to her cleavage, and with obviously experienced fingers he began to flick open the remaining hooks securing her pelisse.

XXXII

"You are a devil! Alec Tyron, you stop that this instant! Let me up!"

"Presently, love," he said soothingly, ignoring her squirming efforts to be free as he unfastened the last of the hooks.

"No, don't!" she cried in near despair, but it was too late. He pushed the edges of the pelisse aside, and looked down with a lurking grin at the hideously inadequate bodice of her gown. To her horror Isabella saw that the too big gown had shifted, exposing even more of her white skin than it had previously. Her breasts rose wantonly above the lower edging of braid, bared by her wriggling almost to the nipple.

"Pray don't look." Blushing, she lay perfectly still and turned her face away. Thus she missed his sudden frown as he saw how truly embarrassed she was.

"Isabella. Look at me."

Gently he caught her chin in his fingers, and turned her face so that she had no choice but to look at him. In that moment her eyes were more gray than blue, cloudy with distress. The prim coil of hair at the back of her head rested against the mottled green of the ground, forcing the front part, usually demurely combed back, to fall forward, surrounding her pinkened face with a brown-gold nimbus. Though she did not know it, she looked very young, very shy and every bit as vulnerable as she felt.

"You are being absurd," he said. "I've already seen considerably more of you than this—" His eyes flicked her chest, and returned again to her face as she reddened still more. "And I will not allow you to make yourself ill because of some ridiculous notion of propriety. It's too damned hot to wear this bloody thing, modesty be damned."

With that he let go of her hands and pulled her to her feet, stripping the pelisse from her with a single ruthless yank before she could recover herself enough to try to stop him. Isabella gasped as the pelisse was dragged down her arms and then lifted away, her hands flying instinctively to cover the exposed expanse of soft white flesh.

"Bully!" she hissed when she'd recovered sufficiently.

"If you like to think so," he answered with a shrug, slinging the pelisse over his arm. Without another word, without even so much as looking at her again, Alec turned and walked back to the carriage. Isabella's smouldering eyes followed him every step of the way. She watched with no small degree of outrage as he tossed the pelisse inside, and then returned with easy strides to settle himself cross-legged beside the picnic basket as if nothing out of the way had occurred. To Alec, obviously, might meant right, and his high-handed assumption of authority infuriated her.

Isabella eyed him narrowly as he bit into a leg of roast chicken with blithe unconcern.

"You are an ill-mannered cur, Alec Tyron."

"Then you have your work cut out for you, don't you, Madame Tutor? As soon as we reach Amberwood, you may busy yourself by attempting to smooth out all my rough edges. But in the meantime, why don't you help yourself to some chicken? The Carousel's cook has a way with it."

Berating the maddening creature was clearly a waste of her time and effort, Isabella decided after a moment in which the state of her temper hung in the balance. Seeing that he was paying her exposed charms no particular attention, and secretly admitting that she was beginning to feel a great deal better now that the hot pelisse was no longer swathing her to her chin, Isabella gave up her ire and came over to sit, legs curled at her side, on the opposite side of the cloth. She was careful to keep one slim hand spread over her shocking décolletage, however. Arranging her skirts around her so as not to expose her ankles, she kept a sharp eye on Alec. If he dared to ogle her . . .

But he seemed far more interested in his luncheon than her charms. Gradually Isabella relaxed enough to find a drumstick of her own and begin, daintily, to eat. Casting fleeting looks down at herself as she picked the meat from the bone, she finally decided that, sitting up as she was, the cutout was not so revealing that she must keep a hand constantly plastered over it. Indeed, she probably looked foolish doing so. After a succession of lightning glances in Alec's direction, each less wary than the one before, Isabella finally allowed her hand to drop.

"Tomorrow you may send for a dressmaker and order yourself a wardrobe, if you wish. I'll stand the nonsense, of course."

His attention still appeared to be concentrated solely on his meal, and his tone was nonchalant. But clearly, from the timing of his remark, he had been watching her more than she knew. His offer, though of course she could not accept it, clearly was meant to please her. Despite his toughness, the appalling conditions of his birth and upbringing, and an infuriating high-handedness that she suspected was inbred, Alec Tyron was at heart a very kind man, she was discovering. Isabella put down the bread she was getting ready to bite into, and smiled at him.

"It's very generous of you, Alec, and you must not think I don't appreciate the offer. But you cannot buy my clothes. It wouldn't be proper."

He met her eyes then for a pregnant moment, and she saw that her answer had annoyed him. "We have already stepped well beyond the boundaries of what you would consider proper behavior, Countess. Besides, who's to know? And you need not fear that I'm short of blunt, because I'm far from that. Buying you a few fripperies will not put me in the poorhouse, I assure you."

Isabella shook her head determinedly. "Your finances are not in question. It's simply that I cannot allow you to pay for my clothes. Why, that would make me . . . make me . . ."

"Yes?" he questioned very quietly, lowering the wing he was getting ready to bite into.

"Less than a lady," she said, and looked away. He made a sound that bespoke extreme vexation, drawing her eyes again. Before he could respond in anger, as she feared he would do, Isabella added hastily, "That isn't to say that I don't realize that I must commission a few decent gowns to wear. Perhaps if you would be so kind as to give me an advance on my salary—I am assuming you do mean to pay me a salary—I could purchase enough for my needs myself."

"Of course I intend to pay you a salary—" Alec broke off suddenly, put the wing back on his plate, and wiped his hands on his napkin. Then he got to his feet, came around the perimeter of the cloth, and hunkered down at her side. Isabella set her own plate on her lap and looked at him wide-eyed. His expression was intent, and there was, besides, a certain impatience in his eyes.

"Hell, Isabella, let's have an end to this farce, shall we?" His voice had an underlying roughness. "You have a care for me, I think, and I . . . I find you more than attractive. You may consider my person and my money at your complete disposal for the foreseeable future, if you wish. I can afford to buy you a wardrobe as grand as a duchess's. I can give you jewels, and your own carriage and horses—whatever you want. I know you're not greedy, love, and I've no fear you'll bankrupt me. You'll have carte blanche to purchase what you choose. I'm a rich man, and I'll see you well provided for in the event we part ways, enough for you to afford to live quite comfortably for the rest of your life. You need never return to St. Just again."

Isabella went very still as he spoke. When he finished,

his eyes sweeping her face for her reaction, she could barely speak. She had to force the words out through her suddenly dry throat.

"I am not sure that I understand you. Exactly what are you proposing?"

He looked at her more carefully then, and something—uncertainty?—flickered for a moment in his eyes. Then he grinned, though the grin was crooked, went down on one knee before her, and placed a hand over his heart.

" 'Come live with me, and be my love, and we will all the pleasures prove. . . .' " His voice, like his posture, was teasingly soulful, but his eyes were intent, and they never left her face.

"You are suggesting that I become your kept mistress." It was a statement, not a question. Despite the heat, Isabella suddenly felt as if she'd been turned to ice.

" 'Tis a crude way of putting it. I prefer to emulate Marlowe and ask you to be my love."

His hand dropped away from his heart to reach for hers. Numbly she allowed him to take her fingers in his, and raise them to his mouth. As if she were no more than an observer of the pretty scene, she watched him press his lips to her knuckles. Coldly, clinically, she took in the bowed, handsome head, the broad shoulders, the muscled thighs that his kneeling position caused to strain against the knit breeches. Dancing sunbeams glinted off gold threads in his tawny hair. . . .

He looked up at her then, smiling. "Well, Countess?"

She stared at him unspeaking for an instant longer. Then her eyebrows twitched together and her mouth turned down violently at the corners. Jerking her hand from his hold, she jumped to her feet, upsetting her plate, which had been resting on her lap. He looked up at her as she stood over him like an avenging fury, surprise plain on his face. Then his expression changed as he too stood.

"Isabella—"

"You may take me back to town, if you please."

"You're angry." He sounded resigned. "I should have

waited, I know, but I wanted to put an end to all these silly games between us. I desire you madly, love."

"Don't dare speak so to me!"

His mouth tightened with impatience. "Very well, if you wish, we'll continue to play out the farce to its end. But you may be very sure that you'll end up in my bed sooner or later, however much you like to pretend that you will not. We want each other too badly, my girl. You as well as I. It's there in your eyes for me to see every time you look at me."

"You're insufferable! Take me back to town!"

She felt as if she were choking, as if she were wrapped about by iron bands that tightened with every breath. There was an ache in the region of her breastbone that she refused to subscribe to a lacerated heart. Pearl had been exactly right: Alec had meant to set her up as his mistress all along. He would enjoy her favors only as long as they continued to please him, and when they no longer did, when her novelty began to pall, he would buy her off. If things were different, if the world could be as she wished it and not as it were, there was nothing on earth that would please her more than to be his love. But love had nothing to do with the arrangement he proposed. It was a business transaction, pure and simple. The irony of it was that it was she who had insisted that their future association be strictly business. Though what he had suggested was certainly not the sort of business she had had in mind!

"It's a common enough arrangement, you know. There's no need for you to act as if I've mortally insulted you. Indeed, you could say it's an honor to be asked. I've never before gone to the trouble of setting up an official *chère amie.*" If he was trying to pour oil on the waters he had disturbed, he failed abysmally. Isabella rounded on him, fists clenched and eyes flashing.

"So I'm supposed to feel honored by your filthy proposition, am I? Well, let me tell you something, you bounder—I feel dirtied by the very suggestion! And if you won't take me back to town, right now, I'll walk every step of the way! So help me I will!'' Furious, she marched toward the carriage. He fell into step beside her.

''Be reasonable, Isabella. I'd no intention whatsoever of insulting you. You're taking this entirely the wrong way.''

''Are you going to drive me back to town or am I going to walk?''

''You can't go back to town. There's no place for you to stay but the Carousel, and you can't wish to stay there; it's not a fit place for you.''

She threw him a glance of such fury that his eyes widened as if from a blow.

''Not a fit place for your mistress? I would have thought that a bawdy house was the perfect place for a whore!''

''Isabella—'' He tried again to calm her, but she wouldn't let him finish.

''Don't even speak to me, you . . . you . . .''

''I don't see why you're so bloody upset.'' He reached out suddenly and caught her arm, forcing her to stop and face him. She swatted ineffectually at his imprisoning hand, but he refused to release her. ''You've bedded me already—of your own free will, and don't try to make me think you didn't enjoy it—and it seems to me that the insult would be if I then went on about my business and never gave you another thought. But did I do that? No. Having already plucked the choicest blossom from the bush, in a manner of speaking, I still offered you free access to both my purse—which is more than plump—and my person, which I've never yet had a female despise. What's the insult in that? Pray enlighten me, because I've no idea.''

As he spoke, she had ceased swatting at him to stare at him with growing incredulity.

''I can well believe you don't see the insult, you blackguard! I'm sure it is very different with your kind, but I was raised to think that 'lady' was more than a courtesy title!''

He stared at her for a moment without speaking. She lifted her chin at him haughtily.

''Ah,'' he said finally. ''So that's the way it is. The insult's not so much in the offer as in the offerer. Would your answer be different if I were a bloody lordship like your bloody murdering husband?''

Pure rage flared from her eyes at that. ''My answer would be the same if you were the Prince Regent, or the King himself! Take me back to town, I said!''

This time she succeeded in knocking his hand from her arm, and whirled away toward the carriage.

He was right behind her. ''Damn it to hell, Isabella, you're being ridiculous, and you know it. Come, let us forget this whole fiasco of a conversation and go back to what we were before! 'Twas a joke merely, I assure you.''

''You meant every word,'' she said fiercely, and stalked on toward the carriage. He made a sound that was halfway between a growl and a groan.

''All right, so I did. Hell and the devil, 'tis a bloody compliment I paid you! Haven't you the sense to know a compliment when you get one, girl?''

Isabella did not deign to look at him. As they reached the carriage she ignored his outstretched hand and clambered into the seat on her own. In cold silence she sat, arms crossed over her breasts, looking pointedly off into the distance as he, standing beside the carriage looking up at her, bit off a disgusted oath.

''All right, have it your own way then. I'll bloody well take you back to town if Your 'Ighness wishes it! I'll drop you off on your bloody 'usband's doorstep! I'm starting to think the murderous bugger's got the bloody right idea!''

His roughening accent told her that he was fast losing his temper, which suited her just fine. She had already thoroughly lost hers! When she didn't reply, but continued to look away from him in icy hauteur, Alec swore again, turned on his heel, and stomped back to gather up their leavings. In moments he was tossing the basket in the carriage with more force than was necessary. It landed with a bounce and a clatter at Isabella's feet, and she shoved it beneath the seat.

Removing the horses' feed bags with more speed than care, Alec threw them into the back with barely controlled violence. Then he climbed up beside Isabella, untied the reins and, with a flick of his wrists, got the tilbury smartly in motion. The only problem from Isabella's standpoint was that they were heading in precisely the same direction as they had been before.

XXXIII

"London," Isabella pointed out coldly, "is the other way."

"Aye, and if I were as big a bloody fool as yourself, Countess, I'd be 'eaded that way. As it is, I'm takin' you to where you'll be out of 'arm's way whether you like it or not."

"And just where is that?"

"Amberwood, as was intended from the first. I'll not change my plans to suit a 'oity-toity miss's distempered freaks."

"As you seem determined to do just as you please with no thought of my wishes, must I expect to be ravished the moment we arrive?" The question dripped icy disdain.

His head snapped around, and the look he gave her told her more than any words could have just how furious he was. Then he was hauling in on the reins, pulling the horses to a sudden stop. He wrapped the reins around the knob at the front of the carriage with quick, angry purpose, and turned on Isabella, who was hanging on to the side with both hands as the vehicle lurched forward, then back. Her eyes widened in the face of his blazing wrath.

"I've 'ad all I plan to put up with of your bloody airs. You'd do well to keep a civil tongue between your teeth, Countess, lest I decide to school you to better manners." He forced the words out through clenched teeth.

"Violence is just what I would have expected from a

canaille like you,'' she responded haughtily, nose in air. ''And you're dropping your *h*'s.''

Like a line stretched to the breaking point and beyond, his temper snapped. Isabella saw it happen, saw the flood-tide of red rush into his cheekbones, saw the sudden fierce flaming of his golden eyes.

''You liked the common touch well enough the other night,'' he growled, and reached for her. Alarmed, she shrank back, but he dragged her toward him, his fingers digging into her soft flesh. He pulled her close and held her there, his eyes alight with a ferocious gleam, his mouth twisted grimly. He meant to frighten her, she thought, and refused to admit even to herself that he was succeeding. Suddenly he was no longer Alec but the Tiger, lord of London's criminals, brutal, savage, in his own world all-powerful as a king.

His mouth swooped toward hers. He meant to punish her with his kiss.

She turned her head away, struggling, but he pulled her halfway across his lap, still holding her in that bruising grip so that she could not get away. As they fought, the horses stirred restlessly, stomping their feet so that the carriage jerked and rattled. Overhead a squirrel set up a raucous chatter. But Isabella was aware of none of this. She was only conscious of the hardness of the upper arm against which her head rested, the strength of the hands holding her, and the predatory gleam in his eyes. He caught her jaw, dragging her head around, holding it still for his kiss. As those golden eyes met hers, she ceased to struggle. Mesmerized, she could only wait for him to deal her the lethal blow.

And it was lethal, she realized even as he took her lips, kissing her with a passion that was at first as much fierce temper as wanting. Lethal to her morals, lethal to her self-respect and the good of her soul. She could not be his mistress, and she would not. But oh, how she wanted him! Never in her life had she thought to respond to a man as she responded to him, instantly, at his slightest look or touch. He dazzled her, blinded her to duty and every sense of what was right and wrong. He tempted her past bearing. . . .

Even as his tongue slid between her teeth, her mouth opened for him, allowing him entry, kissing him back. Her arms, freed now of his harsh grip, slid up to curl around his neck.

When his hand slid inside that shocking neckline to find the softness of her naked breast, she whimpered a wordless protest into his mouth. But her eyes stayed tightly closed and her back arched, pushing her breast more closely into the palm that cupped it.

"Isabella. You feel so sweet." If he had been angry, his anger, like hers, had perished in the flames. He sounded as dazed as she felt, as dizzy with wanting. He kissed her cheek, her ear, her neck, before his lips returned to find hers again.

His mouth was slow and hot, his tongue both gentling her and claiming ownership of the sweet territory it explored. Her mouth met his with helpless rapture, unable to mount even so much as a token resistance. The merest touch of his lips and hand had shattered her defenses like brittle glass.

She was his, to do with what he would. Her kisses, her caresses, all belonged to him. If he wished her to live in glorious shame as his mistress, she was suddenly, dreadfully afraid she had not the strength to resist. . . .

Even as his hand tightened on her breast, his fingers seeking out the tiny bud that thrust hungrily into his palm, the sound of hooves on the road behind them brought Alec's head up. Her eyes opened to find him staring back down the road they had travelled, shaking his head slightly as though to clear it of the mists of passion.

"Hell and the devil, what bloody timing! Though I suppose it's just as well. An open carriage is not really the place for—" He broke off, looked down at her lying across his lap, and with a surprisingly tender gesture removed his hand from her bodice and smoothed back a tendril of hair that had strayed across her cheek. "Here, love, sit up and straighten your dress. We'll sort this whole thing out when we get to Amberwood."

"I won't be your mistress." She was still dazed as he set her off his lap, but not too dazed to manage a faint but pursuing protest at his apparently unchanged plans for her. As the drugging effect of his touch was removed, her resistance improved. She could resist, and she would.

"Are you still arguing?" He leaned over and dropped a quick, hard kiss on her still tremulous mouth even as he picked up the reins. "Hush your mouth, woman, and let me drive. You can argue with me all you want later, when we have a modicum of privacy."

The hoofbeats were drowned out by the sound of their own carriage wheels clattering over the ruts as Alec got the horses moving again. Looking at him, still somewhat befuddled from that heart-shaking kiss, Isabella saw that the anger was totally gone from his face. He looked cheerful, and completely sure of himself again. As he felt her eyes on him, he slanted a glance at her and smiled.

It was a breathtaking smile, warm and intimate and loaded with charm. Isabella felt her heart turn over at the impact of it.

Without a doubt, Alec Tyron was the handsomest man she had ever seen in her life. Just looking at him caused her a physical pang. But his looks, magnificent as they were, were not what drew her to him so strongly. There was something in the man himself that appealed to her, a kind of warmth at which she yearned to thaw her chilled heart.

Giving in to such dangerous feelings would be a major mistake, she knew. She might be young, she might be inexperienced in the love games he played so easily, but she was not a fool. It would be all too easy to fall in love with her dazzling ruffian, and that way lay a broken heart.

Because, sooner or later, she knew she was going to have to give him up, resume her proper place in the world, take up her lackluster life again as the wife of an indifferent earl and the daughter of a less-than-fond duke. There was no place for Alec in her life, her real life, and however little she liked to face it, that was the simple truth. She was of the nobility, and a married lady to boot, and he was a charming nobody from the gutters of London. Even if she had not been wed to Bernard, their liaison would have been impossible. But add a wedding ring to the mixture, and a love affair between herself and Alec became an offense against God as well as man.

Alec's arm brushed hers as he drove, and glancing up at him, she saw that his face had tightened with tension.

The horseman behind them was closing fast. Isabella could hear the hoofbeats clearly, even over the noise of their own carriage. She supposed that was why Alec was pulling the horses up, although it seemed an unnecessary precaution as the road was certainly wide enough for a lone horseman to pass. But that couldn't explain why Alec was grabbing at something under the seat. . . .

Suddenly frightened, she glanced back over her shoulder. A man bent low over the neck of a big roan horse was coming around the bend, moving at a pace that she would have thought too fast for the pitted road. At that speed, she thought, he would overtake them in a matter of seconds. . . .

"Isabella, get down!"

Alec's hand was on the top of her head, pushing her down on the floorboard even as the rider urged his mount abreast of them. Isabella no sooner was pushed to her knees than a terrible trio of sounds separated by no more than a fraction of a second ripped open the peace of the afternoon.

First, a musket exploded seemingly right above her head.

Then another shot, from a little farther away, echoed the first.

And finally, Alec cried out. Her head jerked up just in time to see him fall back against the seat.

XXXIV

Terrified by the sudden explosion of sound, the horses bolted. Even as Isabella struggled to climb onto the seat, to help Alec, whose face, she saw to her horror, was awash in blood, she was thrown back to her hands and knees on the floorboard by the crazed leapings of the carriage. The animals galloped down the road in a wild frenzy of terror, pulling the tilbury behind them as if it were weightless. The flimsy vehicle bounced and jolted over the ruts, the wheels sometimes losing contact with the pitted road altogether. Their speed was such that it made the trees beside the road seem as thick as box hedges.

"Damn it to bloody 'ell!"

Alec's profanity had the novel effect of reassuring Isabella. Surely he would not be swearing so on the brink of death—or would he? She tried again to reach him, only to be sent sprawling by a jolt that nearly catapulted her from the carriage. Only a hasty grab at a side strut saved her. The musket Alec had snatched up as he had recognized their danger bounced from the seat beside him to land with a clatter on the floorboard beside Isabella's hand. Instinctively she flinched. Then she remembered. Alec had fired it—that was the explosion she had heard just above her head. Empty, it was no threat to her, but still she recoiled from it as she would have from a live snake. She was relieved when another series of rattling bounces sent it sliding overboard, to be lost somewhere in the blur of greenery on the side of the road.

"Grab the musket—no! Christ Almighty!"

Alec, seeing the musket go, cursed again, savagely. He grabbed at the reins that trailed loosely over the box, caught them and tried to rise, only to fall back with a groan, one hand going to his badly bleeding head.

"Alec!"

Sheer terror helped Isabella claw her way up the seat. Clinging to the seat back for her life, she leaned over him as he half sat and half lay against the upholstery, his booted feet braced under the box to keep him from being jounced from the carriage. What looked to be a long, jagged cut poured blood from the left side of his forehead. Blood trickled from his chin onto his once pristine shirt, staining the cloth an ugly shade of red-brown. The other side of his face was streaked and spattered with blood too, but what struck her most was the sudden pallor of his skin. He was conscious, certainly, but for how long? People who had suffered fatal injuries had been known to remain alert and even active for some minutes before collapsing and dying. There was so much blood she couldn't even be certain of the depth or dimensions of the wound. She leaned closer, balancing precariously as she sought to see the size of his pupils.

"Sit down, you bloody little fool, before you get yourself killed!"

Isabella sat, not because he ordered her to but because the bouncing carriage threw her back against the seat. He was pulling on the reins, but she thought from the horses' lack of response, he must be dangerously weakened. Ignoring the profanity with which he ordered her to get back down on the floorboard out of harm's way, Isabella reached out to add her strength to his as he sawed on the reins. First they must stop the runaways, or they would both likely end up in the hereafter before they were ten minutes older.

She never even touched leather. Even as Alec bared his teeth at her in another hissed warning to get on the floor, there was the clatter of hooves on planks, and then the tilbury leaped into the air like a startled rabbit. Instants later came another bone-jarring jolt as the wheels touched down on a bridge. The chaise snapped upward again like a stone fired from a slingshot, tethered to earth only by the horses that shrieked and bolted anew in an effort to get out of the way of the airborne vehicle that this time seemed determined to leapfrog them.

Catapulted head over heels from the carriage, Isabella screamed. Bridge and stream and a brushy bank whirled sickeningly below her as she somersaulted toward them. From somewhere just ahead of her and to her right came the rending crash of splintering wood, the screaming of the horses, Alec's yell. But Isabella had no time to wonder at Alec's fate, or the horses', or that of the chaise. The ground rushed up to meet her. She barely had time to shut her eyes before she landed.

Both breath and sense were driven from her body by the jolt. For long moments she remained motionless, barely conscious of lying spread-eagled over a bush, her feet trailing in the icy water of the small creek that had caused their disaster.

In the distance came shrill, shuddering screams.

Alec? With returning awareness came the memory of his being shot, and the knowledge that only the worst kind of mortal agony could wrest such sounds from him.

Gasping at the agony of airless lungs, Isabella nevertheless managed to draw in a deep, shuddering breath that told her that she still lived. Taking the next one was marginally easier, and then, with the screams still ringing in her ears, she struggled to get up. She had to get to Alec. . . .

That thought drove her to her knees, and then, shakily, to her feet. The screams continued unabated. It was not until she had scrambled the short distance up the bank to the road that she realized that the screams were not from Alec at all: they were from the horses.

Isabella had always had a special affinity for animals, and horses were no exception. Her heart twisted at the pained whinnies of the poor, shuddering creatures as they thrashed in a tangle of reins and snapped shafts. Lying on its side, the chaise was little more than a pile of kindling. As they fought to free themselves, the horses lashed it with their hooves, rocking it back and forth. The uppermost wheel, the only part that appeared to be relatively whole, was still spinning dizzily, which meant that her collapse could only have been momentary.

The contents of the picnic basket, her carpetbag and Alec's valise were scattered over road, bridge and bank. The bottle green pelisse that they had disputed earlier floated in the creek.

There was no sign of Alec.

"Alec!" she cried, frightened. Then, louder, "Alec!"

There was no answer save the frightened nickerings of the horses, and the whisper of the slowing wheel. The possibility that Alec might be trapped in the crumpled carriage, or, worse, crushed beneath it, made Isabella survey the wreckage with frightened eyes.

The horses had managed to drag the tilbury to the far side of the narrow plank bridge. What was left of it lay just beyond where the bridge turned again into rutted roadway. Isabella realized that she must have been thrown from the carriage seconds before the actual crash.

Had Alec been as lucky?

"Alec!" she called again, with still no answer. Cold with fear, she hurried to what was left of the tilbury, and peered inside as best she could. She saw no sign of him, though blood liberally stained the seat that had been turned on end, poking out at a drunken angle through the side of the carriage.

If Alec was beneath the tilbury, she would need help to drag it off him. Even in its splintered state, it was far too heavy for her to budge on her own.

There was no help available. At least, no human help. But perhaps she could make use of the horses. . . .

"There, now, hush, shhh." She approached the animals carefully, picking her way through broken shafts and tangled lines. The horse that had been down had managed to get to his feet. Both now stood quietly, heads lowered, sides heaving as they wheezed for breath.

"Poor boys. Good boys." Seemingly indifferent to whatever disaster fate might throw next in their paths, the animals allowed her to get close. She stroked the nose of one—Blaze, she thought, or maybe Boyd—and then, gently, tugged on its nosepiece. It threw up its nose and whinnied in terror. But by pulling on the reins of both horses she managed to coax them to take a single step forward, then another, and a third, dragging the wreckage behind them. The shattered chaise was fortunately lightweight. Though the wood creaked and tumbled in protest, the traumatized horses managed to drag it far enough so that she could be certain that Alec did not lie in the roadbed beneath it.

True panic hit her then. If he was not in the chaise, nor under it, nor anywhere along the bank that she could see, where was he?

"Alec!"

With a cold shaft of fear she remembered the man who had ridden up so fast behind them, the man who had appeared out of nowhere to shoot Alec, and her hands grew clammy. Had he circled back after the wreck and finished the job, perhaps even making off with the corpse? But the wheel had still been spinning when she'd reached the road, so surely there hadn't been enough time. . . .

"Alec!" This time her voice was a shriek. It brought the horses' heads up. Their ears flicked back and forth nervously, their sides quivered.

"Alec!"

"Over here."

At first the voice was so faint that she thought she might be imagining it. Then came a heartfelt, though weak, curse, and Isabella knew that Alec, no matter in what shape he might be, still lived.

He lay on the bank on the other side of the creek from the one she had landed on, nearly hidden by a large lilac that, from its broken branches, had done a great deal to cushion his fall. Blood still oozed from the wound in his forehead, running down his face to soak his shirt, making him, at first glance, a truly gruesome sight. He lay on his back, his eyes closed until he heard her approach. Then, as she knelt beside him, frightened anew at the dreadfulness of his appearance, he opened his eyes and looked at her.

"You hurt?" he asked immediately.

"No. But you—your head . . ." Distressed, she forced herself to look closely at the wound, half-afraid of what she might find. But the ball did not seem to have penetrated. Rather it had gouged out a jagged, six-inch-long gulley on the left side of his forehead that ended just above his temple. It bled dreadfully, but he seemed in full possession of his faculties, and she did not think that the wound was as grave as she had at first feared. But what of the rest of him, flung from the carriage like a sack of meal? Anxiously Isabella ran her eyes and her hands over him, looking for injuries other than the wound to his head. His limbs appeared to be intact, but there was no telling what kind of internal injuries he might have sustained that were invisible to her inspection.

But the first order of business was to stop as best she could the heavy flow of blood from his head. She looked around.

"Lie still; I'll be right back," she said, and went to retrieve one of his shirts that had ended up flung over a nearby bush. It would serve as an adequate bandage until something better could be devised. Returning to him, she swathed his head in the shirt, wrapping the sleeves around twice and knotting them over the wound.

"My skull's thick, praise God. I doubt that the damage is serious." He shut his eyes as she finished, then almost immediately opened them. "The bloody bastard! Did you get a look at him?"

Isabella shook her head. "Not really. It all happened so fast. Are you in much pain?"

"My head hurts, is all. I've had hangovers that hurt worse."

Isabella suspected that he was lying to hearten her, but despite her suspicions, she did feel absurdly comforted.

"I winged him, I think. Christ, when I get my hands on the bloke responsible for this, I'll—" He broke off, lifted his hand to dash a maddening trickle of blood from his eye, then grimaced as he saw the bright crimson that stained his fingers.

"Don't move," Isabella said sharply as he started to sit up. "Just lie still. Please."

"I can't just lie here in this bloody bush forever."

"I think it's best if you stay still while I try to find some help."

Alec made a sound that was equal parts a snort of derision and a groan of pain, and managed to sit up despite Isabella's restraining hands. "We've no time, love. Unless I injured him sore, the bloody bastard could well turn around and come back to finish what he started. He's not likely to find me more vulnerable than at this moment, and if he's a modicum of sense, he knows it."

Shock had stripped some of the polish from Alec's voice. Despite his injury he looked suddenly very formidable, and Isabella had another glimpse of the life-hardened man beneath the surface charm. If the assassin came back, he would have a fight on his hands. Alec, injured or not, would be a fearsome opponent.

But the other man had a gun, while they were unarmed.

Alec winced as he tried to get to his feet. He managed to rise a few inches off the ground before his knees misgave him and he collapsed, flat on his back once more.

"You've the sense of a child, Alec Tyron! Just lie there, do you hear me? And don't so much as move! If you make yourself faint, then what will we do? If you'll just wait, I'll . . . I'll bring one of the horses to you. The carriage is past using, I'm afraid, but we can ride astride."

She thought he hesitated for an instant, but then he closed his eyes and nodded, wincing. "Aye, get one of the horses. They weren't injured?"

"Not that I could see. Just wait here, and be still, will you, please?"

Alec opened his eyes again then. "Isabella, be as quick as you can, and be careful. If you hear a rider approaching, run and hide, do you hear me?"

Isabella met those pain-filled golden eyes, and realized what he was trying to tell her. If he was attacked again, he wanted to deal with the would-be killer alone. There was absolutely no possibility that she would do as he wished, of course, but she had neither the time nor the inclination to argue with him at the moment. So she nodded, and turned away to fetch one of the horses.

It was amazing how quickly she managed to free the animals from the tangled lines, spurred on as she was by the knowledge that the assassin could return at any minute. As she worked, sweating, cold-handed with fear, she strained her ears for any out-of-the-ordinary sounds, but heard nothing except the normal peaceful stirrings of a spring afternoon. The stream gurgled, birds called, the horses stamped their feet, and a slight breeze rustled the just-budding branches of the trees beside the road.

Blaze—or was it Boyd?—seemed the calmer of the two, and she chose him, shooing the other away. The poor animal still shivered in the aftermath of its ordeal, but it was docile enough as she led it down the bank toward where Alec waited.

"Alec."

It was a struggle, she could tell from the way his face tightened beneath the mask of blood, but he managed to sit up as she stopped the horse beside him.

"So you got the bloody beast, hmm?" There was something odd about his tone, but she was too busy wrapping her arm around him and helping him to his feet to think about it.

"Do you think you can get on?"

She helped him the few paces to the animal's side. Without saddle or stirrup, mounting would be tricky, but unless he was extremely weakened, he should be able to heave himself up and over.

"Oh, aye. I think I can do that."

He was swaying, eyeing the horse with an expression

that she couldn't quite fathom. Then he looked from it to her with a grimace that she almost thought looked shamefaced.

"Well, then, get on. Shall I try to help you?"

"Perhaps you'd better get on first, and I'll ride behind you."

"But you may need me to give you a boost, or some such."

"Countess, I need you to steer the bloody beast. I've never done such in my life, and now is not the time to learn."

"What?" The confession was so stunning that she just stood there staring at him, sure she could not have heard correctly.

"I'm a dab hand at driving, because for a while I earned a few coppers as a hackney driver, but I've never had occasion to throw a leg over one of the bloody beasts and ride it. I'm London-bred, remember? There weren't too many horses around for me to practice on when I was a lad."

He sounded defensive, and the look he gave her was truculent, as if daring her to think less of him because he could not ride. To Isabella, riding a horse was as natural as breathing, but she realized in that moment that it was because she had been doing it from the time she could walk. To her knowledge, all members of her class rode, just as they rose up from their beds in the morning and retired to them at night. It was a skill that required no thought.

"Very well then." Isabella thought that she recovered from her momentary surprise with aplomb. Without another word she reached up for a handful of mane and hitched herself astride, which was no easy task without a saddle, and in a narrow skirt to boot. To the horse's credit, he stood still for this indignity—after all, he was a carriage horse, not a saddle horse, and being ridden, particularly bareback, particularly after such a trauma as he had suffered, might reasonably have been expected to send him into high fidgets. Perhaps his senses were still disordered from the shock he had suffered, or perhaps he was just naturally mild-natured. But for whatever reason, he suffered her to mount him with a minimum of trouble. Seated at last, and baring a considerable expanse of stockinged leg, she looked down to find Alec surveying the animal as he might have Mount Kilimanjaro.

She dared say nothing as he heaved himself up behind her. It was obvious from his set expression that his need to depend on her in this situation galled him, but she could think of no way to alleviate his embarrassment. In any case, there was no time for a long, conversational delving into his feelings. Alec had just narrowly missed being murdered, and the killer could well return. It behooved them to make themselves as hard to find as possible, and fast.

Picking up the makeshift rein she had devised from the remnant of the old one, she clucked to the horse. Obliging animal that he was, he immediately began to move up the slope. Behind her, Alec slipped, cursed and closed his hands around her waist, but he kept his seat.

"No, don't take the road. Through the woods," he said in her ear as she would have steered the beast back the way they had come. Of course, Alec was right. If the killer came back, he would look first along the road.

Isabella tugged the horse's head around, and they headed down into the protection of the trees.

XXXV

Alec was weakening, she could tell from the increased weight of him slumped against her back. Isabella tried to fight down panic. If he fell from the horse, how would she ever manage to get him back on again? She could never lift him.

"There's an inn not too far from here, I think. 'Tis called the Trader's Rest. I used to know the bloke who runs it." His voice was hoarse, and her fear for him heightened. She urged the weary beast carrying them to pick up its pace.

Isabella assumed that the inn Alec mentioned did not cater to the quality. Remembering the flash-house where he had taken her to talk to Molly, Isabella shuddered inwardly. Would the Trader's Rest be as bad as that? She prayed not; the thought of seeking refuge in such a place frightened her. But Alec needed care, and soon, and protection from his enemies. To get that for him, Isabella was willing to ride into the bowels of hell itself if need be.

Guiding the horse through the woods with neither proper bridle nor a saddle of any description was not an easy task. Fortunately, Blaze, or Boyd, was exhausted from its earlier exertions, and gave her no trouble. As they rode up a little incline, Alec leaned even more heavily against her back. Glancing worriedly over her shoulder, she saw that his face was utterly white beneath the bloodstains and the scarlet-soaked linen of the makeshift bandage.

Desperately she began to talk to him, talk that demanded his response, praying that he would remain conscious until they reached help. The journey seemed never-ending. Even under the trees it was dreadfully hot. Isabella was drenched in sweat before they had covered a mile. She suspected that terror was at least part of the reason for her distress, but the itchy hide beneath her thighs and the body heat of the man pressed close against her back didn't help.

She was constantly aware of the possibility of pursuit. At every sound in the woods she tensed, though she tried to conceal this from Alec. But she suspected that even in his weakened state he was more alert to the danger than she.

From the position of the sun, Isabella judged that it was late afternoon when they emerged from the woods onto another road that was scarcely more than a dusty track. Some quarter of an hour later, after rounding a bend, the inn at last came into view.

It was small and squat, made of chalkstone with a thatched roof. A weather-beaten sign hung over the entrance. The door was flung wide open, and leaned drunkenly against its hinges. Two small, dirty-paned windows were set like eyes on either side of the door. A low stone wall separated the innyard from the road. To Isabella's horror, the yard was filled to overflowing with a noisy, jostling crowd. Some sort of altercation was obviously in progress. Taken aback, she pulled the horse to a stop.

"Not what you're used to, is it, Countess?" Alec spoke almost in her ear. "Under the circumstances it's the best I can do. Go on; we'll come to no harm here."

"It looks fine," Isabella lied in her teeth, and reluctantly gave the horse a nudge. To tell the truth, the place looked like a thieves' den, and it frightened her even more than she had imagined it would. But what choice did they have?

She urged the tired horse into the yard, doing her best to skirt the commotion. The two men who appeared to be at the center of the disagreement traded insults in bellows that grew increasingly more truculent as Isabella headed the horse around the eddying mob. The crowd seemed to be made up almost entirely of men who certainly seemed to qualify as members of the great unwashed. They were very vocal as they expressed partisanship for one principal or the other.

"Hell and the devil," Alec muttered in her ear. "We've timed this ill. 'Tis a bloody cockfight!"

Only then did Isabella see that each of the principals held a hissing cock, one red and the other white. The crowd cheered then, causing the horse to shy nervously, and formed a rough circle around the two men. As Isabella watched, the men set their bristling roosters on the ground.

With a scream the two birds flew at each other. The crowd yelled hoarse encouragement, as bets, boasts and insults went up on all sides. They closed around the combatants so that Isabella could see nothing but a jostling mass of men's backs. From the roosters, hidden from her view, came enraged shrieks.

"Head on over to the stable. We don't want to attract more attention than we can help," Alec said.

Isabella guided the horse to the rickety wooden barn. No groom ran out to offer assistance; she assumed all the help was engaged in watching the cockfight.

"Can you get down?" Isabella asked.

"Easier than I got up."

Alec straightened away from her, and as she looked around she saw the intense concentration on his face as he forced himself to marshal his remaining strength. Then, grim-faced, he slid one leg over the horse's rump and lowered himself to the ground. For just a moment he stood leaning against the animal's side as if his legs might not support him. Beneath the drying blood he was as white as death itself, but he managed a lopsided smile. Isabella hurriedly dismounted.

"Don't look so scared," Alec said. "The owner is an old friend of mine. Just tie up the bloody horse and let's get inside. I'll bet I've more than one acquaintance in this crowd, and some might not be friendly."

His enemy—enemies?—might be present. That thought made Isabella catch her breath.

"We're safe enough; don't worry. What, don't you trust me to protect you?"

Only Alec would poke fun at his own weakness at such a time. Isabella had to smile, although the effort was a trifle strained.

"Let's get you inside," she said, suddenly realizing how close his strength was to deserting him. For Alec to sway as he pushed away from the horse, he must be close to the limit of his endurance. He must have a bed to lie down upon, and medical attention, very soon.

With Isabella's arm around his waist, they managed to skirt the crowd without anyone noticing them. The noise was deafening; at any other time the profanity would have made Isabella blush. Under the circumstances she was thankful that the attention of the rabble was focused away from Alec and herself. At the foot of the shallow steps leading into the inn they had to stop. A heavyset, grizzled man in a stained white apron was standing foursquare in the doorway, fists clenched and head bobbing as he shouted encouragement to one of the fighters.

"Can you house another pair of travellers, Innkeep?" Alec's voice was surprisingly strong. The innkeeper barely bothered to glance at them. His attention was all on the screaming frenzy of the cockfight.

"Nah. Full up."

"Full up, are you, Hull?"

Alec got his attention this time. The man looked down, his eyes widening on the face that was still dazzlingly handsome and thus easily recognizable despite the layer of blood that coated it.

"The Tiger, as I live and breathe! Come up, come up!" Despite his girth, he jumped down the steps to pump Alec's hand. "Of course we've room! We'll just throw one of the other bloody beggars out! Step inside! Bloody good to see you, Tiger, bloody good. Lord, it's been some years! Looks like you've met up with a bit of trouble, man."

"It's good to see you too, Hull. And the trouble I've met up with is the walking, talking, treacherous kind. It may be that someone'll come looking for us. I can trust you to say naught of my presence, I know."

"You can trust me with your life, Tiger, and you know it. 'Tis not likely I'd forget. . . ."

Hull was ushering them up the steps and into the squalid interior, all but bowing and scraping before Alec. The smell of cooking cabbage, combined with less easily identifiable odors, was strong. Isabella, her arm still around Alec's waist, wondered anew at the power the Tiger must wield to instill such a response in the men who knew him. In his own way, Alec inspired every bit as much awe as her father the duke amongst his tenants, or even the Prince Regent amongst his subjects.

"You make too much of what was but a small service, Hull. You were always a loyal sort, and I do what I can for men I can count on."

"You can count on me, Tiger, like you always done. You saved me from the topping cheat, and I don't forget it. Anything you need, Tim 'Ull's your man."

"Right now he needs a bed. And a doctor," Isabella interjected firmly. Alec was leaning heavily against her, and despite the seemingly easy tone of his conversation with Hull, she could tell by the increasing amount of weight she was supporting that he was getting weaker. Listening to him, looking at him, one would never guess that he could barely stand up. Except for the bandage on his head, and the great quantity of drying blood that adorned his person, he looked and sounded much as always. She supposed that not showing weakness was a survival mechanism he had perfected in his days as one of the rag-tag plague of homeless children who haunted London's streets.

"I've no need for a bloody sawbones. 'Tis naught but a graze."

She looked up at him impatiently. "Don't be a fool, Alec. Please send for a doctor, Mr. Hull."

"Isabella . . ." If there was a warning note to that, she chose to ignore it.

"Either you have a doctor look at your head or I wash my hands of you! Do you hear me, you great looby?" Her eyes flashed at him. It was past time for such foolishness on the part of a full-grown man.

Either the fierceness of her voice or the novelty of being addressed as a looby carried the day.

"Have it your own way, then. But I tell you there is no need." He sounded grumpy.

"Perhaps not. Nevertheless, I insist. A doctor, please, Mr. Hull. And we've left a horse tied to your stable door. If there's someone who could see to the creature . . ."

"O' course, o' course! Liddy! Eh, there, Liddy!"

A tall, thin woman with black hair and a heavily lined face appeared in the doorway to the taproom.

"There's no need at all to shout, Timmy," she said reprovingly. "I can 'ear, you know."

"Ah, you're deaf as a piece o' wood, woman," Tim muttered, then added more loudly, "This 'ere's—"

"I'm an old friend of Tim's," Alec interrupted, smiling rather thinly at the woman. "As you can see, we've met with a bit of an accident. Tim's kindly promised us the use of a room till we recover a bit."

"We're full up," the woman protested, fixing Tim with disapproving eyes. "The rooms 'ave all been bespoke for weeks."

"Not for 'im, we ain't." Tim did not wilt under that daunting look. "Do you go send Mick for the doctor as fast as 'e can run, then turn the big room at the top of the stairs out for 'im and 'is lady. And don't give me no more o' your sass, woman."

"Sass my backside," Liddy sniffed by way of a reply, but with another sour look that encompassed the three of them, she left the room, presumably to do as Tim had told her.

Tim looked at Alec apologetically. "When I wed 'er, she was as biddable a lass as a man could want. Wedlock changes 'em, I swear it does." Then he glanced at Isabella, whose arm was tight around Alec's waist. To outward appearances it was a rather loving pose; Hull could not know that Isabella was all that kept Alec upright. What Hull saw was a slender female who was well enough but no beauty, certainly not the flashy kind of ladybird the

Tiger usually had in keeping. This chit was both dishevelled and downright dirty, her brownish hair tumbling around her pointy, dirt-streaked face, her disappointing bosoms half-bared by a gown that looked like it had been made for someone who could fill it out to better advantage. She was bossy, too, spoke right up like she had the right, in a prissy kind of accent like she thought she was better than she was. Not the kind of female the Tiger usually had in keeping at all.

Hull's eyes widened. "Uh, you ain't wed yourself, are you, Tiger? If you are, I meant no offense."

"I've not yet fallen victim to the parson's mousetrap, thank God. Though I congratulate you on your acquisition of so lovely a wife."

"T'anks. Liddy's comely still, ain't she?"

"She is."

In the face of this purely masculine exchange, Isabella felt suddenly uncomfortable. Her hair had long since escaped its pins, her borrowed dress was ripped and dirty and had the neckline cut down to there, and she was alone in Alec's company. Probably she should feel flattered that Tim Hull might suppose she was Alec's wife. For the first time in weeks, Isabella was acutely aware of the unconventionality of her position. Only a wife or a female relative could respectably travel unchaperoned with a man and keep her reputation. Only a wife could share a man's bedchamber and still retain any claims to the title "lady." Clearly she and Alec were to share a single chamber. Alec seemed to take it as a matter of course, as did the innkeeper and his wife. Requesting a separate room would be ridiculous, even if Hull could be persuaded to cast out another patron to accommodate her. Alec needed tending, and she had no intention of leaving him to anyone else's care. Besides, she had come too far beyond the pale to start worrying now about the proprieties. If ruin was to be her lot, she had already thoroughly embraced it.

XXXVI

Just then a great cry went up outside, making all of them look toward the open door and what was visible of the innyard beyond it.

" 'Tis the red, the red!" screamed a grimy youth perched on the steps just outside the door. Beside him, an equally unprepossessing youth jumped up and down with excitement.

"Mr. 'Ull, Mr. 'Ull, it be the red!" The second lad came streaking through the door, skittering to a halt as he found the one he sought. "Mr. 'Ull, 'tis the red!"

"Bloody good!" Hull pounded the youth's back at the news of the victory. "Blimy, I 'ad a packet ridin' on that one!" Then he remembered his audience. "Jimmy, now it's all over, do you go take care of the 'orse that's left in front o' the barn. And if Mistress 'Ull 'asn't already told 'im, tell Mick to ride for the doctor. We've a guest who needs 'is attention. Tell 'im 'e'll be well paid for 'is trouble."

"Aye, sor."

With a curious look at Alec and Isabella, Jimmy scampered back out the door. Hull's eyes followed him, the expression on his face almost wistful. Isabella guessed that he wished he could follow the youth, and join in the excited celebration that had erupted in the innyard in the wake of the red's victory.

Then, as Hull's attention was distracted, Alec swayed,

making Isabella almost lose her balance as she sought to hold him up. She took a quick step sideways, her arm tightening around his waist, her eyes flying to his face. He was whiter than before, and sweating noticeably as he gritted his teeth. For just an instant he seemed to slump. Then, with what Isabella knew was an effort of sheer will, he pushed himself a little away from her, standing more or less on his own as he fought to conceal the full extent of his weakness from the man whose eyes were even then swinging back to him. Apparently Alec's trust in Tim Hull was something less than one hundred percent.

"Alec . . ." She tried to prop him up unobtrusively with her body.

"I'm all right," he muttered for her ears alone.

But he looked as if he might collapse at any moment.

"Mr. Hull, I'm sorry to hurry you, but I am beginning to feel distinctly unwell. Do you suppose we might go on up, whether the room is quite ready or not?"

By taking the onus upon herself, Isabella hoped to attain two objectives: get Alec a place where he might lie down while at the same time concealing just how weak he was. If Alec did not truly trust the innkeeper, then she would not either.

"Oh, o' course. What a clunch I am, keepin' you standin'! And you injured, too, Ti—"

"Just plain Alec, while we're here."

"Certainly, certainly! I understan' completely. I—"

Before he could get under way again, Liddy reappeared, gliding toward them as silently as a ghost.

"Room's ready," she said brusquely. "And Mick should be back with the doctor anon."

"Good, good. Come on then, Ti—uh, Alec, and I'll show you and the lady up. This way."

With Isabella's support, Alec managed to follow Hull down the dark hall to an even darker one in the rear. A narrow flight of stairs led upward from that, too narrow to permit two to walk abreast. Reluctantly Isabella dropped her arm from around Alec's waist. He didn't even sway. Only Isabella could guess what it cost him to grasp the oily banister with nonchalance and trudge up the steep stairs on his own. 'Twas a performance worthy of a master.

" 'Tis our best," Hull said proudly, throwing open the door to a room just beyond the top of the stairs. It was small by the standards Isabella was used to, furnished with an iron bedstead that might sleep two if they lay very close, a washstand, chest and chair. The walls were simple whitewash, the oak floors bare. The smell of boiling cabbage was everywhere—the odor pervaded the establishment—but the room seemed reasonably clean.

"You've done well for yourself, Hull," Alec said, passing by him into the room. " 'Tis a fine place you have here."

" 'Tis all thanks to you, Tiger. Uh, Alec. If you 'ad not—"

"Excuse me, but I'm very tired and I must lie down. I hope you will not think me rude if I hurry you on your way."

"Oh—oh, no, ma'am, not at all," Hull stuttered, looking at Isabella with as much surprise as if she'd been a two-headed goat. She supposed she had offended him, and didn't much care. Alec was getting weaker by the minute.

Alec shrugged and smiled apologetically, as if to say, "You know what women are." Hull nodded with transparent sympathy as he backed from the room.

"I'll send the doctor up when 'e comes. Can I bring you anything? A meal? The missus is cooking cabbage and hocks."

"A meal would be fine—and Hull, I'd appreciate the loan of a pistol if you have it."

Hull never even blinked. "Anything you want, Tiger, and 'tis yours."

"I'll remember this, Hull."

With that promise in keeping, Hull took himself off. Isabella closed the door behind him and turned the key in the lock. When she turned back to the room, Alec had sunk down on the end of the bed, where he slumped wearily against the chipped footrail.

"You shouldn't have stood about so long," Isabella said in a scolding tone, crossing to the bed and pulling back the covers. She only hoped the bed did not house bugs—but she refused to let such squeamish thoughts daunt her. They were lucky to have found a haven, even such a one as this.

" 'Tis always a mistake to let anyone see you vulnerable. Hull was my man once, but time and circumstance have a way of changing things."

"You don't trust him."

"I don't distrust him. I am just taking reasonable precautions. You learn to, after a while."

With the bed readied, Isabella came to kneel in front of him. Instinctively, as she might have started to undress a tired child, she undid the buttons of his shirt so that she might peel the filthy garment from him. Alec suffered her ministrations without protest, watching her with a queer little gleam in his eyes that she did not see. His shirt fell open, exposing a chest that definitely belonged to a man, not a child. With her head bent over her task, Isabella never even noticed until at last her fingers brushed the warm, muscle-ridged skin of his belly. Unbuttoning his shirt when he was so weak had seemed perfectly natural until she touched his flesh; then tiny sparks seemed to shoot through her fingers all the way down to her toes and back up again. Blushing, she pulled her hands away, leaving the shirt hanging open to his waist.

"There, now, I've unbuttoned your shirt for you. You must do the rest yourself." Her tone was brisk to cover her confusion. She didn't look at him as she stood, but rather turned away to busy herself with the pillows.

"Shy, Isabella?" There was a note to Alec's voice that made her cheeks grow even warmer. She thought of all the extremely coarse remarks he could make about how she no longer had reason to be shy with him, and almost cringed as she waited for one. Instead he said softly, "I appreciate your care of me."

Isabella looked at him then, to find those golden eyes

fixed on her with an odd expression that she could not quite decipher.

"I would do the same for anyone in need."

The words were gruff, because the truth of the matter was that she was lying. There was no one else in the world she would do the same for, unless duty or charity compelled her rather than the tenderness that had come over her when she had looked at Alec, injured and weary. The thought of undressing a weakened Bernard made her shiver with distaste. Her feelings for her husband were in no wise tender. And her father—after years of neglect on his part, she could not truthfully say that she felt for him any degree of tenderness, either. He was her father, and for that he was owed her respect and obedience, but love?

For the first time it occurred to her just how very lacking in love her life was.

"Would you indeed?"

"What?" Lost in thought, it took her a minute to return to the present.

"Never mind. Aren't those pillows sufficiently plumped yet? You've pummeled them to within an inch of their lives."

He was teasing her, as usual, but she was too relieved that he was capable of it to take umbrage. Suddenly her world rocked back into place, and she was able to banish the unusual melancholy that had threatened to overwhelm her.

"You should be abed. If I help you with your boots, can you manage the, er, rest?" Self-conscious, she left off fluffing the pillows.

"I could—if I had any intention of going to bed. I do not." From the obstinate look on his face, she could tell that he meant what he said. Isabella looked at him for a moment, aghast.

"Don't be silly! You've been shot, you've lost a great deal of blood, and you've been looking like you could faint for the better part of an hour. Of course you must go to bed. Immediately."

"I've never fainted in my life. I'll certainly not start now, over this. 'Tis little more than a graze."

"Alec, would you please get into bed?" She was losing all patience with him.

"No."

They exchanged measuring stares. Isabella had to fight back an urge to clout him upside his injured head. He was being a silly, stubborn fool, and to what purpose?

"I assume there is some valid reason that you are refusing to do what any sane man would? Certainly you don't have to prove to me what a brave fellow you are. I assure you, I'm quite impressed already."

"I am waiting until the bloody sawbones that you insisted on comes and goes. I'll not give anyone reason to suppose me helpless unless I must."

"Oh." That aspect of the situation had not occurred to her. With the wind taken out of her sails, Isabella felt vaguely foolish for not having figured that out for herself.

"Understand this, Isabella: these men are like jackals—if they sense weakness, even the most normally trustworthy of them are likely to close in for the kill. I'll not chance it, for your sake as well as mine. Without me, you'd have about as much chance here as a nice, juicy bone thrown into a pit of starving dogs."

"I'd not thought of that, I confess. Very well, then, if you'll not lie down, at least let me wash some of the blood from your face for you."

"Now, that I'll not object to," he said, and essayed a smile. The crooked attempt had an effect on Isabella that was far out of proportion to its relative dazzle. Her heart swelled, and she fairly bristled with protectiveness. Such a reaction frightened her. Not for the first time, it occurred to her that she was growing far too fond of Alec. She must not allow herself to fall in love with him. That way lay heartbreak.

There was water in the pitcher on the washstand. It was stone-cold, and probably stale, but it served to splash her face and wash her hands in. Catching a glimpse of her reflection in the small mirror hanging on the wall above the bowl, she almost cringed. She looked like a witch, or worse. Quickly she set about trying to remedy the damage the day had wrought to her hair. Gathering the trailing ends together, she gave the tangled mass a couple of twists to form a knot and thrust the pins through. Though her reflection did not show a great deal of improvement, under the circumstances she decided that it was the best she could do.

Isabella poured some of the water remaining in the pitcher into the matching porcelain bowl and carried it and a linen towel that had been draped over the towel rack to the bed. Sitting on the mattress beside Alec, bowl in her lap, she dipped the towel in water and reached up to gently sponge his bloody face.

He rested wearily back against the footrail, suffering her ministrations with closed eyes. Blood no longer seeped from beneath the bandage, and that which was on his face was mostly dry. She wiped at it, careful not to hurt him as she cleaned the gore from the chiselled planes of his face and neck. There was dried blood in his eyebrows, in the ear nearest the wound, along the side of his neck. More blood was caked in the curling mat of hair on his chest. By the time she was half-through, the water in the bowl was murky red.

"Can you take off your shirt?" she asked as she stood up to exchange the water in the bowl for fresh.

Alec's eyes opened then. Isabella could feel them following her as she moved.

Again she waited for a comment or jest that would put her to the blush. Again he surprised her.

"You've uncommon gentle hands," he said, then shrugged out of his shirt without another word.

Returning, self-conscious now as he sat before her bared to the waist, his magnificent torso available for her to look at and touch as she would, Isabella knelt at his feet with the fresh bowl of water, the better to get at the blood that had congealed on his chest. His shirt had absorbed a good deal of the gore, but still his chest hair was matted and sticky, and brown streaks anointed his muscled rib cage.

Isabella forced herself to work slowly and carefully, so as not to betray her rising awareness of him. Yet so sensitive was she to the heat emanating from his body, to the silky texture of his body hair and satin sleekness of his skin, that by the time she had finished her pulse was tripping along at twice its normal speed.

When at last she dropped the towel back into the bowl and would have stood up with it, relieved to have it done, he stopped her with a hand sliding around the back of her neck.

"Thank you," he said softly, his fingers caressing the soft skin at her nape.

Startled, her eyes flew to his and were trapped by the intensity of his gaze. By the softly filtered light of the late afternoon sun slanting through the window, she saw that the golden eyes were actually hazel flecked with gold, with the tiniest hint of emerald green near the pupil. Then he turned his head just enough for a dusty sunbeam to strike his face, and his eyes glowed as golden as metal. Isabella caught her breath, mesmerized by the sheer beauty of them. Had he been a woman, those eyes alone would have been enough to assure his reign as an Incomparable. The rest of his far too considerable male beauty was simply a case of a disproportionately generous Mother Nature heaping more bounty on top of an already ample feast.

"You shouldn't look at me that way if you don't mean it, Countess." Those golden eyes never left her mouth as, dipping his head, he kissed her.

XXXVII

Before her lips could do more than flutter under his, there was a knock at the door.

"I've brought the sawbones, Ti—uh, Alec," Hull called through the closed panel.

Alec's hand fell away from Isabella's neck, and she got quickly to her feet. Flustered, she forgot about the bowl and barely managed to save its contents from being spilled all over the floor as she stood.

"Steady," Alec said. And there was the mocking note she had been waiting for.

She supposed it was deserved. After all, it was she who had protested vehemently not more than six hours before at the notion of becoming his mistress. Yet the merest touch of his lips on hers could make her knees turn to jelly, and her hands shake.

Without looking at him again, she opened the door to admit Hull, his wife, who was carrying a covered tray, and an older man in a black suit turned shiny with age whom Isabella assumed was the sawbones.

"Treat 'im gentle, you 'ear, McIver? 'E's a good friend of mine," Hull directed jovially, passing a pair of pistols to Alec as casually as he would have handed over a pair of gloves. Alec thrust one in the waistband of his breeches and laid the other on the bedside table.

"Dinner, such as 'tis," Liddy announced without enthusiasm as she set the tray on the bedside table. She and

Hull then left. The aroma of cooked cabbage emanating from the tray was so strong that there was no ignoring it in the closed room. The sawbones, nose wrinkling, paused in the act of unpacking his instruments to request that they go ahead and eat, which they did, with little enthusiasm for the lukewarm boiled cabbage and pork, and the less than fresh bread. Alec barely managed two bites, and those only at Isabella's urging.

Isabella laid aside her fork when Alec did, and watched with a twinge of sympathy as the doctor went to work on him, poking and prodding and clucking importantly. By the time he had finished his examination, Alec, cursing all doctors with scant regard for this one's sensibilities, was as grumpy as a rooster who'd had its tail stepped on.

Dr. McIver, pronouncing the wound to be superficial but the blood loss substantial, ordered at least a week of bed rest. Alec was determined to be on the road by the next morning, and said so. The doctor shook his head, prophesying dire consequences if his instructions were not followed to the letter. Alec called him a blood-sucking leech, along with other less flattering terms that would have burned Isabella's ears had she not already grown somewhat accustomed to Alec's penchant for colorful language.

Dr. McIver looked outraged at Alec's invective. Isabella shook her head warningly at him when he opened his mouth to, she feared, reply in kind. Thinking better of it, the doctor contented himself with snapping closed his bag and storming out. Isabella followed him into the hall, shutting the door behind her.

"Well, what is it?" He eyed her up and down, looking thoroughly ruffled.

"Please allow me to apologize for Alec, Dr. McIver. He's had some unpleasant experiences with medics lately."

Dr. McIver snorted. "I don't know what he is to you, but if you've a care for yon rude beggar, you'll keep him abed for at least three or four days. The bullet not only tore off a large patch of his skin, it hit his skull with considerable force. Had the bone not deflected it, he would have been killed outright. If he tries to move about, I cannot say with any certainty what the consequences might be.''

''I will do my best to keep him here, and abed. But he is not a good patient under the best of circumstances.''

The doctor's expression told her that he had already reached that conclusion on his own.

''Get this down him at night, and sprinkle this on the wound twice a day. If it does not get infected, and if he stays quiet, I've no fears for his life. More's the pity.'' This last was muttered as the doctor handed over a brown glass bottle full of a milky fluid, and a smaller, powder-filled vial, which Isabella tucked into her sash.

''Thank you for coming, Doctor.'' Isabella reached into Alec's purse—which she had taken from him without a qualm, just like the shameless hussy she felt herself to be rapidly becoming—and handed the doctor a folded pound note. The doctor accepted the money, nodded, and left. Isabella followed him down the stairs. Now that she was out of Alec's sight, she had other business to attend to.

The excitement of the cockfight had calmed somewhat, and the taproom was swarming with men. One or two eyed Isabella, but most were too intent on going over the details of the fight and the amount each had won or lost to pay her any mind. Fortunately she did not have to look far to find Hull. He saw her hovering at the door of the taproom and came hurrying over to her.

''Can I get you sommit, miss?''

''There is a message I need to send to London. Could you show me where I might find writing materials, and then spare a lad to deliver it? There's twenty pounds in it for the messenger.''

''Twenty pounds!'' He looked suitably impressed. ''I don't doubt that my boy George'd be glad of the money—and I've pen and ink at the bar. I'll bring 'em up to you, if you like.''

Isabella shook her head. ''I'll use them down here, if you've no objection.''

Isabella scribbled her message, sanded it, folded it and sealed it with a drop of wax as quickly as she could.

When she finished writing the direction on it, she handed it to Hull.

"If it is delivered tonight, there's an extra ten pounds in it for your boy, thirty in all," she said. "There are instructions to that effect in the note. The messenger will be paid as soon as it's in the right hands."

"For thirty pounds, my boy could make it to France and back, much less London." Hull took the message and squinted at the direction on its back. "He'll get it done for you, don't you fear."

"Thank you, Mr. Hull. You've been more than kind."

She turned to make her way back upstairs, threading through the crowded taproom as quickly and unobtrusively as possible. The last thing she wanted to do was attract attention, but in this she was not successful. One man left his seat and his guffawing cronies to trail after her as she passed.

Isabella was halfway up the stairs before she realized he was behind her. A quick glance showed her a stocky man in a black frock coat and gray frieze breeches who might have been dapper had he been cleaner. But claret spotted his waistcoat, and his neckcloth was grimy, as though it had not been fresh for several days. He was swarthy-skinned, and his features, though not unhandsome, were coarse. Isabella felt a quiver of apprehension as she met bold black eyes, and hurried on up the stairs.

"What's your hurry, sweeting?" the man called after her, quickening his own pace to match hers. Isabella caught her breath as she realized that he was deliberately following her. She froze him with a glance, and went quickly along the hallway to her room. Fumbling for the key, she was not quite fast enough to elude her pursuer. He caught her by the elbow, and turned her to face him.

"How dare you, sir!" she said, jerking her arm from his hold. He stood frowning at her, his brows twitching together over his beak of a nose.

"I'd swear we've met," he muttered. Ignoring him, Isabella thrust the key into the lock and turned it, intent on stepping inside and putting herself safely beyond his reach.

"Hold," he said suddenly, reaching out to catch her arm again and turn her forcibly toward him. Isabella gasped, and shrank away. Every instinct urged her to call out to Alec, but she was loathe to disturb him for something that she could, she was sure, handle herself. Besides, Alec was not up to a fight on her behalf at the moment.

"Let me go, please. My husband is within." She spoke the half lie firmly.

"Who are you?" He completely ignored her words, instead staring intently into her face. "Who are you?"

"My identity is no concern of yours. Pray release my arm before I am forced to summon my husband for assistance."

"I'll have your name." His fingers on her arm tightened cruelly.

"Unhand me. At once, do you hear, or I'll scream!"

"Will you, indeed?" He loomed closer, crowding her against the wall. What act of violence he intended, Isabella never knew. To her utter relief, just at that moment Alec jerked open the door she had unlocked, and stood scowling at her. As he saw her companion, his scowl changed from the irritable to the dangerous. Bare-chested and barefoot, with a fresh bandage wrapped around his forehead, Alec managed nevertheless to look formidable.

"What the bloody hell is going on out here?" His eyes never left the man who had been menacing Isabella.

"God's teeth!" the man gasped, his eyes widening as they locked on Alec. "Alec Tyron, the Tiger, here!" His eyes swept back to Isabella. "Of course, I should have tumbled to it at once. The mystery lady." He paused for a second, then seemed to recollect himself. His eyes slid back to Alec. "I'd heard, of course, that you'd a fresh bird in keeping that was not quite in the common way."

"John Ball." Alec's greeting was cold as stone in winter, and his eyes flicked to the hand that still gripped Isabella's arm. " 'Twere I you, I'd unhand the lady at once. Seeing her mishandled sets ill with me."

"Does it indeed? Then I apologize, of course. To you and to her."

He removed his hand from Isabella's arm. At a gesture from Alec, Isabella stepped around him and inside the room. Violence was in the air, and she feared that Alec, injured as he was, stood little chance should this misbegotten encounter degenerate into blows, or worse.

" 'Tis a good piece from London you are, Tiger." John Ball's tone was affable on the surface, but there was an undertone to it that set Isabella's nerves to quivering with alarm. If ever one man disliked another, John Ball disliked Alec.

"As are you, Ball." Alec's voice was infinitely cold.

"One does one's business where one can."

"Precisely."

"Well. I'll leave you to your labors. From what I've seen of them, they look far more enjoyable than mine."

"Appearances can be misleading."

"Quite."

"Quite."

With that last cryptic exchange Alec shut the door, and turned the key in the lock. Isabella breathed a sigh of relief, then decided she had relaxed too soon. From the stiff set of his wide, bare shoulders, Alec's temper had not improved during the time she had been belowstairs. The muscles of his back stood out sharply, as if he was keeping himself in check with considerable effort. Stiffening her spine, Isabella prepared herself to face the explosion of wrath she was sure must follow. She was not disappointed. When he turned to face her, leaning back against the door as though he needed its solid strength to remain upright, fury blazed from his eyes.

XXXVIII

"Where the bloody hell have you been?"

"Don't you swear at me, Alec Tyron!"

His lips thinned. "I'll swear if I bloody well want to. You step outside for a quick chat with the bloody sawbones and you vanish for near three-quarters of an hour! I've been out of my mind with worry! Do you realize the kind of place this is? The kind of man John Ball is? Hell, if I hadn't heard you at the door, there's no telling what he might have done to you! You're not amongst the bloody nobility here, you know."

"But you did hear me, so no harm's done, is there?" She was determined to make light of the incident. "Shouldn't you be in bed? Dr. McIver left some medicine for you to take."

"Devil take Dr. McIver, and his bloody medicine! I want to know where you've been, and how you came to encounter Ball!"

"Get in bed, and take your medicine like a good boy, and perhaps I'll tell you."

She was being deliberately annoying, she knew, but felt he deserved it for his language, to say nothing of his bad temper.

"Isabella . . ." Alec sounded as if her name was forced out through gritted teeth. His eyes flashed pure temper. But what smote her was his obvious weakness as he leaned back against the door. She had not meant to worry him, nor anger him, nor involve him in an altercation with an uncouth stranger. He had every right to be upset with her, she admitted to herself, although she still took exception to his language.

Sighing, she surrendered her own indignation at his intemperate reception in favor of coaxing him back to bed.

"I will tell you everything, really, and very odd it was, too. But you really should lie down, and take your medicine. Please."

"I'm not a puling infant for you to mother."

Isabella made a face at him, and moved toward the bed. She fluffed his pillow and smoothed the sheets, speaking to him over her shoulder.

"You're acting like an infant, so you mustn't blame me if I treat you like one."

She turned to face him, standing beside the bed with her arms crossed over her chest.

"Get into bed, Alec, or I'll be forced to take stern measures."

Despite his annoyance, that coaxed the beginnings of a smile from him. "You're frightening me to death."

"I should be. I'll have you know that I can be very stern indeed." Encouraged by his smile, she returned it.

"I remember all too well." He reached up to touch his right eye, which still bore the faintest trace of a bruise.

Disconcerted, Isabella felt herself blush at the reminder of the blow she had dealt him, and all that had gone before it, on the never-to-be-forgotten night at the Carousel.

"If you want us to have any chance at all of getting on, you won't remind me of—that." Her tone was constricted. Then she noticed how he still leaned against the door, and how pale he was below the bandage that the doctor had replaced. Her embarrassment vanished, and impatience with his foolishness appeared in its stead.

"Stop being such a wantwit, Alec, and get into bed."

When he still stood there, watching her without moving, she gave a disgusted exclamation and marched across the room to catch him by his ear as she would have a recalcitrant schoolboy.

"Hey!" He looked startled, but stood his ground. "And just what do you think you're doing, miss?"

"Putting you to bed."

"Indeed?"

"Indeed."

Still not appreciating his danger, he didn't move. She tugged. He yelped.

"Ow! You're hurting me!"

"I meant to. Come on."

She tugged again, harder. This time he allowed her to pull him across the room and push him down on the bed. When he was seated, she released his ear with a nod of satisfaction. Alec rubbed his abused ear with a pained grimace.

"You're a cruel woman, Countess."

"Only when I encounter foolish, stubborn men who don't know what's good for them."

The medicine the doctor had given her was still tucked in her sash. She pulled it out, set the vial down and, reaching for an unused glass from the supper tray that still sat on the bedside table, poured a large dose of milky liquid into it from the bottle.

"Drink this." She held the glass out to him. He looked at it with loathing.

"Can we talk about this?"

"No!"

"I was afraid of that."

He took the glass, grimaced, and drank. When he had drained the contents, he made another face, more horrible than the first, and handed the glass back to her.

"Satisfied now, harpy? Then tell me how you managed to run into Ball."

"Get into bed first."

Alec gave her a fulminating look, but other than that, didn't argue. She suspected he was feeling weaker than he liked to admit, even to her. When he was comfortably arranged, his long legs still clad in the breeches he refused to remove—in case of emergency he didn't want to be caught buck naked, he said—stretched beneath the coverlet, his head propped up by pillows, she rewarded him with a wide smile.

"I warn you, if you don't quit beaming at me in that annoying way, I won't be responsible for my actions."

"My, we are ill-tempered, aren't we? Why don't you take a little nap? We can talk later."

His brows snapped together, and he looked as dangerous as it was possible for a man to look all tucked up cozily in bed with a bandage around his head.

"Damn it, Isabella, stop treating me like a child and tell me about Ball!"

There was fire in his eye. Isabella, seeing it, perched meekly on the edge of the mattress.

"He was in the taproom. He saw me and followed me upstairs. He seemed to think he knew me from somewhere."

"What the bloody hell were you doing in the taproom?" It was almost a shout.

"Don't swear, Alec," she protested automatically, clasping her hands in her lap and looking at him reprovingly. "If you must know, I went to the taproom to send a message to Paddy."

"You did what?" The question was explosive.

"I sent a message to Paddy. Before I left, he asked me to let him know if I thought you needed his help. I do."

There was a pause. His eyes measured her. She looked guilelessly back at him. The deed was done. There was no way he could change it.

"Taking quite a lot on yourself, aren't you, Countess?"

" 'Tis your hide I'm thinking of, not mine. That man meant to kill you today."

"He's not the first."

"One of them just may succeed."

"Anything's possible." He shrugged. "But not too bloody likely. I'm harder to kill than a cockroach. Well, I don't say I would have sent for Paddy—I don't need a bloody nanny dogging my every step—but I don't fault you for it, under the circumstances. Let's get back to Ball. Tell me everything he said to you. Exactly."

Isabella complied to the best of her ability.

"So he thought he'd seen you before, hmmm? Where could he have seen you? You've never before been to London, and Ball rarely leaves it."

"Who is he?"

"A London sewer rat. Lower than that. He'll do anything—and I mean anything—for a price. Take you, for instance. He'd sell you to an abbess quicker than you could blink, given half the chance. A real to-the-manor-born lady would fetch a fine price on the market, and he'd know it."

"He'd sell me?" Isabella breathed, half-fascinated, half-horrified.

"After he was through with you himself, of course. He'd enjoy forcing himself on you, making you scream."

"You're trying to frighten me!"

"I'm telling you God's honest truth, my girl. Christ, you're such a baby you're not safe to be let out." He shut his eyes for a moment, then opened them again to fix them on her. "You're not to leave this room again without me with you, do you understand? Not for anything."

"But Alec—"

"Do you understand?" His voice was fierce. "Listen to me, Isabella. Ball's a danger, but he's not the only one. The majority of those men out there wouldn't think twice about pushing you over on your backside and having their way with you, scream you ever so loudly. God knows what else they might do to you. These blokes are scum, most of them, and they'll harm you without a second thought. There are no gentlemen amongst them. Believe me, I know. I was—am—one of them."

"You didn't harm me, when you could have."

"I would have let Parren kill you if he hadn't taken the job under the table. The fact that your life was saved in the process of protecting my turf was just bloody coincidence." The words were brutal.

"You're not nearly as black as you paint yourself, Alec Tyron. And I'd be willing to wager that most of these men are not as evil as you'd have me think, either. After all, people are people, whether they're rich or poor."

Alec made a sound that was a cross between a laugh and a groan. " 'Tis clear you've led a sheltered life, love. Trust me on this, will you? I want your word that you won't leave this room without me."

"But—"

"Your word, Isabella." He was implacable. Looking at him, she had to acknowledge that he must know what he was talking about. She *had* felt uncomfortable in the taproom, and John Ball *had* frightened her.

She nodded. "Very well, I give you my word."

"That's a smart girl. God, my head hurts! If that medicine of yours is supposed to ease the pain, it's not working."

"You should try being quiet. It might perform wonders."

"You've a sassy mouth on you, Countess." He was looking at her narrow-eyed, though a slight smile lurked around the corners of his mouth. She smiled at him, and swept loosened tendrils of hair from her face.

"A sassy, beautiful mouth," he went on, his eyes fixed on the feature he praised. "I don't suppose I could interest you in kissing the pain away?"

"Alec . . ." It was part protest, part warning.

"I thought not. Well, there's no harm in asking, is there?"

Uncomfortable at the turn the conversation had taken Isabella sought to change the subject. "I feel like I'm carrying around more dirt than a garden. Do you suppose this place runs to a bath?"

The lurking smile on Alec's face widened. "You are a mess, love, but a very fetching one. Pray feel free to order a bath. I doubt that it's a request they get very often here but I'm sure Hull will do his best to accommodate you."

His grin was devilish, and Isabella suddenly deduced the reason for his amusement. Of course, they were sharing a room. If she were to bathe, he would get an eyeful It might be possible for her to rig up some sort of screen but the very idea of disrobing in the same room with Alec made her nerves tingle. Better by far to wait until she had some privacy.

"On second thought, I think I'll make do with the water in the pitcher," she said primly.

"You disappoint me," he murmured, and yawned. "Christ, I feel peculiar."

"Peculiar? In what way?"

He yawned again, hugely this time. "My head's spinning, and my eyelids feel like they've been weighted down with coins. The pain in my head's better, but this feeling is worse. I feel like I've been drugged."

Isabella stared at him. His eyelids were drooping, and he tried to suppress another yawn without success. A hideous thought occurred to her. Had the medicine been poison? Under the circumstances, the notion was not as outlandish as it seemed. Danger could lurk anywhere.

She almost ran to the bedside table, snatched up the bottle, unscrewed the lid and sniffed.

"Wh . . . what is it?" His voice was slightly slurred.

" 'Tis naught but laudanum," she said in relief.

"Laudanum!" His eyes flew open and he cursed viciously.

"It won't hurt you."

"Won't hurt—" He ground his teeth. "Isabella, don't open the door to anyone—not anyone!—but Paddy when he comes. If someone tries to enter, warn him off; then if he keeps coming, shoot him with the pistol here. Shoot to kill. Do you know how? Just point it, pull back the hammer, and pull the trigger. Do not open the door for Hull, or his wife, or anyone except Paddy, do you understand? We'll take no chances until I'm functional again."

His fierceness was momentarily staving off the effects of the laudanum.

Isabella looked from him to the pistols in growing horror.

"You don't think Dr. McIver is in on it, do you? How could he be? He didn't even know who you are."

"I doubt it. 'Tis hard to say. But 'tis best to trust no one. Not anyone, Isabella. Christ, I feel like I'm swimming through a thick mist! Don't trust anyone, do you hear?''

His eyelids were drooping. Isabella looked down at him with a dreadful sense of being caught in a nightmare. Could Dr. McIver be evil enough to have deliberately poisoned him?

XXXIX

Isabella spent that night in a chair beside the bed. With Alec deep in a drugged sleep, she refused to lie down for fear that she, too, might fall asleep. In the event, she dozed off in the chair sometime in the wee hours of the morning, only to be startled awake by a sound that she could not at first identify.

Her first thought was of Alec. Blinking, lifting the hair from her eyes, she sat up and checked him. He was still deeply asleep, his breathing quiet and rhythmic. If he had stirred since she had last looked at him, she couldn't tell it.

The sound came again. Heart speeding up, Isabella slowly turned her eyes in the direction from whence it had come.

Slowly, very slowly, the doorknob moved as she stared at it, horrified. A soft creak accompanied the movement. That must have been the sound she had heard.

Someone was trying to get into the room.

Her heart was pounding so furiously she could feel the blood drumming against her eardrums. Her mouth went dry. She licked her lips, trying to put some moisture back into them as she watched the knob turn slowly in the other direction. The knob stopped moving. The door shuddered slightly as if someone was pushing against it from the outside.

"Alec!" Isabella whispered urgently, rising from the

chair and leaning over him to shake him. "Alec, wake up! Please!"

His breath caught, was released in a gentle snore. His head turned on the pillow.

"Alec!" Instinct warned her to be as quiet as possible as she tried frantically to rouse him. She kept a frightened eye on the door. No sound, no movement. Save for the soft rasp of Alec's breathing, and her own frantic whispers, the night was as quiet as the grave.

Someone was out there, listening. She knew it as well as she knew anything.

Suddenly it came to her why her instinct had warned her to try to rouse Alec in silence. If whoever was on the other side of the door realized that he had only her to contend with, his efforts to get into the room might be significantly bolder.

Or did he know? Had Dr. McIver been in cahoots with the assassin? Was it Tim Hull? Would a scream bring help? Or would it cause whoever was listening on the other side of the door to abandon all attempts at subterfuge, break through the door, and murder herself and Alec without further ado?

Alec would not be roused. He continued to sleep heavily, drugged by the laudanum. If someone was to get to him now, he would be slain without so much as a whimper of protest.

A new sound at the door galvanized Isabella. It was the faint clatter of metal against metal.

Something had been inserted into the keyhole. She caught her breath. The key that she'd left in the lock quivered as something probed at it. Thank God she had left it in!

The pistols that Hull had given Alec lay untouched on the beside table. Isabella's eyes slid from the still-moving key to touch on the pistols with almost equal horror.

Never in her life had she fired a pistol. Never had she expected to have to. They were as alien to her as earbobs were to Alec.

But she could not just stand there, hand pressed to her

heart, eyes wide with fright, while some lowlife assassin broke into the room and murdered Alec in his sleep.

The key jerked. Isabella caught her breath, afraid for a moment that whoever was out there might have succeeded in dislodging it. Eyes huge, she waited for it to fall with a clatter to the floor. With the last impediment removed, the assassin would open the door, and charge in to carry out his dastardly mission. . . .

The key held. The lock rattled loudly, as if whoever was outside was growing impatient.

Isabella looked longingly at Alec. He lay on his back, his lips slightly parted as he drew in air between them, a dark stubble roughening his jaw, his tawny hair all on end, falling over the pristine white of the bandage. Crescents of stubby dark gold lashes lay against his cheeks.

He was broad-shouldered, powerfully muscled—and in his present condition, as defenseless as a babe. The knowledge brought all Isabella's protective instincts to the fore.

Anyone who wanted to harm him would have to get through her to do it!

The key rattled again, quivered, jolted. This time whoever was out there succeeded in dislodging it. It hung on the edge of the lock, poised to fall. . . .

Isabella snatched up a pistol, leveled it at the door, closed her eyes and pulled the trigger.

The resulting explosion nearly deafened her. The kick from the pistol sent her stumbling back to land heavily on the edge of the bed. From the other side of the door came a howl, then the sound of running feet. Isabella's eyes flew open. She had blown a hole neat and round as a schilling through the center panel of the door. Other than that, it was still intact, still closed, and, she hoped, locked. The key now lay on the floor.

Alec still slept. If the sound had penetrated the opium mists that held him in thrall, he gave no sign of it.

Beyond the door there was silence. Were all the inhabitants of the inn deaf? Did they all sleep in the drugged blissfulness that claimed Alec? Or were they in on the plot? Could she expect a contingent of men to storm the door at any minute, all considerations of stealth now abandoned?

Heart in throat, Isabella picked up the second pistol and ran to the door. She tried the knob. The lock still held, Fingers trembling, she snatched up the key and inserted it in the lock to block any second key's access. Then she bent and put her eye to the hole she had blown.

Beyond the panel nothing stirred. The dingy passageway, barely lit by a single candle drowning in its own wax in a wall sconce, was deserted. There was not a sound to be heard. All was precisely as it should be in a country inn in the wee, dark hours of the morning.

If it were not for the hole in the door, and her own racing pulse, Isabella might almost have thought that she had dreamt the whole thing.

Straightening, she moved from the door to stand beside the bed. Alec slept unknowing beneath her guardianship. She listened to the even tenor of his breathing, listened to her own heartbeat, listened for a sound more ominous than either.

But there was nothing. Nothing beyond the homely melody of a man sleeping.

When she had fired the pistol, someone had cried out. Clearly she had hit whoever had been on the other side of that door. Had she wounded him seriously enough to deter him from coming back? Or did she have to wait in frozen fear for another try at the door?

A hideous thought occurred to her. If Tim Hull was in on this, her message to Paddy had most likely never been delivered. And she had only one pistol, with one ball in it, left.

The chair was of the hard wooden upright variety, and for the first time that night, Isabella was glad of it. She could not, would not, allow herself to fall asleep until Alec was alert again. Dragging the chair behind the bed so that she could watch both Alec and the door, she sat in it, stiffly erect, pistol in hand, as she strained to hear every sound.

For a long time she sat there, listening to Alec's breathing and her own. If there were other sounds beyond those in the small bedchamber, she never heard them.

Gradually dawn broke. As muddy orange light crept through the windows, Isabella allowed her grip on the pistol to relax. Only as her spine slumped did she realize that she was drenched in nervous sweat.

XL

"Isabella?"

The groggy syllables were the most welcome sounds she had ever heard. She leaned forward eagerly, hovering over the bed.

"Alec?"

"Is there water?"

His eyes were open, but barely. The golden irises were cloudy, the lids with their stubby gold lashes fluttering. Isabella felt a sudden pang in her heart as she looked down into that beautiful, dishevelled face. Last night she had saved his life. This morning she felt as if he belonged to her.

"Yes, of course." She placed the pistol carefully on the side of the bed, and stood up to get him water. When she came back, his eyes were closed again.

"Alec?"

"Hmmm?" His lids lifted. For just a moment he seemed not to register why she was bending over him. Then he muttered, "Oh, the water. Christ, my mouth is dry."

She lifted his head, helped him drink. Then he fell limply back on the pillow, his eyes closing again.

"Alec?" There was a panicked sound to his name this time.

"Hmmm?"

"Don't go back to sleep. Please."

His eyes opened at that. "Is ought the matter?"

"Someone . . . someone tried to get in here during the night."

"What?" His eyes opened more fully, and his voice grew fractionally sharper.

"Someone was at the door, trying to get in. I . . . I shot him."

"You what?" From the sound of it, he was now fully awake.

"I shot him." She pointed toward the door, where the hole in the middle panel was clearly visible. Alec stared at it.

"Good God." His eyes focused back on Isabella. "Why didn't you wake me?"

Isabella gave him a wry look. "If the shot didn't wake you, do you think I could have? I tried, of course."

He said nothing, just looked from Isabella to the door and back in thoughtful silence.

Eventually he said. "Tell me exactly what happened. Everything."

Isabella complied. When she was done he shook his head. "Countess, my admiration for you grows with every passing hour. You continually amaze me."

Isabella blushed with pleasure at his words. Compliments had been a rare commodity in her life, and such a one from Alec she knew she would carefully store in her memory and treasure forever.

"But what do we do now?" The question was almost plaintive. Alec frowned.

"I don't think Hull would be stupid enough to have me murdered beneath his own roof, even if he is involved in this, which I don't believe he is. He's been away from London too long to have any stake in who's running things. However, anything is possible, and to completely rule him out as a suspect could be a fatal mistake. John Ball knows I am here, and would be happy to see me in the ground. But we didn't cross paths until after that bloody sawbones had been here and given you the laudanum, so that would tend to argue against him being the man at the door. Unless the administration of laudanum was just a happy coincidence for whoever wants me dead. . . ."

His voice trailed off. Isabella watched him silently as he stared, lost in thought, at the wall. Now that he was awake and aware again, she felt as if a great burden had been lifted from her shoulders. Alec would know what to do. . . .

He threw the covers back, swung his legs over the side of the bed, and sat up. Immediately he groaned, and dropped his head in his hands.

"You shouldn't try to get up! You know the doctor said you were to stay in bed for at least three or four days, preferably a week." She came around the bed to stand over him.

"I know what the bloody sawbones said. I also know that someone is trying mighty hard to kill me—and will probably be quite happy to kill you as well. We're not safe here, not safe anyplace where the men surrounding me are not handpicked for loyalty. I think our best choice is to head for Amberwood, without letting anyone know we've left. Check the innyard, will you?"

Isabella went to the window and looked down. The sun was just peeping over the horizon, but already a serving girl was feeding a noisy flock of chickens, and a lad was lugging a sack of grain into the stable. A farm cart was hitched in front of the inn; a farmer probably had just gone inside to make a delivery of some kind. Isabella related all that to Alec.

"Well, it won't get any quieter. We'd best be making our move." He got to his feet with obvious effort, holding on to the footrail for support, his face going a ghastly shade of white that was only a degree less pale than the bandage around his head.

"We could wait for Paddy."

Alec looked so unsteady that Isabella had to offer the halfhearted suggestion. He rejected it with a shake of his head.

"If Hull is involved in this thing, your message was never sent. Paddy won't come."

"But—"

Isabella was interrupted by the sound of a galloping horse. Curious, she turned back to the window. Alec's eyes swung in that direction as well.

" 'Ull! 'Ull! Wake up, wake up! Get out 'ere, you overfed suet bag!"

The rider was a tall, thin man on a puffing horse. As he clattered into the innyard, chickens scattered noisily in every direction. The serving girl looked up; two boys emerged from the stable to stare. A mangy dog barked, making daring sorties at the horse's thin legs. Apparently oblivious to the commotion he had created, the rider pulled his horse to a rearing stop just as Hull came hurrying out. From the soap covering half his face, Hull had been in the process of shaving. His wife was behind him, still tying her apron strings behind her back.

"What the devil ails you, Dickon?" Hull boomed up at the rider. His wife muttered irritably.

"Boney's abdicated! The war's over! Praise God, it's over!"

"What?"

"The Frenchies've got the Bourbons back! Louis's on the throne! The war's over, do you 'ear me? Boney's gone and quit!"

Isabella's hand went to her throat. The war that had been going on for nearly as long as she could remember was finally over? The horrifying spectre of France's Little Corporal launching an invasion of England need no longer lurk constantly at the back of her mind? Would that it were true. . . .

"Alec, they're saying Bonaparte has abdicated." Her voice was faint. She barely glanced at him. Her attention was on the activity in the innyard below the window.

"The devil you say!"

Weak or no, he moved swiftly to stand beside her, looking down on the scene below. Liddy was weeping into her apron, while Tim Hull's broad face was wreathed in a beaming smile.

"Are you certain sure?" Hull asked the question as if

he wanted badly to believe the good tidings but couldn't quite let himself.

" 'Tis all the talk in London! Ring the bell, man!"

The rider turned his mount about and clapped his heels to its sides. The horse bounded forward, with the man in the saddle bobbing up in ungainly counterpoint to the animal's frenzied gallop.

"The war's over! Boney's quit!"

Hull embraced Liddy, kissed her cheek, swung her around, all the while yelling the news into the inn. Last night's celebrants came staggering out in singles and bunches, to stand milling about in the innyard. Behind the inn, one of the stable lads began to ring the big iron bell erected to summon help in emergencies.

"Ale for all!" Hull's expansiveness was rewarded with a rousing cheer. Someone rolled a big keg of ale from the inn; someone else created a lug hole by the simple expedient of blowing a hole through the barrel's side. Mugs were produced, thrust under the golden stream. Toasts were drunk. Cheers filled the air. Over all sounded the incessant, joyous clanging of the bell.

"God in heaven, think what this will do to the rates on the Exchange," Alec said pensively. This was such a prosaic reaction to the thrilling news that Isabella stared at him in disapproving surprise. At her expression, his face broke into a slow-dawning smile. "I do have quite a few legitimate business interests, you know. I would be a fool if I didn't consider how a Bourbon restoration is going to affect them."

She continued to stare at him. Even with a bandage wrapped around his head, dirty and unshaven as he was, he was handsome enough to take her breath. His tawny hair, unconfined, was wildly tousled around his face. His eyes gleamed gold with excitement. He was bare-chested, his muscles taut and hard-looking beneath satiny bronze skin, the sun picking out golden glints in the soft wedge of hair on his chest. His breeches rode low on his hips, exposing most of the board-flat abdomen to her view. His feet were bare. Looking at him, it occurred to Isabella that there was no one else in the world with whom she would rather have been at that moment, no one with whom she would rather have shared the momentous news.

"The war's over, Alec," she whispered as the impact of it sank in at last. By way of answer he held out his arms to her. Isabella went into them as if she belonged there. They closed about her, rocking her against him, hugging her tight against his warm, bare chest while he nuzzled the top of her hair with his face. Clinging to him, she closed her eyes. The musky scent of him enveloped her, made her dizzy. It seemed the most natural thing in the world to lift her face for his kiss.

It seemed almost as though he hesitated. Isabella opened her eyes to find him looking down into her face, his expression both unsettled and unsettling. Then, as he met her eyes, the gleam in his suddenly heated. He bent his head, touching her lips with his, drawing her up on her tiptoes so that the entire length of her was molded to his body. Isabella's arms slid around his neck, her fingers twisted in the tangles of his hair. She opened her mouth to his, kissing him with a greedy hunger of which, once, long ago, she never would have believed herself capable.

The sudden escalation of the commotion caused Alec to lift his head. Still held close to his heart, her hands still locked behind his neck, Isabella took a deep, shaken breath and turned her head to see a contingent of men, some on horseback, some in carriages, gallop into the innyard. The carriage in the lead rolled right into the center of the crowd with scant regard for the lives and limbs of the celebrants. Almost before it stopped a man jumped from the interior. He was huge and frowning menacingly, a pistol clutched in his fist. The other men tumbled off their conveyances to form a tight band at his back.

"It's Paddy." Isabella recognized him with a tremendous surge of relief. "Paddy's come."

XLI

Safe at Amberwood. Forever afterward, that was how Isabella thought of it. As soon as she saw the imposing Georgian house, she fell in love with the place. Consisting of thirty-two rooms plus servants' quarters, divided into three wings shaped into a U, the house was large and handsome, built of stone with a symmetrical facade and dozens of multipaned windows. It was set well off the road leading from Horsham to Tunbridge Wells, with many acres of parklike grounds surrounding it. The drive leading up to the front door ended in a circle at the steps.

Alec seemed uncharacteristically diffident when Amberwood came into view. Sandwiched into a chaise between Alec and Paddy, who was driving, Isabella exclaimed with pleasure at the property's beauty.

" 'Tis a lovely place," Paddy agreed, while Alec smiled wryly.

"I always feel like there should be a lord or at least a squire attached to my name when I come down here. The butler who came with the place is swanker than I am."

"But you own it," Paddy pointed out, speaking across Isabella in a tone that told her they'd had this conversation before.

"Aye, I own it." He glanced at Isabella. "I got it for practically naught, in a private deal to keep the previous owner from total financial ruin. At the time I was thinking of moving here—I've investments down this way that could stand keeping an eye on—but after a few visits I decided that I was more comfortable in London.''

''You can take the lad out of the slums, but you can't take the slums out of the lad,'' Paddy finished with a grin.

''Exactly.'' Alec grinned too, while Isabella, looking from the huge man driving to the leaner, handsomer one resting back against the seat, had to fight not to reveal the sudden pang that assailed her heart. The truth was that Alec felt uncomfortable at Amberwood because he considered himself inferior. . . .

''Who was the previous owner?'' she asked, to cover the fierce surge of protectiveness she suddenly felt.

Alec's sideways glance was wry. ''Wondering if you know him? Maybe you do—he's your sort. Lord Rothersham.''

''I don't know him.''

''Well, you've been sheltered. If you ever take your proper place amongst the *haute ton*, you can tell him how much you like his family home. Though I don't suppose you will. If you did, you'd have to tell him how you came to see it.''

Something in Alec's voice—a barely suppressed bitterness?—made her look quickly at him. Before Isabella could answer, Paddy was turning into the circle at the end of the long drive and pulling the chaise up before the door. The rag-tag cavalcade behind them followed suit, so that when the impeccably dressed butler opened the door, it was to see an odd assortment of carriages, horses, well- and ill-dressed men. His eyebrows lifted a mere fraction of an inch. Otherwise his expression was wooden as he surveyed the scene before calling out to someone inside the house.

''Good afternoon, Shelby.'' Alec's manner of greeting his butler was perfectly proper as he ascended the steps with Paddy's unobtrusive support. Isabella, slightly ahead of them, stepped through the door first. The entry hall was floored with marble in black and white squares laid on the diagonal. To the left a curving walnut staircase led upstairs. To the right closed double doors presumably opened onto a salon. The hall was furnished with a settee and a console table and mirror flanked by a pair of chairs. All very appropriate, but lacking . . . warmth?

"Good afternoon, Mr. Tyron. We were not expecting you, sir." Again, Shelby's words were perfectly proper, but like the house, lacked warmth. Only just inside the door, Isabella could well see why Alec had not been able to make this place his home. Owner or not, there was no welcome for him here.

By that evening, Isabella's initial impression had been amply confirmed. The staff, from Mrs. Shelby, the housekeeper, to the lowliest housemaid, all of whom had been kept on from Lord Rothersham, treated Alec with a kind of contempt that was no less evident for being heavily veiled. Isabella herself had requested that Paddy, Alec and herself be served their dinners on a small table before the fire in the enormous master suite, so that Alec, who had grudgingly consented to go to bed for the day, might be comfortable in a dressing gown and slippers. Upon receiving the order, the butler had made the mistake of raising his eyebrows at Isabella, who had responded with a stare so incredulous that the man had hastily decamped.

The meal had been delivered, and properly set out on a table covered with white linen and laid with silver, but the food was scarcely more than adequate. The celery soup, which should have been cold, was warm, and the mutton, which should have been hot, was not. In fact, all the courses were of approximately the same temperature. Isabella was not surprised to see Alec consume his meal without enthusiasm, and lay down his fork when he should have been no more than half-done. Paddy, who with his large frame was by necessity a prodigious trencherman, did a better job on the meal, but he too grimaced at the watery syllabub and pushed it aside barely eaten.

" 'Tis a mystery to me how Rothersham contrived to grow so fat on stuff such as this," Alec muttered wryly as he cut cigars for himself and Paddy in lieu of dessert.

Paddy grinned. "Only think how fat he would have been did he have a cook who could cook."

"True. Very true."

Isabella looked from one to the other. She was itching to take the running of the house in hand, but under the circumstances—after all, what status had she to give orders at Amberwood?—she disliked to put herself forward. Alec lounged back in his chair, a fresh bandage around his head, clean-shaven now with his hair neatly brushed into a queue at his nape, puffing on his enormous cigar. White wreaths of aromatic smoke circled his head. Paddy paced about, clad in boots, breeches and open-necked shirt, puffing on his cigar quite as furiously as Alec. The smell was enough to make Isabella faintly queasy—or maybe the slight sickness was the result of the meal.

"I believe I'll retire, if you don't mind," she murmured. It was obvious that Paddy had much to say to Alec, and it was equally obvious that he didn't like to say it with her present.

Alec removed the cigar from his mouth and looked at her. "I expect you to treat this as your home for the nonce, Isabella. Ring for whatever you need."

"I will. Good-night, Alec. Good-night, Paddy." She rose to her feet and, with a smile, left the room. The room she had been given was just along the corridor from Alec's. If truth were known, she would have preferred to share his—'twas funny how used she had grown to his presence, and how comforting, and comfortable, she found it—but if she shared his room, she would, sooner or later, end up in his bed. And she could not allow herself to sink to the level of mistress. . . .

The chamber she had been allotted was very grand. The walls were hung with yellow silk, the furniture was of fine mahogany, and the rug was an Aubusson. But dust had settled on the surfaces, and a cobweb adorned a ceiling corner. All in all, it was obvious that someone badly needed to take a hand with the housekeeping.

She pulled the bell. When a maid answered—after a wait of nearly a quarter of an hour—she requested a bath. This request, too, was filled slowly. But at last she was seated in a porcelain tub before the fire, rubbing scented soap into her hair and revelling in the blissful sensation.

Her bath complete, she stepped out, dried herself and put on a nightdress and wrapper from the baggage that, with Paddy and the others as bodyguards, they had retrieved from the wreckage. Then she sat on a footstool before the fire, rubbing her hair with a towel and fanning it so that it would dry in the heat. To her surprise, despite the unconventionality of her position, she felt oddly content.

Her hair was almost dry when a knock sounded at the door.

"Yes?" She felt suddenly nervous. The previous night's experience had left its mark on her.

" 'Tis I, Paddy."

"Just a minute." Reassured, she crossed to the door, opened it, and stood looking up at the scowling giant on the other side.

"Alec asked me to send you along to him." His voice was abrupt. Something in the way he looked at her made Isabella color.

"Oh."

Still Paddy stood there, looking down at her with that fearsome scowl. Having deepened her acquaintance with him over the last few weeks, Isabella knew that he was nowhere near as unapproachable as he appeared. Still, that scowl made her uncomfortable.

"Is ought the matter?" she asked finally when he continued to glare at her.

His frown deepened. "Alec talks about you all the time. Isabella this, Isabella that."

"Does he?" She colored even more furiously, and her eyes fell.

"He does." There was a long silence. Isabella finally looked up to meet Paddy's eyes. Those soulful brown eyes were hard, measuring. "I believe 'tis time and past that you went home. Did I have your husband killed, would you be willing to go? You'd have naught to fear, then."

Isabella stared at him in astonishment. "No!" Then, more loudly, "No!"

"No?"

"No! You cannot be serious! You'll have Bernard killed . . .?"

"If that's what it takes for you to be safe in your own world. You've been in ours too long."

"What are you talking about?"

"Alec. Alec is—he's gettin' grand ideas about you. I know him as well as I know myself, and I know he's gettin' set up to be badly hurt. 'Twould be best if you just went back to where you came from."

Isabella stared at him. Paddy met her look with that same fierce frown.

"I forbid you—forbid you, do you hear me?—to have Bernard killed. That's murder, and I won't be a part of it, nor permit Alec to be a part of it on my behalf. As for Alec and his grand ideas about me—I know of none. But our relationship is between him and me."

She met Paddy's gaze without flinching, little realizing how ridiculous it was for a slender, fine-boned young woman to try to stare down that monster of a man.

"Telling me to mind my own business, are you?" Paddy shook his head. "Alec is the closest thing to family I've got. He is my business, and I'd advise you not to forget it."

With a nod, he then headed down the corridor. Isabella watched wide-eyed until he vanished around a corner. For a moment longer she stood stock still, and then she picked up the skirt of her wrapper and went to Alec's room.

XLII

His door was not even locked, Isabella discovered as she turned the knob minutes later when there was no reply to her soft knock. Letting herself in, she saw that Alec was seated in a wing chair before the fire, his head bent over a newspaper that he held before him. So absorbed was he in whatever he was reading that he didn't even hear her enter.

Isabella closed the door with a little snap, and ostentatiously turned the key in the lock. She turned back to the room to find that Alec was looking at her at last.

"The door was not locked," she said in a scolding tone, walking toward him.

"Wasn't it? There's no real need for it. I'm hardly likely to be murdered in my bed. Paddy's got an army of men stationed on the grounds."

His carelessness with his own safety nettled Isabella. "And what if the murderer is already in the house?"

Alec laughed, folded the paper and put it aside. "Who? Shelby doesn't like me overmuch, but I don't see him slitting my gullet as I sleep. After all, I pay his salary. The same goes for the other servants. There's no one else here, except Paddy—and you. And I acquit either of you of designs on my life."

Isabella had to agree that both Paddy and she could be counted as perfectly safe housemates.

"Besides," he added placidly, "I asked Paddy to send

you along. I'll lock the door before I go to sleep, I promise."

Isabella stood beside the wing chair in which he sprawled, looking down at him with a frown.

"What did you want me for? Shall I change your bandage for you?"

Alec shook his head. " 'Tis fine. I expect to dispense with it altogether tomorrow."

"So soon?"

"I've suffered enough wounds in my life to know when one is serious. This one is not, believe me. The most I'll suffer will be a scar on my forehead, and such is not fatal."

"The doctor said—"

"I know what the doctor said." Alec's tone of voice as he interrupted said far more than his words.

"Do you suspect that Dr. McIver had a hand in what happened last night?"

"I don't know. I'm simply covering all the possibilities. I've men talking to McIver now. And to Hull. And John Ball, if they can find him."

"But he didn't know you were there until you came to the door for me."

"That's true. But he's long had designs on some of my crafts, and he's the kind of wily bastard who'd think killing me was the best way to take over. Still, he's only one of any number of suspects."

"Do you think you'll find out who it is—before they get to you? They're bound to try again."

"Aye, they'll try again. But I don't expect them to try at Amberwood. The place is too heavily guarded. And they know I'll be waiting for them this time." His eyes moved over her, widened. "That's a fetching nightdress."

Isabella, startled by the abrupt change of subject, looked down at herself and blushed. Seeing her embarrassment, Alec grinned.

" 'Tis a wrapper, and the most decent one I could find at the Carousel." The words were defensive.

"I'd give a schilling to see the ones you rejected as indecent."

"I'm sure you already have. They mostly belong to Pearl."

At the acerbic note in her voice his eyes rose from their leisurely inspection of her silk-clad body to her face.

"Did I not know better, Countess, I would suspect that what I detect in your voice is more than a touch of jealousy."

"And did I not know better, I would suspect that the wound to your head has addled your wits."

He laughed at that. "Touché, love."

His teasing had annoyed her, and she shifted impatiently, her bare toes curling into the oak floor.

"Was there something you wanted, or did you just call me in here to tease me? If so, I'll return to my own room."

Alec's eyes darkened. "Oh, aye, there's something I want."

There was a note in his voice that made Isabella cease to breathe. His eyes slid over her again, making it clear what he meant, while she drew herself up to her full height and prepared to wax indignant in the face of any indecent proposal he might make to her.

"I've a dressmaker coming tomorrow. You'll oblige me by ordering what you need from her. Everything, from the skin out. You cannot continue to go about in someone else's clothes."

"Very well." Isabella bowed her head. "I'll have a dress or two made up. If you'll take their cost out of whatever you intend to pay me."

Alec made a disgusted sound. "I'll have no more of your nonsense, Countess. I'll pay for what I wish, and you'll accept what I choose to give you with good grace. And that's my last word on the subject."

"Is it indeed?" Her eyes rose along with her indignation. "I—"

"Christ, do you argue this much with everyone or am I just lucky?" He muttered the words even as he caught her hand and yanked. Caught off guard, Isabella was pulled down into his lap without a struggle. She sprawled across his thighs, her bare feet thrashing helplessly, even as her eyes were caught and held by his.

"You have beautiful hair. It gleams like silk in the fire-light."

"Let me up, Alec." The words were a warning. Disregarding it, he lifted one hand to stroke the hair he praised, while the other held her effortlessly on his lap.

"I've grown disconcertingly accustomed to sharing my chamber with you at night. Surely you won't leave me to sleep alone, unprotected?"

"If you're fearful, get Paddy to sleep in here."

Alec grinned wolfishly. "Paddy, I'm afraid, is not quite the kind of companion I have in mind. I like my room-mates soft, and curvaceous, and smelling of lilacs. . . ."

"In short, any female will do," Isabella responded tartly, refusing to be seduced by the velvet voice.

"No." He shook his head. "No. There's where you're wrong, love. Any female definitely will not do. In the last few days I have discovered in myself a decided preference: the female I want must have skin that feels like silk and looks like cream, with an enchanting crop of freckles adding spice across her nose. She must have eyes as gentle as a dove's, and a soft, rosy mouth that begs for kisses even when the words coming out of it deny any such thought. She must have masses of hair that look a prim brown in the daylight, but by firelight take on a hue as lovely and rare as fine wine. She must be slender and delicately built, with breasts no bigger than a teacup, and a derríere that—"

"Stop it, Alec!" Blushing furiously, more than halfway to being seduced in spite of herself, she pulled a hand free and clapped it over his mouth to silence him. "You're wasting your silver tongue on me. I'll not be seduced, so there."

He said nothing, as her hand over his mouth stifled all utterance. But his eyes gleamed brightly gold at her, and to her dismay, his tongue came out to tickle her silencing palm.

"Alec!" Disconcerted, she jerked her hand away. "Let me up!"

His face was very close as he looked down at her, pretending to consider. Then, judiciously, he nodded.

"Very well," he said, making no move to release her. "I will—but you must first pay a forfeit."

"Oh, no." She had had experience with his forfeits before.

"Oh, yes. Or I'll be very happy to keep you just as you are all night."

She looked up at him measuringly. He smiled down into her eyes with beguiling sweetness, but she had seen the jut of that chin before. He meant what he said.

"What did you have in mind?" she asked warily. That sweet smile touched his lips again.

"A kiss," he said persuasively. "A single kiss, nothing more."

"I've no wish to kiss you."

"Now, there you lie. But I'll not argue with you about it. If you wish to get up, you must pay the price, and the price is a kiss."

"You're a swine, Alec Tyron."

"I'll not argue with you there either."

"And no gentleman."

"Definitely not."

It was hard to sound severe when, if truth were told, she was short of breath at the prospect of kissing him. That beautifully chiselled mouth hovered above her with tantalizing promise, while the golden eyes gleamed at her. Surely there was no harm in permitting herself a single kiss? A soft peck on his lips, and then she would be off his lap with temptation behind her.

"One kiss," she said sternly. "And you'll let me go."

"That's the bargain."

"Very well." She looked at him a moment longer, then hitched herself into a sitting position on his lap, slid a hand behind his head, and kissed him. The kiss was quick, a brief butterfly touch, but the feel of those soft, warm lips beneath hers had a galvanizing effect on her body. Quickly she pulled back.

"There."

"You call that a kiss?"

"I do indeed. Now let me up."

His face was scant inches from hers, their eyes almost on a level. One of her hands rested on his upper arm, the other on his shoulder. The silk of his dressing gown felt smooth and cool beneath her fingers. The flesh beneath was hard with muscle. The taste of his cigar was on her mouth. Her chin tingled where it had brushed the stubble on his. Her bottom was nestled in the cradle of his thighs. She could feel the effect that breath of a kiss had had on him. As for herself, her very nerve endings were atremble.

"You don't want to leave me." The words were soft, scarcely above a whisper. They brushed her cheek like a caress. Isabella caught her breath. Her eyes flew to his.

"We made a bargain, Alec." It was all she could do to remain firm.

His mouth tightened. "We did indeed. But I don't feel that you held up your end of the deal properly. This time I'll claim my own forfeit."

He bent his head, slowly, and captured her lips. Isabella didn't even try to turn her head away. Every instinct she possessed shrieked that what she was doing was wrong, dangerous even, that if she let him, he would break her resolve and probably her heart. But she simply could not resist the urge to experience once again the heady delight of his kiss. After all, she reassured herself, what was the harm in a mere kiss?

When his lips touched hers, she knew. When she gasped at the impact, her head tilting back to lie against his shoulder while he kissed her with devastating thoroughness, she knew. When her arms rose of their own accord to lock around his neck, and her tongue stroked his with shameful ardency, she knew. When the waves of rapture started to swell within her, and her reason threatened to be swept away on the tide of it, she knew.

She knew what the harm was. It was not in the kiss, it was in the man.

He was kissing her breathless, stealing her reason, carrying her away with him on a tide of passion too strong to resist. She trembled in his arms, made soft, passionate sounds into his mouth, tangled her fingers in his hair.

When he slid his lips across her face to her ear to nuzzle her sensitive lobe, then moved lower to make a meal of her neck, she could only lie with quivering abandon against his shoulder.

When his hand slid up to cover her breast through the thin layers of her wrapper and nightdress, she trembled from head to toe.

"Let me love you, Isabella," he whispered against her ear.

Her eyes fluttered open. His hand was dark and long-fingered as it splayed over the fragile white silk covering her breast. As she watched, his fingers tightened, squeezed her, sought and found the nub that was her nipple, rubbed it. Fire shot along her nerve endings. Her fingers curled convulsively into his shoulder.

Then from somewhere, she never afterward knew where, she summoned the strength to do what she must.

"No!" she cried, pushing his hand away from her breast and struggling to sit up. "No, no, no!"

Her rejection caught him by surprise. He permitted her to scramble off his lap, while he leaned back in the chair and looked up at her with a flushed face and narrowed eyes.

"I'll not do this, Alec," she said fiercely. "Do you hear? I'll not do it!"

"I hear."

"You promised that our relationship would be strictly business, and I hold you to your word. Do you not keep it, I'll leave, I swear."

He forbore to point out that she had nowhere to go. "I'll not force you to share my bed, Isabella. You need have no fear of that." His head still rested against the back of the chair as he watched her.

"No, I know you'll not force me," she said bitterly. "There's no need for that, is there? No doubt you're used to women melting like butter in your arms. But I cannot do it, do you understand? To let myself become your mistress would kill something inside me. I would be ashamed, Alec, bitterly ashamed. Every time I looked into a mirror I would think 'whore.' Do you have any smallest scrap of care for me, please don't burden me with that. I'm asking you because I know now that I'm weak where you're concerned. But you . . . you can have your pick of women. I'm just a novelty to you, and in a few weeks you'll wonder what you ever saw in me. I . . . I couldn't live with that. So I'm asking you, Alec, please leave me be. Please."

His eyes narrowed, and his lips compressed. "If that's the way you want it."

"It is."

He inclined his head, but his eyes were angry. She looked at him, bit her lip, and turned on her heel.

"Lock the door after me," she said, and let herself out into the hall.

XLIII

By morning Isabella felt positively drained. She had slept very little the previous night, and the coming of dawn was almost a relief. At least she no longer had to lie in her bed and worry. She dressed herself—it was amazing how difficult some of her garments were to do up without the assistance of a maid, but as a mere employee of Alec's, she did not like to presume to ring for assistance—and went downstairs in search of breakfast.

To her surprise, both Alec and Paddy were in the small breakfast room to which Shelby showed her. As she entered, they looked up at her with varying degrees of displeasure.

"Good morning," she said with what she felt was creditable ease. The two men grunted something by way of a reply, but neither stood. Isabella supposed that it was her place to point out this omission to Alec—after all, it was he who had requested her help to turn him into a gentleman—but after the words that had been exchanged between them the night before, she did not feel quite up to launching what she was sure would be another sharp exchange.

Besides, she would not embarrass him by correcting his behavior in front of Paddy.

Isabella helped herself to a rasher of bacon, a spoonful of egg and a cup of tea from the sideboard. When she sat down, across the table from Paddy and at Alec's left hand (she would have preferred to take her meal in solitary splendor at the opposite end of the long, rectangular table, but judged that doing so would have been too impolite), and began to eat, she saw immediately why most of the food still remained on Alec's plate.

The victuals were atrocious.

She put down her fork and sipped her tea, which had the advantage of being hot and strong, at least.

"Pray continue your conversation, gentlemen," she said as Paddy, who had been speaking when she entered, had fallen entirely silent.

Alec nodded. "You can talk in front of her."

Paddy shrugged. "I'll be seeing what I can do then. It shouldn't take more than a week or so, and then I'll be back. If it's concluded sooner, I'll send word."

"Your pardon, Mr. Tyron." Shelby stood at the door. Alec looked at him.

"The seamstress is here for, uh, the lady."

"You may address me as Lady Isabella," Isabella said, rising. In truth, she felt uncomfortable in Alec's company, and was nothing loathe to escape it. As for Paddy, he seemed to regard her with a degree of wariness. Shelby, with his sneering, superior ways, was another source of irritation, but she knew she could deal with him.

"Pray excuse me," she said to the room in general, and swept out. Shelby followed her, his face a study in confusion as he tried to reconcile her obvious quality and the name she gave herself with her presence with his ill-bred master.

"I put her in the little salon, if you will come this way, my . . . uh, my lady."

Isabella followed him. When he would have left her, she smiled serenely at him. "I'm sure Mr. Tyron would appreciate hot, well-prepared meals in future, Shelby. I know the cook must look to you for his orders, so I am confident that you will be able to see to it."

"Certainly, my lady." Shelby sounded taken aback, but Isabella noted that there was no longer any hesitation in his voice as he addressed her properly. As she entered the little salon, Isabella smiled to herself. She had been managing a household for years. Handling servants was one service she could quite legitimately perform for Alec.

The seamstress was a small, timid woman named Miss Stark. She was obviously ill at ease as Isabella walked into the parlor. Miss Stark was the daughter of a minister left on her own to make her way in the world, and she was clearly used to mistreatment by those she served. But Isabella's gentle smile soon put her more at ease, and as she produced her pattern books and fabric samples, she chatted quite volubly.

"There's been such talk in the village about Amberwood lately. You know, you'll laugh, I daresay, but some were saying that Lord Rothersham sold out to a Cit, or worse! Of course, I wouldn't be telling you this if I couldn't tell at a glance that you're of the quality, Lady Isabella. They do say that gossip is a fearsome thing, and now I can go back and quiet their wagging tongues. Oh, do you look at this! This style would be quite ravishing on you, do you not think?"

"It's lovely, but I require something more serviceable than decorative, I'm afraid. Perhaps—"

"Don't be a goose, Isabella." To Isabella's horror, Alec strolled into the room and stood looking down at the pattern book thoughtfully. Miss Stark blushed, and tried to get to her feet, although the heavy pattern book foiled her.

"Pray stay seated, Miss Stark," Isabella said hastily. "Alec, I am sure our business will be concluded much more expeditiously without your presence."

"Are you, indeed?" The look he sent her was mocking. "I, on the other hand, am positive you'll get nothing done without me at all. She has such conservative taste, you see, Miss . . ."

"Stark," Isabella said through her teeth before the little seamstress could reply. "Do go away, Alec."

"Your husband is most welcome on my account, my lady. After all, a gentleman's view of ladies' fashions is not to be despised. We do dress to please them, and I suppose they are the best judge of how we may do that."

"There, you see?" Alec grinned at Isabella in triumph, then disregarded the sizzling look she sent him to turn his attention to the pattern book. Isabella was left without a word to say. Miss Stark's easy assumption that Alec was her husband had thrown her off balance. Of course, if he was anything but her husband or a male relative—and his proprietary attitude had apparently precluded the possibility of that to Miss Stark's mind—then the gossip Miss Stark had related about Amberwood would be reinforced by the lady herself. And Isabella's own character would be irredeemably blackened, although under the circumstances, she didn't suppose that mattered. Best to hold her tongue and let the woman assume as she would.

"Isn't it fortunate that your wife has such a lovely, slim figure? She can wear the new high-waisted styles so gracefully! Take this gown, for instance. My lady would be lovely in it."

"I quite agree with you, Miss Stark. This style would be ravishing on Lady Isabella."

Over Miss Stark's head, which was bent over the pattern book, Alec's eyes met Isabella's. The mocking glint in them made her grit her teeth. He was embarrassing her, the fiend, and he knew it. She was convinced he was doing it deliberately.

"Ordinarily I do not involve myself in ladies' fashions, of course, but I want my wife's wardrobe to be slap up to the nines. She tends to favor quiet shades of blue and gray, but I would like to see her in warm colors: pink, maybe, and lavender, and perhaps soft yellow."

"You have a wonderful eye for color, sir! That is just what I would have recommended myself, had I dared to venture an opinion."

The little seamstress beamed at Alec, and the two proceeded to pour over the pattern book in perfect charity with each other. Isabella, left with nothing to do but silently seethe, was forced to either make a scene—which she was certain would be reported from one end of the countryside to another by Miss Stark's gossip-hating mouth—or acquiesce.

After styles were agreed upon between them—they seemed not to need Isabella's opinion at all, but rather discussed her as if she were not even present—then there was the matter of accessories. Alec insisted on slippers to match each outfit, and reticules, redingotes and even a sunshade to complement particular gowns. To Isabella's protests that she didn't need this or that, and certainly not so many gowns, both turned a deaf ear.

When, after about an hour, Miss Stark packed up her things to depart, Alec had ordered a complete wardrobe, from slippers to stockings to underclothes to outerwear and bonnets. Miss Stark was atwitter with excitement. She had already promised Alec one of the gowns by the following day, and the remainder within three more.

"If I must work night and day, I will," she said heroically as Alec escorted her from the room. "I shall carry out all we have agreed upon, sir, as quickly as it may be done."

"I am sure you will," Alec murmured by way of answer, rewarding her devotion to duty with a dazzling smile. Isabella, left behind, sniffed. Alec's charm had blinded Miss Stark to the truth of his character, just as it had Isabella herself and every other female she had ever seen him exercise it on. He used it quite deliberately, she was convinced, and when he returned to her, smiling, she told him so.

"You're turning into a regular scold, Isabella," he admonished lazily, throwing himself down on the settee he had shared with Miss Stark and stretching his arms up to lock his hands behind his head. He watched her from half-closed eyes, crossing his booted feet at the ankles as though to emphasize how little her displeasure disturbed him.

"Am I indeed?" she responded crossly from the other side of the room. "I suppose you will try next to tell me that a governess needs such a wardrobe?"

"No," he surprised her by saying. "But if you're to have the fun of turning me into as near a gentleman as is possible to do, then I reserve the right to have a little amusement of my own."

"Such as?" She eyed him warily.

He grinned at her, those golden eyes teasing. "Why, I mean to turn you into a regular little beauty, Isabella."

XLIV

"I wish you will stop your everlasting teasing." She crossed her arms over her chest in a gesture of annoyance.

"Believe me, I am very serious." That lazy smile matched his indolent posture.

Fulminating, she looked him up and down. He smiled at her.

"If I am to be your tutor, then I will give you my first lesson in decorum. A gentleman never sits while a lady stands."

"I make you my apologies." With a lurking smile and a handsome leg, Alec got to his feet. "Pray go on."

"A gentleman never, ever, presumes to discuss, er, unmentionables with a dressmaker, or any other lady, for that matter."

"Er . . . unmentionables?" Isabella was quite sure he knew to what she was referring.

"Underclothes," Isabella elucidated, mentally grinding her teeth.

"Oh. Ah, I see. I shouldn't have told Miss Stark that you require a dozen chemises, all of silk, or three dozen pair of stockings, or—"

"Hush, you devil!" Isabella crimsoned, and looked around to make sure that there was not the slightest chance that he had been overheard. Thankfully, they were quite alone.

"Am I embarrassing you?" he asked innocently.

"You know you are."

"Ah. Another solecism. I'm sure a gentleman would never embarrass a lady."

"No. A gentleman would not."

"What else would a gentleman do that I do not?"

"He would not be a dreadful tease!"

"Are you accusing me . . .? Isabella, you wound me; I protest you do!"

Isabella fixed him with virulent eyes.

"You—are—a—" She broke off, unable to come up with a word to properly describe the maddening creature.

"Yes?" he encouraged, grinning.

She set her teeth and refused to answer.

"Bastard? Son of a—"

"Stop!" Thoroughly incensed now, she marched up to him, finger pointing at him admonishingly. "So you want me to turn you into a gentleman, do you? All right, I'll do my level best. On top of the points I've already mentioned, a gentleman does not swear in the presence of a lady. He certainly does not try to provoke a lady into following his despicable example." Her eyes swept him. "You've mud on your boots. A gentleman would never come into a lady's presence in all his dirt without first apologizing, and begging her leave. You are coatless, and you seem to have mislaid your neckcloth as well. A gentleman never comes into a lady's presence unless he is fully clothed."

Her eyes swept him again, took in the breeches and shirt that, being too loose and too well-worn for fashion, had obviously been chosen strictly with comfort in mind. "You need a valet," she pronounced with satisfaction.

"A valet?" His tone was both dismayed and defensive as he looked down at himself. "Me? You aren't serious."

"A valet," she repeated with relish. "A gentleman's gentleman will see that you are well turned out on all occasions. He will help you to dress, and undress, and see that your boots are shined, your linen clean, your neckcloths starched, your hair properly trimmed."

"I don't need a bloody bishop to put my breeches on for me!"

"Ah-ah! Two transgressions! You swore, and you mentioned breeches (they're considered unmentionables, you know) in the presence of a lady! I can see that you're going to have to do a great deal of hard work. You're a sad case, indeed."

Alec's eyes narrowed. "Are you enjoying yourself, Countess?"

"Immensely." She smiled in such a way that it was more a baring of her teeth. "You did hire me to teach you to be a gentleman, did you not? Or, when faced with grim reality, have you taken the coward's route and changed your mind?"

His lips compressed. His eyes met hers, and held. "I'll tell you what, Countess. I'll make you a deal: I will put up with your nonsense if you put up with mine. I'll do whatever you say, within reason (and that means no bloody valet!) to be turned into a gentleman, if you will follow my dictates on how to become a beauty. Whatever I say, mind! Do we have a bargain? Or are you going to take the coward's route and refuse now that the agreement's become two-sided?"

"We have a bargain!"

He had deliberately goaded her into answering in the affirmative, and as soon as the words left her mouth she wondered if she was not being too hasty. Just how did he plan to turn her into a beauty? If he thought that she would fall for being told that the greatest beautifier of all was the exercise involved in warming a man's bed, he was very much mistaken!

"Within reason," she modified cautiously. She didn't trust the tricky devil one bit.

"Within reason," he echoed, grinning, and held out his hand. "I'll have your hand on it, Countess. I'm sure reneging on a deal can't be gentlemanly—or ladylike."

"No," she agreed. "It isn't."

And she gave him her hand. He shook it, briskly, and the deal was done.

As he tucked her hand in his arm and escorted her from the salon, Isabella felt more like a participant in a battle that had just been thoroughly joined than a partner in an agreement. Alec's very manner was unsettling to her nerves. He was acting the gentleman with outrageous punctiliousness, just to tease her again, she knew.

She only hoped that she would not live to regret the bargain they had made. But she was afraid she probably would.

XLV

Alec was as good as his word. The first dress arrived, as promised, late the following morning. To Isabella's dismay, a hairdresser, Mr. Alderson, showed up at Amberwood just after luncheon. Under strict orders from Alec not to cut the mass of her hair, he trimmed the ends and scissored a few strands so that they would curl about her face (despite Isabella's adamant protest that her hair would never, under any conditions, curl), and twisted the rest up on the crown of her head in a soft topknot. The effect, when Isabella was at last permitted to look into the mirror, was astonishing. Piled high, her hair took on a silken gleam that was almost striking. It was still plain light brown, of course, but the way Mr. Alderson had styled it revealed glinting strands of red and gold that she had never suspected she had. To her further astonishment, the small strands that he had cut short around her face did curl, as he had promised, enough to form a flattering frame for her face and bring out the size and shape of her eyes.

"And may I suggest just the suspicion of color on your lips, my lady? If you will permit. . . ." He pulled out a leather-bound box that, to Isabella's horror, contained cosmetics. Never before in her life had she worn such, and never had she expected to do so. Ladies didn't—although females like Pearl certainly did.

Pearl was certainly far more gifted with beauty than she was herself, but the paint helped enhance what nature had wrought. Perhaps it could do the same for her. Isabella was shaken by the sudden strength of her desire to be beautiful. Never before in her life had she minded being plain, but now there was Alec.

"All right, just a touch," she consented, and closed her eyes while Mr. Alderson rubbed a cream into her lips and cheeks, and brushed her eyelashes with what, by the smell of it, was a burned stick. The final touch was the whisking of a hare's foot over her face to, Mr. Alderson promised, eliminate shine.

"You may look now," he instructed.

Isabella opened her eyes.

The face that the mirror reflected back at her was hers. The features were the same, from the too wide mouth to the abominable freckles sprinkling her nose to the too-high forehead and pointy chin. But Mr. Alderson had wrought a miracle of alchemy in those unremarkable attributes. With her hair piled high on her head, her cheekbones suddenly seemed more prominent. The faint touch of pink, which even Isabella wouldn't have known was paint had she not felt Mr. Alderson's deft fingers at work, brought a sparkle to her eyes. Secretly Isabella had always considered her eyes to be her best feature—after all, what was there to find offensive in large eyes of soft blue-gray?—but like the rest of her, they had never been anything out of the ordinary. Now, framed in artfully darkened lashes, their color intensified by the wash of pink on her cheeks, they were positively luminous.

Isabella blinked, then blinked again, entranced at the unexpected effect. Her eyelashes, no longer colorless, were suddenly as thick and sweeping as chimney brooms. Alec had vowed to make her a beauty. He had not succeeded, of course. A beauty, she would never be. But she was certainly . . . pretty. Very pretty. Amazingly pretty, considering that she had sat down on the dressing table stool as a little brown wren. Now, looking at herself in the mirror, she felt as if she'd been turned into a peacock.

"Mr. Alderson," she breathed, "you are a worker of miracles!"

"I have done no more than bring out what was always there, hidden," he said modestly, surveying her reflection in the mirror with a satisfied air. "My lady has by nature a certain something not quite in the common style. It only needed to be shown off."

"Thank you," she said, turning on the stool to smile up at him. He nodded in reply.

"It was my pleasure, truly. I will leave with you the cosmetics you need, and you have only to use them thus"—he demonstrated the application technique of rouge and burned stick on himself—"then follow with a hare's foot just dipped in rice power. Do this each morning, and—*bellisima!*"

With a bow he left her. Isabella touched the little pots of rouge and powder with a hesitant finger. Paint was for hussies and light-skirts. . . . She looked in the mirror again. But the effect was so lovely. Perhaps she would use them, just a little, every day. At least while she was with Alec.

She knew, of course, that their time together was finite. Sooner or later, she would have to end this delightful interlude and return to being herself. Although quite how that was to be managed, she couldn't fathom. Perhaps if she talked with Bernard, and told him that she knew that he was behind her kidnapping and had schemed to get her killed, and that others knew too (no need to mention who the "others" were, because Bernard would certainly scorn the intimidation factor of people of Alec's class), perhaps then Bernard would be frightened into leaving her in peace. Perhaps Bernard now regretted what had happened. She could even, if necessary, petition for a bill of divorcement. Isabella shuddered at the thought of that. She would be the object of scorn and scandal, shunned by everyone, including (probably especially) her own family.

Without money of her own, how would she live?

Perhaps she need never go home. Perhaps she could stay with Alec forever. . . .

"Shall I help you with your dress now, ma'am?" Annie said. Isabella smiled at her. This unschooled country girl she'd taken to maid on Alec's orders was very far from her own dear Jessup, but she was biddable and eager and willing to learn. Isabella felt herself much the elder and wiser of the two, which was nice.

"Thank you, Annie, yes," Isabella said, standing up and removing her wrapper.

Miss Stark had included the necessary undergarments and even shoes and stockings with the dress. Annie was a little clumsy as she fumbled with lacings and buttons, and Isabella had to roll the stockings up her own legs. But when the dress itself was removed from its box and lifted over her head, and she stood looking at herself in the mirror as Annie did up the hooks in the back, she thought—and said—that not even a fine lady's dresser could have done a more creditable job.

"Thank you, ma'am," Annie smiled shyly. "You look a real picture, ma'am."

The woman Isabella saw reflected in the mirror made her catch her breath. The dress was of rose pink muslin with short, puffed sleeves, a scooped-out neck and an elegantly slim skirt. Burgundy ribbons trimmed the sleeves, and tied in a bow under her breasts, leaving the ends to flutter down the front of her gown.

The transformation begun by her new hairstyle was completed by the gown. Isabella's reflection was that of a lovely, fashionable lady of the *ton*.

When she went downstairs to join Alec in the library at the prearranged hour of four o-clock, she felt ridiculously ill at ease. He was sprawled on the blue upholstered settee, his long legs stretched out before him, his attention on the newspaper, which he held before him.

He looked up when she entered. Whatever he'd read in the newspaper had caused him to frown. But as he saw her, his eyes widened. Slowly he folded the newspaper and put it aside.

"By God," he said.

His reaction was everything she could have wished for. She smiled at him, shyly, and he slowly got to his feet. Still he stared.

"Turn around."

Isabella felt a blush color her cheeks as she obeyed.

"Well?" she said when she was facing him again.

He shook his head. "You were lovely before, in your own quiet way, but now—you could be the queen of the Carousel, love. Or anyplace else."

There was no mistaking his sincerity. Isabella looked into those golden eyes, and felt a rush of warmth. He was certainly no gentleman, far from it, in fact, but it occurred to her that he had been kinder to her than had anyone else in her life. Neither her kith nor her kin had ever given her more than the most lukewarm of compliments. Always those most closely related to her had held her to be of little value.

Unexpected tears rose in her eyes. She blinked to disperse them, glad that Alec hadn't seemed to notice. Tears had never been something that she had shed easily, and she did not mean to start for so silly a reason as a compliment.

"You've had your fun for the day. Now I'm to have mine. I've asked Mrs. Shelby to lay tea in the yellow salon."

"I'm agreeable."

"You must offer me your arm, and escort me to the table."

"Ah, I see. I'm to suffer lessons with my tea, am I Well, at least the brew will help wash them down. And will have you to feast my eyes on, of course. Countess?"

He offered her his arm with a gallant air that would not have been out of place from her father the duke. Isabella beamed approval at him, and placed just the tips of her fingers on his arm.

Then he grinned at her so wickedly that the illusion of gentlemanly grace was quite banished. But the reality of his charm—Isabella had to admit that the beguiling creature had that in spades.

XLVI

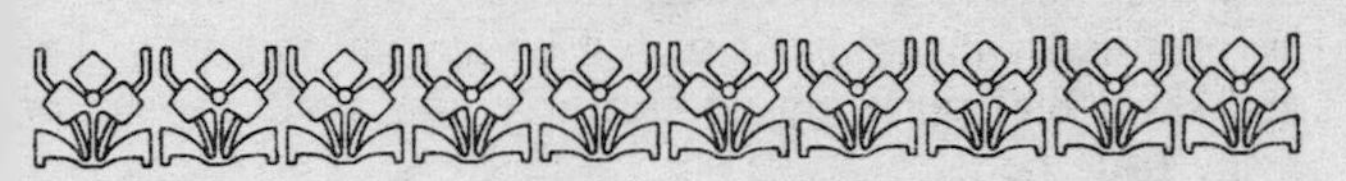

For the next fortnight, while Paddy scoured London for Alec's would-be assassin, and a small army of men lurked in Amberwood's well-trimmed bushes trying to look inconspicuous as they guarded Alec, Isabella was happier than she had ever been in her life. She bedeviled Alec about his manners, provoked him into losing his temper and then reproved him for both his swearing and his lapse of diction, teased him about his disdain for proper attire (neckcloths and coats he preferred to do without much of the time), and generally performed exactly the duties that he had professed to hire her for. Why that should annoy him so much, she said, she simply could not understand. The saucy grin that accompanied her prim words earned her a retaliatory swat on her derrière. Promptly she reproved him for that, too.

If truth were told, though, Alec, for all his occasional lapses in the sphere of formal manners, was very much a gentleman. He made no further attempt to lure, cajole or seduce Isabella into his bed, and was, instead, a delightful companion. Rather than being cooled by this forbearance on his part, Isabella's attraction to him increased by the day. She discovered that she liked her handsome ruffian quite as much as she desired him.

Alec kept his part of their bargain, too, sending Isabella back upstairs when, the day after their encounter in the library, she tried to revert to type. She was more comfortable with her customary hairstyle and with no paint on her face, although the gowns Miss Stark had made up were admittedly far superior to the ones she had requisitioned from the Carousel. But Alec was adamant. If he was to put up with the tomfoolery she insisted on foisting upon him in the name of her "duties," then she must do her part and work at being the beauty. She'd soon get used to it, he promised, and then it would be second nature to her and she'd feel perfectly comfortable as a belle instead of a shy little hen.

One afternoon about three weeks after they had arrived, Isabella had an idea for bedeviling Alec that topped any she had yet thought of. If he wanted to be a gentleman, she announced straight-faced, then he must learn to ride.

"I drive very well, thank you," he said in answer to her suggestion.

"Gentlemen ride as well as drive. Surely it has been an inconvenience to you, as carriages can only go where there are roads. On horseback, you can go anywhere at all."

"London has a very fine road system, as does the countryside. Riding about on an animal's back has never seemed to me to be a necessity. Or even particularly desirable."

"Don't tell me you're afraid!"

"Don't be daft."

"Well, then, you must see that it would be an advantage to be able to ride astride if you wished. And here am I, ready and able to teach you. What could be more fortunate?"

"Ready and able to have a good laugh at my expense when I fall on my arse," Alec said dryly. Isabella's gurgle of laughter brought a reluctant smile to his face, but still he demurred. "I'll not do it, Isabella. Teach me something else."

"I do so love to ride." Isabella looked wistful. "I had hoped you would learn to like it, too. We could have wonderful rides together. But if you refuse to make the attempt, then of course, there is nothing more to be said."

Alec eyed her. "You're a minx, Countess. Don't think

for a moment that you are fooling me with that pitiful expression. But I suppose I will agree. Provisionally. One fall on my arse is all I'm willing to tolerate."

"I wouldn't dream of asking for a greater sacrifice. Let me go change, and I'll be right back."

This conversation had taken place on the terrace at the rear of the house. Less than a quarter hour later Isabella had returned, clad in her new bottle green riding habit, and caught Alec's hand to pull him in the direction of the stable.

"I doubt that I even have any riding horses," Alec said sourly as he let himself be led.

"Certainly you do. I already checked."

"Been planning my comeuppance for a while, have you? How do I know that this is not some fiendish plot to murder me? It's more likely to succeed than all the knives and bullets they've been throwing at me lately."

"You'll love it, Alec, once you get used to it. Trust me."

"I wonder why I don't."

They reached the stables then, and Alec, with a distinct lack of enthusiasm in his voice, ordered two horses saddled. The groom accepted that order with a pull of his forelock, and turned to do Alec's bidding.

After a swift look at Alec, Isabella called after him, "Gentle ones, mind. I'm something of a nervous rider."

"I bought the property intact, servants and livestock included. Had I known then what I was letting myself in for, I wouldn't have done it."

"You're nervous."

"Not at all. I'm perfectly resigned to breaking an arm, a leg, or even my neck."

"You won't, I promise."

The groom led the horses out. A large bay had been saddled for Alec, while Isabella's mount was a dainty sorrel mare.

"What are their names?" Isabella asked.

"The mare's 'Epzebah, miss, and the bay's 'Annibal. 'Is lordship were that fond o' namin' 'em strange." He cast a quick glance at Alec as he spoke, and looked suddenly uncomfortable, as if he feared he might have spoken out of turn.

Alec spoke up unexpectedly. "You're Tinsley, aren't you?"

The groom's discomfort changed to apprehension. "Aye, sor."

"And you've worked for me for—what?—two years now?"

"Three, sor." Tinsley looked even more alarmed. Clearly he feared that he was on the verge of being dismissed out of hand for his unfortunate reference to Lord Rothersham.

"And I haven't been to the stable in all that time, have I? Well, I've been lax, but then, I've been busy. 'Tis a good job you've done, keeping the stable and animals up the way you have with none to oversee. I appreciate it."

"Why, thank you, sor. Mr. Tyron." The groom was near stuttering in surprise. A hesitant smile crossed his face, to be quickly wiped clean as he resumed the proper expressionless demeanor. But Isabella realized that in that brief exchange Alec had gone far toward winning the loyalty of this one servant, at least.

"Shall I 'and you up, miss?" Tinsley offered as Alec made no move to. Isabella glanced over at Alec, to find him eyeing the big bay with carefully concealed misgiving. Casting a quick glance at Tinsley, who awaited her answer, she realized how damaging it would be for Alec to reveal his lack of experience with horses in front of the groom. All the servants, who as a class were notoriously greater snobs than their rightful masters, apparently took Alec for a jumped-up Cit, and despised him accordingly. But even Cits could ride. If it were to be bruited about that Alec could not, the servants' contempt would both solidify and escalate enormously. Amongst the upper classes, children rode almost before they walked. There was no truer mark of a Cit than awkwardness around horses. Alec's lack of any experience in the saddle marked him. Isabella discovered that she hated the notion of a servant or anyone else sneering at Alec, no matter how discreetly. With a sudden fierce surge of protectiveness, she resolved to make the riding lessons completely private, away from prying eyes. Furthermore, she would do her utmost to turn him into a creditable rider.

"Would you mind if we walked the horses a little ways?" she asked Alec with a pretty air of apology, assumed for the groom's benefit. Alec lifted his eyebrows at her, but the very alacrity with which he agreed showed her how ready he was to postpone their lesson. Smothering a smile, she tugged on her own mount's reins.

Hepzebah obediently followed, and Alec, leading Hannibal, fell into step beside her. Neither animal was a bit skittish, and Isabella could only assume that they had been regularly and thoroughly exercised. She suspected that Tinsley had been making use of Alec's absence to ride his horses. On any other property, that would have been grounds for dismissal, but under the circumstances it had been for the best.

As they headed down the lane that led away from the stable, two men fell into step a discreet distance behind them. Alec, seeing them, halted, and beckoned. The two men approached. Both were scruffy fellows, and from their clothes it was obvious that they were not country-bred. Isabella immediately guessed that they were part of the army Paddy had set to guard Alec, and their words confirmed that.

"Aye, Tiger?"

"There's no need for you to dog my every step. Keep watch of the house, and if I've a need for you, I'll fire off my pistol."

"But Mr. McNally said we weren't to let you out o' our sight." The younger of the two, clearly green and eager, protested, only to be silenced by his elder's look of horror, and abrupt shushing motion.

"Mr. McNally tends to be overprotective," Alec replied with good humor. "Now, go on back to the house. Who knows? Someone may be sneaking in a window even now."

''Not bloody likely, with—'' the younger man began, forgetting himself once more. The elder grabbed his arm and dragged him away.

''I make you 'is apologies, Tiger,'' he said over his shoulder, keeping his grip on the younger man. '' 'E's green, and 'e don't know nuttin'.''

Alec waved them away. As the elder dragged the younger off, Isabella heard him say, ''You bloomin' idiot, that was the Tiger. I've seen 'im slit a man's throat that dared to gainsay 'im.''

''Did you really?'' Isabella asked with a sidelong glance at Alec as they resumed their walk.

''Did I really what?''

''Slit a man's throat for arguing with you?''

Alec shrugged. ''I don't recall the incident, but if Buzz says so, who am I to argue? 'Tis how reputations are made.''

''Oh.'' Rarely now did she remember who and what he was, and how he had made the money that had enabled him to buy such as Amberwood. The ruthless criminal had long since been supplanted in her mind by her dear Alec. It was a jolt to be reminded that there was another side to him.

They walked in silence until the lane passed through a small copse of trees to a grassy meadow. The wood hid the meadow from the stable and the house. To Isabella's eyes it was a perfect place for their lesson.

''This will do, '' she said, and led her own horse over to the grass.

''At least the ground looks soft. Oh, look, there are even some blades of grass. Perhaps I won't break my neck after all.''

Isabella gave him a dampening look, and put her own reins over Hepzebah's neck.

''Just do what I do, to start. You mount from the left.''

''I know how to get on the bloody beast. 'Tis staying on that concerns me.''

So saying, he got his reins in position, put his foot in the stirrup, and swung aboard. But he held the reins too loosely, and Hannibal immediately dropped his head and started to crop at the just-sprouting grass. Alec pulled his head up. Hannibal, unhappy over being deprived of his treat, stomped his foot and tossed his head. Alec tightened the reins some more, and Hannibal, with more angry head tossing, began to back up. Alec looked so uneasy and at the same time so determined to prove himself master of the situation that Isabella had to laugh.

XLVII

"Enjoying yourself, are you, Countess?" Alec eyed her narrowly.

"Immensely," said Isabella, not bothering to swallow the huge grin that wreathed her face. "Ease up on the reins, Alec. Hold them loosely, so."

She demonstrated with her own reins. Alec, looking wary, relaxed his grip. Immediately Hannibal stopped backing and stood still.

"Very good." Isabella urged Hepzebah closer. "Now let's try going forward. Squeeze a little bit with your knees and kind of cluck. Like this." She demonstrated, and Hepzebah walked forward while Isabella turned in the saddle to watch Alec.

He followed her instructions, and Hannibal walked sedately after Hepzebah. Isabella had to turn quickly away to hide her laughter.

"What's so funny?" Alec called from behind her.

She turned in the saddle.

"You cluck just like a lovesick pigeon," she giggled. He frowned at her, but in the face of so much merriment he finally had to smile.

"I'll get you for this," he threatened. "Just wait until we're back on the ground. You'll pay in spades."

"Pooh," she said inelegantly. "You don't scare me." She circled Hepzebah around so that she could better observe Alec's seat. "Pull your elbows in and put your heels down. Sit up straighter. There. That's very good."

"I feel a bloody fool," Alec grumbled, and that set Isabella off again. She giggled like a schoolgirl as Alec on Hannibal plodded around the meadow again.

"You'll be riding like a centaur in no time."

Her unenthusiastic pupil completed his third circuit, looking so very put-upon that Isabella could not stop laughing. Her laughter earned her a censorious look as he pulled Hannibal up beside her.

"I think I'll stick with driving, thank you very much."

"You're doing wonderfully. So wonderfully that I think we should try a trot."

He all but groaned. "Couldn't we save that for another day?"

"I have a feeling that on another day I might have a hard time getting you in the saddle. Don't be a pudding-heart, Alec. Come on."

She set Hepzebah to circling the meadow at a placid trot, for the most part keeping her face carefully forward so that Alec couldn't see her huge grin, and watching him via sidelong glances thrown over her shoulder. When the circuit was completed, she did her best to sober her expression, then turned to look at him.

"How was that?"

"Just fine."

The very sourness of his tone threatened to make her lurking grin break forth. With a great deal of effort, she managed to hold it back.

"All right, let's try it again. Watch me."

She urged Hepzebah into a trot, her hands properly bent at the wrist and her back ramrod straight as she adjusted to the horse's movements. For as long as she could remember, she'd been riding, and the basics were as natural to her as breathing.

"Of course, you'll do it a little differently since you're riding astride. Just let your knees take your weight, and adjust your movements to his stride. That's right. Once around the meadow."

Alec had set Hannibal in motion and, teeth set, was bobbing up and down on his back with almost as much grace as a chicken in flight. From the grim set of his chin she could see that what she considered amusement, he considered an ordeal, but she refused to allow him to give it up. All teasing aside, Alec really did need to learn to feel at home on a horse. He was too intelligent, too capable in every respect to be handicapped in such a way.

Despite his grim determination, he was not a natural horseman. If some people were born to the saddle, Alec was definitely not one of them, Isabella decided, watching as her reluctant pupil came back to her. It charmed her to realize that in this area in which she excelled Alec was deficient. The turnabout was a novel experience, and it enchanted her.

"I feel like every tooth I have has been shaken loose," Alec complained as he pulled Hannibal up for the umpteenth time.

"You're doing very well," Isabella soothed. "Try it again."

"Again?" At Isabella's nod, he grudgingly obeyed.

He was looking more comfortable, she judged as he came back to her again, and seemed to have lost much of his initial tenseness. If he would only relax a bit more, his spine would not be forced to endure so many jolting encounters with the saddle, and so she told him.

"You're enjoying this," he accused her, and the grin she could not repress was answer enough.

"Now we canter," she said by way of a reply, and he groaned again.

By the time the afternoon was over, Alec had shown considerable progress. Isabella had to revise her initial evaluation of his abilities again and again. Forced into the saddle, he seemed to develop a sudden determination to master the task she had set him to. Isabella wondered how much of that determination was spurred by a resolve to impress her and how much was innate. Both, she thought. A man without a will of iron would never have made the spectacular climb from the gutter that Alec had. But he was very much a man, and men, like little boys, loved to show off.

"My stomach moans for sustenance. Can we call a halt now, Madame Tutor? Or are you determined to keep me out here until I beg for mercy?"

"We can go back, if you like. You truly did very well. You'll be riding to the hounds in no time."

He snorted, and fell into step beside her as she turned Hepzebah toward the stable.

"I'm more likely to sell every horse in the stable. Tell me, pray, why you insisted on walking the horses to begin with."

The unexpected change of subject flustered Isabella. She had thought he was so thankful for anything that would postpone their lesson that he would not comment on her peculiar behavior in the stable. Glancing at him, she decided on honesty.

"I did not want the groom to know that you are not at home on horseback."

"Did you not, then? And why is that?"

"Because . . . because . . ."

"Because you didn't want him to think the less of me for it, or because you didn't want him to think the less of you for being in my company?"

His perception caught her off guard. Had she once been so full of her own self-importance that she might have felt shame to be seen in his company? If such had ever been the case, it was true no longer. To her, Alec was . . . Alec. He had transcended all boundaries of class and privilege in her eyes.

"I did not wish him to think the less of you, of course. I feel no shame at all in being in your company. On the contrary, in fact."

He looked over at her then, suddenly more at ease on horseback than he had been all afternoon.

"I don't pretend to be more than I am, you know. You need not try to protect my feelings from servants and fools. There are few parts about me that remain tender, and my emotions are not one of them."

"I wonder, then, that you have taken the trouble to educate yourself, to learn to speak like a gentleman, to behave like one. If you are satisfied with what your birth gave you, why, for instance, did you wish me to tutor you in the ways of gentility?"

His mouth twisted. "Because I don't choose to be limited by my birth. Those who are low-born are not intrinsically less intelligent or capable than the nobility, you know. In fact, I am not convinced that the opposite is not true. I'm a gutter rat by birth, spawn of a mother who was likely a whore and a father who could have been any son of heaven or hell. Everything I have, I have gotten for myself. Every mite of education, every schilling, every nod of respect. I'm not ashamed of it, I'm proud. I'd like to see any bloody lordship do what I've done. He'd not have survived his first week on the streets of Whitechapel."

Sudden lines of bitterness appeared in his face. Glancing over at him, Isabella was struck by just how far he had brought himself through sheer force of will. For the self-described gutter rat to have become the owner of all this, and more besides, for him to have retained his humor and human kindness and dignity in the process, was truly remarkable. The circumstances of his youth must have been horrendous to cause such an expression to come over his face when he contemplated it.

"Tell me what it was like, Alec. Your childhood."

The bitterness vanished, replaced by a wry smile. "I had no childhood. Come, let's talk of pleasanter things. Like how lovely you look with the sun shining on your hair. It's a kind of dark gold, with red threads. Most entrancing."

"I have the greatest admiration for you. I want you to know that." She spoke earnestly, ignoring his attempt to change the subject. "I am proud to be in your company."

His face seemed to tighten fractionally, but still he smiled. "Careful, Countess, you'll unman me. Look, we are close on the stable. Do we dismount and walk in, to save me from any possibility of looking the fool? Or do we say the devil take the groom, and ride up bold as brass?''

''Whatever you wish.'' It was clear he meant not to talk of anything sensible, so Isabella let it go.

''I say we ride up.''

And so they did. Tinsley came out to take the horses, treating both Isabella and Alec with equal deference. When Alec swung down, Isabella thought she detected a slight grimace on his face, but he walked her back to the house without complaint.

Inside the front hall, she turned to him.

''I must bathe and change before dinner. Shall I join you in the yellow salon at half past seven?'' A glimmer of a smile touched her face. ''We can resume our lessons then.''

''Do you mean to never let me rest, woman?'' Alec grinned at her good-humoredly as he raised his eyebrows at Shelby, who had come gliding silently up to him.

''Very well then, at half past seven.''

XLVIII

Alec's table manners were acceptable, due as much to his natural fastidiousness as any training his actress friend might have given him. Watching him as they ate, Isabella thought that if she hadn't known his identity and had just met him as a nameless stranger, she would have assumed him a gentleman without a second thought. Impossible to believe that those perfectly carved, patrician features could belong to anything less. Impossible to believe that the humor and intelligence, the quick charm and wit of him, had been bred in the gutters of London.

Dressed in impeccable black evening wear—Alec had flatly vetoed the valet, but Isabella had enlisted a footman to take care of his clothes and, on this particular night, to lay out what she wished him to wear—with the light from a dozen candles turning his hair to the same gleaming gold as his eyes, he was so handsome that just looking at him gave her pleasure.

Her handsome Alec; the thought with all its ramifications of possessiveness both frightened and pleased her.

"The food is considerably better," Alec said, motioning to Shelby for more wine. He'd drunk rather more than was his custom tonight, and as a consequence of having her glass frequently topped off, Isabella had as well.

"I had a word with the cook. I hope you don't mind." It was amazing what culinary prowess could be uncovered by a simple threat to allow the behemoth in the kitchen to look for a position more to his liking.

"If these are the results, I certainly don't mind. In fact, I salute you." Alec raised his glass to his mouth and drained it with the words. At his signal, Shelby was immediately at his shoulder with the bottle to fill the empty glass again.

It occurred to Isabella that she had never seen Alec drink to excess before. She frowned at him.

"Is something wrong? You seem to have developed a powerful liking suddenly for wine."

Alec looked at her almost craftily. Isabella's eyes widened on his face. Their eyes met, Alec's secretive, Isabella's alarmed. Then, suddenly, he grinned.

"What skulduggery are you imagining, I wonder? 'Tis merely that today's lesson was hard on one of my few remaining tender spots, and I was hoping that wine might help dull the pain."

For a moment Isabella didn't understand. Then comprehension, and with it growing amusement, dawned. "Are you telling me that you're saddle-sore?"

"If that's the term for the portion of my anatomy designed for sitting being unable to carry out its function without causing me acute discomfort, then yes."

"Oh, my. I didn't think of that," Isabella confessed. Her eyes began to twinkle, and despite her best efforts, she broke into a wide grin.

"Nor did I. Had I thought of it, not all the fluttering lashes in England would've gotten me on the back of that bloody great beast."

"Don't swear," Isabella said automatically as a footman removed their plates and replaced them with the dessert course. "I'm truly sorry you're suffering discomfort, Alec."

"You look truly sorry. Shelby, break out some of that French liqueur that we purchased very honestly since the cessation of hostilities. This syllabub sets ill on my palate."

"Should you drink so much?"

"Don't worry, I haven't been in my cups since I was a lad of fourteen and almost entered into service in His Majesty's Marines."

"Tell me about it," Isabella begged, enchanted at the tantalizing picture this conjured up.

Alec took a healthy swallow of the greenish liqueur, and complied. "Paddy and I'd prigged a load of French brandy, and sold most of the bottles on the street for thrice their worth. We kept two, one for each of us, and proceeded to down the contents in something under an hour. After that we went prowling the streets—it was night by then, you understand, but not over-late—and happened to cast our eyes upon an advertisement inviting all loyal young men who had an eye for riches and glory to repair to a certain locale, where they might have the honor of being enrolled in His Majesty's Marines. The part about riches and glory certainly caught our eye—before we'd lucked on the brandy, we'd but fourpence between us, and to save our meager horde, had eaten but once in two days. We talked together, and decided that a change of scene was what we needed. Not that we were foolish enough to believe all the bombast in the advertisement, but we thought His Majesty's service might offer honest employment, which generally is rewarded with an honest wage.

"We went up to a street in Westminster, to the location specified in the ad, and found ourselves in due course before a Captain of a marching regiment. He was all for taking likely lads such as ourselves—Paddy in particular caught his eye with his size, but I, being taller than the average for my age, was acceptable too. Fortunately I bethought myself to inquire about the wages His Majesty would pay us for doing his glorious work. Imagine my dismay at being told the pay was but sixpence a day! Paddy, far more than three sheets to windward still from the brandy we had consumed, considered that a great sum, but I, with my wits not quite as befuddled as his, did some calculations and discovered that, in our single night of selling stolen brandy, we had made more blunt than we would have in a year of service with His Majesty's Marines!

"As Paddy was in no case to be reasoned with, I dragged him out of there on the excuse that we needed to answer nature's call and would return forthwith. Needless to say, that was the last that Captain saw of us, although the brandy smugglers soon got to know and loathe us, by reputation if not by name, as we began to regularly relieve them of their wares."

Alec grinned, took another swallow of the liqueur, grimaced, and gestured for a refill. Isabella took a drink from her glass too—quite good, the liqueur was, with a minty taste and smell—and waited for him to continue. When he didn't, but continued to sip at his liqueur with a reflective smile on his face, as though he was reliving old memories, she prodded him.

"You never did enlist?"

He shook his head. "Sober, I found the notion appalling. Why should I—or Paddy—offer myself up as cannon fodder for King and country when King and country had never done ought for me? Sixpence a day was not near enough of an inducement."

"So you peddled stolen brandy instead. Is that how you got your start?"

"You mean, was that my introduction to a life of crime? No. I'd always made my way by thievery, stealing whatever I could lay my hands on, and keeping or selling it as the need and mood struck me. But it was that night that I realized just how much money a clever lad could make. And I was right. We never went hungry again after that, nor had to go begging, nor accept handouts from Pearl."

His careless reference to Pearl was unexpectedly painful to Isabella. Pearl had been there from the beginning, taking care of Alec when he was a ragged, hungry youth, a friend and lover for decades before Alec had ever become aware of Isabella's existence. Once the novelty of her title wore off, how could she ever compete with a relationship like that? Then, shocked at herself, Isabella wondered that she even thought of competing for Alec.

Her world was not his. Hers was sunshine, his shadow. Like Persephone with Hades, she could not spend all her life in her lover's underworld Kingdom. Sooner or later, she must once again seek the sun.

Disturbed, she swallowed the contents of her glass with a gulp worthy of Alec, and stood up. The liqueur immediately went to her head, making her sway slightly. Isabella clutched the back of her chair, and stood her ground.

Alec looked up at her, mildly surprised at her abrupt termination of their dinner. But he drained his own glass and rose too, offering her his arm with a courtly bow.

"Shall we repair to the yellow salon, Countess?"

"That's very well done of you," she answered admiringly, coming around the table to place her hand on his arm in the correct fashion. "The Prince Regent couldn't have done it better."

"But then, Prinny has to contend with a corset, and I do not." He was smiling as he escorted her into the yellow salon and closed the double doors, after shaking his head negatively to Shelby's inquiry about whether they would care for coffee to be served. "What shall we do now for after-dinner entertainment? Should you like to play at cards, or shall we discuss improving tomes we have lately read?"

Isabella considered the possibilities he had funningly proposed, then shook her head. A daring idea had come to her, one that, in the cold light of day, she never would have considered. But it was not day, it was night, and she was locked in the Kingdom of her underworld prince, where everything was slightly unreal. The only certainty was that his arm was warm and strong beneath her hand, he was handsome enough to take her breath, his smile dazzled her with its charm—and she greatly feared that she might be falling in love with him. Certainly some intense emotion must account for the dizziness she suddenly felt when looking up into that unfairly handsome face.

"Then what?" Her hand reluctantly left his arm, and he leaned back against the closed doors, watching her.

She took a deep breath. "I propose that we continue our lessons."

"I've no intention of climbing on the back of another bloody horse—and particularly not after dinner."

"No, lackwit," she said, smiling a little. "I meant another kind of lesson. Like—dancing."

"Dancing?"

"You have heard of it? Ladies and gentlemen do it together—you know, da dum, da dum?"

She swayed and pirouetted in front of him, one hand daintily holding up her daffodil yellow skirt while the other rested on the shoulder of an imaginary partner. The snatch of song she hummed was as light and gay as she was. Her voice had never been known for its musicality, and tonight, under the influence of strong drink and stronger emotion, it was even less on-key than usual. But neither of them noticed, or cared for such a triviality as that.

As he watched her, the light in his eyes flared, then darkened. His arms crossed over his chest. "I do believe you've had more wine than is good for you, my girl."

"Is that what this strange feeling is? If so, then I quite see why gentlemen are so frequently in their cups. It feels quite marvelous. Come, Alec, will you not dance?"

"If you wish." He smiled suddenly, not proof against her pretty persuasion, came away from the door, and held out his arms. Isabella floated into them as if they were the one place she longed to be—as indeed they were. "But I warn you, I've less experience dancing than sitting the back of a bloody horse. I'm likely to trod on your toes, love."

That homely endearment, accompanied as it was by the feel of his arms about her—a feeling that she had both craved and feared for weeks—completed Isabella's intoxication. She smiled up at him radiantly, one small hand resting on his broad shoulder, the other clasping his in the correct stance for a waltz.

"It's easy. Just follow my lead," she breathed into the warm skin of his neck, tugging him in the direction she wanted him to go. "One-two-three, one-two-three, dip, turn, sway—no, it's I who am supposed to sway. Oh, dear, I fear I am teaching you the lady's part."

"No matter. I quite like dancing." His voice, so close to her ear, was husky. Isabella discovered as she steered him through another turn, humming tunelessly all the while, that he was holding her rather closer than propriety—or the dance—dictated. She made no effort at all to pull away. Instead she snuggled just the tiniest bit closer, and led him through the movements of the dance. A sense of breathless anticipation bubbled to life inside her. It felt so good to be held by him again, to have his arm about her waist and his head bent over hers, to feel the tingle of her breasts as they brushed his hard chest. She inhaled deeply, closing her eyes as she continued to hum the rhythm and move her feet in the patterns of the dance. He smelled of soap, and cigars—he had had one before dinner—and man. He was warm, and solid, and strong—and hers.

Hers?

Just then his foot made brutal contact with hers as he had prophesied it would. Isabella, wrenched from her imaginings by the shooting discomfort in her toes, made a pained sound, her eyes flying open as a grimace contorted her face. Alec had lifted the offending foot almost as soon as it had crushed down on hers. Now he pulled away from her, shaking his head in apology.

"I did warn you," he reminded her. "I'm sorry, love. Did that hurt?"

Isabella was surprised to find that, compared to the pain of no longer being held close in his arms, her abused foot hurt not at all.

She shook her head, and held out her arms to him. "It's all right. You haven't crippled me. Shall we continue?"

To her dismay, he shook his head. "I think I've had enough dancing for one evening, thank you. If I don't take care, I fear I may find myself as intoxicated on you as you are on the wine. And that would never do, would it, Madame Tutor?"

His voice was thicker than usual. Isabella absorbed that,

along with the hard, restless glitter in his eyes. The pupils seemed to contract and then expand with some unknown emotion as they slid from her face down the front of her dress and back again. A quivering excitement sprang to life inside her, a sense of herself as enchantress and him as the enchanted.

"So you're tired of dancing, are you?" she murmured, stepping closer so that her breasts brushed his chest again. His hands came up to grip her upper arms, bare beneath the puffed sleeves of her gown, and he looked down at her in a considering way that did strange things to her breathing.

"Isabella . . ."

"I, on the other hand, could dance all night—with you."

"You're more than a little tipsy, love."

"If I'm tipsy, then 'tis a wonderful state." Her hands came up to rest on his chest, palms flat against the pristine white of his shirtfront, head tilted back as she smiled beguilingly into his eyes.

He caught his breath. She heard it quite distinctly.

"You're going to regret this, Isabella." The warning was laced with a note of wry humor, but underneath it lay a hard foundation of gathering passion, of need that burned at least as hotly as hers.

"If I do, it'll be too late, won't it? We'll already have had tonight."

Emboldened by the strength of her desire for him, or the spirits she had consumed—she couldn't say which and didn't much care—she slid her hands up his shirtfront, over the broad, tensed shoulders, to link behind his neck. With her arms around his neck she pressed herself against him, smiling, her head tilted back and her lips slightly parted.

"You're right, of course." He smiled down at her then with devastating effect, the hard restlessness in his eyes flaring into something far hotter and brighter. "Whatever fireworks tomorrow may bring, we'll have tonight."

XLIX

But when he would have kissed her, she shook her head and, with a flickering smile, placed her hand over his mouth to restrain him.

"Dance with me," she whispered as those golden eyes blazed down at her, and began to hum the lilting strain of the waltz once more.

With a laugh and a shake of his head to free it from her hand, he obliged her, his long body moving gracefully in the rhythms she suddenly was certain he'd learned long before this night, twirling and dipping her as he held her far closer than any dance had ever been designed for, so close that she could feel every hard muscle and sinew in his body as it moved against hers. He began to hum the melody too, his voice far more melodic than hers.

"You humbug, you! You waltz like you were born doing it! Why did you not tell me you could dance?" Mildly indignant, she pushed against his shoulder in a vain attempt to take herself out of his arms.

"And spoil your fun? Not I," he responded with a devilish smile, twirling her so quickly that her head spun and much of her indignation was lost in laughing protest. Her hair, insecure in its pins, loosened in the mad whirl and formed a soft halo about her face. With her cheeks rosy from exertion and her blue eyes sparkling with laughter, she was radiantly lovely as she leaned back against his arms to shake her head at him in mock reproach. Before she could give further voice to her sense of ill usage, he swung her about in a series of fast turns that left her breathless.

"Where did you learn?" This as she came up gasping for air.

"Remember Cecily?"

The woman who had taught him to read. Isabella remembered, and nodded. "Yes."

"Besides her many other accomplishments, she was a great devotee of . . . dancing."

Alec pulled her even tighter against him as he said the last word, his hand sliding down from its proper grip on her waist to very improperly explore the curve of her buttocks through her dress.

"Was . . . was she?" That bold caress so unnerved Isabella that she could barely think. Her insides turned to jelly. Her lips parted.

"Mmmhmm. Just as she did with her passion for reading, she passed her passion for . . . dancing . . . on to the lad I was then. I've had more than a passing fondness for it ever since."

He was waltzing her about the room, the steps perfectly proper as his hands explored her body in a way that was anything but. He caressed her buttocks and spine and waist, stroking and squeezing and pressing her ever more intimately against him. Head spinning from a combination of the dance, the wine and the man, Isabella quivered in his arms, pliant and responsive to anything he might ask of her. The hard, sinewy muscles of his body enticed her. Then a movement of the dance brought her in contact with a more intimate hardness, and her knees turned to butter. If it had not been for the support of his arms close about her, she feared she would not have been able to stand. But stand she did, and dance too, because all the while he was conducting the delicious assault on her senses, he never faltered in the steps. He twirled her about like a child's top, humming the haunting refrain in her ear. It was wildly erotic, this waltz that could never be performed on any dance floor. Increasingly helpless in the face of a burgeoning passion the heat of which threatened to incinerate the last remaining shreds of her inhibitions, Isabella could only cling to his shoulders and move as he willed her.

"I really think I must kiss you now, Madame Tutor. You're so very kissable, you see."

"Alec . . ."

"Shhh."

The hand that was not clasping her waist slid up over her bare upper arm, over the silk of her sleeve, over the slight protrusion of her collarbone to cup her neck. Isabella trembled at the trail of fire his hand left in its wake, and when he tilted her chin up with his thumb she made no further demur.

"We're good together, you and I," he murmured just before his mouth came down on hers. "Remember?"

Remember? Oh, did she remember! Never, if she lived to be a hundred, could she forget the white-hot passion that both exhilarated and shamed, that swept her away with it, that changed her world. How could she not remember?

If he said something more, Isabella heard none of it as the roar in her ears from the heating of her own blood drowned out every other sound. Vaguely she realized that they were no longer waltzing, that they were standing in each other's arms, while he pressed her head back against his shoulder with his kiss.

The walls of the room seemed to twirl and then recede as she kissed him back with a hunger so intense it seemed that she could never get enough of him. His lips were hard and hot as they moved over hers, his tongue boldly laying claim to the territory she willingly surrendered. He tasted faintly of the liqueur with which they'd finished dinner. With the part of her mind still capable of functioning, Isabella wondered if that was not part of the reason she felt herself growing ever more intoxicated as she explored his mouth.

But the truth was, she was growing drunk on the man himself.

When he lifted his mouth from hers, she mewled a protest and dug her nails into the back of his neck without ever opening her eyes.

"Careful, now, Madame Tutor. You'll wound me anew," he chided, and then Isabella felt herself being lifted off her feet.

"Alec . . ." Her eyes flew open, and she clung to him as he carried her toward the closed door of the salon. "What are you doing?"

"Taking you to bed, love. I'm too old and too fond of comfort to make love to you on the rug."

"But Shelby, the servants . . ." He had opened the door and was maneuvering her expertly through it as he spoke.

"To hell with Shelby and the servants. I'll do as I like in my own home. Now, close your eyes, and put that pretty little mouth to its proper use and kiss me."

"Yes, Alec." She surrendered to a will that was, for the moment, stronger than hers, closed her eyes, and lifted her lips for his kiss. His mouth crushed down on hers, blocking out all awareness of anything but him. So oblivious was she that she had no notion that Shelby, shocked and muttering something about scandal and bad blood, saw her locked in Alec's arms and retreated into the shadows. She had no notion that Alec was climbing the stairs quickly, as if she were no weight at all, his kisses robbing her of her breath all the while. She had no notion of the desperateness of her hold on him, or the quiescent way she lay in his arms, her head thrown back against his shoulder, her feet dangling. She had no notion when they reached his chamber, or of how they got through the door. All she knew was that his arms were lifting away from her as he set her on her feet by his bed.

She opened her eyes then, looking up at him with a passion so intense that it set the blue-gray depths ablaze, clinging to his shoulders with abandon as her lips once again sought his, brushing the stubbly roughness of his chin and cheek in her quest. Mindlessly her hands sought and found the proper neckcloth that he had worn at her insistence. Now the elegantly knotted folds offended her, and she tugged at them, trying to work them loose so that she might free more of his flesh.

''Gently, gently, love. We've got all night,'' he whispered against her lips as he dropped soft kisses on her seeking mouth. Once the neckcloth was sent flying, to land forgotten on the floor, her attention turned to his coat and she pushed against it, trying to work it down his shoulders. With a quirk of his lips that was not quite a smile, he shrugged out of it. Then even the last semblance of a smile vanished as her fingers went to work on the buttons of his shirt, sliding them free of their holes. The sudden blaze in his eyes was the only warning she had that his desire had reached flashpoint. He drew in his breath, sharply, then yanked at the sides of his shirt so that the remaining buttons popped and she had free access to his chest.

She caught her breath then, too, her eyes and hands moving to the expanse of bare flesh revealed by the forcibly opened shirt. Her fingertips were sensual as they stroked over the sleek contours of his chest, burrowed into the soft wedge of hair. His skin was hot and firm over muscles as unyielding as wood. At the feel of him under her hands, she grew intoxicated all over again. Driven by instinct, she bent her head to press tiny, biting kisses into the rigid muscles of his chest. At last she found the male nipples that were already taut with anticipation, first flicking them with her tongue and then biting them.

''Christ, love, this goes too fast,'' he muttered, catching her head with both hands and pulling her away from him. His accent was roughening, and somehow that less than elegant intonation set the seal on her intoxication. She looked up at him then, with his hands still lying flat on either side of her face. His teeth were clenched in an effort to keep a rein on his burgeoning passion, but even he with his iron will was not proof against the sudden fierce hunger that shone from her eyes.

''Love me, Alec. Now. Please.''

''Oh, God, Isabella,'' he groaned in surrender, and slid

his hands away from her head to catch her arms and haul her up for his kiss.

But she didn't wait for that. She launched herself upward before he could lift her, almost leaping at him as she wrapped her arms around his neck, raising herself on tiptoe as she pressed her breasts against the hardness and heat of his bare chest. With torrid desire she kissed him, her passion made that much the sweeter for all the time she had fought to deny it. Her hands burrowed under his hair to spread out against his skull, holding him to her even though he made no move to lift his head. Her mouth twisted under his. Her tongue invaded his mouth with hungry ardency as the passion she had held in check for so long blazed up to consume them both with its flames. On the morrow, she knew, she was going to regret what she had done. But for now, in the steamy semidarkness of his bedchamber lit only by the dying embers of the fire in the hearth, she was burning with the intensity of her need for him. Lady or strumpet, in the dark it made no matter. She was all a woman, and he was all a man. And oh, how she wanted him!

His hands were shaking as they sought for and found the fastenings of her dress. But the tiny buttons resisted his importunities, and at last he grew impatient. Catching the neck of her gown at the back with both hands, he yanked it open. The material gave with a loud rip, and buttons scattered everywhere, clattering as they hit the floor and rolled.

"Alec. My dress." Her eyes opened at the unexpectedness of his violence.

"I'll buy you another one, love. Dozens, if you like."

He was pulling the gown down her arms, pushing it past her waist so that it fell to her ankles. She obliged him by stepping out of it, and then undoing the tapes of her petticoat while he wrestled with the laces of her stays. When at last she stood before him clad only in the scant protection of her chemise, he looked down at her for a long moment with an expression that made her heart stop.

Then he reached for her again.

Isabella made a tiny mewling sound, and melted into his arms. Her arms went around his back, under the abused shirt, clutching him to her. He lifted her, and laid her on the bed, fumbling with his breeches as he came down on top of her.

''Forgive me, love. I can't wait more,'' he breathed into her ear. Her legs parted for him even as his still-breeched thighs slid between them, and then he was pushing against her for a scant moment until he found the place he sought and thrust inside.

Isabella stiffened as he filled her, fighting to hold back the hot, sweet clamoring that was refusing to be denied. He sensed her battle and went very still, then with a muffled curse began to move, pushing himself inside her again and again as she surrendered with a cry to the abyss that from the beginning had threatened to claim her.

''Christ Almighty.''

It might have been a curse or a prayer. Isabella didn't know. She only knew that he plunged into her at that instant of her deepest joy with a wild hunger and a wilder cry, holding himself inside her as his lean, strong body convulsed with long shudders. Finally he collapsed on top of her. Spent, he lay still, and she wrapped her arms around him, snuggling her cheek against his still-thudding heart.

L

"We never do manage to do this properly, do we?" It was a little while later. Alec lay on his back on the bed, his head properly disposed on a pillow, and a wry smile on his face. He was very much in control again, of his voice and his emotions. Isabella lay close beside him, her head pillowed on his shoulder. His arm was around her, and she was, at the moment, feeling very much content with the world.

"Is there a proper way to do it?" she asked, interested. Her hand, resting against his chest inside the buttonless shirt he still wore, stroked his skin idly.

He slanted a look down at her. There was a wry twist to his mouth as he smiled. "We might try it with both of us naked. And slowly. Very, very slowly. So that I can savor every square inch of you."

"You're putting me to the blush."

She suited the action to the words. He laughed as he saw the truth of her statement, hugged her closer and kissed the top of her head.

"I like a woman who can blush. It opens up all kinds of interesting possibilities."

"Such as?"

Alec sat up. Dislodged from her resting place, Isabella made a sound of protest as she was left lying forlornly on the mattress. Surveying himself rather ruefully, he gave the hitch to his breeches that was needed to make him minimally decent. Then, feeling her watching him, he looked up to meet her eyes. Pouting at his absence, Isabella had shifted so that her head rested on the pillow his head vacated. His eyes swept her as she lay there, legs sprawled, sleepy-eyed in the aftermath of their loving. Suddenly self-conscious, Isabella tugged down the shift she still wore so that she was covered to midthigh. His eyes took on a gleam as they surveyed her. Seeing that gleam, and remembering what he'd said about being naked, she felt a languorous twinge deep inside as that part of her she had thought was sated awakened once more.

"Such as, would you blush if I kissed your toes?"

He ran his hand down the length of her bare leg as he spoke, half teasing but still sending tremors up her spine in the wake of that warm touch. To her surprise, he captured her ankle, shifted position a little, and lifted her foot to his mouth to nibble on her small bare toes.

"Alec! Stop!"

Isabella wiggled her toes in shocked protest, while he held her ankle and kissed them one by one, drawing the big toe into his mouth and sucking on it for good measure.

"She does blush. Interesting," he observed with a devilish glint as he lifted her foot higher to press kisses on the sensitive instep.

"Stop kissing my foot! It tickles, and it's . . . it's embarrassing!"

"If you insist."

Obligingly he desisted, but she relaxed too soon. Retaining his grip on her ankle, he slid his mouth up over her ankle to nibble his way up her calf to her knee, where his mouth rested for a long moment, hot and wet against her skin. Isabella, blushing furiously now at both his action and the immodesty of her posture with one leg lifted high, pulled down the hem of her chemise with one hand and sought to scoot into a sitting position with the aid of the other.

"Would you stop?"

She was laughing a little at the sheer foolishness of him,

but she meant it too. What he was doing was . . . exciting. But far too wicked to be permitted.

"Remember our bargain?"

"What bargain?"

"You were to turn me into a gentleman and I was to turn you into a beauty?"

"What does that have to do with anything? Alec, stop kissing my knee!"

"A beautiful woman is one who looks well and thoroughly loved. I'm just trying to keep my part of our agreement." He accompanied that with a devilish smile.

"I knew you'd come out with something like that sooner or later. Well, if you think I . . . Alec, you can't do that!"

His mouth left her knee to crawl up the inside of her thigh as she spoke. The scorching journey made her break out in goose bumps from head to toe. Again she tried to pull her ankle free of his hold. Again he refused to release her while his mouth inched closer to that part of her that he had already claimed very thoroughly as his own.

"It isn't decent! You musn't!"

He lifted his head at that to regard her intently. "For a married lady, Countess, you're very innocent. Didn't you and St. Just ever have fun in bed?"

"No!"

"He did bed you. You weren't a virgin that night in the Carousel, I know full well."

"No, of course I . . . Oh, do we have to talk about this?"

It was almost a wail. If her blush got any hotter, she'd go up in flames. It didn't help that the whole time he was interrogating her, his hand, almost absently, stroked up and down the inside of her captured thigh.

"I think so. You were a virgin when you married, I'm certain. So all you know about sex is what you learned from St. Just—which doesn't seem to be a hell of a lot—and me. Am I right?"

"Yes!"

Distractedly she tried again to pull her ankle from his

hold. He retained his grip without effort, watching her embarrassed struggles to make herself decent.

"I gather that his idea of a good time in bed was ten minutes rutting in the dark?"

"Alec!"

Shocked at his crudeness, she stopped struggling and sat up straight, staring at him. The flickering firelight painted his chiselled features in shades of bronze, while his hair gleamed like old gold from the reflected light of the flames. With his shirt loose and open, and his breeches unbuttoned to expose his belly a considerable number of inches past his navel, he looked very handsome—and more than a little debauched.

"Well?"

He clearly meant to have an answer. Isabella, feeling herself turn seven shades of red, muttered resentfully, "Yes."

"I thought so."

He began to rub her thigh again, then pressed a kiss on the inside of it just above her knee. To her surprise, he released her ankle, and sat looking at her meditatively. Isabella drew her legs out of his reach, scrambling up into the bed until she was sitting with her back pressed against the headboard, watching him with as much wariness as a rabbit might watch a hound.

"This calls for a different type of approach," he said after a minute. "Surely you cannot be shy of me still, Isabella?"

"It depends."

That wary response surprised a smile out of him.

"Canny, aren't you, my girl? But you've no need to be shy of me after bedding me twice, and pretty hotly too. The way I see it, you're eager to learn but a little uncertain of what you're about. And green as grass. The first thing you've got to understand is that tumbling about in bed with a man is fun. Let me teach you that, Isabella. Let me teach you how good it can be between a man and a woman."

She moistened her lips with her tongue. He was seducing her again, with words alone, without even touching her. And she . . . was she willing to be seduced?

"I won't do . . . anything indecent. Like . . . like . . ."

Her voice trailed off as she found herself at a loss to describe what she suspected he had been meaning to do to her.

This time he laughed outright. "Oh, Isabella, you are a delight! Do you know, this is as new for me as it is for you? I've never had a virgin, or anything approaching one. My previous bedmates have been at least as experienced as I, if not more so. So you see, we can learn together."

Her wariness increased when he sat down on the end of the bed, pulled off his boots, and then, barefoot, stood and held out his hand to her.

"Come on."

"Where to?"

"Nowhere. Right here."

"Why?"

He sighed. "Just trust me, will you please? I promise I won't do anything you don't want me to. Anytime you want, you can tell me to stop. And I'll stop. I give you my word."

Isabella looked at him for a moment, hesitating. Then she held out her hand, and let him pull her from the bed. With both of them barefoot, facing each other, linked by their clasped hands, he stood at least a foot above her. It struck her for the first time how tall he was. Next to Paddy, as she was used to seeing him, he looked no taller than the average, but she herself was a little above average height, and the top of her head did not even reach his chin. The very handsomeness of his face tended to blind one to the sheer muscular power of his body, but standing so close to him, Isabella was totally aware of how helpless she would be against him if he should choose to exert his strength against her. But this was Alec, whom she had grown to rely on more than anyone in the world. He had given his word to stop anytime she chose to call a halt.

"What do you want me to do?" she said low.

He smiled, then reached out and caught her other hand to pull her closer.

"Let's do it properly this time," he said in a husky voice that was scarcely above a whisper. "Let's have this thing off you."

He let go of her, and reached for the hem of her chemise. Though she knew it was foolish, knew he'd already seen all there was to see of her that night in the Carousel, she panicked suddenly at the idea of standing naked before him, washed in gold by the dying fire, her body revealed to his eyes with no secrets left to her. Swallowing, she shook her head.

Immediately he withdrew his hands. "All right then. How about if you undress me?"

Catching her hands, he placed them against his chest. Isabella was conscious of the heat and strength of that chest, of how she had caressed and kissed it not an hour ago.

She took a step closer, so that little space separated their bodies. The warmth of him, the smell of him, enticed her. His hands were at his sides now, as he waited, quiescent, for what she would do.

Earlier, he had talked of making love naked. Isabella realized that the very idea of Alec naked made her throat go dry.

Without a word she slid her hands beneath the sides of his shirt and slipped it from his shoulders. It fell to the floor at his feet. Then, as his eyes darkened, her hands slid from his shoulders over his chest and belly to the waistband of his breeches. The buttons were still open, and it was no great task to push the breeches down his hips to his thighs. His manhood sprang free, huge and ready, and he sucked in his breath as it did. Still he made no move to touch her, just stood there as she tugged the breeches down his thighs until he could step out of them and kick them aside.

She straightened, her eyes flickering over him, touching him everywhere, drinking in the sheer physical perfection of him. His shoulders were wide, his hips narrow. His legs were long and corded with muscle. From the evidence between them, he was once again eager to push her on her back and pump out his lust, but he was as good as his word. He let her look, just look, and made no move to touch her.

His very willingness to let her take the lead, to let her learn about his body without interference, excited her. She reached out, touched him gently, her finger just brushing that enormous man-part of him. He groaned, and jerked as if she had hurt him, but still he made no move to grab her.

Isabella made a decision. She would trust him, trust him to teach her about his body and her own. From him, she would hold nothing back.

As he watched her, his eyes blazing hotter than the fire, she reached down, caught the hem of her chemise, and drew it over her head.

"Teach me, Alec," she said simply, and threw the garment on the floor beside the fire.

LI

It was dawn before they fell into an exhausted sleep. When Isabella awoke hours later, it was to find that the curtains had been opened to permit sunlight to blaze into the room, and the ashes had been swept from the hearth. Apparently the maid whose daily tasks included these duties had seen no reason not to perform them just because her master was still abed, and with his female houseguest yet. At the thought of anyone, even a maidservant, seeing her lying in Alec's arms, Isabella felt a surge of shame. But then, she told herself, such was the lot of mistresses.

A mistress. By her actions last night she had taken on that role. The first time, in the Carousel, she might have excused herself on the grounds that she had lost her head. But last night . . . last night she had been willing, nay, eager, to lie with Alec. Eager to make love with him until they were both too sated to do anything more than fall into a stuporous sleep. The unaccustomed amount of wine she had consumed might serve as a convenient excuse for her behavior, but Isabella knew the truth: she had done nothing she had not desperately wanted to do.

The bedroom door was closed. Isabella made sure of that, then sat up. The sheet fell about her waist, but she made no move to cover herself with it. Alec was asleep, and except for him, she was alone. Besides, she supposed that covering herself in front of Alec was now a waste of time.

Mistresses certainly could not be modest.

He was lying on his back, one arm flung up above his head, the other hidden beneath the rumpled pile of bedclothes. His mouth was open, his jaw was dark with stubble, his hair was wildly tousled. By all rights, looking at him on this, the morning after, should have repulsed her.

But it didn't. Her eyes moved over him assessingly. Even ungracefully asleep, the man was breathtaking. Some master hand had carved each feature and, putting them together, formed a flawlessly handsome whole. Had he been less than the man he was, his face could only have been a drawback in the world from which he had sprung.

Like herself, he was naked. The coverings came midway up his chest, but his broad shoulders and the upper part of his chest were bare above them. Dark hair with just a tinge of gold tufted under his upraised arm. The hair on his chest was a shade or so lighter.

His shoulders were heavy with muscle. From intimate experience Isabella knew that the rest of him was equally powerful. Had they been wed, she would have felt a swelling of pride every time she looked at him, to know that this gorgeous man was hers.

But they were not wed.

She had not been raised to find herself as a man's mistress. Any man's, be he lord or commoner. Her mother had been a devout churchgoer, a woman of unshakable principles. Although she had died before Isabella had been more than half-grown, her influence on her only child had been strong. And Pressy, dear Pressy. How horrified her faithful governess would be if she could know to what depths her charge had sunk.

Pressy, raised in the Church of Rome, would be sure that Isabella was destined for eternal hell-fire. Adultery was a mortal sin, after all. If she could see her charge now, Pressy would be saying fervent prayers for Isabella's soul.

Restless, Isabella got out of bed, found her chemise on the floor, and put it on. Her petticoat was in one piece. She put that on, too. Then she pulled the ruined dress over her head, picked up the remainder of her garments, and took herself back to her own chamber to wash and dress for the day.

She did not spare Alec so much as a single look as she let herself out the bedroom door.

Later, disdaining breakfast, she went out to walk in the rose gardens at the back of the house, and ended up wandering down to the pavilion that overlooked the lake. It was in that pavilion, seated pensively on the stone bench, that Alec at last found her.

She was dressed in lavender. The gentle shade made her skin look very white, and her hair a color softer than gold, but brighter than brown. Her face was turned away from him as he approached along the path from the house. As she stared out over the small ornamental lake at the back of the property, her expression was almost sad.

"Isabella."

She turned to look at him then, smiling faintly. Was it his imagination or did the smile not reach her eyes?

"Good morning, Alec." Her voice was very composed, remote even. He looked at her more closely. Was she angry at him?

It surprised him to discover that he, who had faced bullets and knives and violent men and angry women by the score over the course of his life, should be made so ill at ease by one slender chit.

"Have you breakfasted?" The prosaic was the only way he could think to approach her.

She shook her head. "I wasn't hungry." Then her eyes left his face to travel out over the lake once more.

He was left staring at the elegant curve of her back, the long white stem of her neck, the soft roll of hair at her nape. Of her face he could see only the curve of one pale cheek, and the dainty outline of her nose and chin.

Suddenly he was conscious of a dull, thudding pain in the region of his heart.

"Isabella." He gave up trying to pretend that everything was as usual and came around to sit on the bench beside her. "Do you regret last night?"

She looked at him then, her lovely eyes widening as though she was surprised at the question. Her hair formed a nimbus as soft-looking as a cloud around her face. Her expression was serene. That luscious mouth which she considered a fatal flaw and he thought was too erotic to look at without kissing was curved in a faint smile.

"Do I regret last night?" she repeated musingly. "Do I regret behaving like a wanton and coming into your bed though I have no business whatsoever there? Do I regret violating my marriage vows and my own honor? Do I regret the wicked things I did?"

He went very still then, his eyes on her face, feeling himself vulnerable as he had never been before. He was sore afraid she was sorry.

"No," she said softly. "If I could relive the evening again, I wouldn't change a thing. Not one thing."

Speechless for what must have been the first time in his life, he picked up her hand and carried it to his lips.

"Isabella." His voice was hoarse. "Isabella."

"I'm in love with you, you know. I never meant it to happen, but it has."

Unable to speak, he kissed her hand again, laid it against the side of his face. Her fingers were very cool against his skin. His eyes met hers, and he tried to speak but couldn't. A scratchy dryness in his throat threatened to unman him. Never in his life had anything affected him like her sweet voice speaking of loving him.

She went on. "You needn't look so worried. There's no future for me with you, and I know it as well as you do. You don't have to try to pretend otherwise. It's funny, though. I wouldn't be your mistress for a home, or security, but I'll do it for love."

Love. The word was like a sword piercing his heart. He kissed the palm of the hand that rested against his cheek, and held it.

"What do you mean, you don't have a future with me?" If his voice was rough, he considered himself lucky to be able to talk at all. For the first time since he was a tiny lad lost in a frightening world, he felt the sting of tears at the backs of his eyes. She was so brave, and so beautiful, and so gallant, and his heart ached with wanting to keep her safe beside him forever.

"You've as much a future with me as you want to have. Do you think I don't have a care for you? Hell, I would wed you tomorrow if I could." His lips were as dry as his throat. He moistened them, and looked at her with a humility as foreign to him as the tears burning the backs of his eyes. That she should love him . . . He had never expected that.

"You would . . . marry me?" Her eyes searched his face. Her hand quivered in his. "You needn't try to make things easy for me, you know. I'm perfectly prepared to be your mistress for as long as you want me. You needn't make pretty speeches that you don't mean."

He smiled then, crookedly, as the aching in his throat eased. "I never make pretty speeches I don't mean. At least, not to you. I love you, Isabella, and I've never in my life said that nor wanted to say it to another human being. So how's that for a pretty speech?"

The crooked smile went even more crooked as her eyes met his. Her lips trembled. Her fingers curled around the hand that held hers.

"Do you mean it? Really, truly?" she asked low.

"Aye, I mean it," he said gruffly, and took her in his arms.

LII

They had a week. A single, glorious week. All thought of shame, and sin, Isabella banished from her mind. She loved, and was loved in return.

Never in her life had she expected to experience such happiness.

The daylight hours were spent in a golden glow of bliss, walking around the estate, continuing Alec's riding lessons that were tenderly hilarious now, playing at cards or some other game. But after dinner—which was served early on Alec's orders—they retired to his room, together. And in his room, in his bed, Isabella awakened to what it truly meant to be a woman in love.

It was early May now, and the few times that Isabella thought of it, it seemed incredible that three months ago she had been living very much retired at Blakely Park. The plain, unloved Countess of Blakely seemed like a different human being altogether, with no connection besides a name with the Isabella who danced and laughed and played with Alec.

When thoughts of the future threatened to rear their ugly heads, she banished them. The present was too unbelievably wonderful to worry about what might happen at some distant time. The future would just have to take care of itself.

Then the message came from Paddy.

"I'm going to have to go to London for a day or two,"

Alec told her ruefully, looking up from the screw of paper that one of his men had just brought in to him. They were seated on opposite sides of a small table in the library, playing at piquet. Under Alec's coaching, Isabella was becoming quite proficient at the game. Occasionally she even won a hand, although she suspected him of—and he loudly denied—cheating to let her win.

She put down her hand of cards and looked at him with a gnawing disquiet. The first intrusion into their Eden. Of course, he had businesses to run, things to see to. Had she really thought that the two of them could stay here at Amberwood, undisturbed, for the rest of their lives?

"This is from Paddy," he said, displaying the note. "He wouldn't send for me if it wasn't urgent. I'll be back as quickly as I can."

"I understand, of course." And she did, really she did. But the sense of reality intruding on their idyll was strong.

"I'll leave most of the men here, to keep an eye on things. Don't stray far from the house."

"No. I won't."

He looked at her closely then, and frowned.

"Isabella." Pushing his chair back, he stood up and came around the table to rest his hand on the vulnerable nape of her neck, bared by the elegant new upsweep of her hair. " 'Twill only be for a day or two, love."

The warmth of his hand cradled her neck. With his index finger he absently stroked the tender skin just below her ear, the caress both coaxing and stirring. Isabella looked up at him then, determinedly smiling even if the smile was a trifle forced.

"I know. I'm being ridiculous. It's just that . . . I'll miss you." Her voice went husky on the last words.

"I'll miss you too, love; never doubt it." As her smile faltered the golden eyes took on a gleam with which Isabella was becoming totally familiar. "What say we skip dinner tonight, and turn in early? I can leave for London in the morning."

His hand slid from her neck to fondle the soft curve of her shoulder where it was bared by the fashionable décolletage of the taffeta afternoon dress. It took no more than that—the glint in his eyes and the most decorous of caresses—to kindle longings that she had never, before Alec's expert tutoring convinced her otherwise, dreamed she possessed.

"All right."

Alec pulled back her chair for her, and with a rustle of skirts Isabella got to her feet and turned to face him. Still determined to put a brave face on it—how ridiculous to feel so devastated by the prospect of a few days' separation!—she essayed another smile. As her eyes met his, the smile faltered and died. He was regarding her intently, his eyes twin flames of gold, his mouth straight and a little compressed.

"I will be back, Isabella. Not all the catastrophes in the kingdom could keep me away. And you've no need at all to fear for my safety. I've been taking care of myself quite adequately for longer than you are old, if you care to remember."

"Of course you have, old man that you are," she managed to reply cordially, having to use real resolution to resist the idiotic urge to weep instead. His prickliness about his relative youth made the topic foolproof fodder for her teasing, and in the halcyon days just past she had needled him about it often, with frequently delightful results.

"Wet-behind-the-ears miss," he retorted as he always did, smiling crookedly even as he reached for her.

That heartbreakingly familiar smile was her undoing. It brought home to her just how very dear he was to her, and how fragile was their hold on each other. A million circumstances could conspire to force them apart. . . .

"Oh, Alec!"

Feeling as though that smile had stabbed her clear through to the heart, Isabella abandoned all attempts at bravery and flew into his arms. They closed around her, pulling her against him in a hug that threatened to force the very air from her lungs. Even as her arms wrapped around his neck, his mouth came down on hers, kissing her with a fierceness that told her that, for all his brave words, he dreaded their coming separation as much as she did.

The knowledge made Isabella shiver.

She tightened her arms around his neck, answering his kiss with a desperate hunger as her fingers clenched in the raw silk of his hair. With the urgency of parting looming over them, she couldn't seem to get him close enough. She wanted to imprint on her mind and body forever the hard masculinity of the body to which she clung; the feel of his chin and cheeks which all these hours after his morning shave had grown rough again, abrading her sensitive skin; the faint taste of ale that clung to his tongue, and the warm smell of man that enwrapped her as completely as his arms.

Holding him close, she could pretend that she never had to let him go. Then he lifted his mouth from hers to press molten kisses along the line of her jaw.

''I love you,'' she breathed into the hollow between his shoulder and neck, her hands releasing their death grip on his hair to slide across the broad planes of his linen-clad shoulders and then down over the long muscles of his back.

By way of reply he muttered something unintelligible into the soft skin of her neck, where he was tracing tiny devouring kisses from her ear to her collarbone, his arms tightening around her so fiercely that Isabella would have feared for her ribs if she had been in any condition to think of something so mundane. But she was not. Instead she pressed herself so closely against him that she could feel his heartbeat pounding against her breasts through his shirt and her gown, feel the urgent hardness that trumpeted his need of her more clearly than any bugle call, swollen and enormous against the softness of her belly.

''Alec,'' she whispered his name, going on tiptoe to press a kiss into the vulnerable skin just below and behind his ear.

''Isabella.'' His voice was hoarse. ''See what you do to me.''

Reaching for her hand, he guided it between them, pressing it against the front of his breeches with blatant sexuality. Only a few days before, Isabella would have been shocked speechless. But in the brief time since she had thrown her cap over the windmill and admitted her love for him, Alec had tutored her well. She felt the familiar tightening in her body even as her fingers closed willingly around him, squeezing and stroking as he had taught her despite the barrier of cloth.

His tongue was in her ear, tracing the convoluted whorls with delicious effect, so she could very clearly hear the moment his breathing went ragged. Her fingers were opening the top button of his breeches, crawling down the hair-roughened, board-hard warmth of his abdomen to free the second. . . .

''Oh, God, Isabella,'' he groaned, and then he was lifting her off her feet and laying her down on the carpet before the fire with more haste than care, freeing himself from his breeches with shaking hands even as he came down on top of her. Impatiently he pushed the rustly taffeta skirt out of his way, and then he was thrusting into her while he groaned and she cried out his name.

The fierceness of their need was so intense that neither could wait, and their mating was over in moments. Alec lay on his back before the fire, spent, his clothes askew and his breathing only gradually returning to normal. Isabella curled at his side, her head on his shoulder, one hand resting comfortably on his chest. A thought occurred to her and made her smile.

''What's so funny?''

Isabella looked up to find his golden eyes fixed on her face. Her smile widened.

''I thought you were too old and too fond of comfort to make love to me on a rug.''

He frowned slightly, and then as he remembered, his lips twitched.

''Words spoken in haste are usually repented.''

''Are they indeed?''

''Yes, ma'am. I now see that I could make love to you on a rug forever.''

"You're not too old?" Her fingers slid between the buttons of his shirt to tickle his chest as she teased him.

"Minx," he said, catching her hand and bringing it to his lips for a kiss. "Let's go upstairs."

His eyes were on her. From the growing gleam in them, Isabella realized that despite the fierceness of what had just passed between them, his desire for her was far from sated.

She sat up. "Certainly not. At least, not until I've had my dinner. I find myself suddenly extremely sharp-set."

"Worked up an appetite, have you?" He grinned suddenly, and got to his feet with easy grace, reaching down a hand to pull her up beside him. "Well, so have I. We'll tell Shelby to bring us up a tray. I just might be able to wait the length of time it takes us to eat."

Isabella laughed. Smoothing her skirt and then doing what she could to restore her maddening hair, she watched with interest as Alec made repairs to his own appearance. "He'll think us scandalous."

"I'm sure he does already. Do you care?"

She shook her head. "No," she said, surprised to find that it was true.

"I'll make a wanton out of you yet, Countess; see if I don't," he said, grinning, and sliding an arm around her waist, he hugged her close. Arm in arm, her head on his shoulder, they walked from the library.

The next morning came all too soon. Knowing that she was being idiotic, Isabella nevertheless could not stop herself from weeping as she stood on the front steps watching as Alec prepared to leave. The sight of her tears as he swung his portmanteau inside the closed carriage made him groan, and curse, a rush of red staining his cheekbones as he glanced around at the interested audience of Shelby, a footman and half a dozen of his men. But to his credit he ignored them, coming back to her and holding her close, kissing her and whispering sweet love words into her ears. But his tenderness only made her dread of losing him worse, and the more he tried to soothe her, the more she sobbed, stricken by the fear that if he left her now, she would never see him again.

"I must go, love," he said finally, putting her away from him and stepping up into the carriage with a signal to the driver. Alec had agreed to the precautions of a closed carriage complete with armed driver and a small vanguard of his men with much reluctance, to ease her fears that he might be attacked en route.

But not even these safeguards could quiet Isabella's growing sense of impending disaster. As she stood on the steps, one hand shielding her eyes and the other brushing the tears from her cheeks, watching the carriage until it was out of sight, Isabella trembled with the strength of her conviction that their parting was not for a day or two, but for good.

That night Isabella slept in Alec's bed, her arms clutching a pillow that she could not, with the best will in the world, successfully pretend was him. Staring sleeplessly into the dark, she realized that she had never, not even on the dreadful morning after her marriage, felt so alone in all her life.

With the rising of the sun her spirits lifted slightly. After all, Alec had promised to be gone no more than one or two nights. With luck, he might be home before she had to spend another sleepless night in his bed. Clinging to that thought, she dressed in the rose pink muslin that she knew was a favorite of his and took extra care with her hair, in the hope that he might make it home that afternoon. If somewhere deep inside her dwelled the conviction that he would never return, she refused to allow herself to acknowledge it. Such megrims! she scolded herself, and chalked up the inner dread she could not completely banish as one of the exigencies of being head over heels in love.

Restless after luncheon, she went for a walk along the lane. If Alec was to arrive at all today, it would not be until much later, she reasoned. Alec's men were about somewhere, she knew they were, but they kept discreetly out of her sight, and she felt herself very much alone as she strolled along. The sun shone brightly, the trees were in leaf, and spring flowers bloomed in colorful profusion along both sides of the lane. It was a beautiful day, and Isabella's spirits rose to match it.

In the sparkling sunlight her fears were exposed as the ridiculous things they were. Alec would be back soon, and they would go on just as before. To fret herself into a headache was absurd.

She wandered down past the stable, waving at the groom who had become a friend. A little farther along, near the meadow where Alec had had his first riding lesson, she stopped to pick a bunch of bachelor's buttons for her dressing table. Inhaling deeply of the soft blue blooms, she became aware of the sound of carriage wheels approaching.

Alec! He was home even earlier than she could have expected! It had to be he, for who else would be bowling along a private lane?

Smiling foolishly, she moved to the side of the road, watching as the carriage came into sight. It was travelling at a moderate speed, but as it approached her, it slowed. Pressing the small bouquet to her bosom, she waited with breathless anticipation for Alec's tawny head to appear.

It was only as the carriage was almost upon her that Isabella noticed that it was not the same vehicle in which Alec had left. And the stone-faced driver was a stranger. . . .

The carriage pulled up next to where she stood on the thick carpet of grass at the side of the lane. The door swung open, and a man jumped out. He was of medium height, stocky and blunt-featured. Isabella had never seen him before in her life.

She gasped, and took a step backward in surprise and fear as he boldly approached her.

"This 'er, guv?" the man spoke over his shoulder, to someone who suddenly appeared behind him in the ca riage door. Isabella glanced at this second man, and felt her heart stop.

"That's her. That's my wife," Bernard answered grimly. Isabella was so shocked that she hardly protested at all as she was dragged into the carriage to face her husband.

LIII

To Alec's vague surprise, Paddy was taking dinner with Pearl in her suite when he arrived at the Carousel. He joined them, glad to be back in his old haunt but feeling as though something was slightly amiss. He supposed he must be missing Isabella, and felt absurd. He was a grown man, not a callow youth.

"Alec!" Pearl cried as he entered, abandoning her mea to envelop him in a hug. Alec hugged her back, and re- turned her more than enthusiastic kiss, but his heart an mind were both elsewhere.

"Alec." If Paddy sounded less enthusiastic than Pearl Alec, with the heightened senses of the newly in love suspected it was because his old friend had quite a tendr in that direction himself, and was getting tired of seein the object of his adoration fawn upon his best friend.

"Paddy." He grinned and shook Paddy's hand, the availed himself of Pearl's offer to join them at their meal

"So how's the little countess?" Pearl asked with jus the faintest hint of malice as he sat.

"Isabella," Alec said, stressing her name, "is jus fine." Then, over a dish of creamed mutton, he looked a Paddy. "What did you want to see me about?"

Paddy was frowning, his eyes on Pearl, but at that h looked at Alec.

"I had a bit of luck the other day. A bloke what wa trying to get in with us came to me with some news: 'ti

Rothersham who's behind the attempts to put you in your grave."

"Rothersham!" Alec stared at Paddy. "Are you sure?"

Paddy shrugged. "It all fits. According to the bloke, Rothersham don't like it that you bought his house. Been in the family for generations, and all that. Didn't he make you an offer to buy it back a year or so ago and you turned him down? Well, he didn't like that. So like the gentleman he is, hating to get his hands dirty, don't you know, or maybe just a bit of a pudding-heart, he put out the word that he was willing to pay to see you dead.

"John Ball heard of it, got in touch with him, made the deal, and hired Rat-face Hardy to murder you. Only Rat-face died, and you didn't. Instead you hid out here, and no one could find you. Until John Ball happened to be in the Carousel that night that your lady ran out into the hall. He got a glimpse of me, too, I would imagine, and figured out where you were. So he tried again, with two operatives this time for a good measure. Only you didn't die again. So he set a man to watching the Carousel, and when you went down to Horsham, he was right behind you.

"You winged that bugger pretty good, by the way. I hear he won't be ridin' a horse again, ever. But Ball followed him down, to make sure the deed really was done that time. He must not have been able to believe his luck when he stumbled across you at the Traveler's Rest. He tried again—did it himself, this time—only to have a hole blown through his shoulder by the countess. So he ran away, but he didn't give up.

"When I got to him he was making plans to bribe one of the servants at Amberwood. Well, he's no longer a threat, but as long as Rothersham is willing to put up the money to see you dead, he'll find takers. If you don't want to be dodging musket balls the rest of your life, we'll need to take care of him."

"Damn it to hell and back," Alec said thoughtfully. "I was looking in entirely the wrong direction."

"So was I. If this bloke hadn't come to me and talked, I never would have tumbled to it."

"You did good work, Paddy, and I thank you." Alec saluted Paddy with his wineglass, and got a wry smile in return. "You know, I gather, where Rothersham might be found?"

"I know," Paddy said grimly, and took a sip of his own wine. "He's a member of Boodle's, and he's engaged there tonight. I suggest we have someone waiting outside when he leaves."

"No. This one I want to handle myself."

"I thought you might. Well, then, shall we make use of the card rooms here until midnight? No point in hoping to catch Rothersham until after that."

"You're coming?"

"Would I let you go without me? You're a might too hot-headed for my liking, Alec. You need a calm head at your back."

"And that's you," Alec said, grinning.

"That's me," Paddy agreed tranquilly, and pushed his chair back.

LIV

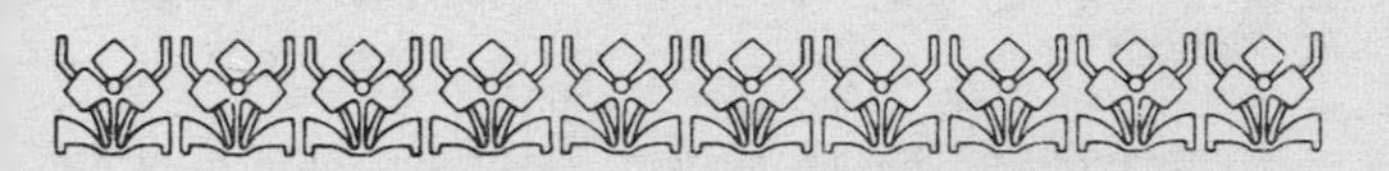

The night was, to say the least, eventful. Alec took a certain grim pleasure in the look on Rothersham's face when he and Paddy stepped out of the shadows and pulled his nobleness into their carriage instead of the one that waited for him. Rothersham, faced with two of London's most dangerous men, confessed everything and cried like a baby for mercy. Paddy was all for killing him and throwing his body in the Thames. Alec, mellowed perhaps by the throes of true love, seriously considered Paddy's suggestion, but in the end contented himself with getting in a few well-placed body blows and giving Rothersham the fright of his life. Toward dawn, they threw him out of the carriage in the worst section of Whitechapel to fend for himself amongst the street carrion and find his way home as best he could. Alec was confident that they'd done all that was needed to remove the threat Rothersham posed.

"If anything happens, or almost happens to me, he knows he'll be the first one we'll visit," Alec said nonchalantly to Paddy as they rode in well-upholstered comfort back to the Carousel. "I don't think he'll soon forget that."

Paddy shook his head at him. "You're getting soft, Alec. I never thought I'd live to see the day. Is it the countess?"

Alec scowled, his eyebrows meeting fiercely over his nose so that he looked ferocious in the uncertain light of the carriage lamp. But Paddy, who had known him longer than anyone, was unimpressed. Finally Alec succumbed to a reluctant grin.

"Maybe. Women are the very devil, ain't they?"

"They are." Paddy was silent then, doubtless thinking of whichever female had caused his heartfelt agreement to Alec's wry pronouncement. Alec had a sudden feeling that he knew exactly who had brought the unaccustomed gloom to Paddy's face.

"Is it Pearl you're hankering after?"

Paddy's head came up at that. He looked almost guilty, and his face turned beet red. Finally he nodded, a quick, shamefaced jerk of his head. "Aye, the saucy bawd's got me tied up in knots. Do you mind?"

With that question Paddy acknowledged Alec's prior claim, and silently offered to bow out of the picture if Alec did mind. But Alec shook his head.

"I've other fish to fry. Pearl's a good girl, one of the best, but she and I . . . it's never been true love between us. Though I've a care for her, of course, and always will. But you may have her, and welcome."

"Aye—if only she felt the same," Paddy said gloomily. "She's willing enough for a quick tumble, but I—fool that I am, and I know it—I don't want her bedding anyone but me. Can you see me telling Pearl that? She'd laugh in my face, and I wouldn't blame her. She's done as she's pleased since she was a wee lass, and if she's ever fancied anyone enough to give up the gents entirely, it's you. But I can't stomach the idea of her being so free with her favors. Sometimes, when I know she's got a man with her, I have to leave the Carousel to keep from committing a bloody murder. So how's that for a fine laugh?"

Alec grimaced sympathetically. "I'd say you're in quite a fix, my friend. Pearl fancies you—I think even more than she knows. But for her to be faithful—that's like asking a bird not to fly. She's a lusty wench; it's just her nature."

"Don't you talk about Pearl like that!" Paddy said, firing up.

Alec held up a quieting hand, then grinned. "You're in

a sad way, aren't you? You know I love the chit like a sister, and meant no disrespect."

"Aye, I know it." Paddy sighed, relaxed back against the squab, and shook his head in disgust at himself. "It's just that she's got me so tied up in knots that I scarce know if I'm going or coming."

With another deep sigh Paddy pulled a cigar case from his pocket, offered it first to Alec, who extracted a fat brown cigar, then helped himself to one. After lighting them on the carriage lamp, both men sat puffing in silence for a while. Then Alec took the cigar from his mouth.

"Hell, Paddy, were I in your shoes, I'd keep her so busy that she wouldn't have time to even think of other men, much less do anything else with one. Bed the wench morning, noon and night until she begs for mercy. Stake your claim, and let her know you mean business. If she squawks, don't take no for an answer, just pick her up and carry her to bed. When you have her there, tell her you're mad with wanting her. Females like that."

Paddy glanced over at Alec, an arrested expression on his face. Then his brows lifted quizzically, and he began to grin around the cigar.

"Now, there's an idea," he said. "Provided she don't shoot me. But if I stake my claim, and she ups and turns those great eyes of hers on another man—even you, my friend—it'd be all I could do not to break her bloody neck. Or his. Or yours."

"Noble sentiments," Alec said approvingly. "I know just how you feel. But you'll never know how Pearl feels until you put it to the touch."

"Maybe I will." Paddy chomped down on his cigar, and frowned at the seat opposite him. "Maybe I just will."

And with that they arrived at the Carousel.

Alec meant to make the drive back to Amberwood as early as possible after breakfast, and it was already close to dawn, so he went straight upstairs to his chamber and undressed for bed. Paddy stayed below, Alec presumed to search out Pearl and start staking his claim. Grinning as he anticipated the fireworks that were certain to ensue, he blew out the lights and crawled between the sheets. But despite the lateness of the hour, and his exhaustion, he couldn't sleep. God, how he missed Isabella!

Thus when the key turned stealthily in his lock, and his door swung open, he was still awake.

It was too dark to see anything of the intruder, but as the door closed behind whoever it was, Alec knew with a certainty that didn't depend on sight that he was no longer alone.

Someone was in the room with him.

Christ, had they made a mistake in blaming Rothersham? But the slimy toad had confessed; there was no possibility of error. Could this be another would-be-assassin, so soon after he had eliminated the first?

Alec almost groaned aloud. He was getting bloody tired of constantly fighting for his life.

He stiffened, readying himself for a spring as the intruder approached his bed. Just when he was ready to launch himself at the stranger's throat, he got a whiff of perfume. Then, before he recovered from the sheer surprise of it, he was enveloped in the voluptuous scent of her as she plopped herself down on his bed and wrapped her arms around his neck. Even as her lips sought his, his hands closed over her arms and held her away.

"Good God, Pearl, you might give a man some warning," he growled, thwarting her efforts to rub her breasts against his chest with more dexterity than tact. "Stop it, now! Be still! Christ, do you realize I nearly throttled you?"

"Quit grumbling, Alec, and kiss me, do! Oh, I've missed you, lover!" She strained toward him, and he leaned so far back in an effort to ward her off that he hit his head on the wall with a solid-sounding crack.

"Hold on now . . ." he ordered, wincing.

"Don't you want to kiss me?" she pouted, still pursuing. Then, when he didn't laugh and pull her against him, as she expected, she jerked free and got to her feet to stand arms akimbo beside the bed. "You *don't* want to kiss me! Do you?"

"Now, Pearl," he placated feebly, rubbing the back of his head. "Don't take a pet. 'Tis not that I don't want to . . ."

"Then what is it?" She sounded thoroughly affronted. She was close enough for him to make out the luscious shape of her through the shadows. Her question had an ominous ring to it. Cursing himself for a want-wit, Alec sought frantically for an answer that would pacify her. On this of all nights, he realized he should have been expecting her. For years now she had been his most constant bed partner. He had been away from her for some weeks, and she fancied herself more than a little in love with him, he knew. Of course, on his single night in town before returning to Amberwood, she would seek out his bed. And ordinarily he would have welcomed her with open arms. But now—there was Isabella. And Paddy. Why he had failed to anticipate this highly embarrassing situation, he couldn't fathom, but he had. And now he had to get over heavy ground as lightly as he could.

" 'Tis obvious you wish me at Jericho," Pearl said with an edge to her voice as he failed to answer. "Knowing you, I should've guessed that bedding with a real live countess would spoil you for us gutter folk. That's it, ain't it? I'm not good enough for you anymore! Tell me, is she better in the sack than she looks? I would've thought 'er a dull piece, myself, but then, what would a 'ore know about a *lady?*"

"Now, Pearl, hold on." As familiar with her temper as he was, Alec was quick to try to placate her. The last thing in the world he wanted was for her to give way to a screaming tantrum that would inevitably bring Paddy charging to the rescue. "Let me light the candle, and we'll talk a bit."

"Talk!" she sputtered as he touched flint to steel and lit the bedside candle. The wick caught, and as the soft pool of light spread over the room, he looked up at her. Her hair was loose and well brushed so that it glinted in the candlelight as if it had been sprinkled all over with the dust from a million diamonds. Her lovely skin glowed white above and through the diaphanous gold bedgown she wore. Her face was as beautiful as it had always been. Her body was as breathtakingly magnificent as ever. But she stirred nothing in him save acute embarrassment, and regret that he must hurt her.

What he felt for Isabella must be love if it left him totally cold to Pearl's dazzling array of charms.

"Sit, Pearl, please." Alec patted the side of the bed invitingly.

"So that we can *talk?*" She spoke through her teeth, her arms crossing beneath her nearly bare bosom so that the luscious globes threatened to burst forth in all their naked glory with every indignant shake of her head.

Her eyes flashed warning sparks as they ran over him, returned to his face. "That tells me all I need to know, I guess. You're a 'orny bastard, usually. Does the little countess's blue blood make up for 'er lack of a chest, or 'ips, or any other female attraction? She looks kind of puny for your taste, but then, she's a countess, ain't she?"

"Quit spitting at me like an angry cat, and sit down here and listen." Impatient now, Alec reached up, caught one of her hands, and tugged.

"Let go of me!" Pearl was a strong woman for all her blatant femininity, and succeeded easily in freeing herself of his grip.

"Damn it, Pearl!"

Determined to get things straight between them while he had the chance, he leaped out of bed stark naked, then wrapped his arms around her to hold her still.

"Get your bloody 'ands off me, or so 'elp me God, I'll scream the place down!"

That was a very real threat, although she didn't know it. Visions of Paddy bursting through the door danced through Alec's head. Of course, he had no doubt that his old friend would accept the situation for what it was rather than what it looked like once he had the chance to explain, but in the state he was in, Paddy was unlikely to wait for explanations. The thought of coming to fisticuffs with

Paddy made him clamp a precautionary hand over Pearl's mouth. Good God, what a damnable coil!

She was struggling in his arms, furious now, so he wrestled her to the bed, pushed her down, and fell on top of her to hold her there, one hand pinioning her wrists.

"Damn it, Pearl, will you be still and listen?" he hissed into her enraged face. She tried to knee him by way of answer, and he shifted himself just in the nick of time. Still, the blow made him angry, and his eyes blazed down at her as he pressed her deeper into the bed.

"If you scream, I'll gag you," he threatened, and lifted his hand, holding it just millimeters from her mouth so that he could replace it quickly if need be.

"You're a whoreson son of a—"

Alec clamped his hand over her mouth again. She continued her furious tirade against the human gag. Rolling his eyes heavenward, Alec got a firm grip on his temper and tried again.

" 'Tis Paddy," he said as she squirmed mightily beneath him, knowing himself for a coward but not daring to admit to his feelings for Isabella as a reason for fobbing off the vixen beneath him. Like himself, Pearl had a wicked temper when roused, and was capable of God knew what degree of mayhem. He'd known her once to have set a man's breeches on fire—with the man in them.

"Paddy—he's besotted with you, crazy with wanting you. He loves you, Pearl. Truly loves you. And what you and I have together can't stand up to that."

She went very still as he spoke, staring up at him with narrowed, suspicious eyes. Encouraged by the fact that she was no longer fighting him, Alec lifted his hand from her mouth again.

"Do ya take me for a flat, Alec Tyron?" she demanded furiously as soon as she could speak.

" 'Tis God's honest truth. I swear it," Alec said sincerely. "Paddy's been hankering after you for a long while; it's been as plain as the nose on your face. And tonight he told me plain that he loves you, girl. He also told me he'd murder any other man who bedded you, even me."

Pearl snorted. "Paddy's a great oaf, and you're no more afraid of 'im than you are of the air you breathe. 'Tis that bloody little Isabella what's come between us, and don't try to tell me otherwise! She's turned your 'ead with 'er simpering airs, that's what it is! You've always 'ad a 'ankering to be better than you are, and you think she's just the ticket! Well, I've news for you, my fine buck: she may think you're great between the sheets, but to a lady like 'er, that's all the likes of you are good for! Once she gets back to her blue-blooded kin, she won't give you the time o' day! Then what will you do, eh? Don't come cryin' to me, 'cause I won't 'ave you!"

"What I'm telling you about Paddy is true, so you can just leave Isabella out of this," Alec began, nettled, when Pearl, with an enraged cry, managed to throw him off her with a single mighty heave. She bounced to her feet beside the bed, and turned on him like a spitting fury.

"It is 'er!" she hissed. "I knew it! You've lost your bloody fool 'ead over 'er, 'aven't you, you bloody idiot? So protective you are! 'Just leave Isabella out of this,' " she mimicked nastily. Her sneer changed to an expression of utter rage. " 'Tis in love with 'er you think you are, don't you, you great fool? Well, mark my words, she'll never 'ave you, not for nothin' more than a stud, and after this, I won't either! You can get down on bended knee to me in future, and you won't get me into your bed again!"

"Pearl . . ." Alec came off the bed and approached her, knowing that he had handled her badly but helpless to think of a way to retrieve the situation. Reaching out, he caught both her hands and tried to pull her to him.

"You can just keep your 'ands bloody well off me!" she cried, jerking them free and jumping back out of reach. Then, to Alec's horror, Pearl burst into a torrent of tears. Good Christ, how much more could a man take in a single day?

"Aw, Pearl, sweetheart, won't you just—"

"You're so full of shit you stink, Alec Tyron!" Pearl shrieked, the suddenness of it making him jump. "I 'ate you, do you 'ear? I 'ate you! And I 'ate that bloody scrawny bag of bones you're doin' it to, too! By God, I do!"

With that she ran to the door, jerked it open, and fled along the corridor, her nightdress billowing behind her like a shimmering golden cloud. Alec followed her as far as the door, then hesitated, watching thoughtfully as she disappeared down the stairs.

Perhaps this was something that Pearl was best left to work out alone. He knew that once she was herself again, she would hate the idea that he had made her cry. Pearl was a proud woman, independent, feisty. Alec suddenly threw up his hands, shut the door, propped a precautionary chair beneath the knob, and went to bed, thanking God that it was Paddy who had to sort this particular female out, and not himself.

The next morning, neither Pearl nor Paddy put in an appearance at breakfast. With a mental shrug—perhaps Paddy was at that very moment taking his advice—Alec ate a light meal, then, with only one stop in town, drove back to Amberwood in a natty high-perch phaeton. He'd bought it before all the attempts on his life, and had scarcely had a chance to drive it. He thought exploring the countryside in it might tickle Isabella's fancy. As he neared Horsham he patted the securely wrapped package in his pocket and whipped up his horses, absurdly anxious to see her again. He shook his head at his own foolishness. At near enough to thirty as to make no matter, he was behaving like a green lad in the throes of his first infatuation. But he had to admit, it felt good.

Grinning, he imagined Isabella running down the steps of Amberwood to greet him, imagined enfolding her in his arms, presenting her with her present, and carrying her off to bed. Later, they'd laugh at how she had cried when he'd left, and she would model the necklace of a dozen robin's-egg-sized amethysts set in silver he'd bought her, along with matching earbobs. At the thought that he might be able to cajole her into wearing just the jewelry and nothing else for him, his heart speeded up. God, he'd missed her a ridiculous amount just to have been absent from her for less than two days. But making up for lost time together might have definite rewards. . . .

As he pictured Isabella, with her soft mouth and softer body, her eyes almost exactly the color of the stones in his pocket, his grin dimmed somewhat. Something about that delectable picture was bothering him. He thought of Isabella and he felt . . .

His blood ran cold as he realized that what he was feeling was that omniscient tingle of danger again.

LV

Isabella walked into the inn at Tunbridge Wells with Bernard right behind her. She was cold with fear, but clear-headed too. If he was taking her into a public inn, he could not mean to murder her out of hand. Could he?

This inn was called the Pelican. It was a fashionable establishment, outfitted with crystal chandeliers and soft carpets, obviously used to catering to members of the quality. Upon their entrance the innkeep hurried up to Bernard, obsequious as he inquired if he could help my lord in any way. Bernard waved him away with an impatient look.

The taproom was all but deserted at this hour in the afternoon. Bernard, with a heavy hand on her elbow, escorted Isabella to a private parlor that he must have previously reserved. The knowledge that there would be few people within earshot should she be in trouble heightened the panic that she was fighting hard to control. If Bernard had schemed to have her murdered, and the evidence said he had, what were the odds that he would try again? Surely, if he had tracked her down merely to kill her, he would already have dispatched her in the carriage. If he was squeamish about doing the deed himself, the cretin accompanying him, who obviously had been hired as muscle, could have done the deed. The man looked capable of any violence, and stupid to boot. So perhaps she was safe, at lease for the nonce. Then again, maybe she was not.

The contrast between the Pelican and the Traveler's Rest could not have been greater. The Traveler's Rest had been squalid, malodorous and downright dangerous. But Isabella would have exchanged her present elegant surroundings for it in a heartbeat, if she could have exchanged her present escort for her previous one at the same time.

Alec. She clung to the image of him arriving to rescue her as to a lifeline. Alec would be returning to Amberwood soon, she knew. He would miss her, of course, almost immediately, and start to search. But had anyone seen the coach, and her abduction? Would he even know where to begin to look? Would he guess that Bernard had found her? Or would his initial assumption be that she had suffered an accident or some such mishap?

She had to face the fact that it could be hours, or even days, before Alec managed to track her down. At the realization, she cast an apprehensive look at her stone-faced husband.

So far Bernard had spoken not one word after he had identified her to the thug accompanying him as his wife. Isabella, too, had remained silent out of a mixture of prudence and fear. After all, what was there to say between an adulterous wife and the husband who had in all likelihood paid to have her killed?

In a ridiculously incongruous gesture under the circumstances, Bernard opened the door to the private parlor and then courteously stood back to let her precede him into the room. Even if he planned to kill her, Bernard, a gentleman to his fingertips, would observe the courtesies to the end, she knew. Before she bowed to the inevitable and entered, Isabella cast a despairing eye back down the corridor. Should she scream for help now, before he got her alone?

But then, she had to remember that Bernard could not know that she knew that he had planned to have her killed. It was possible that he might suspect that she had some inkling of his plans—and then again he might not, because his opinion of her intellect had never been strong—but he could not know for certain that she knew. Safety lay in pretending ignorance of his intentions until she could get away, or until someone came along to rescue her.

Isabella took a deep breath, entered the room, and crossed to the unlit hearth (the weather had continued unseasonably warm). Then, schooling her features so as not to show the fear that made her nervous as a bird around a cat, she turned to face her husband.

For the first time in almost a year, they were alone together. Bernard had closed the door, and as she watched him, he locked it. Then he turned to look at her, his hands still resting behind him on the knob, his back leaning against the door.

Had she ever thought him handsome? Isabella wondered, marvelling at herself as her eyes swept him. The lowering answer was, yes, she had. She had once found his tall, slender elegance admirable. His face was thin and clever, with aquiline features and an olive complexion. Lines scored it from nose to mouth and, to a lesser extent, around his eyes. But never until this moment had she thought to wonder if those lines had resulted from too many nights of dissipation. His hair was black, with distinguishing wings of gray above either ear. His eyes were rather slanted, and dark brown. On this day, as on every other occasion that she had seen him, he was elegantly turned out, in a coat of blue superfine and biscuit-colored breeches. His Hessians gleamed like mirrors, and sported white tops and tassles. His linen was immaculate. Whatever else he was, Bernard St. Just was every inch a gentleman.

"Now, wife. Now you may tell me where, and with whom, you've been."

He made no move toward her, but his eyes glittered with malice. Isabella had never in all the years she had been wed to him heard him raise his voice, and he did not now. But there was an icy note underlying his words that warned of rage barely suppressed. She was reminded again that he had wanted her dead, and with difficulty held back a shiver. But she had to brave it out. Her life might very well depend on it.

"I . . . I was kidnapped. Surely you know that."

"You were kidnapped, yes. Unless, of course, you staged the whole thing, which I never, until I received word that you were living incognito with your lover, considered. But even allowing that the kidnapping was genuine, that does not answer the question of where, and with whom, you have been for nigh on three months. The ransom was paid, in full, less than a week after you vanished. You never appeared. We—your father and I—feared you were dead. You father had Bow Street Runners searching for you. Indeed, Alpin, who accompanied me in the carriage, is a Runner. When I came upon you, you were clearly not being held against your will. You were free to return home anytime you wished. Yet you did not. If you do not wish to feel the full force of my wrath, you will explain yourself, madame, and quickly."

His voice was silky, but the very silkiness of it frightened her. He sounded capable of any violence. . . .

"Well?" He rapped out the word when she didn't reply at once. Isabella jumped at the sharpness of it.

"I . . ." she began, desperately searching for an excuse. Would he believe that her dreadful experience had addled her brain, so that she had forgotten who she was? Not likely. But she could not tell him about Alec, or that the reason she had not returned home when she could have was that she feared he would try again to kill her. Quickly quickly, she must think of some other, reasonable, excuse

"Don't bother trying to think up a lie," he snarled coming away from the door with a lunge and crossing the room with two long strides to grab her by her upper arms and give her a shake. "I know where you've been: you've been with a lover. Who is he? By God, you'll tell me that!"

He spat the last words in her face, holding her on tiptoe so that her face was only a few inches below his.

Terrified by the white fury that blazed from him, she said nothing.

"Who is he? Who is he?" he hissed. "By God, to think

that I've been cuckolded by a gray little mouse of a chit who never had two words to say for herself! I—"

There was a knock at the door. Isabella had never been so glad of an interruption in her life. As Bernard looked toward the solid portal, Isabella made up her mind there and then that, whoever it was, she must ask for help. Bernard was beside himself with rage. She felt herself in terrible danger. . . .

"What is it?"

"Bernard? You in there? Let me in!"

"Charles!"

Isabella's mouth closed with a snap. She knew that voice.

"Papa!" she cried, her knees weakening with relief. Her father had never cared for her overmuch, but he would not stand by and see her murdered in cold blood. She need no longer draw each breath in fear of her life. . . .

Bernard, shooting her one last murderous look, released his grip on her arms by shoving her away from him so hard that she stumbled backwards. He strode to the door. As he turned the key in the lock, Isabella steadied herself by holding on to the corner of a table. The best way to safeguard herself would be to lay the whole story before her father, who would know how to protect her. Perhaps the marriage could be dissolved. . . .

"Papa!" she said again as he stepped into the room. Hurrying forward, smiling at him with relief and affection, she would have thrown herself into his arms. But the expression that came over his face as he beheld her made her falter and stop while she was still some feet away. Crossing his arms over his chest, her father fixed her with a look of utter loathing.

"So it was true," the Duke of Portland said bitterly. "That a daughter of mine could so disgrace our name—I cannot credit it. I would not have believed it did not my own eyes give me the evidence." His eyes shifted to Bernard. "I make you my apologies, Bernard. The gel wasn't raised to be a whore."

"Papa . . ." She addressed him almost piteously. Both

men ignored her as completely as if she weren't even present.

"I take it that you, too, received a letter informing you of where, and in what circumstances, our prodigal could be found." The violence had left Bernard's face, to be replaced by nothing more threatening than cool good breeding as he looked at the duke.

"Indeed I did! I didn't believe it, of course, but it was strange, arriving out of the blue like that when I'd just brought Sarah up to London. So I took it around to your place only to have your man tell me you'd left this morning for the Pelican in Tunbridge Wells. Figured you must have got something of the same, because Tunbridge Wells is too close to Horsham for it to be a coincidence. Figured if you took it seriously enough to travel here out of season, I should come along too. Not that I expected there to be anything to it, of course. Isabella's never been much to look at, but she was a good, biddable gel. Who would have thought she'd bring this disgrace upon us all? I suppose it was true? She was with a man?"

Bernard nodded. "At least, I never saw the man—not that I don't mean to; I'll call the whoreson out for dishonoring my wife—but I wanted to get Isabella out of it first, without any trouble. I didn't really expect to find her, you see, so I wasn't armed. But there she was, right where my anonymous correspondent said she'd be, walking as merrily as you please along a lane outside a place called Amberwood. Rothersham's seat, you know, sold to a Cit or some such a few years ago." Bernard deigned to look at her, his eyes dark with anger. "Don't tell me you've sunk so low as to take a Cit as a lover. Gad, I can't even call the fellow out! Take a horsewhip to him, more like."

"Papa!" Isabella clasped her hands in front of her, ignoring Bernard's slander as she looked at her father beseechingly. "Papa, you must listen. I—"

"Be silent," the duke said coldly, hardly bothering to glance at her. "Now that you've got her back, what do plan to do with her?"

"I see no recourse to a bill of divorcement. . . ."

The duke had a round, rather florid face topped by a shoulder-length fall of crisp, snow white curls. Hearing that, his face went almost as pale as his hair.

"I would greatly oppose any such action. A divorce is unthinkable! The scandal would ruin us all! I know the gel deserves to be ruined, but you would be tarred with the same brush. So would we all, Sarah and my innocent children included."

Bernard's eyes took on a sudden gleam that Isabella, watching him with growing horror, thought might be described as cunning. She had never considered the possibility that her father might refuse to hear her side.

"I'll not keep a wife who's played me false. Why, she might be with child! A bastard child, to be foisted off as my heir! We've been cronies a long time, Charles, and I'm sorry for it, but you must understand when I tell you that I can't keep an adulteress as my countess. Every feeling is offended."

"Papa—"

The duke shushed her with an impatient gesture. "I know it's a hard thing I'm asking, but I'm willing to pay to get what I want. You keep my gel as wife, and help me hush up any scandal, and I'll make you settlement enough to keep you in funds for the rest of your life. I'm prepared to be generous about this, Bernard."

"Well . . ." Bernard pretended to consider. Isabella knew it was pretence because she had at last been able to put a name to the gleam in his eyes: it was greed, pure and simple. But her father could not, or would not, see. His vision of Bernard was forever clouded by what he thought a gentleman born and bred should be. Desperate, she walked up to her father, and shook his sleeve determinedly.

"Papa, he was behind my kidnapping. He paid a gang of men to kidnap me, hold me for ransom, and then, when it was collected, kill me. He meant to have me murdered in cold blood! He's had losses at the gaming table, huge losses, and he used what was left of my marriage settlement to cover them. With the money gone, I wasn't worth anything to him anymore, so he decided to kill me and wed another heiress. I'm sure he already had someone in mind.''

Isabella repeated the story that Molly had told her, and Alec had amplified on, coldly, clearly, her eyes steady on her father's frowning face. She was rewarded by the sudden riveting of both men's attention on her.

Bernard recovered first. His face, which had gone white, crimsoned. ''Why, you lying little . . . So that's how you think to cover up your fornicating! Pray don't think your father—or anyone else!—is fool enough to swallow such a tale as that!''

Isabella's eyes never left her father. ''It's true, Papa. I swear on my mother's soul it's true!''

The duke's mouth tightened, and his pale blue eyes glittered icily. Before Isabella knew what he was about, he lifted a hand and slapped her hard across the face.

She staggered back, her hand flying to her cheek, tears springing to her eyes. That he could so contemptuously dismiss her without even considering what she had to say hurt more than the blow. '' 'Tis the truth! He paid them to kill me. . . .''

''What bloody poppycock!'' her father snorted, and shook his head at Bernard. ''I don't know where she comes by it. There's no bad blood on either side of the family that I know of it. Her mother wasn't much, but she was good *ton.*''

''I don't hold you to blame, Charles, you may be sure.'' Bernard, with a single glinting look at Isabella, reassured the duke almost affably. Helplessly Isabella cradled her abused cheek and looked from her husband to her father. Neither had as much care for her as they might have for a stray dog.

''You'll put aside the notion of divorce? Beat her a dozen times a day if you have to to keep her true, but spare the rest of us the scandal. I beseech you.''

''Papa, you must listen! I—''

''One more word out of you, and I'll take a stick to

you. 'Tis what you deserve, with your fornicating and your lies."

Bernard lifted the back of his hand as if to strike her while her father looked on, if not with approval, at least without objecting. Isabella took an instinctive step backwards. Further pleas obviously would be useless. There was no persuading her father to her cause. He had never cared for her overmuch, and now he was completely on Bernard's side. But at least, with her accusation of attempted murder made public, Bernard would not be likely to try again . . . would he?

As her legal husband, he could treat her however he wished. He could beat her, lock her in, starve her, rape her—and the law would be on his side. Only if he actually murdered her—and it could be proven—would a kind of justice be done. But then, of course, it would be too late to do her any good.

It was a hard lesson, but Isabella learned it in those few moments. If she wanted to save her skin, she had best meekly accept whatever plans these two hatched for her future until she could discover an alternative. Or until Alec could arrive to save her. . . .

"You must take her to Paris," her father was saying. "All the world's there, now that Louis has got his throne back. Who's to know that she hasn't been there all the time, when you bring her back to England at last? Nobody ever saw her in town anyway. There was some rumor about the gel being missing—fellow actually had the gall to ask me to my face at White's if my daughter'd shown up yet—but with Boney exiled and all the excitement, it'll be forgot in a trice. What a blessing that you held off on sending that death notice to the paper, eh, Bernard? I told you not to write the gel off so fast."

"To Paris?" Bernard frowned, then nodded. "That might serve. Though it will be costly, and my funds are tied up at present. I foresaw an opportunity to make a good investment, now that the Bourbons are back on the throne, and I daren't withdraw the funds yet. They're just starting to increase."

"I'll stand the nonsense," the duke interrupted gruffly. "And make the settlement I spoke about besides. Paris is the answer. Sarah and I will join you, to give the gel a bit more countenance. We'll take her about a bit so that she's seen and everyone knows she was in Paris with her family. Then in a couple of months you can send her back to Blakely Park, and all this will be forgotten."

The duke held out his hand to Bernard, while Isabella, feeling sicker by the second, watched.

"By God, you're a game'un, sir!" the duke exclaimed, and shook his son-in-law by the hand.

LVI

Not more than twelve hours after Alec had driven cheerfully away from the Carousel, he was bursting back through the front door in a rage fueled by sheer terror.

"Get out o' my way!" he snarled at the obsequious Sharp, who tried to hold the door open for him. Eyes widening, the butler stumbled back just in time to keep from being hit by the door, which crashed into the elegantly papered wall behind it.

"Where's Mr. McNally?" Alec barked, the glittering menace in his eyes frightening the old butler so much that he blanched.

"Uh, uh, with Miss Pearl, in her rooms, sir," Sharp answered.

Without giving him a chance to say another word, Alec turned on his heel and strode furiously down the hall.

"Sir . . . sir, wouldn't you rather I fetched him for you?" Sharp quavered with a desperate air, almost running as he tried to keep up with Alec and at the same time gesture frantically to the half dozen footmen on duty. This early in the evening, the gaming rooms were thin of company, but the few patrons who had decided to try their luck looked around at the commotion. Alec no more saw their speculative stares than he saw the glowing candles or the fine gilt mirrors or the high-polished floor. A horrifying sense of urgency drove him, making him blind to anything that was not connected with his objective.

"Go on about your business, you blathering idiot!" Alec ordered over his shoulder, and dismissed with a murderous glare the footmen who had started to close in on him. Hired partly to provide protection for the establishment and its mistress, they recognized the Tiger and fell back. Sharp, apparently realizing that he had as much hope of detaining Alec as he did of stopping the sun from rising in the morning, shrugged fatalistically and returned to his post by the door. Alec reached the door to Pearl's suite, turned the knob, found it unlocked, and burst through it without ceremony. It bounced back on its hinges, crashing into the wall with a resounding bang.

From the bedroom beyond the sitting room came a man's curse and a woman's scream.

Alec saw nothing more of the sitting room than a blur of white, and then he was standing in the doorway of the bedroom, looking into the mouth of a pistol pointed at his head by his best friend.

"Alec!" Paddy sounded both dumbfounded and relieved. Alec saw without any interest at all that his friend was stark naked, and that Pearl, sitting up in the wide bed in which Alec had passed many a pleasant hour, was naked too. Paddy lowered the pistol, and shook his head. " 'Ave you lost your bloody senses, man? I could've done for you!"

"I need your 'elp. It's Isabella. She's gone." His voice had an odd rasp to it, probably because he could hardly talk around the lump in his throat.

"What do you mean, gone?"

"Gone, disappeared, vanished! Someone's taken 'er! A groom saw 'er walking along the lane in front of the 'ouse, and then when 'e looked again, all 'e saw was a carriage turning back the way it 'ad come! 'E'd already set men after 'er when I got there, but they never found a trace. Not a trace! Oh, God!" Alec broke off, fighting not to give way to total panic as he tried for the hundredth time in an hour to imagine who could hate him so much—and know him so well—that they would attack him through Isabella.

How many who knew him, or of him, were even aware of her existence?

"Rothersham, do you think?" Paddy asked tersely, laying the pistol on the bedside table and reaching for his breeches, which were crumpled on the floor beside the bed.

"If I thought so, I'd kill the bloody bastard by inches—but the man's too much a coward, and too thoroughly frightened, to 'ave done such a thing."

"Then who?"

"God, I've racked my brain and I can't come up with any answer to that!"

"There's no need to be in such a taking, Alec. I'm sure the countess 'as come to no 'arm." Pearl rose from the bed, sublimely unconcerned with her nakedness until she caught Paddy's darkening eye upon her. Then, with a conciliatory little moue in his direction, she picked up her white silk wrapper from the chair by the bed and shrugged into it, tying the ribbons and shaking her hair loose from the collar as she came toward Alec.

"Darlin', what makes you think anything's 'appened to 'er? 'Ow do you know the little—Isabella—'asn't just decided that she's 'ad enough of an adventure and gone back 'ome? Or maybe she's found another lover. Some of us do that, you know."

There was the barest undertone of malice to that, telling Alec that Pearl had not forgotten their recent quarrel.

"Isabella would no more do such a thing than she would fly," he said positively, dismissing the suggestions as not even worth considering until something—*something*—in Pearl's expression struck him as odd. He'd known her long, and he'd known her well, and he'd seen that cat-with-the-canary-in-its mouth smile before.

"Damn you to bloody 'ell and back, Pearl," he swore savagely, reaching for her and dragging her forward to stand in front of him, both hands closed tightly around her soft upper arms. "What 'ave you done?"

" 'Ave you lost your mind, Alec? Take your 'ands off 'er!" Paddy was beside him, towering over him, glowering threateningly, but Alec paid him no mind. Pearl was looking frightened now, the malicious amusement that had shone from her eyes moments earlier replaced by an apprehension that was obvious to those who knew her as well as Alec—and Paddy—did.

"Good God, woman!" Paddy muttered, one look at her face convicting her for him as well as Alec.

"What 'ave you done?" Alec growled again, and when Pearl still didn't answer, he shook her furiously. "What 'ave you done? You'll tell me, or I'll . . ."

"Ow, Alec, you're 'urting me, you are! Paddy, are you goin' to let 'im treat me this way? You said you loved me! Ow!"

Alec was beside himself, ready to wrap his fingers around her neck and squeeze the answer out of her if need be. Paddy, seeing the fury in his friend's face, placed a restraining hand on his arm.

"Leave off now, Alec. Leave 'er to me."

"And welcome," Alec said bitterly, thrusting Pearl toward him. Like Alec, Paddy held Pearl's upper arms in his huge hands, but his grip was gentler. She looked up at him, her white-blonde hair spilling down her back, her midnight blue eyes wide and frightened. She looked very young suddenly—and very guilty.

"Pearl?" Paddy questioned softly, his eyes fastening on and holding hers.

Pearl looked up at him for a long moment without speaking. Then her face crumpled and she burst into noisy tears.

LVII

In a week Isabella found herself in Paris. The city was in an uproar, as Royalist troops searched out the last of the Bonapartists who, unable to escape with their master, had gone into hiding. Soldiers in their tall shakos and fine pelisses marched the streets at all hours. Homes were summarily searched, and scores of people were arrested for no greater charge than having been loyal to Napoleon. The Tuileries, returned to the Bourbon King, glittered every night with festivities as all those in Paris—the French citizenry and the English who flocked into the city to be present at this triumphal moment—celebrated the Bourbon restoration. If some of those present would have just as joyously welcomed the return of Napoleon, no one could have told it from the dedication with which they celebrated the new regime.

The Duke of Wellington had been named Ambassador of Paris, and all the talk was of the assassination attempt against him that had gone awry. Isabella, receiving afternoon callers with her stepmother in the sitting room of the house Bernard had leased in the fashionable rue de la Printemps, listened as Colonel Tynling told the tale yet again:

"The assassin placed himself in the Rue Royale, just outside the gateway of the courtyard of Nosey's hotel. Just as Nosey's carriage turned into the gateway, the fellow commenced firing his pistol at the duke; then when the weapon emptied he ran up the street and made his escape before he could be seized by the sentries who were on duty at the hotel's entrance. The Minister of Police—a Frenchy, of course—made a great noise about discovering the criminal, but the man got clean away, to Belgium it is said. Of course, he had help from those who employed him."

"Do you think he was hired? Who would do such a thing?" One of the other guests, a petite little redhead named Miss Brantley, breathed in wide-eyed fascination. That her fascination was more for Colonel Tynling than his tale was well-known, and obvious even to one as new to their company as Isabella. But the Colonel, feeling himself properly appreciated, visibly swelled.

"There are those who would have Bonaparte back, who would stop at nothing to send fat Louis packing."

"Oh, my!" Miss Brantley gasped, apparently awe-stricken. It was all Isabella could do not to roll her eyes in disgust. This, her first taste of Society, was likely to give her a disgust for it that no amount of time could eradicate.

The six days since their arrival in the newly liberated city—the party consisted of Bernard, herself, the duke and his wife—had been spent largely in an orgy of shopping. Isabella, escorted by Sarah and a "footman" named Lambert whom Isabella suspected had really been employed to keep an eye on her, had visited mantua-makers by the dozen. Without Alec to dazzle, she contented herself with restoring her accustomed appearance. Thus it was that, for all her wardrobe's expense, it consisted of quiet blues and grays and mauves. Once again she faded into the background, attracting no notice. Her hair she styled as she had for years, scraped back into a tidy knot at her nape. The fringe that Mr. Alderson had so cunningly fashioned still framed her face, hinting at the quiet beauty that she didn't care enough to let shine, but in the general drabness of her appearance no one noticed. She was sensible Isabella again, and determined to remain so.

"She's such a . . . a nothing," Sarah complained to the duke that evening, after Isabella had spent the entire afternoon seated on the small settee with hardly a word to say for herself. "She's an embarrassment, Charles, really. Why must I do this?"

Isabella, who had come into the hall behind Sarah, was neither hurt nor surprised by this overhead outburst. Indeed, she felt nothing at all as she listened to her hitherto despised stepmother's words. If Sarah was ashamed of her, then good. She herself had no love for Sarah. But to her surprise, Isabella found that she no longer either hated or feared her, as she had as a girl. She felt only indifference. Sarah had lost her power to wound at last.

"To protect our name, of course. Do you want it bruited about that our daughter spent months in the company of a man not her husband? Think of that, my dear, and be thankful that Isabella is not one to attract much attention. No one will remember just when she was and was not in Paris, as they would if she were a raving beauty."

"I had not thought of that," Sarah said, frowning. Then their carriage arrived and they left.

Isabella and Bernard were to join them at the Elysée that evening, to pay their respects as new arrivals to the King, but they would not leave until half past ten, and at the moment it was only five. Bernard was not in the house—indeed, she had seen him only in company since that first shattering confrontation in the Pelican—and would likely arrive at the house just in time to change into evening clothes before going out. He treated her with courtesy in public, and ignored her in private, which put their relationship back on a footing similar to that which had always existed between them. Appeased by the healthy bribe her father had bestowed on him, and made a little wary by her open accusation of attempted murder, Bernard seemed to have abandoned any notion of ridding himself of his wife.

For the time being at least.

Glancing out through the glass sidelight by the imposing front door, Isabella saw that Lambert was stationed by the front steps. She wondered what he would do if she simply walked out the door, down the steps and away . . . away to England, Amberwood and Alec.

Stop her, of course. Without ever putting it to the test, she knew.

Suddenly Isabella was afflicted with the most dreadful headache. Or was it heartache that sent her to her room to rest?

LVIII

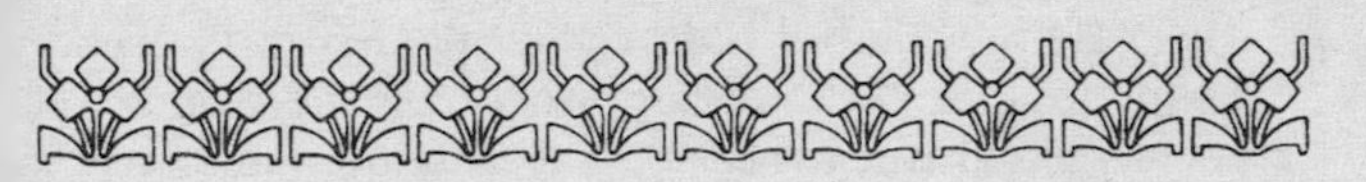

It was late afternoon two days later. At Sarah's insistence, Isabella had joined a party of her friends watching a balloon ascension from a carriage in the Place de l'Etoile. Nearby stood the half-completed Arc de Triomphe, which Napoleon had intended to stand as a symbol of his victories and which had been hastily abandoned. As the balloonists were having some trouble getting their craft in the air, Isabella stepped down from the carriage to join Miss Brantley and Sarah in viewing the symbol of the deposed Emperor's waning fortunes. Colonel Tynling and Viscount de Lile, who formed the rest of the party, stayed behind to watch the adventurers' efforts, so the ladies ventured forth alone.

The carriage was only a few yards from the monument, but many people had crowded into the square to watch the promised spectacle, and it took some time to pick their way through the crowd. Isabella found herself jostled mercilessly, and when a hand caught her arm, she was hardly surprised.

"Please release my . . ." she began, turning to treat her assailant to a frosty stare. But then the words died in her throat. The square with its noisy crowd faded into nothingness.

"Alec," she said. Then again, helplessly, "Alec."

He looked down at her, those golden eyes intent, then

without a word, turned and pulled her by the hand through the crowd.

Isabella followed him, blindly obedient, her heart pounding so fiercely that she could scarcely breathe, let alone think. She fastened her eyes on the back of that tawny head, and drank in the sight of him.

Alec had come at last.

He pulled her into a little walled garden in the nearby Champs Elysées. Then at last, when they were totally secure in their privacy, he stopped walking and turned to look at her. Those golden eyes moved over her face as if he were starved for the sight of her. His hands caught hers and he pulled her close, their bodies almost touching.

"My God, Isabella, I've been going out of my mind," he said quietly. And then she was locked in his embrace, her arms sliding around his neck to clutch him as if she would never let him go. They kissed tenderly, fiercely, as if they would die if they didn't.

When at last he lifted his head, he still held her pressed against him, his arms around her, his mouth in her hair.

" 'Twas Pearl," he said. "She confessed when Paddy taxed her. She was jealous, crazy jealous, and when she knew that I'd be coming up to London and you'd be at Amberwood alone, she sent messages to that whoreson husband of yours and, to her credit, to your father, thinking that way to at least save you from being murdered on the spot. I near strangled her when she admitted what she'd done. Only Paddy stopped me, but he was wroth with her too. She said when I found you I should tell you she was sorry for what she did."

"Oh, Alec," she murmured foolishly against the solid warmth of his chest. She didn't seem capable of saying anything else. Just his name, again and again. Like a litany. His words went completely over her head. She barely heard them. All she cared about was being back in his arms. She felt suddenly whole once more, as if half of her that had been missing had been found.

"Has the bloody bastard harmed you?"

"No. He had no more reason to, you see. My father

has given him a fortune not to divorce me. For adultery. With you.'' The absurdity of it struck her then, and she gave a hysterical little giggle.

As inured as she was to his language, the word he said then made the tips of her ears burn. Pushing a little away, she looked up at him. Her eyes touched every chiselled feature, caressed every well-loved plane and angle of that handsome face. His broad shoulders blocked her view of the rest of the garden, but she wouldn't have cared if there had been a hundred spectators. She rose up on tiptoe and kissed him full on the mouth, softly and tenderly, with exquisite feeling. Then, as his arms tightened around her and his mouth took control of the kiss, the tenderness blazed into throbbing passion.

''Oh, Alec,'' she said again when she could talk, her forehead bowed against him, resting just below the hollow in his neck. ''I feared never to see you again.''

''No chance of that, my girl.'' He was still holding her, but more loosely now, and his voice had recovered some of its normal aplomb. '' 'Twas France that threw me off, or I'd have come for you sooner. As it was, I had men scouring every nook and cranny of England. Finally a chap in Portsmouth remembered seeing a lady of your description boarding a ship. After that it was easy.''

''I've missed you so.''

''And I've missed you. It embarrasses me when I think how much. But enough of this. We'll have time and more for this kind of foolishness once I have you safe away.''

He dropped a kiss on her hair, then another on her nose, then a third on her mouth. His arms dropped from around her waist. He caught her hand, and would have herded her from the garden. Beyond him, just outside the shoulder-high stone walls, Isabella caught a glimpse of a hulking giant and perhaps half a dozen others. Alec had brought a small army of his own, it seemed. With Paddy and the rest guarding the entrance to the garden, no wonder she and Alec found themselves completely alone.

''No, Alec,'' she said gently. She knew that what she was doing was the only possible thing, but still she felt as though she were being stabbed clear through to the heart. For just a moment she allowed herself to imagine what it would be like to go with him, back to Amberwood or wherever he wished, to live with him and be his love as he had once asked her to. But then, in a blinding flash of reality, she knew that such an existence, while beautiful to imagine, would be impossible in real life. If she were to disappear again, after this time being so visible in Paris, there would be a scandal. Bernard and her father would inevitably turn up at Amberwood in a matter of days. Even if she and Alec were to go elsewhere, they would be found.

Alec, Bernard and her father would meet. There would be bloodshed. Alec would quite likely emerge the victor, but could she come to him with the blood of her legal husband or her father on his hands?

As long as Bernard lived, she had to remain his legal wife. Marriage was a sacrament, not to be put lightly aside. Alone, she could not hope to win a bill of divorcement. If Bernard divorced her—and she considered bloodshed far more likely than divorce, since an open scandal would touch his honor—the disgrace would haunt her family forever.

She shouldn't care, but she did.

"I can't come with you," she said, lifting her chin in a proud gesture meant to stave off incipient tears.

"What?" He looked dumbfounded.

"I can't come with you," she repeated.

"You can't come with me? Why the hell not?"

"Because I'm married, whether I like it or not. Because, although I love you, my place is with my husband."

"What bloody tripe is this?" he all but roared. "Your bloody husband tried to have you killed!"

"I told you, I don't think he'll try again. He's got money now."

Alec stared at her. Those golden eyes bored into hers as if they could see into her very soul. "Either you're crazed or I am. Of course you're coming with me. I've moved heaven and earth to find you again, my girl."

Arguments about bloodshed and scandal would not move him, she knew. He had no scruples about one, and cared nothing about the other. She had to fall back on the only weapon she had that she knew would infuriate him enough to drive him away.

"Listen to me, Alec," she said in a low voice, obstinately resisting when he would have dragged her with him by main force. "Please, just listen. What we had together was a dream, a beautiful, beautiful dream. I'll treasure the memory of it all the days of my life, but it's time for me to wake up now, to return to reality. For both our sakes, the dream has to end."

"Why?" He sounded stunned, and hurt, and angry. The golden eyes were beginning to shoot sparks. Looking at him, her heart aching, Isabella knew she had to deliver the killing blow. For his sake more than her own, being cruel now would be kinder in the end.

"Because of who you are . . . and who I am," she said softly, and had the doubtful satisfaction of seeing all the fires of hell blaze to life in his eyes.

"Because I'm a bastard gutter rat and you're a bloody countess," he clarified, and dropped her hands. His expression was bitter, hating, furious. "Why not just call a spade a spade?"

"All right then, yes. That's why." The look in his eyes was killing her. If he was hurting half as much as she was, then he was in mortal agony. But it had to be done, and it was best done quickly.

"You snobbish little bitch," he said then, his lip curling in a furious sneer. "I wish you joy of your bloody murderous blue-blooded husband, then, Countess. When he runs short of money again, I'll be sure to come to your funeral."

With that he turned on his heel and stalked from the garden. Watching him until he vanished from sight, Isabella's heart bled.

LIX

Later that night, in a bustling little *pensione* off the Rue de la Paix, Alec sat bleary-eyed at a table in the taproom, systematically drinking himself into oblivion. Paddy, opposite him, eyed his friend sympathetically as he nursed his own drink, knowing that it would be up to him to steer the pair of them safely to their beds in due course. In the near quarter century that he had known Alec, he had never seen him in such a state as he had been since the little countess had so brutally spelled out the facts of life to him in the garden that afternoon. Paddy shook his head. He wasn't much of a judge of women, he would be the first to admit that, but he wouldn't have thought the lady had it in her to be so cold-hearted. Alec had been wild after, half-crazed with anger and a kind of . . . grief.

Women were the very devil, and that was the simple truth. Paddy took a long swig of his drink, and shook his head again, mournfully.

"Christ, can you believe it? She flat-out don't want me, Paddy. She said so," Alec muttered as he had all evening, speaking more to the golden liquid in his glass than to his friend. "Pearl was in the right of it after all. The bloody little bitch wanted me to warm 'er bed for 'er, but when it came right down to it, that's all she wanted! She said she's too good for me! A countess can bed a gutter rat but she won't run off with one!" He laughed bitterly.

"Don't fash yourself so, Alec," Paddy said, feeling

helpless in the face of what he knew was Alec's very real pain. "She's not worth it. 'Ell, she's not even a beauty; far from it, in fact! When we get 'ome again we'll get you a real dazzler, and you'll soon be wondering what you ever saw in such a scrawny, 'oity-toity little miss!"

"Aye," Alec said, looking up to meet Paddy's eyes at last. "God, I'd like to wrap my 'ands around her throat and choke the life out of 'er! When I think of 'ow bloody I was to Pearl, and 'ow I ran all over England looking for the ungrateful little bitch! 'Ell, I should send Pearl a bloody thank you note! She did me a bleedin' favor, and I was too dumb to see it!"

"Pearl did wrong, and I admit it, but you were over-'arsh with 'er. She cried."

"She's cried before." Alec was indifferent to Pearl's heartburnings at the moment. His own heart was too sore to allow him to worry about anyone else.

"Aye, well, be that as it may, I don't like to see it."

Alec shifted his attention back to his glass, emptied it, and filled it again from the bottle on the table.

"You're in love, my friend. Be careful, it's a 'orrid state."

"Aye." Paddy drank to that, and refilled his own glass. Swirling the contents thoughtfully, he cast a considering look at Alec. "Mayhap you should go talk to 'er again on the morrow. Females are subject to queer starts, you know. Mayhap she didn't mean it."

"Oh, she meant it, all right." Alec gave that humorless laugh again, downed the contents of his glass in a single long gulp, and refilled it for what must have been the dozenth time that night. "She meant it. No, I'm for 'ome at first light. I've business to see to. I've neglected things shamefully over the last few months. Things 'ave gone to 'ell in a 'and-basket, and it's time I set them to rights."

Paddy said nothing, and Alec nodded with determination.

"Aye, I'll go 'ome, that's what I'll do, and the little bitch can rot in 'ell along with 'er whole blue-blooded family for all I care!"

Alec fell silent after that, drank until he passed out, and was finally carried off to bed by the slightly less inebriated Paddy.

In the morning, still obdurate, Alec climbed into a hired carriage with Paddy shortly after noon. Though his head was splitting, Alec insisted that the journey had to be begun that day. Long-suffering as ever, though his head pounded nearly as badly as Alec's, Paddy grumbled but agreed. The men they had brought with them lined up behind the carriage, looking uncomfortable on a motley collection of post horses.

''To Le Havre,'' Alec instructed the driver, while Paddy settled back against the seat for the duration. But the carriage had scarcely reached the outskirts of Paris before Alec sat bolt upright, cursing, and banged sharply on the roof to get the driver's attention.

''What the bloody 'ell . . . ?'' Paddy began, startled, but Alec ignored him.

''Pull up,'' Alec bellowed out the window, then searched for the words in French. Paddy said nothing more, just looked at him narrow-eyed as the carriage rocked to a halt. At the expression on his friend's face, Alec smiled wryly. Paddy looked as if he knew perfectly well what Alec was about before Alec even said a word of explanation.

''Well?'' Paddy cocked his head, crossing his arms over his chest, and waited.

''Fool that I am, I find that I can't just leave the troublesome little bitch to St. Just's less than tender mercies after all.''

Paddy sighed. ''I thought as much. Well, tell the man to turn around.''

Alec shook his head. ''No, you go on home and make things right with Pearl, and take care of business for me. 'Twould be nothing short of idiotic if we both stayed in Paris on account of one snot-nosed little chit. Though I'll keep what men are already here with me. I may have need of them.''

''You sure you don't want me to stay? You won't d

something bloody stupid, will you?'' Paddy asked, frowning.

''Have I ever? Go on, now.'' Alec opened the door and stepped down into the road, then, with a final wave at Paddy, told the driver to move. As the carriage rolled away he strode back to the men who had pulled up behind the carriage, commandeered a horse, and with his little band riding in silent confusion behind him, made his way back to the heart of Paris.

LX

One month passed, then another, and a third. Finally, it was December. The gray, bleak weather exactly matchec Isabella's mood. Since she had sent Alec away, the num- ber of times she had laughed could be counted on the fingers of one hand. Give it time, she told herself eacl and every day. Surely she would not always suffer sucl excruciating emotional pain. She would adjust to the way things had to be, and look back on her too brief interlud with Alec with no more than gentle nostalgia. Of cours she would. No heart could ache like hers did forever.

Outwardly, she had little trouble adapting to the far mor social role she was expected to play in Paris as Bernard' countess. At Blakely Park, there had been no one to pleas but herself, and Bernard on the few occasions when h had put in an appearance. But in Paris there was a contin uous round of afternoon calls, soirees, and balls. Plainl dressed, quiet and unassuming, she would never be on of Society's leading lights, but she was accepted withou question everywhere, and the scandal her father had s feared never materialized. No one seemed much intereste in her whereabouts before arriving in Paris, and if he relationship with her husband was cool, why, then, so wer the relationships of most fashionable married couples- when they weren't actively warring.

Isabella had even made a few friends, the closest (whom was Miss Brantley, who had become engaged t

Colonel Tynling and whom she now called Ellen. Even such a high stickler as Sarah had termed Miss Brantley (the niece of the Duke of Richmond) unexceptionable, and Isabella was allowed to go about pretty much as she pleased in Ellen's company. Of course, the ubiquitous Lambert was always in discreet attendance, as was Ellen's maid, but that was no more escort than was proper for ladies jaunting about Paris on their own, and aroused no curiosity.

Her relationship with Sarah had improved to the point where the two women could spend several hours in each other's company and emerge still on civil terms. Isabella got the impression more than once that, however horrified Sarah might profess to be by her stepdaughter's indiscretion, she was also secretly envious that Isabella had dared to so flout convention as to actually take a lover.

For the first time it occurred to Isabella that Sarah, who was only a few years older than herself, should be pitied rather than despised. Sarah was less than thirty, and Isabella's father was nearing sixty. It could not be easy being married to a man so much older than oneself, and one who was, besides, more than a little corpulent, bluff-mannered and overfond of port to the extent that he was frequently victim of the gout. To share the intimacies of the bedroom with such a husband . . . Well, like Isabella, Sarah doubtless had been raised to believe that to submit herself to her husband was a woman's lot. Isabella shivered to realize that she would still be ignorantly enduring Bernard's invasions of her body, knowing nothing of the rapture that could occur between a man and a woman who truly loved, were it not for Alec.

Alec. She could not think of him without pain. Closing her eyes, she willed the all too vivid image of him to go away. But even as the image obligingly faded, the question haunted her: If she were to find herself back in that garden with Alec, would she again send him away?

Or would she flee with him back to their wonderful, shining dream world, and love him and be loved in return for as long as the fates permitted?

She had made the right choice, the only sensible one. But knowing that didn't even begin to make the pain of living without Alec go away.

On that particular windy December afternoon, Isabella was rambling along the granite cliffs that rose in towering majesty above the sea near Boulogne. From where she walked on a flat plateau covered with brown tufts of grass, it was a sheer drop to the water far below. The rocky shore had dug in under the cliff so that the ground on which she wandered formed a kind of overhang. Foaming waves rolled in from far out at sea to crash against the shore. Like the sea, the sky was gray. The line at the horizon where the two met was so similar in color as to be blurred. Overhead, a lone seagull wheeled and cried.

Isabella followed its flight with her eyes, shivered, and tugged the velvet-lined hood of her dark blue cloak closer about her head as she walked on.

She and Bernard had been invited, along with her father and Sarah and perhaps two dozen other guests, to make up a Christmas house party at the centuries-old chateau of the Marquise de la Ros. Heloise, as the marquise insisted Isabella call her, was a well-preserved, very wealthy widow in perhaps her mid-thirties. While she was too sharp-featured to have ever been a beauty, with her raven hair and slender figure she was elegant as few Englishwomen ever were. She and Bernard were quite friendly in a discreet, one-following-the-other-from-the-room-ten-minutes-later type of way. Isabella suspected, without caring one way or another, that Bernard had set the marquise up as his latest mistress. Or perhaps, given the marquise's autocratic ways, it had been the other way around. In any case, the chateau and its grounds were beautiful, and as Isabella had had absolutely no desire to spend Christmas alone with her husband, she had not been sorry to come

Although the evenings were crammed with entertainments designed to amuse the guests, the afternoons were free to spend as each individual preferred. The rest of the party variously napped, read or played quietly at cards but Isabella had found that she was too restless for any o those pursuits. Instead she had spent nearly every afternoon since their arrival just as she was now doing, walking alone along the cliffs. The solitude soothed her bruised spirit while the fresh, cold air cleared her head.

Isabella had been walking for some time when she got the feeling, as she had more than once in the last few weeks, that she was no longer alone. Glancing uneasily around, she saw that the chateau looked quite small in the distance, silhouetted as it was against the lowering sky. To her left, perhaps a hundred feet away, was a dense woods of small pines. To her right was the sea. Behind her was the chateau, and before her was more flat, grassy ground.

The sense that someone was watching her was very strong. It made her so uneasy that, after resolutely traversing a few more yards, she decided that she had walked enough for that day and turned about to retrace her steps, moving quickly now where before she had merely ambled.

To her surprise, as she hurried along, she saw a man heading toward her along the cliffs. Clearly he had come from the chateau. He was too far away to have been the cause of the niggling discomfort she had felt. Indeed, the sense of an invisible presence seemed to emanate from the woods, and as she walked in the direction of the man, she glanced over at the thick wall of pines more than once. The thought of wolves occurred to her, to be firmly dismissed before she could do more than shiver.

As the man drew closer, she identified him as Bernard. Her steps lagged slightly, but still the thought of what might be watching her from the woods kept her moving toward him. Even an encounter with her husband was better than being devoured by a wild beast.

"Isabella." Bernard greeted her without noticeable enthusiasm. Although they had spoken hardly two dozen sentences to one another during their months in Paris, he was invariably courteous to her, as befitted a gentleman toward a wife. The pattern of their relationship had reverted to what it had always been, except Bernard had made no attempt whatsoever to come to her bed, for which

Isabella was thankful. She did not know what she would do if he did; thinking about it made her physically ill, so she tried not to think about it. Sooner or later, however, the situation was bound to arise. Bernard would want an heir, and she was his wife whether she loved him or not.

As weeks had passed and he had remained the courteous if remote nobleman she had been wed to for nearly seven years, it had grown increasingly more difficult for Isabella to remember that Bernard had really, truly tried to have her killed. In his soft-spoken presence it seemed more like a bad dream than reality.

"Good afternoon, Bernard." Like him, she was polite, if cool. It had surprised her to discover, many weeks ago, that despite the fact that she positively knew he had connived at her murder, she didn't hate him. She felt absolutely nothing for him at all save a mild wariness.

Which feeling, she thought wryly, would probably intensify once he had time to spend the money her father had settled on him. Unless and until he should find himself under the hatches again, she considered herself relatively safe.

And her father had settled a great deal of money on him.

"Will you walk with me a ways? There's something I wish to discuss with you."

"I was headed back to the chateau. . . ."

"It's quite important, I assure you. Indeed, I came out specifically to meet you so that we might have this conversation in private."

Bernard took her arm, drawing her along to walk with him in the direction she had been going originally, away from the chateau. Isabella bit her lip to keep from protesting. He was her husband, after all. She would not disturb the eggshell peace that existed between them over such a trifle as a few minutes' private conversation, or a hand on her arm. They walked on in silence for some little while, until at last she could contain her impatience no longer.

"If you have something to say to me, please do so."

Despite her resolution not to disturb their fragile accord, the words were abrupt.

With the advantage of his superior height, Bernard was able to look down his aquiline nose at her. Isabella saw that his eyes had narrowed at her tone. They looked darker than usual, almost black in color instead of their normal dark brown. The cold air had brought unaccustomed color to his olive skin.

"Are you enjoying the house party?"

The question was innocuous enough, but to exchange polite small talk with her was not the reason he had braved the cold. Isabella nodded stiffly without replying.

"As am I. Heloise is a very charming woman."

Again Isabella merely nodded.

"And a very rich one, too. No wonder she's quite the toast of Parisian society. Like you, she's far from a beauty, but she has a certain *je ne sais quoi* that you do not. One must be born with it, I suppose." He sighed, as if pitying her lack.

Isabella stopped walking and pulled her arm from his hold. "If you have nothing of more import to discuss with me than our hostess, then I must beg you to excuse me. 'Tis chilly out, and I would return to the chateau."

Bernard stopped walking too, and turned to face her. The silver wings in his dark hair had spread, she noticed as she looked at him, really looked at him, for the first time since their confrontation in the inn at Tunbridge Wells. His hair was almost more gray than black now. Isabella remembered that he was closer to her father's age than her own, although his slender, stylishly turned out person made him seem far more youthful than he was. As always, he was immaculately dressed. His neckcloth was snowy white and perfectly tied, his pale blue coat fit his shoulders without so much as a crease, his biscuit-colored breeches clung to his thighs as if they had been poured there, and his highly polished Hessians sported not so much as a single speck of dirt despite the fact that he had walked the same terrain she had, and her own slippers were stained with both mud and grass. Bernard was a noted Corinthian, a pink of the *ton,* acclaimed by many as a remarkably handsome man. And yet he left her utterly cold.

Well, no one had ever accused her of having impeccable taste.

"So you want the matter with no bark on it?" As he spoke, Bernard's eyes darted over her shoulder and all around. Isabella looked around too, to see what he was looking at, and noticed for the first time that in the course of their walk they had rounded the small promontory that jutted out and then curved back in from the sea. The deep green of the pine forest now stood between them and the chateau.

Isabella suddenly felt uneasy. "Yes," she said, and without even knowing precisely why she did so, took a small step back from him.

"Very well, it shall be as you wish. I have been doing considerable soul-searching over the past weeks, and I have decided that, despite your father's pleas on your behalf, you are no longer worthy of the title Countess of Blakely. My decision cannot be unexpected; my reasons are well known to you. Charles is a friend, but not even he can expect me to get my heirs on a female who has soiled herself beyond redemption. My son must not have an adulteress for a mother."

The insults, if they were intended to wound, fell wide of their mark. As Isabella caught the gist of what she thought he was leading up to, she felt a vast surge of relief.

"Are you suggesting that we . . . divorce?"

Once the thought, with its implications of scandal and ostracism, had been frightening. Now the idea of freedom at whatever price had a dazzling appeal. Alec would care nothing for the shame that would be attached to her as a divorced woman. . . .

"No. I'm not suggesting that."

"Then what . . . ?"

His eyes met hers, held. There was an expression in them of—what? Even as she registered that it was odd, he reached out and caught her hand.

"So much scandal attaches to divorce," he said regretfully. "And I've still my heir to think of, you know. Besides, there's Heloise."

"Heloise?" She parroted him almost stupidly, because something about the way he was looking at her was sending cold chills down her spine. Surely she was not in physical peril. . . . Even if he wished to harm her, he would not do it here and now. He was far too fastidious, too much the gentleman, to murder his unwanted wife himself. He would employ underlings for that. For the moment, at least, she was safe. She had only to get back to the chateau. . . .

"I believe she'd consent to wed me, if I was free. She's very rich, and very exciting. And still young enough, I believe, to bear me a child."

"Bernard . . ." Her certainty that he would not personally harm her was fading, to be replaced by a burgeoning fear. Something in his tone caused her blood to freeze. And his eyes—never before had she seen that particular expression in his eyes. They glittered, and she realized suddenly that the reason they seemed so unusually dark was the pupil had dilated until it threatened to overwhelm the encircling iris. "If you divorced me for adultery, all the onus would fall on me. No one would blame you."

Isabella knew she had to keep calm, had to keep him the same way until she could get back to the safety of the chateau. Once there, she would pack her bags and flee to England—and Alec. Every instinct she possessed warned her that if she did not put herself quickly beyond Bernard's reach, she would find herself in mortal danger. The thought that it might already be too late reared its ugly head, and refused to be dismissed. Isabella took a deep, steadying breath—and tried unobtrusively to free her hand from his. His fingers entwined with hers, holding them fast.

Bernard shook his head regretfully. "I'm sorry about this, you know. I never disliked you, as I did my first wife." Bernard shrugged, and smiled at her with chilling sweetness. "It's funny, nobody suspected that I poisoned Lydia. Even her family was quite willing to put her death down to a weak heart. What a tragedy, everyone said—and how sympathetic you were then, looking at me with your big eyes when I would come to play chess with Charles. When we wed, though I needed the settlements you brought, of course, I quite liked the idea of taking you to wife. I kept thinking you might grow up into a beauty, with those big eyes and that funny little face. But you disappointed me; you never did. And then you cuckolded me—I never would have expected that from you, Isabella. No man should have to put up with an unfaithful wife. So I really don't know why I regret having to do this. Maybe because Charles is a friend. But then, I doubt he'll grieve for you overmuch."

His hand slid down to encircle her wrist. His hold on her was as unbreakable as if she'd been imprisoned in an iron shackle, Isabella discovered to her horror as she tried, more urgently this time, to pull free.

"Bernard, you're not thinking . . ." she said desperately, realizing finally that she had been foolishly, fatally wrong. He was going to kill her himself despite everything she had been thinking to the contrary. Indeed, it was terrifyingly obvious now that he had followed her from the chateau with just that purpose in mind. Fear threatened to cloud her mind, but Isabella forced it back. If she caved in to panic, she would be finished. He had only to lift her and heave her over the cliff to the rocks below, an easy task for a reasonably strong man when the victim was as slightly built as she. If she wanted to survive, she had to keep him talking, buy herself some time. . . .

"Come, Isabella; I'm sorry for it, but there's really nothing else I can do. You've brought it on yourself, you know." With an elegant little shrug he began to tug her toward the cliff edge. It occurred to Isabella to wonder if Bernard was not quite, quite mad.

"My father . . . If you kill me, he's bound to know you did it. I told him how you tried to have me killed before, remember? He'll know you did it, Bernard. And he'll see you hang." Her voice was hoarse as her throat went dry with fear.

"I doubt it. Think of the scandal. Charles always does."

Bernard chuckled then, and tugged again on her hand, insistently. Despite her deliberately gentle resistance, Isabella found herself a few steps closer to the cliff edge. She took a deep, shaking breath, trying to fight down the panic, consciously biting back the scream that she feared would only precipitate his violence and ultimately her own end. Desperately she looked around, hoping against hope that someone—anyone—might have also decided to take a walk that afternoon. But the landscape was deserted. If she was to survive, she would have to save herself.

"Come along. One never knows when one's privacy might be interrupted." With another terrifyingly sweet smile Bernard gave a yank that propelled her at least a foot closer to the precipice.

"No!" Isabella pulled against him, trying frantically to find purchase for her slippers in the soft ground. "Bernard, wait! Think what you're doing. . . ."

"You'll not talk me out of it, my dear." He sounded almost pitying. "Don't worry, just a few seconds of fear and then it will be all over. Or are you going to make me hurt you? I really don't want to hurt you, Isabella, but I will if I must."

"Bernard, please . . ."

He turned on her then, the glint in his eyes telling her that she had run out of time. Abandoning all thought of restraint, Isabella screamed, shrill as a steam whistle, and dug the nails of her free hand into the hand that imprisoned her.

He cursed, and snatched his hand away.

Quick as a cat Isabella was running, running as she had never run before in her life, not even in the forest that time from Alec, because never before in her life had she been so desperately afraid. She rounded the promontory, and the chateau was once again in sight. If she could only reach it . . . if only someone would step outside and see . . .

"Come back here, you little bitch. Come back, Isabella, do you hear me? Come back!"

She'd always been fleet afoot, but he was almost as fast. In the end her billowing cloak was her undoing. He caught the end of it, yanked—and she fell screaming to her knees. Then Bernard was upon her.

"Bitch. Bitch."

Isabella screamed again as he dragged her upright, her hands flying up to protect herself from the blow she saw coming. But it was too late. Savagely he punched her in the face with his fist. Pain exploded in the right side of her jaw. Then he was swinging her up into his arms. . . .

Knowing that she must not pass out, Isabella fought him like a creature gone mad, biting and scratching and kicking in a frantic effort to survive. She clawed at his eyes, and with a vicious curse he half dropped her, then forced her the rest of the way to the ground. Even as she tried to scramble away, he loomed over her again. Isabella looked up, cringing, screaming, and saw the jagged-edged rock in his hand.

Almost as soon as she saw it, he slammed it into her forehead with a sickening crunch. Isabella shrieked at the pain of it, at the knowledge that she would die, at the horror of feeling her own head burst open like a melon beneath the savage blow. The rock fell a second time. She must have blacked out for an instant, because when she became aware again, she was being carried in his arms, not more than a yard or so from the precipice.

And they were no longer alone.

"Put her down, St. Just," Alec said evenly, and as Isabella blinked disbelievingly at him, she saw that he had a pistol pointed squarely at Bernard's head.

LXI

"Who the devil are you?" Bernard spoke quite normally, as it he didn't have the wife he intended to murder, bleeding and hysterical, held tight in his arms less than a yard from the edge of a hundred-foot drop.

"I said put her down. Now."

There was blood in her eyes, and in her mouth, but Isabella shook her head to clear it and fastened her eyes on Alec. Her situation was still precarious; it was possible that Bernard might be able to toss her over the side before Alec got a shot off—if he was mad enough to sacrifice his own life to do it. But just knowing that Alec was present took some of the edge off her terror. He would keep her safe, if anyone could. She tried to say his name, but the blood in her mouth made it come out all garbled.

"Haven't I seen you somewhere before?" Bernard, looking faintly puzzled, had his eyes on Alec's face rather than on the pistol.

"It's possible. Put the lady down, and we'll try to discover where."

"In London, I think. A hell, maybe? I've got it—the Golden Carousel."

"I said, put the lady down. I won't repeat it."

The pistol lifted ominously, its tiny black mouth pointed right between Bernard's eyes. At such close range it would be impossible for Alec to miss. Isabella wondered if Bernard was too crazed to realize that.

Bernard glanced down at Isabella almost as if he had forgotten her existence. Then, with a regretful grimace, he bent and placed her gently on the ground. Relief rushed through her, and for an instant she lay there, unmoving, her eyes closing as she realized that she would not die today, after all.

"Isabella?" Alec sounded far away suddenly. "Damn it, Isabella, answer me."

"You know her?" Bernard asked with a surprised frown.

"Al-ec." This time she managed his name. Those golden eyes flickered over her, fastened again on Bernard, the light in them savage.

"Yes, I know her, you swine." His voice was even, but the glitter in his eyes told Isabella that he was dangerous with rage. "Step back from her. Do it!"

"But how? She's never been to London, never been anywhere except Blakely Park and Paris. Except for . . ." Bernard's eyes met Alec's, and he seemed to realize his danger, because he retreated a few steps. Alec walked forward until he stood over Isabella. Dropping to one knee, keeping the pistol trained on Bernard all the while, he touched her face gently, his expression a grimace when the fingers he withdrew were wet with blood.

" 'Twill be all right, love," he said, his voice low. "I've got you now. 'Twill be all right."

"Al-ec." Blood pooled in her mouth. Gagging, she tried to spit it out, and choked. Alec's mouth twisted savagely and he stood up.

"You bloody piece of slime, you'd better say your prayers, because you'll not live out the hour." Alec spoke through his teeth. The hand holding the pistol lifted.

"It was you! You were her lover!" Bernard howled, and sprang. Alec smiled, with what Isabella thought was grim satisfaction, and the pistol exploded.

The ball caught Bernard square in the throat. His hands clawed at the wound from which blood spurted as if from a fountain, pouring over the pristine neckcloth and stain ing it bright red. Isabella was too shocked to even breathe as he staggered backwards, clutching his throat, and then, without even a cry, he toppled over the edge of the precipice and vanished from her sight.

LXII

"Good God! Good God!" The voice belonged to her father and Isabella looked around to find him red-faced and puffing as he skidded to a walk not ten feet away. Behind him, running as Isabella had never thought to see either of them run, came Sarah and the Marquise de la Ros, both cloakless and unprecedentedly dishevelled. Behind those two a motley assortment of guests loped toward the scene.

"Isabella! Isabella, good God, gel, we were in the garden and heard you scream—gad, we saw the whole thing! Oh, dear Jesus, look at her! I wouldn't have believed it of him if I hadn't seen it with my own eyes!"

Alec lowered the pistol and thrust it in his belt as the white-haired duke gained Isabella's side and dropped to his knees, staring from his daughter's battered face to the precipice over which his son-in-law had vanished. The ladies fluttered up, bent over Isabella as well, their faces pale and their eyes wide with horror as they surveyed the damage done her. Isabella scarcely looked at any of the expanding group that clustered, exclaiming, around her. Her eyes were all for the tawny-haired man who stood a little back from her now, watching the scene with narrowed eyes.

"Al-ec." His name was not much clearer than before but he heard. Mouth twisting, he walked toward her, knelt and shouldering aside her father and the others, gathered her up in his arms.

"Who the hell . . ." her father blustered, looking affronted as Alec, ignoring him and the rest of them, started to walk toward the chateau with Isabella held protectively against his chest.

"He saved her life, Charles. Didn't you see?" Sarah put her hand on her husband's arm.

"I saw. I saw. Damn, I wouldn't have believed it of Bernard. The gel was telling the truth all along! I can scarcely credit it even now. But who is he?"

The majority of the guests fell into step behind Alec, leaving the marquise to stand alone at the precipice, staring down at the water far below. If her eyes held tears for Bernard, they were the only ones that did.

"Alec." Isabella could not manage to say more than that, but it was enough. Alec's face twisted at the sight of the slender body draped so bonelessly in his arms.

"Don't fash yourself, love; you're going to be all right. They'll take good care of you, and you'll be as lovely as ever before you know it."

"Bernard . . . ?"

"He's dead. You don't have to fear. He'll never bother you again, I swear."

"Thank you." Held securely in his arms, she rested her head against his chest, and her eyes closed. Darkness threatened to claim her, and she let it. It was safe to do so now that Alec was there.

When she regained consciousness, she was lying on the bed in the bedroom she had occupied since coming to the chateau, and a strange man, whom she gathered from the efficient way he was wrapping a bandage around her head was a doctor, was leaning over her.

"Alec," she said fretfully.

"Do not try to talk, Madame la Comtesse. You have been sadly injured, but with luck, there should be no permanent damage. But you need to lie quietly, and rest."

"Alec," she repeated stubbornly. Suddenly Sarah materialized behind the doctor's shoulder.

"He's outside, in the hall. Indeed, he's been there for the past two hours, refusing to even go downstairs until he's been assured by Monsieur *le docteur* that you're going to survive. It was all I could do to chase him out of the bedroom."

The doctor turned away from the bedside to dispose of some bloodstained cotton with which he had staunched the wound in her forehead, and Sarah leaned closer, whispering.

"My goodness, Isabella, he's a gorgeous man! I can quite see . . . But your father is scandalized! Only think, Mr. Tyron tells us that he has been having you watched for months, just in case Bernard should . . . well, do what he did. He even had what he calls one of his men infiltrate the house staff here when we came to stay, and had another man actually living in the woods. It's positively romantic, and I don't care what your father says, I don't blame you a bit!"

"Your pardon, madame, but Madame la Comtesse needs quiet, not gossip," the doctor said sternly, returning to Isabella's bedside.

"Please, Sarah, get Alec," Isabella pleaded, forcing the words out through a mouth so swollen that it was, perhaps fortunately, numb. Her head throbbed, she was nauseous and dizzy, and her face felt huge and shapeless, as if the skin would split if she opened her mouth or eyes too wide. She knew she must look dreadful, but she didn't care. She had to see Alec.

"I'll do my best, dear, but your father is outside too and they're glaring at each other like two dogs." Sarah patted Isabella's shoulder, then crossed to the door while the doctor gathered his things together.

From the hall Isabella could hear her father bellow "Damn it, Sarah, you can't wish me to let him go into her bedchamber alone! God, think of the scandal already And you know perfectly well he's . . ."

Whatever else her father had to say, Isabella missed entirely, because the bedroom door opened and Alec walked in. The doctor took one look at him and left. Alec closed the door, and walked toward the bed. Isabella tried a welcoming smile. It hurt, and she winced.

"You saved my life." Her voice was no more than a hoarse whisper.

"Think nothing of it. 'Tis getting to be quite a habit with me." He was looking down at her, his handsome face harsh as he surveyed her injuries. Instinctively seeking to give comfort, Isabella groped for his hand. His fingers curled around hers, and she took solace from the warm strength of his grip.

"You didn't go away after all." It hurt to talk, but she was afraid to stop. There was so much she had to say, so much he needed to hear. She didn't have the strength for it, but from somewhere she would find it.

He grimaced. "Did you think I would leave you to the tender mercies of that bastard of a husband of yours? I've had a man watching you since the day after you decided to stay with him rather than go with me. 'Twas only bad luck that we didn't get to you sooner today. I had a man in the woods with me, but when you started toward the castle, we pulled back to blow a cloud. We never even saw you with that whoreson until you screamed." His hand tightened over hers, and his lips clenched. "God, you gave me the fright of my life. I didn't know if I could get to you in time."

"There won't be any trouble? For you, over Bernard?"

Alec shook his head. "There'll be an inquest, of course, but with you in the state you're in and the fact that half a dozen witnesses saw him jump toward me, I doubt there'll be any kind of charge. Obliging of him, really. I'd have killed the son of a bitch even if he hadn't made another threatening move, for what he did to you."

The bedroom door opened without ceremony, and the duke entered, scowling at Alec as he approached the bed. "Here now, you've had enough time. There'll be gossip aplenty without more to add to it. Gad, none of us will ever live this down as long as we live!"

"I'm sorry about the scandal, Papa," Isabella offered in a small voice.

The duke looked down at her, and his brow contracted. He reached out to pat her arm, then scowled at Alec anew as he saw that Alec held his daughter's hand.

" 'Tis I who should apologize to you, daughter. I should've known no chit of mine could be an adulteress. Although who this . . . fellow . . . is, I admit I don't quite understand."

He looked Alec up and down with obvious dislike. Alec looked back at him with a nearly identical expression.

"Alec saved my life. Today, and when Bernard tried before."

"I understand that. What I don't understand is—"

"Isabella's in no state to be making explanations to you or to anyone else. Look at her, for Christ's sake! That bloody husband you forced her to take came within a hair's breadth of beating her to death today!"

"Now, listen here, sirra, I'll not be spoken to in such a way by the likes of you! And who gave you permission to be so free with my daughter's name, and her hand, I'd like to know? You're overstepping your bounds, and—"

"Pardon, Monsieur le Duc, but Madame la Comtesse must be left to rest or I cannot be answerable for the consequences." The doctor glided up to Isabella's bedside and regarded the two combatants reprovingly. Her father broke off in mid-tirade to stand glaring at Alec. Disregarding that basilisk stare, Alec carried Isabella's hand to his mouth and softly kissed the back of it. Watching, the duke made a sound much like a hiss.

"I'll leave you to rest, then." Alec placed her hand with gentle care back atop the coverlet, and turned to go.

"Alec!" Panic filled her. She had not said near what she had meant to. . . .

"You must rest, madame," the doctor insisted, and pressed her back into the pillows when she would have tried to sit up.

Isabella watched anxiously as Alec, followed by her father, left the room.

There would be time later to talk to him, she comforted herself as the doctor forced her to take a sleeping draught

But even as she drank it, and sank almost immediately into unconsciousness, the fear remained that there was no time left. . . .

Her fear proved well-founded. When she awoke again, near thirty-six hours later, and asked for Alec, she was brought instead a small package that he had left for her.

The package contained an exquisite necklace of large, circular amethysts set in filigreed silver, and a matching pair of earrings. Sarah, watching as Isabella unwrapped it, exclaimed over the contents with wonder. It was a magnificent gift, and one Isabella knew from the color of the stones Alec must have purchased specifically for her.

Only after she opened the package did she see the crumpled screw of paper that accompanied it. Isabella read the terse note, then sat looking from the jewelry on her lap to the paper in her hand as if she had been suddenly dealt a stunning blow. As Sarah watched helplessly, tears filled Isabella's eyes and began to roll unchecked down her face. The doctor finally had to be summoned to administer a sleeping draught to quiet her. But not even drugged oblivion could take away her pain.

Alec never intended to see her again.

"I've set you free, so be happy," was what the note said.

LXIII

Two months later Isabella was largely recovered from her injuries. A puckered, pinkish scar still marred the skin of her forehead, but with her hair cut in a fashionable fringe, it was hidden from view. Her speedy recovery had been motivated by a steely determination to find Alec.

And once she did, she would box his ears soundly for the torment he had put her through by his noble renunciation of her, and beg him to love her again. As Sarah had pointed out, a man did not have a woman watched for three months, and traipse around a freezing cold wood himself for days on end, unless he loved said woman madly.

Isabella only hoped that Sarah was right.

Her father had been dead set against her returning to England. He tried everything, from threats to bribes, to persuade her to remain in France, but for the first time in her life, Isabella was obdurate. When she was well enough, she was returning to England—and Alec. Nothing her father could say could persuade her otherwise.

Whenever Alec's name came up, the duke denounced him long and vigorously. The kindest thing he had to say about the man his daughter loved was that he was not a gentleman.

Isabella didn't care a fig for that, and told her father so She also told him that whether Alec was a gentleman or not, she—yes, she, the daughter of a duke—meant to wed her gutter-born criminal if he'd have her. And there was absolutely nothing on earth her father could do to stop her. Sarah whispered later that Isabella's unaccustomed defiance had nearly sent the duke off in an apoplexy.

But as a widow, and with a comfortable jointure (at the time of his death Bernard had not had time to spend much of the settlement Isabella's father had made on him, so those funds were now hers), she was no longer subject to her father's will. And she told him that, too.

For the first time in her life, she was free to do as she pleased.

She had arrived in London only that afternoon, and gone straight to the St. Just townhouse, which, as Bernard's widow, she now owned. She had walked up the steps as bold as brass, been admitted by the butler, who introduced himself as Kirkland, and been treated with obsequious courtesy by all the staff. Of course, she was their employer now.

Common sense dictated that she should wait until the morrow before setting out in search of Alec, but Isabella was too impatient to put her future to the touch to pay much heed to common sense. She did take a nap, and awoke refreshed shortly before six o'clock. After a light dinner which she ate alone at the vast dining table, she had the upstairs maid, whose name was Marta, prepare her bath, and help her dress.

Deciding what to wear was easy. Alec had always fancied her in lavender.

The dress she chose was beautiful. Isabella had purchased it in the Rue de la Paix before she left Paris. Of a silk so fine that it shimmered in the light, it was simply cut to make the most of her slender figure, with a straight skirt and tiny bodice caught up beneath her breasts by a ribbon of deep purple satin. Her hair was brushed until it shone and piled high atop her head, where it was tied up with purple ribbons that exactly matched the ribbon on the dress. Her fringe served the dual purpose of hiding the scar on her forehead, and at the same time bringing out the size and shape of her eyes.

Around her neck she wore the amethyst necklace Alec had left with her. The matching earbobs dangled from her ears.

"If I may so say, you look a real beauty, my lady," Marta said shyly. Isabella thanked her with a smile as she draped a cobwebby shawl about her shoulders. Then, her toilette complete, Isabella left the room and went down the stairs, where the imposing carriage with the St. Just crest—hers now—awaited.

If the coachman—York, he said his name was—was appalled at the address she gave him, why, he worked for her and her alone, and did as he was bid. Being a widow had much to commend it, Isabella decided, although she hoped she would not enjoy the state for very much longer. Smiling at that thought, she settled back in her seat.

It was not long before the coach pulled up before the deceptively respectable façade of the Golden Carousel. If Alec was not within, Pearl would know where to find him, although Isabella was uncertain of the kind of reception she could expect from Pearl.

"Shall I wait, my lady?" York asked, looking nervously around at the darkened, deserted street as he helped her to alight. It was just past dusk, and a lamplighter was touching his taper to the torch at the corner.

"Yes, please," Isabella said, and then walked up to knock on the heavy oak door.

In response to her second summons, the small panel through which visitors were viewed before being admitted slid back.

Isabella smiled serenely at the pale blue eye that blinked at her.

"Pray let me in, Sharp; I've business with Miss Pearl," she directed, and with a sound like a gasp, the butler closed the spy-hole and opened the door.

"Miss—miss, ma'am, uh . . ." Sharp stuttered unhappily as Isabella walked in and looked about. From the appearance of things, the evening's guests had not yet started to arrive. Footmen moved about straightening table covers and lighting candles, and packs of cards lay uncut and ready on the tables inside the parlors.

"Is something the matter, Sharp?" Isabella asked, as the butler looked desperately over his shoulder toward the left front parlor. Sharp was spared having to reply by the rustling of skirts behind Isabella. His expression became one of obvious relief, and Isabella turned to behold Pearl.

For a moment the two women stared at each other without speaking. Pearl was as breathtaking as Isabella remembered, dressed for an evening's work in a gown of scarlet satin trimmed with black lace. As usual, more of her magnificent bosom was on display than was covered, and the front of her skirt was slit to the knees to reveal a filmy black petticoat.

Isabella was obliged to concede defeat. She could never compete with Pearl's spectacular beauty. But she could compete with her for Alec.

"Hello, Pearl," Isabella said quietly, breaking the silence.

Pearl's lower lip quivered, and then she rushed forward, to catch Isabella by the upper arms and press her cheek to Isabella's in a hug designed to spare both maquillage and gown, but that was no less sincere for all that.

"Oh, angel, will you ever forgive me?" Pearl said, stepping back. Isabella saw to her amazement that there were real tears in Pearl's midnight blue eyes. "I was out of my mind jealous, to do what I did. I never meant you to get 'urt, never. Paddy and Alec, they tore a rare strip off me for that. But I'd be sorry, even if they 'adn't. I truly would."

Such disarming candor made it hard for Isabella to hold a grudge. Indeed, unless Pearl had succeeded in appropriating Alec during the last two months, Isabella bore her no ill will at all.

"Of course I forgive you," she said readily. Then, a small smile breaking forth, "That is, unless you tell me that you have Alec cozily tucked up in your suite."

Pearl grinned, relieved. "Paddy'd 'ave a thing or two to say about that, I guess! No, as beautiful as Alec is, I've 'ad to give 'im up. 'E 'asn't been worth much since 'e met you, anyway, so I don't regret it."

"You'd better not," a voice growled from the doorway to her left, and Isabella looked around to see Paddy, his huge form incongruously clad in elegant evening finery. Sharp let out an audible sigh of relief upon seeing him, and returned to his duties beside the door. Isabella smiled at Paddy, genuinely glad to see him. He'd been a true friend to Alec, and any friend of Alec's was a friend of hers.

"It's about time you came to put Alec out of his misery. He swore it was over between you two, but I didn't believe it for a minute. You don't look the fickle kind to me. Not like my wench, here." Paddy gave Pearl a lopsided grin as he slid a proprietary arm around her waist. She pinched his wrist in retaliation for his teasing, but then rested contentedly against his side. Looking at the pair of them, Isabella realized that she didn't have to compete with Pearl anymore.

"Is he here?" Her mouth went dry as she asked the question. It was foolish, she knew, but she got butterflies in her stomach at the idea that Alec might be no farther than the next room.

Paddy frowned suddenly, and shot a quick look down at Pearl. She twinkled saucily up at him. The look Paddy gave her was admonishing.

"He is. Pearl, why don't you take her along to your rooms, and I'll bring him down to her?"

"You think 'e can still walk?" Pearl asked, grinning. Then she poked Paddy in the ribs with her elbow. "Go on, let 'er go up. Alec needs to be shaken up a little, and she'll sure do that." Pearl looked at Isabella again. " 'E's been a regular bear since 'e came back from France. If you can sweeten his disposition, 'alf of London'll fall on your neck."

"I'll try," Isabella said, smiling in turn. Pearl, for all the havoc she had caused, had a charm that was irresistible. "Where is he?"

"I'll take you up. Come on, angel." Pearl turned in the direction of the stairs.

"But, sweetheart, don't you think—" Paddy protested, sounding worried.

"Oh, pooh! Go on about your business, you great oaf, and leave matters of the 'eart to us what knows about them! Go on now, shoo!"

Paddy, still looking unhappy, shrugged and took himself off into the parlor from which he had emerged.

"What was that all about?" Isabella asked as she followed Pearl up the stairs and along the second-floor corridor.

"Oh, Alec's been trying to drown 'is sorrows as men do. He's drownin' 'em right now, as a matter of fact, and Paddy likely thought you'd take a pet if you found out. But I think you're made of stronger stuff than that, angel. You give that man a good strong clout on the ear, and tell 'im to behave 'imself in future. 'E'll do it, for you. I've known Alec a long time, and I've never seen 'im in such a case over anything as he's been over you."

Pearl stopped walking then, put a finger to her lips, and opened a door at the end of the corridor. Looking over her shoulder into a sumptiously furnished bedroom, Isabella was shocked to see two nearly naked females ministering to a totally naked man sprawled out in a bathtub before the fire. The man, whose back was to the door, had tawny hair, a fat cigar dangling from his mouth, and a bottle of brandy in one hand. As she watched, he pulled the cigar from his mouth with one hand and tilted up the bottle with the other, swilling down a large mouthful without so much as bothering with a glass. Alec! Isabella recognized that hair and those broad, bare shoulders with a sense of shock. Then the shock lessened, replaced by a bubbling of anger. She'd come all this way to lay her heart at his feet, only to find him disporting himself with a pair—not one, mind, but a *pair*—of Cyprians! Her fists clenched involuntarily at her sides as she absorbed the scene before her.

One scantily clad young woman was at that moment

engaged in adding a bucket of hot water to what was already in the tub. The other scrubbed Alec's back. Both looked up as the door opened, although Alec, taking another swig from the bottle, remained oblivious. Pearl silenced the surprised girls with a gesture, then beckoned them from the room. As they spared speculative looks for Isabella, Pearl pushed her into the room in their place.

"Don't be too 'ard on 'im, angel. 'E's been breaking 'is 'eart for you, truly 'e 'as," she whispered, then left, closing the door behind her.

LXIV

"Dahlia, sweetheart, where'd you go? My back still needs washing."

Clearly unaware that the adoring handmaiden he addressed was no longer present, Alec plopped the cigar back in his mouth and flexed his wide shoulders in anticipation. Standing behind him, Isabella eyed that tawny head, and debated whether or not to make her presence known. But she felt suddenly, ridiculously shy. Perhaps it would be better to let him discover her presence for himself. So she walked up to the procelain tub, picked up the sponge Dahlia had abandoned, and began to run it over his back without a word.

"Ummm, that's nice. Can you get a little lower?" Without waiting for a reply, he leaned forward so that she could scrub the small of his back. Isabella eyed that broad, bare back with an expression that was halfway between amusement and anger. He could consider himself lucky if she didn't squeeze the sponge out over his head, the wretch!

"That's good. Ah, you smell nice, sweetheart." His back apparently scrubbed to his satisfaction, Alec leaned back again, his neck lolling on the lip of the tub, his head tilted up. His eyes were closed, and a wreath of smoke from the cigar encircled his head. Even sprawled naked in a bathtub, puffing on a filthy weed, he was still the handsomest man Isabella had ever seen in her life. Just looking at him made her heart contract.

Still she said nothing, obediently sloshing the sponge over his shoulders and the wide, hair-roughened upper reaches of his chest as she waited for him to open his eyes and discover her.

"A little lower here, too," he murmured sensually, and reaching for the hand that held the sponge, guided it down beneath the level of the water to where the male part of him waited, already semierect.

"You libertine!" Isabella gasped, dropping the soaking sponge full in his face.

"Christ! Isabella!" Swatting the sponge from his face, blinking furiously to rid his eyes of the soapy water, Alec sat bolt upright. Although his vision was somewhat blurry, he discovered to his amazement that his ears hadn't deceived him. Isabella stood before him, cheeks and eyes blazing with temper, fists on hips and arms akimbo as she greeted him with the fiercest scowl he'd beheld in months. He stared at her, dazzled. With that frown, she was certainly no mirage.

"Isabella! My God, how did you get in here?" He looked quickly around, saw that they were alone, and began to smile. She was the most wondrous sight he had ever beheld in his life, scowl and all. He got to his feet, not caring about the huge wave that sloshed onto the floor, and stepped out of the tub. The bottle of brandy was dropped, forgotten, to add what remained of its contents to the mess on the floor. The cigar he pulled from his mouth as he approached her.

"You blackguard! You were going to . . . to . . . to make love with that . . . that girl!" She backed away from him as he drew closer.

If he'd harbored any doubts that his senses were playing tricks on him, and Isabella was not really there, her choice of epithets erased them. No one but Isabella talked like that.

"Now that you're here, of course, I won't," he murmured wickedly, knowing that it would enrage her further and chuckling inwardly at the prospect. God, how he'd missed her! More than he'd ever thought possible. He loved the bloody girl, and that was the truth of it. Hell, he was so besotted that he had lurked about that bloody French wood when his own presence was unnecessary—he'd already posted a man to keep an eye on her—just so that he could get a glimpse of her on her daily walk. So besotted that all he could think of now was pulling her into his arms. . . . Even if her leaving broke his heart, he'd make the most of the time while she was here.

"Don't you dare touch me!" she spat. He laughed, and caught her up in a great bear hug, pulling her up off her feet and swinging her around in a wide arc that made her skirts bell out.

"Alec . . . !"

He silenced her with a kiss. When she sighed into his mouth and locked her arms around his neck, he knew it was safe to release her.

"You've got me all wet," she said with mild dismay as he let her go at last. Alec realized as her eyes ran over him that he was stark naked, clutching a stogie and grinning at her like a damned fool. Reality descended on him like a thunderclap.

He took a step backwards, and the grin faded from his face. As she had said once, it was time to awaken from the dream, however painful that might be.

"What are you doing here?" he asked, quietly this time, and stuck the cigar back in his mouth. It was going to be all he could do to let her leave again, and he cursed her for taking him unaware. If he'd had any inkling she might come, he would have prepared himself for this.

"I thought you might be . . . missing me," she said softly, those huge eyes that had taken on the lavender hue of her gown looking up at him with the soft innocence that never failed to drive him wild.

"As you saw for yourself, I've managed to keep myself entertained." His voice was cool, and he congratulated himself for it.

At that her lips compressed, and a militant glint entered her eyes. She hadn't liked finding him with Dahlia and Daisy; that much was obvious. For a moment he silently conjured up a day of reckoning with Pearl for letting such a thing happen. Then he decided that it was all for the best. Isabella mustn't even begin to guess how much he still cared.

"Pearl said you were drowning your sorrows."

Alec's eyes narrowed dangerously. Damn Pearl for talking too much, as usual!

"Did she now? And what else did Madame Gossip say?"

"That you'd been breaking your heart for me."

That soft statement jarred into his gut with the impact of a knife and twisted there.

He essayed a jeering laugh. He only hoped it sounded better to Isabella's ears than it did to his own.

"Pearl's a regular fount of misinformation, isn't she? Perhaps my heart was a little bruised, once, but I've found consolation, as you saw."

Isabella wet her lips. The sight of her small pink tongue moving over that wide, tender mouth caused an unwanted—and obvious—physical reaction that for the first time in his life embarrassed him. Scowling, he returned to the tub, and sat.

She walked forward until she stood beside the tub looking down at him. Her small hands gripped the lip of the tub, nervously, he thought.

"I didn't mean what I said that day in the Champs Elysées. I don't care a fig about your birth. I love you."

This was going to be harder than he thought. Alec fought the urge to close his eyes. It wasn't fair, that she'd said the very words he'd been dying for months to hear.

He sat up very straight and met her eyes head-on.

"What are you saying, Isabella? That you want to be my mistress whenever you're in London? Hell, I'm willing. Take off your clothes and climb into bed and I'll join you as soon as I'm done with my bath." This he capped with another snide laugh.

The look she gave him was reproachful, and his fists clenched beneath the water where she could not see. It was all he could do not to grab her and pull her into the tub with him and kiss the life out of her and love her and refuse to ever let her go.

But for the second time in his life—the first being when he had killed her bastard of a husband for her, then left her to enjoy her rightful place in society without the encumbrance of a gutter rat like himself—he was going to do the noble thing. He was going to set her free if it killed him.

"I said I love you, Alec."

"Damn it, Isabella, you're bringing this on yourself. I didn't want to hurt your feelings, but the truth is that whatever we once had, it's over. What you need is a husband, a nice, noble husband, and what I need is a string of wenches who are ripe and ready to please. Not a silly little girl who fancies herself in love with the first man to show her a good time in bed."

"You could do it again."

"What?" He eyed her, not quite sure of her meaning.

"Show me a good time in bed."

She caught him by surprise, he had to give her that. Alec sat in the rapidly cooling water, gaping at her. To his astonishment she smiled at him, and then, just as coolly as if she did it for a living, she reached behind her and began to unfasten her dress.

"What the devil do you think you're doing?"

"Getting naked. Didn't you tell me once that that was the proper way to make love?"

If she'd meant to shock him, she succeeded. His eyes widened as she slid the lavender dress down over her arms, then started on the tapes of her stays. Alec swallowed, and frowned direly.

"Damn it, Isabella, didn't you hear what I said? I don't want you! It's over between us! Go home!"

She smiled at him, took off her stays, dropped them on the floor, and slipped out of her petticoats. Unwillingly, Alec's eyes ran over her. She was clad only in a flimsy chemise, white silk stockings and ribbon garters that left the tops of her creamy thighs bare. Unable to help himself, he took a deep breath, and fought to keep his bodily urges under control.

"If all you want is a mistress, then I'll be your mistress. But it might be rather hard to explain to the children."

"What children?"

"Ours."

She was peeling her stockings off, one by one. Alec shut his eyes in sheer self-defense, but it didn't help. The image of her next door to naked burned through his closed lids. Christ, if he got any hotter, he'd catch fire!

He felt her slide into the water beside him, and his eyes shot open. She was half sitting up, half lying on him, smiling beguilingly into his eyes. To his horror Alec felt his limbs begin to shake.

"Love me, Alec," she whispered, and that throaty whisper was his undoing. For a long moment he battled his impulses, but the fight was lost before it had even truly begun. Cursing his own weakness under his breath, he yanked her against him, not gently because she was driving him mad, flipped her onto her back, and took her right there in the water while she clung and moaned and called his name.

When it was over, he buried his face in her hair and inhaled her fragrance. And then he acknowledged it: with the best will in the world, he was never going to be able to let her go again.

"Do you still mean to send me home?" she breathed into his ear. From the sound of her voice Alec realized that she was teasing him. She knew the truth of how he felt as well as he did. He sat up, eyeing her askance, but she continued to loll against the side of the tub, smiling at him in a droll way that was pure enchantment.

"I didn't mean it. You know I didn't mean it. Christ, I was thinking of you."

"That was very noble of you, darling," Isabella acknowledged gravely. "But don't you think we've both been noble long enough?"

"Meaning?"

"Marry me," she said, and her eyes blazed purple fire at him. Alec caught his breath.

"Isabella . . ." he began, but then she was coming away from the side of the tub, catching him by the ears, and planting a remarkable kiss on his mouth.

"Do you love me or not?" she demanded a little shakily when she lifted her lips from his.

"Oh, God, more than my life," he admitted, surrendering with not even a fleeting regret. "But marriage . . . Love, you can't marry me. I'm a gutter rat, remember. Countesses don't marry gutter rats."

"Don't you want to?" She looked wounded. Alec shook his head, stood up suddenly, and picked her up in his arms.

"Of course I want to," he growled, stepping out of the tub with her and carrying her toward the bed. "But—"

"Alec Tyron, you told me once that you would marry me if I was free. Well, a promise is a promise, and I'm not going to let you go back on it!"

"Isabella . . ." He pulled the covers from the bed, dropped her on the mattress, and rolled in beside her, yanking the covers back up over them both. Chilled and damp, she cuddled close to him, and he wrapped his arms around her and pressed his mouth to her hair.

"Do you mean to keep your promise or not?"

She was a persistent little thing, he had to give her that.

"Isabella . . ."

"Would you stop saying 'Isabella' in that ridiculous way and give me an answer? Yes or no? and I warn you, if you say no, I'm going to put my clothes on and go home."

"Hell," he said, giving up. "Hell, yes. I'll marry you, tomorrow if it's possible and the next day if it's not, and the rest of the world can go hang."

"That," she purred contentedly, "is what I was hoping you'd say."

Her hand curled around the back of his head, and she pulled his mouth down to meet hers. And then they didn't talk again for a very long time.

When he surfaced at last, it was because he was too physically exhausted to continue. He leaned back against the pillows with her cradled on his shoulder, his eyes possessive as they studied her slender, naked body.

Suddenly it occurred to Alec that he was seeing her just exactly as he had fantasized on that long-ago trip from London to Amberwood: naked except for the amethyst necklace and earbobs he had given her.

For the first time in a long time, Alec genuinely smiled.

"What's so amusing?" Isabella asked sleepily.

" 'Tis merely that I'm happy, love," he answered innocently, and, still grinning, leaned over and kissed the softness of her exquisite mouth.